"If you apolo
Zora glared at Lucky.

He laughed, an unexpected rumble that rolled right into her heart. "That's my Zora." A bout of hard breathing reawakened the hope he might finally kiss her, but instead he sucked in a gulp of air and held it. "Okay. Better."

"Better than what?"

He ignored the question. "Since I inveigled you into working today, let me buy you lunch to celebrate."

"You're on." The heat in her body hadn't exactly dissipated, but it had faded into her normal pregnancy-enhanced high temperature. As for Lucky, clearly he didn't, couldn't and never would accept Andrew's babies as his own.

As common sense reasserted itself, Zora was suddenly glad nothing had happened. Going any further would have been yet another in a long line of mistakes she'd made with men. Gathering her possessions, she waited until Lucky locked up, and they sauntered out together. Friends again, nothing more.

Which was obviously how they both preferred it.

His Twin Surprise

USA TODAY BESTSELLING AUTHOR

JACQUELINE DIAMOND

&

CARRIE NICHOLS

2 Heartfelt Stories

The Baby Bonanza
and *His Unexpected Twins*

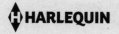

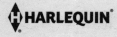

ISBN-13: 978-1-335-47331-8

His Twin Surprise

Copyright © 2022 by Harlequin Enterprises ULC

The Baby Bonanza
First published in 2015. This edition published in 2022.
Copyright © 2015 by Jackie Hyman

His Unexpected Twins
First published in 2019. This edition published in 2022.
Copyright © 2019 by Carol Opalinski

Recycling programs
for this product may
not exist in your area.

For questions and comments about the quality of this book, please contact us at CustomerService@Harlequin.com.

Harlequin Enterprises ULC
22 Adelaide St. West, 41st Floor
Toronto, Ontario M5H 4E3, Canada
www.Harlequin.com

Printed in U.S.A.

CONTENTS

Medical themes play a prominent role in many of **Jacqueline Diamond**'s one hundred published novels, including her Safe Harbor Medical miniseries for Harlequin. A former Associated Press reporter and TV columnist, Jackie lives in Orange County, California. Visit Jackie at jacquelinediamond.net and say hello to Jackie on her Facebook page, Jacqueline Diamond Author. On Twitter, she's @jacquediamond.

Books by Jacqueline Diamond

Harlequin American Romance

Safe Harbor Medical

Officer Daddy
Falling for the Nanny
The Surgeon's Surprise Twins
The Detective's Accidental Baby
The Baby Dilemma
The M.D.'s Secret Daughter
The Baby Jackpot
His Baby Dream
The Surprise Holiday Dad
A Baby for the Doctor
The Surprise Triplets
The Baby Bonanza
The Doctor's Accidental Family

Visit the Author Profile page at Harlequin.com for more titles.

The Baby Bonanza

JACQUELINE DIAMOND

Chapter 1

It was the first time Zora could recall agreeing with Lucky Mendez about anything. Although their truce surely wouldn't last long, she appreciated his good judgment this once.

"No way are you letting that creep move into our house," the male nurse told their landlady and housemate, Karen Wiggins. With his striking dark hair, muscular build and flamboyant tattoos, Lucky made an odd contrast to the pink streamers festooning their den.

"Everybody hates Laird Maclaine," Zora added as she arranged baby shower prizes on a side table. Being seven months pregnant with twins, she had to avoid any strenuous activity. In fact, as one of the shower's honorees—along with two of their former housemates—she could have dodged setup duty, but she refused to take the easy way out.

Ever.

"He's the only one who responded to the notice I posted on the bulletin board." Atop a step stool, Karen tied a bunch of balloons to a hook. In shades of pink and purple, each balloon proclaimed: Baby!

"We have a vacant room and the rent's almost due," she continued. "It's either Laird, or I post on the internet and we fend off the loonies. Unless you guys can produce another candidate, fast."

Lucky hadn't finished castigating the topic of the conversation. "One drink and Laird's telling raunchy jokes. Two drinks and he's leering at any lady who walks by." His lip curled. "Three drinks and we call the police."

"For a staff psychologist, he doesn't have a clue about how decent people act," Zora threw in.

"I don't care for him, either, but there are bills to pay." Karen, a financial counselor at Safe Harbor Medical Center, where they all worked, had inherited the five-bedroom home from her mother the previous December. Forced to take out a loan to repair the run-down property, she'd advertised for roommates. The arrangement had worked well despite the diverse personalities who'd signed on.

So far, three of the women had become pregnant, but the other two had married and moved out, unlike Zora. There was little chance she would marry the father of her babies, because he was already married. He was also her ex-husband, with whom she'd foolishly and, just before finalizing their divorce, trustingly had sex in the belief that her on-again, off-again high school sweetheart still loved her.

Zora rested her palm on her bulge, feeling the babies

kick. How ironic that she'd gotten pregnant by accident at the worst possible time, after she and Andrew had tried for more than a year to conceive. They'd been on the point of seeking fertility treatments when she'd discovered he was cheating on her.

"We have plenty of other colleagues," Lucky persisted. "You guys are in a better position to meet them than me, since my office is out in the boonies." Lucky worked in the medical office building adjacent to the hospital.

"I've tried, but... Oh, yuck!" Karen broke off as a breeze through the rear screen door carried a fetid whiff of decomposing vegetation and fish from the estuary behind the property.

Zora nearly gagged, too. Karen praised the marsh ad nauseam because it provided critical habitat for plants and small animals, as well as for California's migratory birds. However, despite the cooling weather at the end of September, it stank. "Who left the door open?"

"I must have forgotten to close it after I swept the patio." Lucky shut the glass slider with a thump. "How about renting to that receptionist in your office?"

"She declined." Descending from the stool, Karen stood back to assess the position of the balloons. "She prefers to save money by living with her parents. Speaking of money, if we don't find anyone by next month, I'll have to divide the room rent among you guys and Rod."

Their fourth and newest housemate, anesthesiologist Rod Vintner, had gone to pick up the party cake. He'd also gone, in Zora's opinion, to avoid anything approaching hard labor, although he *had* promised to clean up afterward.

"We could use the spare room as a nursery." Lucky

cast a meaningful gaze at Zora's large belly. "If someone would inform her ex-husband that he's about to be
a father and owes child support, she could afford the
extra space."

"Don't start on her," Karen warned, saving Zora the
trouble. "Go set up the chairs in the living room."

"Yes, ma'am." With a salute, Lucky strolled off. Zora
tried to ignore the muscles rippling beneath his T-shirt
and the tight fit of his jeans. The man was a self-righ-
teous pain in the neck, no matter how good he looked.

Surprisingly, he hadn't brought home any dates since
they'd moved into the house last February. Or none that
she'd observed, Zora amended. Since Lucky occupied
the downstairs suite, he could easily slip someone in
late and out early without the others noticing. Men did
things like that.

"You can stop staring at his butt now," Karen said
dryly.

"I wasn't!"

"You can lie to anyone else, including yourself,
but spare me." The older woman—forty-two to Zora's
twenty-nine—tightened the ponytail holder around her
hair, which she'd dyed black this month. "Was that the
kitchen timer?"

"I didn't hear anything." Zora adjusted a gift-
wrapped box with a slot for envelopes. The front read:
Nanny Fund. They planned to share the services of a
specialist nanny among the three new moms and their
collective total of six infants. Well, they *did* work at a
hospital noted for its fertility treatments, although only
one of the pregnancies had high-tech origins.

The timer buzzed. "There!" Karen said with satisfaction. "I knew it would sound any second."

"You must be psychic." Zora waddled behind her past a table displaying shower-themed paper plates and napkins.

"I have a well-developed sense of when food is done. Call it experience." In the kitchen, Karen snatched pot holders from a hook and opened the oven, filling the air with the scents of orange and lemon, almonds and balsamic vinegar.

Karen set the tins of Mediterranean muffins on the stove to cool. "I'd better start on the finger sandwiches. Only two hours before the guests are due, and I have to dress." She tied an apron over her blouse and long, casual skirt.

"I'll finish the vegetables." From the refrigerator, Zora removed the containers of celery, carrots and jicama that she'd cut up earlier, along with sour cream to mix for the dip and peanut butter to fill some of the celery sticks. "Would you get the olives and an onion soup packet from the pantry? I'm too big to squeeze in there."

"Gladly." Karen angled her slender shape around the narrow bend that led to the storage area. "Just black olives, or green ones, too?"

"Both." Zora lowered herself onto a chair, grateful she could still reach the table around her abdomen. A railing underneath allowed her to prop up her swollen ankles, but nothing alleviated the strain on her lower back. It ached more each day.

She hid her discomforts, determined to continue working as long as possible. Being an ultrasound tech meant standing on her feet all day and angling her midsection so she could scan the patients, but she was saving her paid maternity leave for after the twins' birth. Two months left—if they didn't arrive early.

After retrieving the requested items, Karen spread out her sandwich fixings on the counter. Through the kitchen's far door, Zora heard the scrape of folding chairs being opened and placed around the front room. She respected Lucky's work ethic; he always pitched in with an upbeat attitude. If he could only master the art of minding his own business, he'd be…well, tolerable.

Footsteps thudded on the carpet, announcing Lucky's return. His short, military-style haircut emphasized the strong planes of his face, which reflected his Hispanic heritage. "Where are the chair covers hidden? Someone else stored them after Anya and Jack's wedding."

"Upstairs in the linen closet," Karen said.

"Can I ride the stair lift or is that only for mommies?" Lucky teased. Both women narrowed their eyes at him, and he lifted his hands in a yielding gesture. "Just asking."

"Go play somewhere else," Zora muttered.

"Alone? That's no fun." With a rakish grin, he dodged out.

"You two should swap rooms so you could be downstairs," Karen observed from the counter. "Let him ride the stair lift if it gives him a thrill."

"I can't afford the extra rent." Lucky's large room commanded a correspondingly larger price. While Zora didn't care about having a personal patio exit, she did envy him the private bath. Karen had one, too, upstairs in the master suite, while Zora shared a bathroom with Rod and Melissa. Or, rather, with Rod and whoever moved into the room Melissa had vacated when she'd remarried her ex-husband.

Some people have all the luck. A sigh escaped Zora. Too late, she tried to cover with a cough.

"A pickle chip for your thoughts," Karen said.

"No, thanks." Zora popped a black olive into her mouth.

"You really are entitled to support," Karen observed. "I wonder whether you'd have faced your ex by now if Lucky weren't such a nag."

"He has nothing to do with it."

"You're stubborn," was the reply. "Seriously, Zora, how long can you keep this secret? I'm amazed Andrew's mother hasn't spilled the beans."

"Betsy doesn't know." Zora's former mother-in-law was the nursing supervisor at the hospital. The kindhearted lady had suffered through the loss of two beloved daughters-in-law, thanks to her son's faithlessness.

Zora wondered whether Betsy was being more cautious about bonding with Andrew's third wife, a Hong Kong native he'd met on a business trip while he was married to Zora. Unexpectedly, tears blurred her vision. *How could he cheat on me? And then, just when I was ready to let him go, trick me into believing he still loved me?*

"Betsy sees you in the cafeteria every day," Karen reminded her.

"She's aware that I'm pregnant," Zora agreed. "But she has no idea who the father is."

Karen stuck a hank of black hair behind her ear. "She isn't stupid."

"But I doubt she believes Andrew is capable of…of being such a grade-A jerk." Damn those tears stinging her eyes again. "Aside from my closest friends, most people accept my explanation that I made a mistake after my divorce. I let them assume I picked up a guy in a bar."

"And that's better than admitting you slept with Andrew?"

"It's better than admitting I'm a complete chump."

More footsteps, and Lucky reappeared. "They aren't there. Let's skip the seat covers."

"I refuse to have guests in my house sitting on ugly folding chairs," Karen said.

The man tilted his head skeptically. "What's the big deal? People have been sitting on folding chairs without covers since the dawn of time."

"No, they haven't." Hastily, Zora shielded the relish tray from his attempt to grab a carrot. "Hands off!"

"Evidence found in caves throughout northern Europe indicates that Neanderthals shunned folding chair covers as a sign of weakness," Lucky said. "And why so stingy with the veggies?"

"I'm still arranging these. Go eat a corn chip." Zora indicated a bag set out to be transferred into a large bowl.

"I'm a vegetarian."

"Corn is a vegetable."

"Corn chips do not occur in nature," he responded. "Just one carrot. Pretty please."

She flipped it toward him. He caught it in midair.

"Try the closet in my bathroom for the covers," Karen suggested to Lucky. "Top shelf."

"I have permission to enter the inner sanctum?" he asked.

"It expires in sixty seconds."

"Okay, okay." He paused. "Before I run off, there's one little thing I should mention about today's guest list."

Zora released an impatient breath. "What?"

"I invited Betsy."

"You didn't!" Keeping her ex-mother-in-law in the dark at work was one thing, but around here the babies' paternity was no secret.

Karen turned toward Lucky, knife in hand. "Tell me you're joking."

He grimaced. "Sorry. Spur-of-the-moment thing. But your motto *is* the more the merrier, and besides, Betsy's a widow. If she's interested in renting a room, that would solve all our problems." With a carroty crunch, off he went.

"Unbelievable," Karen said.

If she hadn't been so huge, Zora might have given chase. She could easily have strangled Lucky at that moment. But then they'd have to find *two* new housemates.

"I'd say the cat's about to claw its way out of the bag," Karen observed. "Might as well seize the bull by the horns, or is that too many animal metaphors?"

"Considering the size of the rat we live with, I guess not," Zora growled.

Karen smiled. "Speaking of rats, if you'd rather not confront Andrew-the-rodent yourself, don't forget you can hire Edmond to do it." Edmond Everhart, their former roommate, Melissa's husband, had been Zora's divorce attorney.

"That'll only create more trouble." Zora scraped the onion dip from the mixing bowl into a container on the relish tray. "Andrew'll put me through the wringer."

"If that's your only reason for not telling him about the babies, I'd rate its validity at about a three on a scale of ten." Karen trimmed the crust from a sandwich.

Zora dropped the spoon into the mixing bowl with a

clunk. "He's the only man I ever loved. I want to give him the benefit of the doubt."

"Zora, what benefit of what doubt?" Karen retorted. "He dumped you in high school, married someone else, then cheated on *her* with you after he ran into you at your class reunion. Let's not forget that he then cheated on *you* with what's-her-name from Hong Kong. Why on earth would you entertain the fantastical notion that Andrew will ever transform into a loving husband and father?"

With a pang, Zora conceded that that was exactly what she *did* wish for. While her rational mind sided with Karen, the infants stirring inside her with a series of kicks and squirms obviously missed their father. So did Zora.

"It can happen," she said. "Look at Melissa and Edmond. Three years after their divorce, they fell in love again."

"They'd quarreled about having children. Neither of them cheated on the other," Karen persisted. "Andrew can't be trusted, ever."

She spoke with the ferocity of a divorcée who'd survived an abusive marriage. It had taken more than a decade for Karen to trust a man again. She and their housemate, Rod, were still easing into their relationship.

"People can change." Despite a reluctance to bring up her family, Zora wanted Karen to understand. "Did I mention I have a twin?"

"Really?" Leaning against the counter, Karen folded her arms. "Identical or fraternal?"

"Identical." Zora wasn't about to reveal the whole story, just the important part. "But we quarreled, and we aren't in touch anymore. All I know of her is what

Mom passes along." Their mother, who lived in Oregon, loved sharing news.

"Go on." After a glance at the clock, Karen resumed her food preparation.

"Nearly ten years ago, Zady ran off with a married man." Zora inhaled as deeply as she could, considering the pressure on her lungs from the pregnancy. "They live in Santa Barbara. He split with his wife and now he's devoted to Zady. They have a beautiful house and a couple of kids."

"Was there a wedding in there?" Karen asked dubiously.

"I'm sure there was, although she didn't invite me." The rift had been bitter, and there'd been no move toward reconciliation on either side. In fact, her mother said Zady had chuckled when she'd learned about Zora's divorce.

"So the guy married her, and you believe that if lightning struck your twin, it can strike you, too?" Karen murmured.

Zora's throat tightened. "Why not?"

"Because Betsy's about to arrive with her antennae on high alert. If I'm any judge, that woman's dying to be a grandmother."

"And she'll be a terrific one." The elder Mrs. Raditch did all the right grandmotherly things, such as baking and crocheting, a skill she'd taught Zora. "But…"

"You're running out of *but*s," Karen warned. "Unless you count Lucky's."

"I don't!"

"The way you guys battle, you're almost like an old married couple."

"We're *nothing* like a married couple, old or otherwise." Zora could never be interested in a man with so little class. Outside work, he flaunted his muscles in sleeveless T-shirts and cutoffs. While she didn't object if someone had a small tattoo, his body resembled a billboard for video games. On the right arm, a colorful dragon snaked and writhed, while on the left, he displayed a buxom babe wearing skimpy armor and wielding a sword.

Whenever she pictured Andrew, she saw him in the suit and tie he always wore as an international business consultant. He had tousled blond hair, a laser-sharp mind, sky-blue eyes, and when he trained his headlight smile on her, Zora understood why some poor fools became addicted to drugs, because the euphoria was irresistible.

At the image, vague intentions coalesced into a firm decision. "Andrew's the man I married. This…this *liaison* with what's-her-name is an aberration. Once the kids are born and he holds them in his arms, what man wouldn't love his own son and daughter?" *And their mother.*

Even Zora's own father, a troubled man who'd cheated on her mom, had stuck around while his kids had grown up. Well, mostly—there'd been separations and emotional outbursts that left painful memories. But there'd been tender times, too, including a laughter-filled fishing trip, and one Christmas when her father had dressed up as Santa Claus and showered them with gifts.

She longed for her children to experience a father like that. With Andrew's charm, he could easily provide such unforgettable moments.

For a minute, the only sound was the chopping of a

knife against a cutting board as Karen trimmed crusts. Finally she said, "So you plan to hold it together until then, alone?"

"I have you guys, my friends." Zora struggled for a light tone. "All I have to do is stay on an even keel."

"Like a juggler tossing hand grenades on the deck of a sinking ship?" On a platter, Karen positioned sandwiches in a pyramid. "Well, it's your decision."

"Yes, and I've made it." Zora studied the relish tray through a sheen of moisture. Andrew would come around eventually. He had a good heart, despite his weak will.

"I'm happy to report that I found the chair covers and they look fine." Lucky's deep voice sounded almost in her ear, making her jump. "What do Neanderthals know, anyway?"

"Speaking of Neanderthals, how dare you sneak up on me?" she snapped. "I could go into labor."

"No, you won't." The corners of his mouth quirked.

"How would you know?"

"I'm a nurse, remember?" he said.

"Not that kind of nurse." He worked with a urologist.

"Pregnancy care is part of every nurse's basic medical training." His expression sobered. "Speaking of medicine, you're sure Cole's coming today?"

Dr. Cole Rattigan, the renowned men's fertility expert Lucky assisted, had been away this past week, speaking at a conference in New York.

"He and his wife RSVP'd," Karen assured him. "What's the big deal?"

"I can't discuss it. It concerns a patient."

"Why would you confer about a patient on your day off?" Zora asked.

"That's confidential, too." Grabbing the tray of sandwiches, Lucky whisked out of the room so fast it was a miracle the sandwich pyramid didn't topple.

"That's odd," Karen said. "I wonder what's going on."

As did Zora, but Cole, and in particular his wife, a popular nurse, were a touchy subject for her. As the first Mrs. Andrew Raditch, Stacy hadn't hidden her resentment toward Zora-the-husband-stealer, and most staffers had sided with her.

Among them, no one had been more hostile than Lucky. He'd eased up since he and Zora had started sharing this house, but in a showdown there was no question that his loyalty lay with Cole and his spouse.

Zora wished that didn't bother her. Well, she had more important things to deal with, anyway…such as facing the grandmother of her children in less than two hours.

Chapter 2

Lucky wove between clusters of chattering people in the living room, removing soiled paper plates and cups. Although he was enjoying the party, he wished he and his housemates had kept a tighter lid on the guest list. Only half an hour into it, the place was filling up—and not all the choices had been wise.

Inviting Betsy Raditch had seemed a clever trick to prod Zora into finally accepting the help she needed. Instead, the younger woman kept dodging her ex-mother-in-law, who sneaked longing gazes at Zora's belly but maintained a respectful distance. The would-be grandmother's wistful expression sent a guilty pang through Lucky.

And he hadn't counted on Karen inviting Laird, but here he was, fawning over Zora. The psychologist's colorless eyes—okay, they were gray, but a very *light* gray—lit up whenever she so much as flinched, providing an excuse for him to offer her a chair or a drink. Was the man flirting or just trying to charm his way into the house? Either way, he had a very strange notion of what women found appealing.

When Zora winced, the guy reached out to rub her bulge. Stuck in a knot of people across the room, Lucky barely refrained from shouting, "Hands off!" To his relief, Keely Randolph, a dour older nurse Lucky had never much liked until now, smacked Laird's arm and loudly proclaimed that people shouldn't shed their germs all over pregnant women.

After scowling at her, Laird gazed around, targeted Karen and approached her with a smarmy expression. Lucky caught the words *exquisite house* and *can't wait to move in*.

Rod Vintner came to Karen's rescue, his wiry frame and short graying beard bristling with indignation. "Who's moving in where?" he growled with a ferocity that indicated he'd willingly stick one of his anesthesiology needles into Laird's veins and pump it to the max.

Satisfied that the jerk was batting zero, Lucky glanced toward the front window. He never tired of the soul-renewing view across the narrow lane and past the coastal bluffs to the cozy harbor from which the town took its name. You couldn't beat the beauty of this spot.

Yet he might have to leave. And that had nothing to do with Laird or any other roommate.

Lucky had worked hard to earn a master's degree in nursing administration, which he'd completed earlier this year. Now he sought a suitable post for his management skills, but there were no openings at Safe Harbor

Medical. Which meant he'd have to move away from the people he cared about.

They included Zora, who over the past few months had needed his protection as she struggled to deal with an unplanned pregnancy and a broken heart. They hadn't intended to grow closer; he wasn't even sure either would openly acknowledge it. Which was just as well. Because having once failed in a big way to be there for the people he loved, Lucky had vowed never, ever to take on such responsibility. Because he'd only fail again.

Still, he couldn't imagine moving away. His best hope for staying in the area would be the expansion of the men's fertility program in which he worked. Any minute now, its director, Cole Rattigan, would arrive. Most of the staff thought Cole had just been in New York to deliver a speech, but Lucky was more interested in hearing about his boss's private meeting with the designer of a new device.

It offered a slim possibility of helping one particular patient, a volatile billionaire named Vince Adams who was considering a major endowment to expand the hospital's urology program. If that happened, it might create a nursing-administration position for Lucky. Also, it would realize his doctor's dream of building a world-class program.

If not for Cole, Lucky might not be working for Safe Harbor Med at all, he reflected as he carried empty plates and cups to the kitchen. Two and a half years ago, when the newly arrived urologist had interviewed for office nurses, Lucky hadn't believed he had a chance of being hired. After his previous doctor retired, Lucky's tattoos had repeatedly knocked him out of the running for jobs. He'd been considering expensive and painful treatment to remove the evidence of his youthful foolishness.

But the tats hadn't bothered Cole. He'd asked a few questions, appeared pleased with the responses and offered the job on the spot. After that, Lucky would have battled demons if they'd threatened his doctor.

In the den, he poured himself a glass of fruit juice and noted that the sandwiches, chips and veggies were holding their own despite modest depletions. No one had cut the sheet cake yet, leaving intact the six cartoon babies, five with pink hair ribbons and one with blue.

"Aren't they adorable?" The soft voice at his elbow drew his attention to Betsy.

Lucky shifted uneasily. Despite his conviction that Zora ought to be honest with her children's grandmother, he had no intention of snitching. Still, he *had* invited the woman. "We ordered it from the Cake Castle."

She indicated the Nanny Fund box bordered by a few wrapped packages. "I didn't realize most people would be contributing money as their gift. I hope it's all right that I crocheted baby blankets."

"All right?" Lucky repeated in surprise. "The kids will treasure those keepsakes forever."

Betsy's squarish face, softened by caramel-brown hair and wire-rimmed glasses, brightened at the compliment. Why didn't Zora level with the woman? A doting grandma could provide the support a young single mother needed. Considering that Zora's own mother lived in Oregon, she'd be wise to take advantage of Betsy's yearning for grandkids.

"I'm glad to hear it," she said. "Also, much as I approve of the nanny idea, I suspect new mothers could use furnishings and toys."

"Oh, there's plenty of that." Lucky had been forced to park in the driveway for weeks due to the overflow in the garage. "Practically the entire staff has donated their baby gear. Anya and Jack got first pick, since she's already delivered, but they only have a singleton. There's plenty left."

"They're a lovely couple. So are Melissa and Edmond." Betsy indicated the long-legged blonde woman ensconced on the sofa, flanked by her doting husband and seven-year-old niece, Dawn, who lived with them. This was a rare outing for Melissa, who in her sixth month with triplets looked almost as wide as she was tall. "I'm thrilled that they remarried. They obviously belong together."

Was that a hint? Surely the woman didn't believe her son might reconcile with Zora. Aside from the fact that he had a new wife, the guy was the world's worst candidate for family man. "I'd bet in most divorces the odds of a happy reconciliation would be on par with winning the lottery."

"If that was for my benefit, don't bother," Betsy told him.

"Sorry." Lucky ducked his head. "I tend to be a mother hen to my friends. Or a father hen, if there is such a thing."

"At least you aren't a rooster like my son," she replied sharply.

"No comment."

"Wise man."

On the far side of the room, Zora circled past the staircase and halted, her eyes widening at the sight of

Lucky standing beside Betsy. Lucky nearly spread his hands in a do-you-honestly-think-I'd-tell-her? gesture, but decided against it, since Betsy didn't miss much. She must be suspicious enough already about the twins' paternity.

While he was seeking another topic of conversation, his landlady bounced into the den from the kitchen. "Who's ready for a game?" Karen called. "We have prizes." She indicated a side table where baskets displayed bath soaps and lotions, while a large stuffed panda held out a gift card to the Bear and Doll Boutique.

"What kind of game?" Dawn asked from the couch.

"I'm afraid the first one might be too hard for a child," Karen said. "It's a diaper-the-baby contest."

"I can do that," the little girl proclaimed.

"Yes, she can," Melissa confirmed. "Dawn has more experience with diapering than Edmond or me."

"I used to help our neighbor," the child said.

"Then please join in!" Karen beamed as guests from the living room crowded into the den. "Ah, more players. Great!"

Among the group was their former roommate Anya, her arms around the daughter she'd delivered a few weeks earlier. "Nobody's diapering Rachel for a game."

"Certainly not," Karen agreed.

"However, volunteers are welcome to stop by our apartment any night around two a.m.," put in Anya's husband, Dr. Jack Ryder.

Rachel gurgled. A sigh ran through the onlookers, accompanied by murmurs of "What an angel!" and "How darling!"

"I'd be happy to hold her for you," Betsy said. "You can both relax and enjoy the food."

"Thank you." Anya cheerfully shifted her daughter into the arms of the nursing supervisor.

When Zora hugged herself protectively, Lucky felt a twinge of sympathy. She'd refused to consider adoption, declaring that this might be her only chance to have children, but the sight of little Rachel must underscore the reality of what she faced.

Children required all your resources and all your strength. How did this woman with slim shoulders and defiant ginger hair expect to cope by herself?

He reminded himself not to get too involved. Lucky didn't mind changing a few diapers, but he might not be here long, unless Dr. Rattigan brought good news. Now where was the doctor?

Waving a newborn-size doll along with a package of clean diapers, Karen detailed the rules of the game. "You have to remove and replace the diaper. I'll be timing you. Fastest diaper change wins."

"That doesn't sound hard," Laird scoffed.

"Did I mention you have to do it one-handed?" Karen replied, to widespread groans. "If you drop the baby on the floor, you're automatically disqualified."

"For round two, contestants have to diaper the doll blindfolded," Rod added mischievously. A few people laughed, while Dawn's jaw set with determination. That kid would do it upside down and sideways to win, Lucky thought. With that attitude, she'd go far in life.

Then he caught the sound he'd been waiting for—the doorbell. His pulse sped up. "I'll get it."

Someone else reached the door first, however, and friends rushed to greet the Rattigans. Despite his impatience, Lucky hung back.

With her friendly manner and elfin face, Stacy had

a kind word for everyone. Her mild-mannered husband said little; Cole's reticence, Lucky knew, stemmed partly from the urologist's discomfort in social situations. It was also partly the result of having a brain so brilliant that he was probably carrying on half a dozen internal conversations with himself at any given moment.

Lucky could barely contain his eagerness to speak with the great man privately and find out if the device lived up to its promise. However, he drew the line at elbowing guests aside.

Stacy oohed over Anya's newborn and hugged Betsy, her former mother-in-law. The room quieted as the first Mrs. Andrew Raditch came face-to-face with the woman who had cheated with him before being discarded in turn. Most of the staff had cheered at Zora's misfortune, believing she was receiving her just deserts. Lucky was ashamed to admit he'd been among them. Now he wished he could spare her this awkwardness.

"Wow! Look at you." Stacy patted Zora's belly. "Have you chosen names yet?"

"Still searching," she said with a tentative smile. "For now, Tweedledee and Tweedledum."

This light exchange broke the tension. With her new marriage, Stacy had clearly moved on, and with her courtesy toward Zora, she'd brought her old nemesis in from the cold.

Silently, Lucky thanked her. Cole had chosen a worthy wife.

The game began, with guests lining up to participate. Seizing his chance, Lucky approached his boss, who spoke without prompting.

"I know you're anxious for news, Luke." Cole used Lucky's formal name. "Let's talk."

"We'll have more privacy in here." Lucky led the way into the now-empty living room.

Zora had no interest in diapering a baby. She'd be doing more than her share of that soon.

Stacy's display of friendliness left her both relieved and oddly shaky. Having been treated as a pariah by much of the hospital staff for several years, Zora still felt vulnerable as well as guilty.

Also, Stacy's question about the names reminded Zora of her idea to leave the decision until they were born. She'd figured that if Andrew had a chance to choose the names, it might help bond him with the little ones. Today, however, the prospect of what lay ahead was sinking in.

For starters, what was she planning to do, call him from the delivery room and break the news of his paternity over the phone while writhing in agony? This kind of information should be presented in person, and she ought to get it over with now. Yet being around Andrew brought out Zora's weakness for him; the ease with which he'd seduced her when she dropped by with their divorce papers proved that.

If only Lucky would stop poking at her, she'd be able to think clearly. It might be unfair to focus her anger on her housemate, but this was none of his business. And why had he, one of the party's hosts, hustled Dr. Rattigan off in such a hurry?

Hungry as usual these days, Zora munched on a peanut butter–filled celery stick from the snack table. Keely drifted alongside, following her gaze as Lucky vanished. "Nice build," the older nurse observed in her nasal voice.

Amused, Zora said, "I don't believe he's dating anyone. Interested?"

Keely snorted. "Not my type."

Zora didn't dare ask what that was.

A hint of beer breath alerted her to Laird Maclaine's approach. The psychologist must have downed a brew before arriving, because they weren't serving alcohol.

"We're discussing Mendez?" He addressed his question to Zora, ignoring Keely. "If he snags a better job with that new master's degree of his, I'd love to rent *his* room. I hear it has an en suite bathroom."

"En suite?" Keely repeated. "What a pretentious term."

Laird rolled his eyes.

"He isn't leaving." While Zora understood Lucky's desire for advancement, she couldn't imagine him abandoning his friends.

The psychologist shrugged. "Either way, this is a fantastic party house. I'm expecting to move in next weekend."

Astonished, Zora slanted an assessing gaze at the psychologist. From an objective viewpoint, Laird wasn't bad-looking, although bland compared to Lucky, and she respected him for initiating and leading patient support groups. But it would be annoying to have to run into this conceited guy every morning over breakfast and every night at dinner.

Impulsively, she addressed Keely. "We have an empty room that used to be Melissa's. Any chance you're interested?"

"It's taken, by me," Laird rapped out.

"Nothing's settled," Zora said.

"Don't you already have two men living here?" Keely inquired. "You and Karen should bring in another woman. I'd join you, but I couldn't do that to my roommate."

"You wouldn't fit in, anyway," Laird growled.

That remark didn't deserve a response. "Who's your roommate?" Zora asked Keely. "Do I know her?"

"Oh, she doesn't work at the medical complex," the nurse responded. "She's a housekeeper."

"I admire your loyalty to her."

"Anyone would do the same."

A stir across the den drew their attention. It was Dawn Everhart's turn at the game. Deftly, the little girl rolled the doll with an elbow, tugged on one diaper tab with her fingers and caught the other in her mouth, all while onlookers captured the moment with their cell phones.

"Unsanitary," Laird protested.

"But clever," Rod responded from his post beside Karen. "Besides, it's a doll."

"And she's beating the pants off everyone else's time," Edmond observed, beaming at his niece. "Literally."

Her feet having swollen to the size of melons, Zora wandered into the kitchen and sat down. Through the far door, she detected the low rumble of masculine voices in the living room.

What were Lucky and his boss discussing so intently? Had Cole made job inquiries at the conference for his nurse's sake? Although she'd instinctively dismissed Laird's comment about Lucky moving, the man couldn't be expected to waste his master's degree.

If Lucky departed, who would run out for ice cream when she had a craving? Lucky had promised to haul two bassinets and a changing table to the second floor as soon as she was ready for them. Without him around, who would cart her stuff up and down the stairs? She certainly couldn't count on Laird pitching in.

Well, she'd survive. In fact, she shouldn't be relying on Lucky so much, anyway. Zora hated to depend on others, especially someone so controlling and critical and arrogant and judgmental. She might not have the world's best taste in men, but she knew what she *didn't* like, and Lucky epitomized it. Now what were he and Dr. Rattigan talking about so intently?

No matter how hard she strained, she couldn't follow the thread of conversation from the living room. Just when she caught a couple of words, a burst of cheering from the den obliterated the rest of the doctor's comments.

Judging by the clamor, Dawn had edged out Anya's husband, Jack, by two seconds. "I can visualize the headline now—Seven-year-old Defeats Obstetrician in Diapering Contest!" roared Rod, who, as Jack's uncle, had the privilege of ragging him mercilessly. "I'm posting the pictures on the internet."

"You do that and you'll never see your great-niece again," Jack retorted. He spoiled the effect by adding, "Will he, cutie?" apparently addressing the newborn.

Zora lumbered to her feet. She was missing all the fun and worrying for nothing.

Probably.

Chapter 3

Feeling miles from the festivities in the den, Lucky struggled to concentrate on Cole's account. He kept wishing that, if he focused hard enough, the results would be more encouraging.

"The new stent won't fix what's wrong with Vince Adams." The slightly built doctor ran a hand through his rumpled brown hair.

"Are you certain?" Lucky pressed.

Cole nodded. "It won't do anything for a patient who has that much scar tissue."

During the summer, Cole had used the latest microsurgical techniques in an unsuccessful attempt to open the billionaire's blocked sperm ducts. As the office nurse, Lucky hadn't assisted at the operation, but he'd read the follow-up report. The procedure hadn't been able to reverse the extensive damage left by a long-ago infection.

However, Vince continued to press them for options. Cole had told him about a new dissolvable, medicine-infused stent, and Vince had been excited that Cole would get an advance preview of the device. "We have the world's top urologist right here," the millionaire had trumpeted. "And I'll be the first guy he cures."

The higher the hopes, the harder the fall.

"Do you think his interest in Safe Harbor is entirely based on restoring his fertility?" Lucky asked.

"It's hard to say," Cole replied. "His intentions tend to shift with his emotional state."

A private equity investor, Vince Adams was powerful and rich. But wealth hadn't compensated for his inability to sire children. Over the years, he'd paid dearly for treatments without success, and others had paid dearly for his desire for fatherhood.

After several turbulent and childless marriages, Vince had wed a woman with two young daughters. Determined to adopt them, he had used his financial clout to overwhelm Portia's first husband in court.

The man he'd gleefully trounced was Lucky's housemate, Rod Vintner, who'd faced a doubly devastating loss. First, during his divorce, he'd learned that his daughters were actually the genetic offspring of his unfaithful wife's previous lover, now out of the picture. Second, Rod had been outspent and outmaneuvered fighting for joint custody.

For years, he'd been forbidden to talk or even write to his daughters, who lived a ninety-minute drive away, in San Diego. Then, earlier this year, the older girl had run away from home. The twelve-year-old had contacted Rod, who'd enlisted the aid of the girls' maternal grandmother here in Safe Harbor.

Although officially Rod was still banned, Grandma Helen had arranged for Tiffany—now thirteen—and her younger sister to visit her more often. Whenever possible, she let them meet with Rod, and, faced with Tiffany's threats to run away again, the Adamses pretended not to notice.

Vince's search for fertility, however, provided him with another avenue for keeping Rod in line. While Vince's interest in the hospital stemmed in large part from his discovery that one of the world's foremost urologists had joined the staff, it also ensured that Rod didn't dare become too much of an annoyance. An anesthesiologist would be a lot easier for the hospital to replace than a billionaire donor.

Lucky hated that the staff had to curry favor with Vince. Still, he felt compassion for a man desperate to produce a baby. The billionaire's motives might be self-serving, but his comments had made it clear that he would treasure his child. As long as parents offered a loving, secure home, it wasn't anyone else's right to pass judgment.

However, if Cole couldn't help him, it seemed likely Vince wouldn't follow through on his major donation. "Suppose he drops us," Lucky said. "Surely there are others we could approach."

"The world is full of rich people, but Safe Harbor tends to lose out to more prestigious institutions," Cole responded. "I admit, Luke, being at the conference whetted my appetite for better research facilities, more lab space and money for fellowships. In fact, I received three excellent offers to relocate."

Lucky's heart nearly skipped a beat. "You'd take another position?"

Alarm flitted across the doctor's face. "I shouldn't have said that."

Nevertheless, he *had* said it. "If you go, the program will never recover." *Neither will I. On many levels.*

At a burst of laughter from the other room, Lucky flinched. His friends had no idea that he was standing here with the ground crumbling beneath his feet.

Cole's brow furrowed. "I joined Safe Harbor with the intention of building a standout program. Although I'm no longer sure that will be possible, this is my wife's home, and mine, too. I haven't given up yet." But there was no mistaking his distress.

"Nothing else at the conference might be useful?"

"I'm afraid not. Perhaps we should suggest Mr. Adams cancel next Saturday's appointment and save himself a trip." The billionaire tended to arrive with plenty of pomp and circumstance by private plane or helicopter. On other occasions, Vince roared up the coast in a high-performance car that cost as much as many houses.

If only Lucky could find a solution, for his sake and for his doctor's. It would also be important to the medical center to achieve its goal of becoming a major player in the fertility field. Major gifts attracted additional donors; a lack of progress might, by contrast, eventually consign Safe Harbor to secondary status. And this place had been good to Lucky when he'd needed help the most.

"Don't cancel," he said. "That's a week from now. Things could change."

"I suppose you're right." Cole stretched his shoulders. "In any event, my patient deserves to hear the news from me in person."

To Lucky, it was a reprieve. He had a week to figure out the next move.

* * *

Zora had never seen Lucky abandon a party before. After talking to Dr. Rattigan, he'd spent the next hour in a corner of the living room, fiddling with his phone. Searching the internet or texting people? But why?

In view of the doctor's wistful expression, it didn't take a genius to recognize that they'd suffered a blow. They must have been counting on the New York conference for some reason.

Zora tried to shrug off Lucky's absence while she and her fellow moms-to-be opened gifts. Most people had contributed money, but Betsy's gifts were special.

Zora's throat constricted as she held up the soft pink and blue blankets. Her former mother-in-law had created these precious heirlooms even without being sure of her relationship to the twins.

Zora was glad now that Lucky had invited Betsy. To learn she'd been excluded from the baby shower would have been an undeserved slap in the face.

Catching Betsy's eye, Zora said, "These mean more than I can say."

"I'm glad." Wedged among the other guests, the older woman added, "If you need anything, please call me."

"You're a sweetheart." But Zora wouldn't ask for the other woman's help, not until after the babies were born and she revealed the truth to Andrew. When she did, she hoped Betsy wouldn't resent having been kept in the dark.

Her gaze drifted to the diamond-and-emerald ring on her ex-mother-in-law's right hand. Zora had worn the family heirloom during her marriage, treasuring both its beauty and its significance. After the divorce, she'd returned it, with regret. Neither of Andrew's other wives had worn it; there'd been a special bond between Betsy and Zora that had begun in her high school days.

Now, its glitter reminded Zora of how much she'd lost. Not only her husband, but a woman who'd been as close to her as family. Well, perhaps someday she and Betsy could be close again.

She hoped her children would meet her twin sister, too. That depended on whether Zora was ever secure enough to handle Zady's inevitable gloating at her downfall. For now, distance was best. Nobody could inflict as much pain as the people nearest your heart.

After the last guest departed, the adrenaline that had powered Zora all afternoon faded. She collapsed on the living room couch while, inside her, the babies tussled.

What a blessing it would be when they were born and her body returned to normal. And what a joy to hold them and see their sweet faces.

At this point, Lucky should have arrived to offer her refreshments. She missed his coddling, even though it was often seasoned with criticism.

Instead, he bustled about collecting trash as if she weren't there. From the kitchen, Zora heard Karen opening and closing the fridge to put away food, while in the den, Rod ran the vacuum cleaner. Zora would have pitched in if she'd had the energy.

As Lucky removed the white linen covers from the folding chairs, his dark eyebrows drew together like storm clouds. The dragon protruding from beneath one sleeve appeared to be lashing its tail.

Zora broke the silence. "Won't you tell me what happened?"

He tossed a cover onto a pile of laundry. "What do you mean?"

"You've been upset since you talked to Dr. Rattigan."

Lucky snapped a chair shut. "Doesn't concern you."

Zora tried a different tack. "Laird speculated you might move out of town to take a better job. He's angling to get your suite." She deliberately baited Lucky with that reference to the obnoxious psychologist.

Lucky grimaced. "I'd rather not discuss that lowlife."

"Then let's discuss what's eating you."

"Like I said, it's none of your business."

Any second, flames were going to shoot out her ears. "Oh, yes, it is!"

"How so?" he growled, wielding a chair as if he was prepared to thrust it at her.

The guy sure was prickly. "It's obvious Cole brought bad news from the conference."

Lucky set the chair down. "I can't discuss anything involving a patient."

He was right to safeguard the man's privacy, Zora conceded. Medical personnel were required to do that, by law and by hospital policy as well as by simple decency. Still, he'd dropped a clue. Now, why would a patient's condition bother Lucky so much?

From the kitchen, Karen's voice drifted to her. "I'm looking forward to having your girls in town next Saturday. Should we invite them and Helen for lunch?"

"I doubt there'll be time," Rod replied dourly. "They're only being dropped off at their grandma's for an hour or two while Vince sees his doctor."

"Is he having problems?" Karen asked. "I don't usually wish anyone ill, but he's an exception."

"You can wish that jerk as much ill as you like." Rod's voice rose in anger. "Tiff and Amber loathe the man. He may not physically abuse them, but he's a bully, and emotional scars can be the worst kind."

As the rumble of the garbage disposal cut off further eavesdropping, Zora put two and two together. Everyone knew—because the billionaire had discussed it openly—that Dr. Rattigan was treating him. And the men's program counted on his support.

"It's Vince Adams," she said. "No, don't answer. I realize you can't confirm it."

Lucky stacked the chairs to one side. "Are you still mad at me for inviting Betsy? Is that why you're harassing me?"

Zora tried to hug her knees, but her bulge was in the way. "I'm glad you invited her."

"So we're good?" His fierce brown eyes raked over her.

"No. What if you leave?" she burst out, surprised by her rush of emotion. "We're having enough trouble finding one roommate, let alone two. We'll *have* to take Laird."

A knot in her chest warned that she was less concerned about Laird than she was about Lucky staying until the babies were born. Until Andrew hopefully came to his senses and fell in love with his children. *Until hell freezes over.* No, but if hell did freeze over, she'd counted on Lucky to be there with a warming blanket.

As a friend, of course. He'd been just as helpful to Anya—maybe more so—when they'd moved into this house. It was in his nature.

Lucky stopped fiddling around. "You shouldn't upset yourself. It might shoot up your blood pressure."

"Then talk to me."

He plopped his butt on the arm of the couch. "About what?"

"You've been delving into your phone all afternoon, trying to find a solution, right? But if Dr. Rattigan can't fix Vince—I mean, Patient X—neither can you."

"So?" Lucky folded his arms. They were muscular arms, and he folded them across a broad, powerful chest. Too bad the movement also flexed the shapely legs of a cartoon woman, which rather spoiled the effect for Zora.

"We have to figure out another way to keep the Adamses involved with Safe Harbor," she blurted.

"We?" Lucky was addicted to monosyllables today.

She'd surprised herself by saying that. But didn't she owe Lucky a favor, considering how much support he'd given her?

"Yes, *we*," Zora retorted, and, to cut off any argument, she added, "Some people have a ridiculously hard time accepting help, to quote a person I know."

That produced a tight smile. "What do you imagine you, or we, can do regarding this alleged situation?"

"I have an idea." Fortunately, a possibility had hit her. "I'll share it on one condition." She might as well benefit from this.

"Which is?"

"You stop nagging me about my personal choices, however stupid you may consider them."

Lucky didn't answer. Then, abruptly, he burst out laughing. "Sometimes I actually like you."

"Why?" she asked suspiciously.

"Because you're a tough little cookie. If only you would apply that quality to he-who-shall-remain-nameless."

"That's breaking the rules," Zora retorted. "No nagging and no smart-aleck remarks, either. Well?"

"You're draining all the fun out of our relationship." Lucky raised his hands in mock surrender. "I agree. Now, what's the suggestion?"

The sight of him leaning close, intent on her, sent a thrill across her nervous system. Must be the maternal hormones running amok. "Remember when Edmond gave that speech about trends in family law?"

Melissa's husband served as a consultant for staff and patients on the legal aspects of fertility issues.

"Sure." Another one-syllable response.

"Afterward, Vince approached him for advice." Zora had heard the story from Melissa. Quickly, she added, "It was in a public place. No attorney-client privilege."

"Advice about what?"

"About persuading Mrs. Adams to agree to in vitro." If Vince produced even a small amount of sperm, it could be extracted and injected into an egg, bypassing the need to fix his blocked ducts. "She refuses to undergo in vitro, however."

"He can afford to hire a surrogate," Lucky pointed out.

"He objects to bringing in a stranger while his wife is presumably still fertile." Although Zora detested Portia for Rod's sake, she understood why a woman approaching forty wouldn't be eager to undergo a process involving hormone shots as well as uncomfortable procedures to harvest her eggs and implant the embryos. There were also potential health risks from a pregnancy complicated by multiple babies.

"What does this have to do with us?" Lucky asked.

"Talking to Edmond renewed Vince's enthusiasm

for Safe Harbor." According to Melissa, the hospital administrator had phoned later to congratulate Edmond on saving the day.

"Renewed his enthusiasm how?" Lucky persisted. "His wife still hasn't agreed, as far as I know."

"I'm not sure, but judging by what Rod says about him, he enjoys power trips," Zora observed. "He hates to lose. If we figure out how he can win in this situation, it might keep him engaged with Safe Harbor."

"Any suggestions?"

"Ask Edmond what *he* advised."

Lucky considered this in silence. At close range, Zora noticed an end-of-day dark beard shadowing his rough cheeks. Although she preferred men with a smooth, sophisticated look, she had to admit there was something appealing about Lucky's male hormones proclaiming themselves loud and clear.

What was wrong with her? At this stage of pregnancy, she ought to have zero interest in sex. Or men. Or sexy men. Or… *Stop that.*

"Any idea which days Edmond's at the hospital?" Lucky asked.

"Afraid not."

In the adjacent dining room, Karen rose after stowing a tray in the sideboard. "Monday mornings and Thursday afternoons. Why the interest in Edmond?"

"It's private," Zora and Lucky said simultaneously.

Descending the few steps to the living room, their landlady gathered the pile of chair covers. "That's unusual, you guys being on the same page."

They both returned her gaze wordlessly until she sighed and departed. Zora chuckled. That had been fun.

Lucky held out his hand. As her fingers brushed his,

a quiver of pleasure ran through her. On her feet, she lingered close to him for a moment, enjoying the citrus smell of his cologne underscored by masculine pheromones. Then in the recesses of her mind, she remembered something he often said: *it's Andrew who should be helping you, not me.*

Even without speaking, he projected criticism. Glowering, and ignoring Lucky's puzzled reaction, Zora headed for the stair lift.

Chapter 4

On Monday mornings while Cole performed surgeries at the hospital, Lucky replenished supplies, scheduled follow-up appointments with patients and prepared for office procedures in the afternoon.

He'd hoped to slip out to talk to Edmond, but the attorney was fully booked and could only spare a few minutes at lunch. It would have to do. But the morning turned out to be busier than expected, due to a special request from the fertility program director, Dr. Owen Tartikoff. A new urologist, a specialist in men's reconstructive surgery, would soon be joining the staff and Dr. Tartikoff needed someone to review the applications for his office nurse. Due to Lucky's administrative degree, Cole had recommended him.

Pleased at the responsibility, Lucky sifted through digital résumés to select the best candidates. The final choice would be left to the new physician, since the relationship between a doctor and his nurse was crucial. The right person eased the doctor's job, increased efficiency and decreased errors.

The wrong person could cause all sorts of unwanted drama. Hospital lore included a by-now-legendary clash between Keely Randolph and Dr. Tartikoff shortly after his arrival a few years ago. There'd been a spectacular scene when the abrasive Dr. T had dressed her down for an error and she'd blown up, calling him arrogant and egotistical before stalking out.

In view of her long history at Safe Harbor, she'd received a second chance with another obstetrician, Paige Brennan. Miraculously, the chemistry between them had proved stable rather than explosive. Keely spoke of her doctor in glowing terms, which in Lucky's view was how a nurse should behave.

He smiled, remembering how Keely had stood up for Zora at the party, staving off Laird's attempt to touch her. While his attentions hadn't necessarily been sexual, Lucky wouldn't put it past the man.

An image of Zora filled his mind as he recalled her unexpected offer to aid in his quest to expand the men's program. Her teasing grin was irresistible, and who would have imagined a mother-to-be could radiate such sexy vibes? True, she'd been cute before she got pregnant, but Lucky had been too caught up in resenting her for Stacy's and Cole's sakes to take more than a passing notice.

Not that there was any risk of a romance developing between him and Zora. He would never fall for anyone who led such a messy life, and he didn't appear to be her type, either. Judging by Andrew, she went for slick and manipulative, hardly adjectives that applied to a tattooed guy from a rough part of LA.

A guy who'd committed his share of mistakes and was determined not to repeat them, especially if a wife and children were at stake. If he were ever so blessed, Lucky vowed to be sure his family's circumstances were as close to perfect as humanly possible. He'd give them a financial buffer. A protective circle of love, commitment and security. If he couldn't be sure he could provide those things, he'd rather not risk marrying at all.

Lucky focused on the résumés on the computer screen. There were a number of nurses eager to work in such a prestigious environment with regular hours and benefits. He struggled to view them through the perspective of an employer instead of as a fellow nurse who'd spent a year on his own job search. More than ever, he appreciated Cole's willingness to bring him on board.

Clicking open a new résumé, Lucky frowned in confusion. Was this a joke? Someone had inserted a slightly altered photo of Zora. Her face was narrower, but he'd recognize her anywhere.

Only the name on the file was Zady Moore. *Zady, huh?* He read on, prepared for humorous remarks, but the data seemed straightforward. This so-called Zady had grown up near Safe Harbor, just like Zora. Same age, too. In fact, same birth date.

She claimed to have a nursing degree and to work for a urologist in Santa Barbara, a couple of hours' drive north of here. Switching to the internet, Lucky confirmed that there was indeed a Zady Moore listed in connection with that urologist's office. If this was a hoax, someone had gone to great lengths.

The name Moore struck him as familiar. Oh, right. He'd seen mail addressed to Zora Moore Raditch.

Could Zora have a twin she'd never told him about? Or did she have a cousin with an eerily similar appearance and the same birth date?

The alarm on his watch shrilled, a reminder of his meeting with Edmond. Lucky set aside the résumé with several others marked for further consideration.

From the fourth floor, he took the stairs to the medical building lobby and strode out past the pharmacy into the late September sunshine. A salty breeze wafted from the ocean a mile to the south, while seagulls wheeled overhead.

Next door, the six-story hospital rose in front of him, a lovely sight with its curved wings. Remodeled half a dozen years earlier to specialize in fertility and maternity services, it had established a national reputation by hiring distinguished doctors such as Cole and Dr. T, and by adding state-of-the-art laboratories, surgical suites and equipment. As a result, the side-by-side buildings were bursting at the seams with staff and patients.

Lucky glanced across the circular drive at the vacant dental building that had been mired in bankruptcy proceedings. Once the bankruptcy judge allowed a sale, it would be snapped up fast. The corporation that owned Safe Harbor Medical Center had expressed interest in buying it, but had balked at the high price.

When Vince Adams had expressed interest in funding the growth of the men's program, he'd seemed a gift from fate. Since then, Vince had demonstrated mood swings and a knack for throwing everyone off balance, but his donation remained the hospital's best chance of acquiring the building and boosting the men's fertility program to the next level.

Lucky entered the hospital via the staff door. Instantly, his senses registered tempting aromas from the cafeteria. Also nearby, the chatter of childish voices drifted from the day care center, to which he presumed Zora would soon be entrusting her babies.

As he shoved open the door to the stairs—Lucky seized any chance at exercise—he wondered how long he could go without nagging her. *Somebody* had to advocate for those kids, who deserved their father's financial support even if he was incapable of acting like a real dad.

What about this Zady character? If she was a family member, Zora could sure use the help.

On the fifth floor, Lucky passed the executive offices and entered a smaller suite. The receptionist had apparently gone to lunch, and an inner door stood ajar. The placard read, Edmond Everhart, Family Law Consultant.

Lucky listened in case a client remained inside. Hearing no one, he rapped on the frame.

"Come in." From behind the desk, Edmond rose to greet him. In his early thirties, like Lucky, and also about five-ten, the guy was impeccably dressed in a suit and tie. Only his rumpled brown hair revealed that he'd had a busy morning. All the same, there was nothing glib or calculating about him.

After shaking hands and taking a seat, Lucky went straight to the point. "I understand Vince Adams was souring on Safe Harbor until he talked to you. You spoke with him in public, so I presume client confidentiality doesn't apply."

"That's true." Leaning back, the attorney removed his glasses, plucked a microfiber cloth from the drawer and polished the lenses.

"I'm curious how you won him over, because—" Lucky couldn't go into detail, since it involved Vince's treatment "—just in case he changes his mind again. What upset him in the first place?"

"He felt disrespected because the whole hospital is aware that he has fertility issues," Edmond said.

"A fact that he's publicized with his own…statements." Lucky had nearly said *big mouth*.

"Be that as it may, he believed people looked down on him because he can't father children."

"How'd you reassure him?"

"I shared a few personal details that put us on a par." After a hesitation, Edmond continued, "I explained that I'd had a vasectomy and later regretted it." His wife, Melissa, was carrying embryos donated by another couple. "I also asked his advice as a stepfather about parenting my niece while her mom's in prison. I'm not sure why, but the conversation eased his mind."

"My guess is that he felt you respected him," Lucky mused. "Did he bring up anything else?"

Edmond reflected. "Yes. He's frustrated with his wife's refusal to consider in vitro. She wasn't present, so I have no idea how she views the matter."

Lucky recalled Zora's comments. "And he rejects hiring a surrogate?" The hospital maintained a roster of screened candidates.

"That's right."

Wheels spun in Lucky's head. "If we persuaded Mrs. Adams to change her mind, that ought to solve the problem."

"It might," Edmond said. "But is it wise to try to manipulate a woman into having a child she might not want?"

"I believe she's worried more about the medical risk than about having another child." At a previous office visit, a successfully treated patient had arrived to show Cole his newborn son. In the waiting room, Portia Adams had reached out to touch the baby's cheek and studied the child wistfully. Catching Lucky's eye, she'd murmured something about missing those days now that her girls were growing up.

"Perhaps there's a compromise position that might satisfy them both," Edmond said. "What if his wife provided the eggs but didn't carry the pregnancy?"

Lucky hadn't thought about separating the two aspects of in vitro. "It's worth a try."

"Good," Edmond said. "Any other questions?"

"Yes, although it's unrelated." While Lucky had promised not to pressure Zora, he hadn't promised not to encourage others to do so. "Zora hasn't broken the news to her ex about the twins. You're her attorney. How about pointing out that the man has legal obligations?"

The attorney laced his fingers atop the desk. "I assure you, I already have."

"You may have to get in her face, so she can't brush you off."

Edmond tilted his head. "May I share something with you that I've discovered about relationships?"

"Sure." Lucky admired how much Edmond had grown and changed while reconciling with Melissa. "Lay it on me."

"It's important to respect her choices," Edmond said.

"Even if you disagree with them?"

"Especially if you disagree with them." Thoughtfully, the lawyer added, "And especially when she's the person who has to deal with the consequences."

"But Zora keeps repeating the same boneheaded mistakes," Lucky protested.

"I suspect she understands her ex-husband better than either of us," Edmond said. "Legally, she'll have to inform him about the babies once they're born, but until then, she might have reason to be cautious."

Lucky only knew Andrew by reputation. "I suppose it's hard to predict how a guy will react to that kind of news."

"Exactly."

The circumstances might not be perfect, but this was a situation of Andrew's own making. Any decent guy would accept responsibility. However, the man had proven repeatedly that he didn't care about honor *or* decency. "Thanks for the words of wisdom."

"You're welcome."

"Oh, one more thing," Lucky said as they both rose. "Does Zora have a sister named Zady?"

"I believe that's her twin," Edmond said.

"Thanks." A twin. Damn! By applying for the job, Zady had put Lucky in a delicate position. He felt as if he ought to alert Zora, but her sister's application was confidential.

He set off for the cafeteria, anxious to arrive before Zora finished eating so he could get her opinion about his discussion with Edmond. As for her mysterious twin, he'd better leave that hot potato alone.

Being around perfect people filled Zora with a sense of inadequacy. It was balanced by a fervent desire to figure out how they did it.

Take her obstetrician. Six feet tall with dramatic red hair

and green eyes, Paige Brennan was a doctor, mother to an eighteen-month-old daughter and wife of the head of a detective agency. Everyone admired and adored her, including her nurse, Keely, who could barely stand most people.

Busy as she was, Dr. Brennan had fit in Zora's exam during her lunch break. The woman was a step from sainthood.

As she sat on the examining table, Zora doubted she could ever develop such an air of confidence. As for inspiring others, she'd settle for earning their good-natured tolerance.

"Surely you have *some* questions," the doctor said after listening to the babies' heartbeats and reviewing Zora's weight gain and test results. They were fine considering her stage of pregnancy. "You never mention any problems."

"Am I supposed to?" Zora had been raised to consider complaining a sign of weakness.

"Frankly, yes." The tall woman draped her frame over a stool. "At thirty-two weeks with a multiple pregnancy, you must be having trouble sleeping, and your ankles are swollen. As I've suggested before, you should be on bed rest."

"I can't afford it," Zora said. "I don't have a husband to wait on me."

"What about the rest of your family?" the doctor asked.

"My mom and stepfather live in Oregon." She'd rather not have either of them around. And there was no sense bringing up her twin, perfect Zady with her ideal husband and kids, whom their mother never failed to mention when she talked with Zora.

The doctor's forehead creased. "Is your mom flying down for the birth?"

"Not if I have anything to say about it." Her mother would expect to be catered to, regardless of the circumstances. She'd be no help with a baby. At home, Mom waited on Zora's surly, demanding stepfather, but her attitude toward her daughters—toward Zora, at least—was just the opposite.

Dr. Brennan regarded her with concern. "Have you chosen a labor partner?" At every visit, she'd recommended Zora sign up for a birthing class.

"I won't need one for a C-section." Although twins didn't always have to be delivered surgically, Zora preferred to play it safe.

"If that's what you want, okay." The physician nodded. "But remember that what we call bed rest doesn't necessarily require staying in bed. You can relax at home and perform routine tasks as you feel capable."

"I feel capable of working." To forestall further objections, Zora added, "And providing ultrasounds doesn't harm the babies. It's not like X-rays or mammograms."

"But it does require standing on your feet all day. And for safety's sake, you should stop driving." Paige raised her eyebrows commandingly.

Zora *was* having trouble reaching the pedals in her car. "I could ride to work with my housemates." Rod, whose car frequently broke down, cadged rides from others, so why shouldn't she?

Keely chose that moment to step in from the hall. "I can drive her."

"Excuse me?" Paige blinked at the unexpected comment.

"If I rent a room in their house, Zora can ride with me." The nurse mustered a faint smile.

"I thought you had a roommate," Zora said.

"So did I. Can we talk at lunch?"

"Sure."

The obstetrician cleared her throat. "Keely, would you provide Zora with an after-visit summary and schedule an appointment for her in two weeks?"

"Yes, Doctor."

The doctor typed a note into the computer. "Zora, call me if you have any problems, such as spotting or contractions, even if they don't hurt. Okay?"

"Will do." Zora accepted the nurse's assistance in rising from the table.

Once she was dressed, she tucked the printed summary into her purse and walked to the elevator with Keely. With her neck thrust forward, the woman's aggressive stance reinforced the impression of her as a difficult personality. Zora hoped she hadn't erred by suggesting Keely move in with them.

"What's the situation with your roommate?" she asked as they descended. The office was only one flight up, but in Zora's condition, that might as well be ten stories.

"She's in Iowa taking care of her mother," Keely said. "She only planned to stay a week but that's changed. Last night she emailed and asked me to ship all her stuff to her."

"That was short notice. Your rent must be due next week." It was the first of the month.

"That's right. I'm glad you mentioned the vacancy."

"Everything's subject to Karen's approval," Zora warned.

"I'll stop by her office later."

It sounded like a done deal. At least Keely would be an improvement on Laird.

In the cafeteria, the blend of voices and aromas filled Zora with eagerness to share this new development with Lucky. Where was he? Her gaze swept past the food serving bays and across the crowded room.

She spotted him sharing a table with a thin and most unwelcome companion: Laird. The psychologist was talking a mile a minute, oblivious to Lucky's irritated expression.

Zora would rather not discuss Keely in front of the competition. "Hold on," she said, turning.

Too late. Keely was stomping right over to the table. Judging by the set of her shoulders, she didn't plan to be subtle, either.

Chapter 5

Lucky had often heard the flow of gossip referred to as a grapevine, but in a hospital, a more appropriate comparison would be the circulatory system, with its arteries and veins. And its heart, the pump through which all rumors flowed, was the cafeteria.

As a rule, he enjoyed the hum of conversations, among which his ears caught intriguing snatches of news—about hirings and firings, love affairs and broken hearts. Once in a while the drama expanded to include the doctors.

Until today, however, Lucky hadn't understood the embarrassment of landing in the middle of a scene that drew all eyes. It started when Keely announced, without preamble, "I lost my roommate. I've decided to move into your house!"

People peered toward them. The story of Karen's home, its assorted occupants and the resulting pregnancies and marriages had already set many a tongue wagging.

Laird choked, although Lucky couldn't figure out on what. The psychologist hadn't stopped yammering long enough to eat anything. Instead, he'd plopped his butt into a chair at Lucky's table and begun citing his plans for throwing parties.

He'd also proclaimed that his huge TV screen would transform their outdated living room into game central. Not that Lucky would mind, but the guy apparently didn't consider it necessary to solicit *Karen's* opinion.

"Like hell you're moving in!" Laird finally blurted in a voice that rose to a squeal. "Whatever gave you that idea?"

"I cleared it with Zora." Keely indicated that red-haired person, who gazed warily from the hot food line before ducking out of sight.

Lucky nearly bellowed, "Get over here!" but more heads were swiveling. Not his doctor, mercifully. Through the glass doors, he spotted Dr. Rattigan out of earshot on the patio.

"It's a party house!" Laird, his usually pale face reddening with anger, didn't appear to care who heard him roar. "You're the last person in Safe Harbor anyone would invite to a party."

Silence fell save for the clink of tableware and glasses. The chatter of a man talking on a cell phone sounded abnormally loud, and then that too ceased.

"Let's skip the insults, shall we?" Lucky deliberately employed a soft tone in the hope the others would follow suit.

The effort fell flat. "Oh, really?" Keely boomed. "I was invited to the baby shower, in case you forgot. As for you, Laird, you can take your grabby hands and go live in a brothel."

Lucky wouldn't show cowardice by retreating from the scene. But he could remove himself from the line of fire on the pretext of assisting the pregnant lady.

"Excuse me." Springing up, he narrowly restrained the temptation to break into a run.

Behind him, Laird snarled something about Keely being jealous because nobody made passes at her. Whatever the nurse responded, Lucky shut it out.

"Let me help with that," he told Zora, who had set down her tray as she paid for her lunch. He seized the tray without waiting for permission.

She stepped away from the register. "People are staring."

"Can you blame them?" Lucky halted as a tableful of volunteers arose, blocking their path. Grateful for the delay, he smiled encouragingly at an elderly lady, a gift shop regular who creaked to her feet at glacial speed. To Zora, he asked, "How'd you hook up with Keely?"

"She glommed on to me at Dr. Brennan's office," she explained.

"You had to see the doctor? You aren't having problems, are you?"

"Routine checkup."

"You sure?" He searched her face for signs of pain. She had a bad habit of toughing things out, but she looked well enough today.

What a sweet face, he thought, with a full mouth and a youthful sprinkling of freckles. Standing this close to Zora was having a weird effect on him. In light of their new pact, he wasn't sure how to respond to her. It had been easier when he could drop a comment about

Andrew into any conversation and receive a predictably angry retort.

"Did you promise Keely she could move in?" That ought to stir a response.

"Yes, but I warned her Karen has the final say." Biting her lip, Zora peered toward Keely and Laird, who were continuing to insult each other. They'd lowered their voices a notch, but at this stage it only meant other diners leaned forward in their seats to hear them. One orderly went so far as to cup his hands around his ears. "She'd be a zillion percent better than Laird," Zora said.

"For once—twice, actually—we agree on something. Let's not make it a habit."

"Certainly not," Zora replied. "Life would get boring."

"I'm sure we'll find plenty to squabble about." Lucky dodged away as the elderly volunteer snapped her cane to the floor inches from his foot. "Hey!"

She ambled out, not hearing him. Another volunteer responded with a quiet, "Sorry."

"Excellent reaction time," Zora observed.

"Thanks."

They resumed their journey toward the table, where Laird and Keely stood with arms folded, as if whoever was victorious in their staring contest would win the privilege of moving into the house. Around them, conversations slowly resumed.

"Isn't Keely eating lunch?" Lucky murmured. "She didn't stop to pick up anything."

"Look on the bright side," Zora said. "They can't have a food fight."

"I'd enjoy a food fight," he teased.

"Of course you would."

"I didn't say I'd participate." He lowered her tray onto the table beside his. "Guys, how about easing off?"

"Not till we settle this," Keely said.

"We can't do that without..." He broke off at the approach of their landlady, who projected authority despite being no taller than Zora. Maybe it was this month's black hair or the distinctive long skirts she favored, but more likely it was the quelling expression she wore. "Hey, Karen," he ventured.

Her frosty gaze swept the four of them. "Have a seat, everyone, and stop creating a spectacle."

They obeyed. "Now, what is this about?" Raising a hand to stop a barrage of words, Karen said, "Starting with Keely."

As the nurse explained about her roommate departing on short notice, Lucky watched Zora tuck into her food and thought about her twin. How could there be a carbon copy of her anywhere in the world? Surely no one had the same fiery temperament, or the same gift for frustrating the hell out of him while appealing to his masculine instincts. And why was Zady seeking to work near her sister, when the two appeared to be estranged?

Still, twins were supposed to have a special bond, in contrast to Lucky and his older brother. He didn't even know where Matthew lived now or whether he was still serving in the navy, and he didn't care.

Best friends during their teens, they hadn't spoken in sixteen years. Their last fight, after their parents' deaths, had been too bitter for either of them to forgive. Lucky deeply regretted his mistakes, but that didn't give his brother the right to make vicious, unfair accusations and repeat them to other family members. As a result,

Lucky had distanced himself not only from Matthew but also from his aunts, uncles and cousins.

When Keely paused for breath, Laird jumped in. He insisted he had a prior claim and that the household needed him to liven things up.

"I wasn't aware we were dull," Karen snapped. "Frankly, after the behavior I just witnessed, I'd drop you both from consideration, but for financial reasons, I need someone to move in next weekend."

Laird lifted his chin. "Considering my position as staff psychologist, I outrank this woman."

Didn't the jerk realize he'd insulted Lucky, who was an RN on a par with Keely? And Karen herself held the middle-level post of financial counselor.

"This isn't a promotional position," she said. "No offense, Laird, but I think having a nurse across the hall from a pregnant woman would be the most sensible choice. However, I won't approve anyone without the consent of my other renters. Lucky? Zora?"

Nobody wished to become Laird's enemy. Nevertheless, Lucky tilted his head toward Keely, as did Zora. Turning, Karen pinpointed Rod. The anesthesiologist, who was sitting with his nephew and several other doctors, mouthed, "Kee-lee."

If Lucky imagined they'd fallen below everyone else's radar, a rustle of movement proved otherwise as people shifted to observe Rod, then moved their attention back to his table.

"I'm sorry," Karen told the psychologist. "The group agrees with my rationale."

Laird scrambled to his feet. "I hope you'll keep me in mind if there's another opening. Keely might not fit in as well as you assume."

"You're the one who doesn't fit in," the nurse sneered.

"You'll regret this." Noticing everyone's reaction to this threat, Laird added, "I mean, it wouldn't surprise me if they threw you out in a few months."

He stalked off, leaving his dirty dishes. Nostrils flaring, Keely watched him go before excusing herself to buy food.

"Alone at last," Lucky teased after Karen, too, departed.

Zora swallowed a mouthful of milk and wasted no time changing the subject. "Did you talk to Edmond?"

He sketched what he'd learned about Vince and Portia Adams. "My plan is to encourage her to donate eggs and him to hire a gestational surrogate."

"Splitting the difference? Excellent," Zora said. "I suspect you're right about Portia's maternal instincts. During Tiffany's last visit, she mentioned that her mom's developed a fascination with her friends' babies."

"Any suggestions how to nudge her further in that direction?"

"Talk to Rod," she advised.

First she'd recommended he consult Edmond, now Rod. "Why?"

"He used to be married to Portia. If anyone can comprehend how her mind works, it's him." Having polished off her entrée, Zora tackled her custard.

He should have thought of that, Lucky mused. But a marriage that had ended bitterly half a dozen years ago hardly qualified the anesthesiologist as an expert. "You're a mom, or soon will be. Put me into her perspective about this pregnancy business."

"She's a fashion plate who I'm sure injects stuff into her wrinkles and suctions her flab," Zora said. "It's partly ego but I also think she feels she has to compete for her husband's affection. How's she going to fend off gold diggers ten years younger when she has a big round pregnant body?"

"But donating eggs might be okay?"

"Better, although those hormone shots and the mood swings aren't fun," Zora said.

Lucky sighed. "Well, thanks for bouncing ideas around with me."

"Glad to do it." Abruptly, Zora set down her fork. "Something just hit me."

If it would help bring the Adamses together, he was eager to hear it. "Yes?"

"I—" She broke off as a ringtone sounded and she took out her phone. "This is Zora."

Lucky could happily have smashed the device for interrupting them. "Don't lose that thought!"

Frowning, Zora answered. "Yes? Now? Okay. I'll be right there." She clicked off. "It's radiology."

How frustrating. "Before you go, tell me what occurred to you."

"No time. We can discuss it tonight." Hands on the table, Zora hoisted herself upright. "Will you dispose of my dishes? I'd hate to be a slob like Laird."

"Of course," he said. "But—"

"It's a patient of Dr. Tartikoff's," she explained. "The tech went home sick, and he's waiting with her."

Nobody wished to cross the imperious head of the fertility program. "I understand."

"Thanks, Lucky," she said. "I can always count on you."

It was on the tip of his tongue to note that she ought to be able to rely on the father of her children, but he'd promised to lay off that subject. And Lucky found it rather gratifying that he and no one else was the person she counted on.

* * *

Talking to Lucky was more fun now that he no longer poked at her sore spot, Zora reflected as she lumbered along the sidewalk to the medical office building. And even though she hadn't planned it, she'd rather enjoyed needling him by withholding information.

On the third floor, she entered Dr. T's medical suite and headed for the room set up for the ultrasound. Nurse Ned Norwalk, a surfer type with a deep tan, appeared around a corner. "You?" he demanded.

"Me, what?" Zora asked. Although she and Ned moved in different circles, she'd never had any problems with him.

"There wasn't any other tech available?" He obviously didn't expect an answer. "Never mind. Fair warning—Dr. T hasn't eaten lunch."

Great—he'd be crankier than ever. "I'll tiptoe around. Where's the patient's chart?"

"The doctor has it. The patient has a mass on her right ovary. You'll be doing a transvaginal ultrasound."

"Okay." Sonograms to examine ovarian cysts—fluid-filled pockets in or on the surface of an ovary—as well as other growths were commonplace. While most cysts vanished on their own, some caused pain, and there was the scary possibility that an ovarian growth could be cancerous. The best view of the ovaries was obtained by inserting a probe into the patient's vagina. "Is she pregnant?"

"No. But—you're sure there wasn't anyone else available?"

"If you doubt me, call radiology."

"Never mind."

Zora had often assisted Dr. T's patients. She didn't understand why Ned was making a big deal of this, but she didn't intend to question him and keep the great physician waiting.

Ned opened the door and retreated. Near the small ultrasound machine paced a scowling Dr. Owen Tartikoff. Even his russet hair seemed to be sizzling with impatience. "Finally," he growled.

"Sorry for the delay. The scheduled tech went home sick." Zora's gaze shifted to the dark-haired woman lying on the examining table, her lower half covered with a paper sheet.

When almond-shaped brown eyes met hers with a jolt, Zora struggled to catch her breath. The patient was Lin Lee Raditch, Andrew's third wife.

Although they'd never been introduced, she'd seen the woman with him around town, and judging by the other woman's reaction, Lin recognized Zora, as well. That explained Ned's attitude. Either the scheduler hadn't noticed that they shared a last name, or had no other options.

"Is there a problem?" The doctor's cross tone slapped at her. He didn't seem aware of their connection.

Zora darted a glance at Lin. The patient had the right to object to an inappropriate care provider. And for the sake of her own emotional state, Zora wasn't sure she ought to go through with this.

Lin's lips pressed tightly. Was she reluctant to offend the celebrated doctor? Then Zora noticed tears glittering in the patient's eyes. *She's frightened.*

In that instant, Lin transformed from the jezebel for whom Andrew had abandoned Zora into a scared woman who might face a terrifying diagnosis.

"This won't hurt," she assured the patient, and went to work.

Chapter 6

"These appear to be fluid-filled cysts," Dr. Tartikoff told the patient as Zora finished her scan. "However, before recommending a treatment plan, I'll have the radiologist review the images."

"It isn't cancer?" Lin's body had gone nearly rigid, although Zora had encouraged her to relax during the procedure.

"I doubt it." The obstetrician continued studying the screen. "If these were solid, or partially solid, I'd be more concerned."

The patient swallowed, evidently still worried. "Will you have to remove my ovaries?"

"It may be possible to perform a cystectomy, excising only the largest cyst." Dr. T patted Lin's shoulder reassuringly. "Or we might remove one ovary, leaving the other in place."

"I can still have children?" Lin's slightly accented voice trembled.

"Yes, but first let's deal with the discomfort you've been suffering."

"Thank you, Doctor." She regarded him gratefully.

How ironic, Zora thought, that Andrew's wife was concerned about being able to bear his children, while Zora herself stood there with his babies thumping inside her. Nevertheless, her heart went out to the anxious young woman.

Did life have to be so complicated? It would be easier if Zora could simply blame Andrew's faithlessness on his new wife. Instead, she related to Lin's pain. Carrying twins was hard, but being unable to bear children would be worse.

"The radiologist's report should reach me within a few days. I'll review it immediately," Dr. T advised. "Please set up an appointment for next week. Your husband should accompany you."

Lin's smile vanished. "He travels and is very busy."

"You're his wife. There's nothing more important than your health." In his intensity, Zora heard the conviction of a man devoted to his wife and children. "Would you like me to explain the situation to him?"

"No, no, Doctor, that isn't necessary." Lin sounded anxious.

"You're sure?"

When she again declined, Dr. T excused himself and left.

"I'll be out of here in a minute so you can dress," Zora said. She shifted the equipment cart away from the examining table.

Lin touched her arm. "Thank you for being gentle."

Astonished, Zora wondered what the woman had expected. "You're welcome."

"I am wondering…" She indicated Zora's expanded midsection.

Was she asking about the father? Zora pretended not to pick up the hint. "Twins," she said. "Due in late November."

"You are fortunate to be fertile." The patient sat up. "I am desperate for children to bind my husband to me and prove my family is wrong."

"Wrong about what?" Zora asked.

"They believe I married a man who will treat me badly." She sniffled. "And they're angry that I moved to another country after they sacrificed to send me to college. My mother will not talk to me on the phone."

On the verge of inquiring why Lin was sharing this with her of all people, Zora realized how isolated the woman was. "That must be difficult." She handed over a tissue.

Lin wiped her eyes. "Pardon me, but also, I wonder why you are pregnant when you did not want children."

A weird sense of déjà vu swept over Zora. During her marriage, Andrew had claimed his first wife had refused to have kids. Only later had she learned that the opposite was true: Stacy had longed for children but delayed pregnancy at Andrew's request.

Same lies, same manipulations. Pain knifed inside Zora. *Lucky's right. I must be the most gullible person on earth.*

"What is wrong?" Gathering the paper covering her, Lin eased off the table. "The babies are hurting you?"

This show of compassion undid her. Suddenly Zora couldn't hold her secret inside for another instant.

"Andrew lied to you. These are his children, except he doesn't know that yet."

Lin stood frozen with her bare feet on the linoleum. "That is impossible. He had a vasectomy. You insisted on it."

"No, I didn't. When...?" Zora gave a start at a tap on the door.

Ned Norwalk entered, holding a sheet of paper. "How's everything in here?" The nurse halted at the sight of them obviously engaged in a discussion. "Are you okay, Mrs. Raditch?"

"I'm fine," both women said.

"The current Mrs. Raditch."

They glared at him.

He blinked, registering the unexpected collusion, and, to his credit, decided to respect their privacy. "I'll be at the nurses' station if anyone wants me."

After Ned beat a strategic retreat, Zora refocused on her companion. "If Andrew had a vasectomy, it wasn't at my request. And these *are* his children."

"You are wrong," Lin insisted. "He showed me the scar."

Zora preferred not to think about the location of that scar or the intimate circumstances under which he'd displayed it. "When was that?"

The other woman, a few inches shorter than her, considered briefly before saying, "Eight months ago, while we were engaged. Before you became pregnant, if you are in the seventh month."

Could he have faked the scar? Then a better explanation occurred to Zora.

"After a vasectomy, a man's sperm count doesn't immediately drop to zero. It can take a month or more before the sperm is completely gone." She absorbed a lot of medical information in her work. "We were still married—barely. He must have been fertile, because I haven't slept with anyone else."

Lin steadied herself on the edge of the examining table. "These babies, they really are his?"

"I'm afraid so. It all makes more sense now. No wonder he didn't insist on contraception—he'd had a vasectomy." Zora had assumed that, at some level, Andrew had wished to father a baby with her. Instead, he'd believed he was safe.

Lin hugged herself and shivered. "You will take away my husband."

That was precisely what Zora had fantasized. Now, witnessing the other woman's distress, she faced the fact that Andrew had coldheartedly plucked Lin from her family and country, then lied to her and manipulated her. He'd also played on Zora's love for him, using and discarding her yet again. Why? For ego's sake?

The man had no heart and could never be trusted. Zora was truly alone in this pregnancy. Except for Lucky. And her other friends, of course.

To her astonishment, the primary emotion pumping through her was relief. She didn't have to pretend any more. She could tell the truth, to herself most of all.

"I don't want him back," Zora said.

The dark-haired woman studied her in confusion. "But you carry his babies."

The man isn't capable of loving anyone except himself. A burden lifted from her shoulders, filling her with unaccustomed lightness despite the weight in her womb. "You can keep him with my blessing."

A couple of quick steps and Lin flung her arms

around Zora. "You are my sister in spirit. I shall try to be strong like you."

Zora hesitated only a second before returning the hug. When she and Andrew broke up, she'd been utterly friendless. That experience intensified her empathy with this woman whose world was collapsing. "What will you do?"

Lin breathed deeply before replying, "I will think hard."

"If you need a divorce attorney, I recommend Edmond Everhart," Zora said. "He's a consultant on staff at the hospital."

"That is good advice," Lin said.

"Best of luck."

As Zora exited, she ignored a questioning look from Ned in the hall. Struggling to sort through what she'd learned, she wished she didn't have to endure Lucky's comments when he heard about this encounter.

And yet, she felt liberated. "Sorry, babies," Zora whispered. "We're all better off without your dad."

Then fear quivered through her. How could she raise these kids without a father? Her own might have been flawed, but she'd always sensed that he loved her and Zady.

Unlike her dad, Andrew lacked the capacity to care about others. Zora had to accept that and move on, no matter how badly it hurt.

She hoped she wouldn't have to put up with any I-told-you-so taunts tonight from Lucky, who would no doubt hear about this entire scene via the gossip mill. With her heart aching and her mood unsettled, she was in no mood to tolerate his sniping.

* * *

With everyone eager to chat about Keely's pending arrival, Lucky and his three housemates gathered at the dining room table earlier than usual on Monday night. While they ate, they relived the scene in the cafeteria and speculated about Laird's not-so-veiled threat.

Would he try to intimidate Keely to keep her from joining them? Did he honestly believe they'd accept him if he did?

Karen related that Keely had paid a deposit and arranged to move in Saturday afternoon. Her only question had been whether the nearness to the estuary caused illness among the residents. Karen had assured her that, despite the smell, they all stayed remarkably healthy.

Questions and comments flew, but the usually talkative Zora didn't join in, Lucky noted. Instead, she downed her soup and salad while avoiding his gaze. Was she annoyed at him?

Perhaps she'd found out about her twin applying for a job. After reviewing the remaining résumés, he'd confirmed that Zady's qualifications merited a spot among the top half dozen contenders and had scheduled her for an interview next week, when the new urologist would be visiting. But if that was the problem, why wasn't Zora interrogating him?

During a lull in the conversation, she slanted a glare at him. He'd done nothing to deserve that, Lucky was almost certain. "What?" he demanded.

"What do you mean, what?"

"I mean, why are you scowling at me? I haven't done anything." *Recently.*

"You will," she muttered.

"Suit yourself." Lucky let the subject drop. If he'd offended Zora, it was her responsibility to be frank about it.

Rod and Karen finished eating and carried their dishes into the kitchen. As Zora started to rise, Lucky recalled her hasty departure from lunch and the idea she'd mentioned. "Hold on a sec."

She grimaced. "We might as well get this over with."

"Get what over with?"

Still not meeting his gaze, she said, "I refuse to make it easier for you."

He was growing more confused by the minute. She'd been friendly at lunch, and Lucky had been too busy during the afternoon to ruffle anyone's feathers. To compensate for his absence at the convention, Dr. Rattigan had squeezed in so many patients that Lucky had skipped his coffee break and stayed at the office late.

"Is this about your—" He nearly said *sister*, but caught himself. Besides, there was another thing he'd been waiting to discuss. "Idea about the Adamses?" he finished.

"What idea about the Adamses?"

"In the cafeteria, you said something hit you, and then you took off to see a patient," Lucky reminded her.

"Did I?" Zora rested her chin in her palm. Pregnancy had darkened her cute freckles and rounded her cheeks. Her hair had thickened and taken on a shine, as well.

"Please don't tell me you forgot the idea."

She frowned so hard that Lucky feared she'd get a headache. Then she brightened. "I remember!"

"Shoot."

"Portia has mixed feelings about pregnancy because she fears it will turn Vince away from her, but she might change her mind if she realizes it could save her marriage," Zora said.

"Why is she so afraid of losing him?" Lucky countered. "In a divorce, she could take her husband to the cleaners."

"There's always the possibility that she loves the guy. Besides, from what I've read, Vince's previous two wives didn't fare very well," she replied.

Lucky recalled news reports about the man's insistence on prenuptial agreements. Nevertheless, the women had been left financially comfortable by ordinary standards. "A few million apiece might not be much compared to his billions, but it ain't too shabby."

"It's not only the money." Rod joined the conversation from the kitchen entrance. "Portia loves having a ringside seat at New York Fashion Week, being invited to A-list parties and hobnobbing with celebrities. A couple of million dollars doesn't do that. Being married to Vince Adams does."

Lucky supposed Rod knew her better than any of them. "Wouldn't having a baby interfere with all that partying?"

"Not when you can afford live-in nannies," he growled.

"You can be a devoted mom and still hire a nanny," Zora said. "Don't forget, she has lots of free time during the day, since she doesn't work."

"Portia will do whatever she believes is in her best interest, and to hell with anyone else," Rod snarled, and ducked out of sight.

While Lucky had a less jaundiced view of Mrs. Adams than Rod, he did agree that she'd fight to save her marriage. "Interesting point," he told Zora. "It's worth bearing in mind."

Silence descended, aside from random noises in the kitchen. Zora poked at the remaining bits of lettuce on her salad plate. "Stop torturing me."

He might as well take the bull by the horns, Lucky decided. "Is this about your sister?"

"My sister?" Her blank expression indicated he'd missed the mark.

He had to cover his mistake, fast. "I heard you have a twin sister."

"From who?"

He couldn't cite the job application and he'd rather avoid implicating Edmond, who'd merely confirmed what Lucky had already stumbled across. "Informed sources."

"She's none of your business," Zora snapped. "We aren't in touch. Stop changing the subject."

Rod stuck his head through the door again. "Oh, seriously, Lucky, quit acting coy. Everyone's dying to find out what happened between the two Mrs. Raditches."

That was what had gone down today? And he hadn't heard a word.

Lucky threw up his hands. "I skip my coffee break for one afternoon and miss the gossip of the century. You went mano a mano with the new Mrs. Raditch?"

"She's a patient. I can't discuss…" To his dismay, Zora's face crumpled, and tears rolled down her cheeks.

Lucky scooted over and put his arms around her, enjoying the warmth of her pregnancy-enhanced body. "You discovered she's no more a demon than you are, and Andrew's an even bigger rat than you realized. Am I close?"

"I feel bad for her." Zora scrubbed her cheek with the back of her hand. "Her family rejected her when she married him. She's alone in a foreign country. And he lied about me, like he lied about Stacy. As if we're interchangeable."

To Lucky, there was nothing interchangeable about Zora and any other woman on the planet, including her twin. That was irrelevant, however. "You're crying for her sake?"

"And because what I learned means he'll never love these babies. Before today, I believed that deep down, he wanted them." Her gray eyes darkened with sorrow. "Ever since I've been steeling myself for you to say, *I told you so*. Go ahead and get it over with."

Cradling her against him, Lucky said, "Okay. I told you so."

A painful whack in the ankle sent him jolting backward, nearly overturning his chair. "Ow! How'd you do that from this angle?" Releasing her, he rubbed the spot where she'd kicked him.

"Public opinion agrees that you deserved it," noted Rod, who'd resumed snooping from the doorway.

"Beat it," Zora ordered him.

"Me?" Rod feigned innocence.

"This is between me and this pain in the neck," she retorted.

"Pain in the ankle," Lucky corrected.

From behind Rod, a feminine hand gripped his shirt collar and tugged him out of sight. Lucky wafted a mental thanks in Karen's direction.

"If my shin is black-and-blue tomorrow, I'll sue for assault." He moved to a chair at a safer distance.

"Felled by a pregnant midget?" Zora wisecracked. "What a wimp."

Footsteps moved through the den and around to the

front. The stairs creaked as their housemates ascended, leaving them in privacy.

Once Lucky heard Karen's door close upstairs, he felt safe to ask, "What's your next move?"

Zora stretched her legs under the table. "I talked to Edmond. He says Andrew has to pay half of the uninsured costs for my pregnancy and half the child-care expenses."

"You'll let the attorney deal with him?" That seemed wise.

Zora nodded. "I'm still not sure how I'd react to Andrew in the flesh."

"More importantly, how would he react to *you*?" Lucky's hands formed fists at the idea of the man bullying Zora.

"I hate being weak." She dabbed her eyes with her napkin.

"There's nothing weak about using good judgment," he said. "You don't have to prove how tough you are."

"That's not what I mean." She indicated her enlarged abdomen. "When I'm alone with Andrew, he slips past my defenses. Here's the living proof."

"You can seize control if you're determined." Surely she could resist the man after everything he'd put her through. "Zora, you're strength personified with everyone else."

"Am I?" She gazed into space. "My dad used to swing between being a jerk and being the most loving father in the world. No matter how hard I resolved to stay angry, I couldn't."

"Did he drink?" In Lucky's observation, alcoholism was often associated with that sort of behavior.

"Yes, sometimes." Zora inhaled deeply. "I used to

long for a family I could rely on, where people were actually happy. That's still my dream, I guess."

It was Lucky's, too, he reflected with a lump in his throat. Money had been tight for his family when he'd been young, and his parents had struggled to keep their store profitable. There'd always been love, but there'd been stress and long work hours, too.

While nothing could excuse the way Lucky had let them down, the pressure to help support the family had been difficult for him to handle as an immature teen. Before he risked establishing a family of his own, he'd make sure their finances were on a secure footing and find a wife who shared his values. Those included careful planning, postponing having kids and communicating honestly.

"What happened to your dad?" Lucky knew Zora's mom was a widow, but had never heard any details.

"When I was twenty-two, they had a big fight and he moved out." She paused, and then the words spilled out. "Mom claimed he'd cheated on her, which to me was such a betrayal of the whole family that I refused to speak to him. A few months later, he dropped dead of a heart attack. We never said goodbye."

"I'm sorry." What a burden of guilt that must place on her. "It wasn't your fault."

"If you love somebody, shouldn't you keep trying to rescue the relationship?"

"But past a certain point, you're only enabling him." Lucky eased farther away in case she tried kicking him again.

Instead, Zora lurched to her feet. "Well, I'm done enabling Andrew. Edmond can handle him from now on."

"I agree in principle." Reaching over, Lucky collected her dishes and piled them with his. "You can't avoid him forever, though."

"I can try." A pounding on the front door sent Zora's hand flying to her throat. "Oh, my gosh, you don't suppose that's him, do you?"

The thuds grew louder. "Stay there. I'll get it." After depositing the dishes in the kitchen, Lucky went to answer.

On the porch, hand raised for renewed hammering, stood a man of about thirty, a tailored suit jacket failing to disguise his pudgy gut. Blond hair, blue eyes, sneering expression. "Andrew Raditch?" Lucky guessed.

"Where is she?" The man stomped in. Had Lucky not dodged him, they'd have collided. "I insist on talking to my wife."

"Which wife would that be?" Finally, here was the man who'd created endless trouble—and, Lucky conceded, a measure of entertainment—over the past few months. Andrew was shorter than he'd imagined, and not nearly handsome enough to explain his appeal to women.

"Don't mess with me, mister." Feet planted in the entry, Andrew bellowed, "Zora, where the hell are you?"

How could this rude oaf be the son of Betsy Raditch? But then, he had alcohol on his breath.

From around the corner of the staircase, Zora regarded her ex-husband coolly. "What's your problem, Andrew?"

"What did you say to Lin?" the man demanded. "She admitted to my face that she talked to you."

As if that were a crime, Lucky thought.

"So?" Still half in the living room as if prepared to dodge away, Zora watched him guardedly.

"She packed a bag and walked out on me," Andrew said. "She was crying. Did you enjoy hurting her?"

"I'm not the one who hurt her." Zora remained admirably calm, in Lucky's opinion.

"You must have filled her head with lies!" Andrew smacked his hand against the wall.

"You accuse *me* of lying?" Zora stood her ground. "You should study the definition of truth. It seems to be an alien concept to you."

"Cut the crap." Andrew prowled toward her. "You call Lin right now and apologize."

"For what?"

"For whatever you…" As Zora stepped into full view, big belly and all, Andrew's jaw worked without producing another sound.

Lucky enjoyed the man's shock. Finally, Andrew had discovered he was going to be a father.

Chapter 7

To Zora, Andrew seemed different tonight. Was it the extra height of the ceiling that dwarfed him or the contrast between him and Lucky? Andrew's muscles from playing high school football were running to fat—in contrast to Lucky's well-toned build—and his once-thick blond hair had begun receding at the temples.

As for his blustering manner, usually it yielded to calculated charm as soon as he saw that he'd intimidated her. Tonight, though, with Lucky on hand and the memory of the afternoon's anguished scene still raw, she remained in control of her emotions. No intimidation, and hence no charm to obscure his true reaction.

For a revealing moment, she watched Andrew's expression shift from disbelief to anger to disdain as he weighed his response to her pregnancy. Before today, while Zora had recognized the self-serving motives that rippled below the man's slick surface, she'd soon been sucked under by his charisma. Tonight, the curl of his lip and the flare of his nostrils might have belonged to a stranger. A stranger she disliked.

"Now I understand what you dropped on Lin." With a wave of his arm, he indicated—and dismissed—her pregnancy. "You persuaded her it was mine, didn't you? I can't imagine how you fooled her. She knows I had a vasectomy."

Behind him, Zora caught Lucky's startled blink. Funny how keenly she registered her housemate's responses, and how grateful she was for his protective stance.

"Your doctor did warn you that a vasectomy doesn't instantly render you sterile, I presume," she said.

"It takes a few weeks," her ex responded confidently. "I gave it a month."

He'd calculated the timing, or so he believed. "I have two words for you," Zora told Andrew. "Paternity test."

"You went out and slept with someone else," he sneered. "No doubt right after I signed the divorce papers."

"Did your doctor confirm that your sperm count had dropped to zero?" Lucky asked. In response to Andrew's who-the-hell-are-you? scowl, he added, "I work in a urologist's office. It takes ten to twenty ejaculations to completely clear the sperm."

Andrew paled. "The baby *can't* be mine."

"Babies, plural," Zora corrected.

"Beg pardon?"

"I'm carrying twins," she said. "And in California, a paternity test isn't necessary for you to owe child support. According to my attorney, if the parents are married, by law the husband is automatically the father. And we *were* still married that night."

At the memory, pain threatened her detachment. She'd dropped by Andrew's apartment to urge him to sign the divorce papers after weeks of him playing games. Instead, he'd sworn that he regretted cheating on her, declared that she was his true love and drawn her into his bed. A few nights later, while she nursed the hope that he planned to cast off his fiancée and stay with her, he'd dropped the signed divorce papers on her porch and fled.

"You waited, what, seven months to inform me?" His other tactics having failed, Andrew assumed the mantle of outrage. "Any man would doubt these children are his. I refuse to pay for what isn't mine."

"If you insist, I'll arrange for a test." Might as well seal the deal.

That didn't appear to be the answer he'd expected. "You'd risk your babies' safety by sticking a needle in there?"

"You're out-of-date, man," Lucky announced. "It doesn't take an invasive test to establish paternity anymore. They can extract the baby's DNA from the mother's blood with ninety-nine-point-nine percent accuracy."

Andrew grimaced. "Fine. Whatever."

Zora seized on his apparent consent. "The test's expensive and insurance won't cover it. Since you're insisting on it, you can pay."

He shifted on the balls of his feet. "Half."

She supposed arguing the point would be futile. Instead, she added, "Okay, but legally you also owe half of my other maternity-related expenses." Oh, drat, her voice was trembling. Did the man feel absolutely nothing after learning that he'd fathered two children-to-be? He hadn't asked their genders, or Zora's due date, or whether she'd selected names.

Names. She'd planned to let him choose those in the absurd belief that doing so would strengthen his connection to the twins. After tonight, though, Zora resolved that he'd have nothing to do with selecting the names if she could help it.

"Let's run that test before you start counting my money," Andrew snarled. He turned abruptly, sidestepped Lucky and stalked out of the house.

Zora struggled to catch her breath. Since learning of her pregnancy, she'd imagined this scene repeatedly, in a thousand variations. Anger and awe, apology and acceptance—she'd credited Andrew with those feelings. Well, he'd shown the anger. Aside from that, however, the only other thing he'd displayed was utter indifference to his own kids.

"High five or knuckle bump?" Grinning, Lucky raised his hand for her response.

She burst into sobs.

"What's wrong?" The man looked flummoxed. "Zora, you were magnificent. You stood up to every trick he threw at you. Didn't you hear me silently cheering you?"

She struggled for control. "How could I hear something silent?"

"It was written all over my face." His dark eyes glowed. "Tonight, I witnessed a miraculous transformation. Right here in our living room, you became a kick-ass superhero."

His praise felt wonderful. It also filled her with wariness, because she didn't deserve it. "I forced him to agree to a blood test, that's all."

"And hit him up for half your expenses."

"He hasn't paid yet."

"Zora!" Lucky gripped her gently under her arms. "I'd swing you around to celebrate, only I doubt the twins would appreciate it."

"You're right." The duo were squirming. At this stage, she'd read, their auditory functions had developed enough for them to hear the argument. How sad that on their first exposure to their father's voice, it had been filled with rage.

Already, the babies might be forming lifelong impressions of masculine and feminine behavior. She hoped that Lucky's gentler tones offset Andrew's harshness. "He didn't ask a single question about his children. Maybe it hasn't sunk in yet."

"And maybe he's a self-centered prick. If I accidentally fathered babies, I'd be determined to give them the best," Lucky assured her.

"You'd take care of their mother, wouldn't you? You'd never let her down." Zora caught her breath, unsure why his answer mattered so much.

"I certainly wouldn't whine and try to weasel out of my obligations," Lucky responded. "But I'm doing everything in my power to avoid running that kind of risk. I won't be ready for a family till I pay off my education loans and save a down payment for a house. My kids deserve a happy childhood with two parents who're mature enough to provide them with stability."

Zora's spirits plummeted. During the confrontation with Andrew, she'd drawn strength from Lucky's nearness, from having a man care about her without making demands. Well, of course he didn't make demands, because he didn't want anything from her, as he'd just indicated. He wanted the perfect wife, the perfect family, and she was far from perfect.

Why can't he love me, messy life and all?

What was wrong with her? She didn't love Lucky. Or if she did, it was the casual, friendship kind of love. He wasn't her type. Too rough around the edges and too judgmental. Still, the way he'd stood by her these past months had been more than kind. It had been… fatherly. And maybe more.

He was still holding her. Still gazing at her fondly. "I wish my children had a father like you," Zora blurted.

Lucky stared down at her for a moment. Then he released her. "I appreciate the compliment, but these are Andrew's kids."

She was on the verge of pointing out the obvious, that her ex-husband didn't want them, when it struck her what Lucky really meant—that he couldn't or wouldn't be their father, either.

The discovery chilled Zora. How naive she'd been, to believe even for an instant that Lucky could fill the void in her heart. How utterly unrealistic. *Typical of me, I guess.*

"I'd better lie down," she said.

"I didn't mean to upset you," he responded. "I only meant…"

Zora waved away the explanation. "Don't bother. I'm a total idiot when it comes to relationships."

"Did I miss something?" Lucky asked.

How adorably clueless he was. "I'm tired. It's been a long day."

"It's only eight thirty."

Zora struggled to ignore his worried gaze. "That's late, for a pregnant woman." A pregnant woman whose last lingering illusions had been shattered.

Until tonight, her bond to Andrew—imaginary though it had been—had shielded her from any other man like a brick wall. Now, vulnerable and hurt, she seemed to be stumbling over a bunch of loose bricks. "Good night."

"If you're sure."

"I am." Zora hurried away, although she wasn't sure about anything. Okay, about the no-more-Andrew part, yes. But as for Lucky, somewhere along the line, love had mushroomed in the dark. What defense did she have against her best friend?

In her bedroom, she dropped onto the floral bedspread, grabbed a dainty pink pillow and began punching the stuffing out of it.

Too bad standing up to her loathsome ex-husband had exhausted Zora when she ought to be celebrating, Lucky thought. And how typical that Andrew hadn't bothered to consider how his actions might affect a woman coping with a multiple pregnancy.

What a joy to witness Zora bravely tackling that creep. How frustrating it had been these past months, watching such a smart, feisty woman repeatedly yielding to foolish delusions.

Yet, unfortunately, she might still forgive the jerk. If Lucky had learned anything about Zora, it was that her emotions regarding her ex-husband seesawed like crazy. Once the babies were born, if Andrew showed any paternal instincts at all, her resistance would probably crumble.

That remark about wishing her kids had a dad like Lucky...for a split second, he'd wished the same thing. Then he'd faced reality. To her, the twins would always belong to Andrew.

Lucky sighed and clicked on the lamp in his bedroom, which was spacious enough for his video games and exercise equipment. During the day, when he opened the curtains, the sliding glass doors revealed a splendid view of the gray-and-green wetlands with their ever-changing tableau of wildlife. Tonight, by contrast, the lamp—on a ceramic base enlivened by a turquoise-and-black geometric pattern—bathed the room in a cozy radiance.

When he'd moved in here, Lucky had purchased several Hispanic-inspired accents, including the rainbow-striped serape draped across a chair as well as a ceramic Aztec calendar plaque that hung on the wall, its buff background covered with red-and-black designs. Although his family was three generations removed from its Mexican-Indian roots, Lucky valued his connection to ancient traditions. He'd worked hard to master Spanish both because of his heritage and to assist patients.

Overhead, the floor creaked, a reminder that Karen and Rod were awake. Lucky tried not to speculate about what they might be doing in Karen's suite. Whatever it was, he appreciated that they'd remained out of sight during the verbal fireworks with Andrew.

If only Zora had more energy, Lucky would have enjoyed sharing a late snack with her, teasing her across the table. It had been fun earlier tonight, figuring out how to persuade Vince to stay involved with Safe Harbor.

How sharp of Zora to note that Portia would do whatever was necessary to preserve her marriage. Especially since, in Lucky's observation, the woman's longing for a baby might tip the scales in favor of undergoing fertility treatments.

Whatever happened at Saturday's appointment, his involvement, if any, had to be discreet. Unhappily, he acknowledged that all this head scratching and cogitating might be for naught. It was possible that, upon receiving Cole's bad news, Vince would simply haul his wife out of there and bid Safe Harbor adios.

It would help to have a second set of eyes and ears. Zora had proven perceptive, and if she were around…

Why not? In addition to working weekdays, Zora filled in occasional evenings and weekends. Cole hadn't scheduled a full roster of patients for Saturday morning. Lucky could identify a few men due for ultrasounds who might be glad to move up their appointments. He'd request that Zora be assigned.

Satisfied with that plan, he changed into exercise clothes and switched on his elliptical machine.

While growing up, Zora had never had a close girlfriend. Her twin, who should have been her dearest pal, had become a rival because their mother had constantly pitted them against each other with criticism and shifting favoritism. By high school, Zora had transferred that competition to other girls as well, a view reinforced by Andrew's flirtations while they were dating.

Then she'd started working at Safe Harbor and, during the lowest period of her life, met Anya. She'd never understood why bubbly, popular Anya had defied the staff's general hostility to Zora and invited her to share an apartment, but she'd been deeply appreciative.

Sharing confidences and movie nights with a friend had been a revelation. A year later, after their rent increased and they moved into Karen's house, they'd continued to be best friends. Zora had been the first to learn that Anya was carrying Jack's baby, and it had been Anya who accompanied Zora to buy a pregnancy kit and discover her own impending motherhood.

Anya's marriage a few months ago, followed by the birth of her daughter, meant that Jack and little Rachel came first. Lonely again, Zora had drifted into Lucky's company, despite his irritating attempts to run her life. But now that her feelings toward him had changed, being around him was dangerous.

Zora needed a friend. And although Keely was far from the warm, cuddly type, she had a kind side. Late Tuesday afternoon, when Zora stopped into Dr. Brennan's office to inquire about paternity testing, the nurse immediately arranged for the doctor to order the lab test. She requested Andrew's email address and promised to send him the information, as well.

"The results take eight working days after you both provide blood." The older woman refastened the pink barrette in her hair. "Say, are you driving home with Karen today? I saw you arrive together. In case she has to stay late, I'd be glad to take you."

A hint of anxiety in the nurse's expression, as if the response really mattered, touched Zora. Not only did she need a friend, but Keely did, too. Also, Karen had texted that she'd be delayed about an hour and hoped Zora didn't mind waiting. The alternative—calling on Lucky—went against Zora's resolve to steer clear of him.

Dr. Brennan's warning about safety had resonated

with her on the drive home yesterday, when she'd found that she could no longer reach the pedals without her baby bulge pressing against the steering wheel.

Thank goodness her housemates had volunteered to pick up the slack, and now Keely was joining in. "Actually, I *could* use a ride, if it's not too much trouble."

The lines in Keely's face softened. "Let's do it!" They arranged to meet in the medical building lobby in fifteen minutes, after Keely got off work. Zora had finished her shift an hour earlier.

At the lab, she had blood drawn. Thank goodness for the newer technique, which extracted fetal DNA from her blood plasma and compared it to the father's DNA. All the same, she'd be willing to bet that Andrew would complain about it. Too bad he didn't have to endure the doctor's poking, the morning sickness, the sleepless nights and the labor pains.

As she rose to leave with a small bandage on her arm, Zora supposed that women from the dawn of time had resented men for escaping the painful consequences of pregnancy. She wouldn't resent Lucky, who took care of her, though. But as he'd pointed out, these weren't his babies.

Recalling that she ought to alert Karen to the change in plans, Zora sent the other woman a text. When she reached the meeting place, Keely was already there, pacing. "Am I late?" Zora asked.

"No. I wasn't sure you'd be here."

"Why not?" Stupid question. Keely's low self-esteem spoke for itself. "I mean, you're doing me a favor. Of course I'm here."

"I'm parked in the main garage," the nurse said. "Is that too far? I could pull around."

"The exercise is good for me. And it's not far." As they set out at a slow pace, Zora asked, "Are you ready for the move this weekend? Did your landlord hassle you about the short notice?"

"Not after I explained the circumstances with my roommate." Keely brushed a speck of dust off her navy uniform. "And told him it was my birthday."

"It's your birthday?" Zora wondered about her new friend's age. It seemed rude to ask, though.

"Last Sunday."

"You should have mentioned it earlier! We'd have celebrated."

"Why?" Keely's eyebrows drew into a dark, straight line. "Turning fifty isn't anything to cheer about."

Well, she'd answered *that* question. "Every birthday is precious," Zora said as they passed a flower bed crowded with red, white and purple petunias. "Considering the alternative."

"What alternative?"

"Dying young."

Keely snorted, which appeared to be her manner of laughing. "Never thought of that." Halting at the garage's elevator, she pressed the button. "I can't afford to get old and sick, without a family to lean on." She punched the button again, although it was already lit.

"Fifty isn't old," Zora ventured.

"My mom was fifty when she had to go on disability." Keely's forehead creased. "I moved in with her after Dad died. She was forever consulting one doctor or another. Aches and pains, high blood pressure, swollen ankles. They ordered her to exercise and quit drinking. She insisted the booze was medicinal and that it hurt to move around."

"To move around at all?" Zora asked. "What did she do, spend the whole day on the couch?"

"Pretty much. I did the shopping and cleaning, while working full-time."

No wonder the nurse had a grumpy attitude. "Is she living?"

A shudder ran through Keely. "I'd rather not talk about it."

"I didn't mean to pry."

The elevator arrived and they rode up in silence. Had she offended Keely? Zora wondered. The woman had a reputation for being touchy.

At last the nurse spoke again. "I take it back. It's better for you to hear the truth."

"About what?"

They exited onto the third level. "About what happened to my mom," Keely answered. "I got arrested and lost my last job because of it."

That sounded shocking. Zora struggled to contain her reaction as they strolled between rows of vehicles. Behind them, an SUV pulled out cautiously. Ahead, a woman beeped open her sedan. Although there was a faint smell of exhaust, the garage's open-air design dissipated the fumes.

"What happened?" Quickly, Zora added, "Obviously, the police made a mistake." *Or did we agree to share our house with an ax murderer?*

"One morning Mom claimed she sensed a heart attack coming on." Keely's voice echoed off the hard surfaces around them. "She was constantly saying such things and complaining to the neighbors about how I neglected her. I'd missed too much work already, running Mom to doctors for no reason. I told her to call nine-one-one if her symptoms worsened."

"Oh, dear." Having grown up with a mother who insisted on being the center of attention at any cost, Zora empathized.

Keely's eyes glittered with tears. "After work, I found her stone cold in her favorite chair. A neighbor told the police I'd been abusing her."

"You must have been devastated." If Zora had ignored her mother's complaints and then she'd ended up passing away, she'd be overwhelmed by guilt.

"The clinic fired me as soon as they heard I'd been arrested." Keely paused at a bend in the row. "There I was, out on bail, handling my mother's funeral arrangements and terrified of being sent to prison."

"That's horrible." Zora's heart went out to the woman. "What did you do?"

The nurse sucked in a long breath before continuing. "Mom's doctors explained to the investigators that I was always bringing her in for one symptom or another. The district attorney decided not to prosecute."

"What about your job? Surely they offered to hire you back."

"I wouldn't work for those doctors again. They were cruel and unfair." Lifting her chin, Keely resumed walking. "I got a job at Safe Harbor. It was a community hospital in those days, before the remodeling. If the top brass now had any idea I'd been arrested for elder abuse, I doubt they'd put up with me."

"But the DA cleared you," Zora responded.

"Dr. Tartikoff hates me. If it weren't for Dr. Brennan…" Keely broke off. "Oh, no!"

She was staring at a boxy brown sedan with bumper stickers that read, Ask Your Doctor—Not Your TV Commercial, Cancer Cures Smoking, and Get Off Your Phone and Drive. The car also sported four flat tires.

"That's yours?"

Keely nodded grimly.

Four flat tires couldn't be a coincidence, Zora thought. "This is vandalism. We should call the police."

Keely shifted for a closer inspection. "They aren't slashed." Her jaw tightened. "Somebody let the air out. It's a nasty prank kids used to do to me in high school."

Keely had been bullied as a teenager, and someone was bullying her again. That aroused Zora's fury, along with her sympathy. "We should at least tell security."

"I'll call the auto club. They'll handle it." Keely swung toward her. "Please don't hold it against me that you have to wait."

"I wouldn't hold it against *you*!" Zora protested. "You're the victim here."

"I appreciate that."

Near the curve where they'd stood talking a moment ago, a motor started and a blue hybrid with a bike rack on top pulled out. It occurred to Zora that the perpetrator of this so-called prank might have lingered to observe—and enjoy—the consequences. "Do you recognize that car?"

"Afraid not."

In the dim light, Zora could see only enough of the driver to be fairly sure it was a man. Then, as the car drove off, she noticed that Keely wasn't the only staff member to display bumper stickers.

The one on the hybrid read, Psychologists Do It on the Couch.

Chapter 8

"Thanks for calling me," Lucky told Keely after parking his car across from hers in the garage. She'd phoned to alert him to what had happened and asked if he could drive Zora home.

Reclining in Keely's rear seat with the door open, Zora eyed him askance. "You're both very kind, but I'm not a fragile doll."

Not a doll, but more fragile than she was willing to admit, Lucky thought, assessing her swollen calves and the weariness in her gaze. He was tempted to stroke a damp strand of hair from her temple, but her stubborn expression warned him against fussing over her.

"The auto club could take half an hour," Keely responded tartly to Zora. "Meanwhile you're breathing auto fumes. It's bad for the baby."

"She doesn't always exercise the best judgment," Lucky agreed.

"I'm right here! Please refrain from talking about me in the third person," Zora snapped.

Ignoring the complaint, he continued addressing Keely. "I notified security. A guard should be here soon to take a report."

Keely shrugged. "Fine. I have nothing else to do till the auto club arrives, but we can't prove Laird did this."

"Motive plus bumper sticker equals Laird," Lucky replied.

"*We* know that," Zora said. "But who else will believe a psychologist would stoop to such juvenile tricks over being bumped from a room rental?"

"Anyone who heard him squabbling with Keely in the cafeteria." Realizing that his comment might seem insulting, Lucky added, "No offense. I meant that he was the one squabbling."

Keely waved off the apology. "Don't bother soft-pedaling, Lucky. I'm tough. I butted heads with Dr. Tartikoff and survived, in case you forgot."

"How could anyone forget?" he teased. "You're a hero."

"Heroine," Zora corrected.

"You planning to argue with everything I say?" Lucky didn't mind, though, as long as she was safe. No sooner had he clicked off the call than frightening scenarios had rampaged through his head. What if the vandal had tampered with Keely's brakes and they'd crashed? "Keely, as a precaution, have the auto club tow your car to Phil's Garage to check the brakes and engine. I think they're open till seven."

"And spend my hard-earned money for nothing?" She shook her head. "I doubt the louse would go that far."

"I recommend playing it safe, but it's your decision." Reaching out, Lucky helped Zora rise.

He was glad he'd replaced his old low-slung coupe with a practical black sedan he could drive for years. And which didn't force a pregnant woman to pretzel herself into the front seat.

"All set?" He leaned inside to adjust Zora's seat belt.

A slap on the wrist knocked his arm away. "No touching the merchandise!"

"The seat belts can be tricky." He didn't attempt to assist again, however.

As a rule, Lucky preferred mild-mannered women, but Zora's peppery manner had its pluses. Never boring, for one thing. Also, no stored-up complaints to be unleashed later. One ex-girlfriend had unloaded on him out of the blue, calling him an arrogant muscle head before breaking off their relationship. Until that evening, Lucky had believed they were doing fine.

Zora didn't hesitate to lob insults at him on the spot. In fact, *arrogant muscle head* was mild by comparison to some of her descriptive phrases. But at least he knew what she thought of him.

Yet despite her feisty spirit, she had a knack for landing in scrapes that begged for a rescue. If he had to move elsewhere for a job, who would show up on a moment's notice? *Somebody* had to take care of her.

As he navigated the curving ramp, Lucky glanced at the resolute mommy-to-be beside him. The full lips, the curving line of her lashes—spicy and sweet, like hot chocolate with a dash of cayenne pepper.

It occurred to him that he hadn't yet updated her on the latest twist to his plan. "Did you hear from the radiology scheduler about working Saturday morning?"

"No. Will I?"

He explained that he'd requested her. "You'll be nearby when the Adamses are here."

"To do what?" Zora demanded. "I doubt I'll get anywhere near them."

"I'd like your insight." Belatedly, he asked, "Do you mind?"

"I suppose not, but next time, ask me first." She flinched as, ahead, a car shot back into the aisle, blocking their path.

Lucky tapped the brake. "I saw it."

"Of course you did."

"You doubt me?"

"Always."

He chuckled. "About the Adamses, you might observe something I miss."

"Seriously?" When they emerged from the garage, lingering daylight glinted off the coppery highlights in her hair. "I thought you considered me a borderline drooling idiot."

"That's a wild exaggeration," he said.

"Which part—the drooling or the idiot?"

"The borderline."

She laughed. "I should have figured."

Heading south on Safe Harbor Boulevard, they crested a coastal bluff. Before them spread the shimmering harbor and adjacent stretch of sand. The arrival of October's cooler weather meant less traffic and smaller beach crowds, a situation Lucky relished.

Growing up, he'd been accustomed to his family's flat, landlocked neighborhood in LA. But after living in Safe Harbor, he'd never be satisfied being far from the expanse of the ocean.

Zora lowered her window. "That sea air smells wonderful."

"Better than exhaust?"

"Thank you for picking me up, if that was a hint." She stretched her shoulders. At this stage of her pregnancy, she ought to have regular massages to ease her discomforts. Lucky nearly volunteered, but the notion of running his hands over her body struck him as dangerously intimate, especially since she was sexy as hell.

"I'll drive you to and from work the rest of the week." He swung left onto Pacific Coast Highway. "Karen can alternate with me, but your hours are more in line with mine. Next week, after Keely moves in, I'll coordinate my schedule with her."

"You sure are bossy," Zora joked.

"Save your grousing for the Sunday meet-up." The residents of Casa Wiggins, as they referred to Karen's house, assembled once a week to review plans and problems.

"Keely will be there, which means I'll have an ally," she said.

"I'm used to you and Anya ganging up on me," Lucky replied calmly. "I can handle it."

"Handle it? You enjoy having women around even if they aren't bowled over by your tats," Zora said.

"That's true. Women share ideas and support each other more than most men do." Living in Casa Wiggins had taught him the value of friendships with the opposite sex. He'd grown up in a predominantly male household, with a strong-minded father and brother. His mom had been quiet by comparison, with a steady, low-key temperament. Lucky wished he'd had a chance to know her as an adult, but he'd lost her, a painful memory he'd rather not dwell on. "So, have you set up the paternity test?"

"None of your business."

He grinned. It felt normal to bicker with Zora. And he was glad she'd agreed to be at Dr. Rattigan's office on Saturday. Whether or not her input proved helpful, he was glad she'd be there.

Throughout her shift on Saturday morning, Zora stayed attuned to the activities in the rest of the office. Usually she only paid attention to her patients, but today she noted Lucky's familiar footsteps, registered the steady tone of his voice, and picked up the fact that Vince Adams was late. Very late.

Perhaps he and his wife had abandoned the possibility of a pregnancy under any circumstances, or decided to use a surrogate in San Diego. All of Lucky's planning could be for nothing.

He might have to leave. How would she handle that?

The sight of him at the garage on Tuesday had been far more welcome than Zora had expected. Since then, riding beside him to and from work, she'd been keenly aware of his powerful thigh close to hers and his muscular arms controlling the steering wheel. Fortunately, their habit of verbally poking at each other made it easy to hide her reactions.

Today, they'd arrived together but then separated to attend to their duties. The schedule kept Zora busy with a series of male patients.

During Zora's training, performing scrotal ultrasounds had required considerable getting used to. She had to adjust the patient's penis and scrotum, apply gel and move the paddle to obtain varied views.

During the procedure, the man often stared at the ceiling, responding to her requests as if commanded by a robot. Others cracked jokes to cover their embarrassment during the twenty-to thirty-minute procedure. Occasionally, she encountered a man whose sexual innuendos crept toward harassment. Her crisply professional manner and request for a nurse to observe had always sufficed to dampen the patient's ardor.

Zora preferred it when the wife accompanied her husband, which was the case with her fourth patient of the morning. A thin fellow in his late fifties, he gripped his wife's hand as Dr. Rattigan checked him before departing.

During the sonogram, a booming voice from the hall alerted Zora that Vince had arrived. Why did he trumpet every word? The man behaved as if everyone else, except a select few such as Cole, was not only invisible but also deaf.

Then a door closed and silence fell. Ominous silence. Scary silence.

Suddenly Lucky's faith in her powers of observation seemed ridiculously misplaced. His future and the expansion of the men's fertility program at Safe Harbor might be crashing and burning, and unable to see or hear what was happening, Zora had nothing to contribute. If only she could do *something*.

"How does it look to you?" The patient's question broke into her thoughts.

Instead of dwelling on the obvious fact that she wasn't a doctor, Zora tried diplomacy. "Dr. Rattigan will review the results with you personally. He takes great care with his patients."

"Yes, but..." The man broke off as his wife patted his shoulder. "I can't help worrying."

"We're almost finished," she told him. "Am I hurting you?" The procedure was painless unless the man was especially sensitive. However, asking the question ought to distract him from further inquiries.

"No, no. Thank you."

While she did observe some anomalies in the man's images, Zora wasn't qualified to interpret what they meant. Entering the medical field, she'd dreamed of helping others rather than simply clocking in to a routine job each day. And often, she *did* help them. She hoped that whatever was wrong with this patient could be put right.

The early loss of both her grandparents had inspired her interest in health care. She cherished memories of her mother's parents, who'd adored her and Zady. Unfortunately, they'd smoked, avoided exercise and ignored symptoms of heart and lung disease until it was too late for lifesaving treatments.

Zora didn't hold an exalted position like a surgeon, but she was part of a team that improved people's lives. She wouldn't trade her career for anything.

Once she'd finished the exam, she gently wiped off the conductive gel. "You can resume normal activities immediately."

"I think a leisurely lunch at Salads and More is in order," the wife said. "Don't you, honey?"

"How about Waffle Heaven?"

Their gazes locked. "Papa Giovanni's?" she countered.

"Done," he said.

Zora envied their easy rapport. How wonderful to

have a spouse with whom you communicated in shorthand and who stood by you through life's ups and downs. The way Lucky did with her…but that was temporary.

"You may get dressed," she told the patient. "I'll be out of here in a minute."

"No hurry."

As she bent to retrieve a cord, her babies squirmed. Did they sense she was hungry? Pushing the cart out of the room, Zora smiled at the idea that her growling stomach had awakened them.

In the hall, she nearly ran into a bulldog of a man. His powerful frame corded with tension, Vince Adams scowled at the elegant woman beside him. Model thin, Portia Adams wore a svelte pink suit and to-die-for designer shoes. She struck Zora as determined and apprehensive.

Apparently the couple had finished their meeting with the doctor. Most patients avoided private discussions in the hallways, but not these two.

"You call that a compromise?" Vince demanded of his spouse. "I've told you I won't tolerate a surrogate! No stranger will be carrying my children. That's what I have a wife for."

In Portia's smooth face, only her eyes betrayed her fury. "I agreed to hormone injections and egg retrieval," she said in a low voice. "And I want a baby, well, almost as much as you do. But at my age, to take on a possible multiple pregnancy…" She shook her head and let the sentence drift off.

Spotting Zora, the billionaire maintained his glare for an instant before his expression softened. "Excuse me," Zora said, and eased the cart to the side to clear a path.

Instead of picking up the hint to exit, Vince bathed her in a smile. "What a beautiful sight you are, miss. Frankly, I find a pregnant woman's body irresistible."

"Thanks." Zora gritted her teeth, eager to escape.

Vince advanced toward her. "Your husband must be thrilled."

His wife glowered. Her twisting mouth conveyed resentment, but there was also a trace of fear in her eyes. Was she really that afraid of losing her husband?

"I don't..." Zora cleared her throat.

"She isn't married. She lives in that house with Rod," Portia snapped. She and Vince had attended Anya and Jack's wedding there when their daughters—Jack's cousins—had served as flower girls.

"You're not married?" Touching his thumb to Zora's chin, Vince tipped her face up. "The men around here must be blind."

Okay, that's enough taunting of your wife. She stepped back. "I'll remove this cart so you can get past."

"You do that," Portia snarled.

Before Zora could squirm farther away, however, Vince laid a meaty hand on her abdomen. "Boy or girl?"

"One of each." She wished she dared smack his arm.

To her dismay, he caressed her bulge with relish. Enjoying his wife's discomfort, or Zora's? Or both? "They're active little rascals, aren't they?"

Behind him, Lucky appeared. Mercifully, the interruption allowed Zora to break free and dodge behind the ultrasound equipment.

Unfazed, Vince addressed his wife. "Well, honey?"

The threat was unmistakable. If Portia didn't yield to his demands, he'd find a woman who would.

A long breath shuddered out of the socialite. "You don't care about the risk to me? Never mind, I already know the answer."

"You're exaggerating the dangers," her husband retorted. "You're only thirty-nine. Lots of women in their forties have babies."

Lucky intervened politely. "There is an increased risk, Mrs. Adams, but if there are no underlying health issues, it ought to be manageable with careful monitoring. You should discuss that with your doctor."

Her nose wrinkled. "What does a man know? He doesn't have to carry a baby."

Lucky didn't miss a beat. "We have excellent female obstetricians on staff."

Portia gripped her purse. "Do any of them perform in vitro?"

"Several," he said.

Vince faced Zora again. "Who's your doctor, honey?"

"Paige Brennan," she said.

"Dr. Brennan often works with in vitro patients," Lucky added. "You'd find her sympathetic, Mrs. Adams. She underwent fertility treatment herself in order to have her daughter."

That was none of their business, Zora thought. However, Dr. Brennan *had* spoken publicly about that aspect of her medical history.

"And she's married?" This appeared important to Portia. Did she think her husband so lecherous that he'd chase her obstetrician? Of course, he *had* just groped an ultrasound tech.

"Quite happily," Lucky assured her.

Portia gave a reluctant shrug. "I suppose she's acceptable."

Triumphantly, Vince draped an arm over his wife's shoulders. "Well done. Why don't we stay an extra day and attend that charity event you mentioned? I'll buy you a new outfit at South Coast Plaza."

"Not that I'll fit into it for long," his wife muttered, but quickly rallied. "Thank you. I suppose this might work out okay. A baby really will be a lot of fun."

To Lucky, her husband said, "Set up an appointment with Dr. Brennan. My wife can send you her schedule."

"Glad to." Judging by the light in Lucky's eyes, he was barely keeping a lid on his excitement.

While he escorted the wealthy couple to the front, Zora stowed the cart in its closet. On her return, she found Lucky performing a victory dance around the nurses' station. Fortunately for his reputation, there was no one else present.

He beamed at her. "I have no idea how you persuaded them, but you were brilliant."

"I didn't do anything." *Except let him grope my baby bump.* However, Zora supposed that Vince's behavior fell within what many might view as acceptable limits. A lot of people assumed—wrongly—that it was okay to touch a pregnant woman's belly.

"Too bad it's illegal to shoot off fireworks in a doctor's office." With a whoop, Lucky caught her. "We did it!"

Zora's discomfort evaporated. Close to him, she felt safe and sheltered. How easily she could forget everything and everyone, except… "Isn't Dr. Rattigan around?"

"He had to perform emergency surgery." Lucky

rubbed his cheek over her hair. "He left right after talking to the Adamses."

"An emergency in urology?" Unlike obstetrics, the specialty rarely dealt with life-or-death situations.

"A patient suffered injuries in a car crash." Lucky mentioned a nearby hospital that handled trauma patients. "The lead surgeon called Dr. Rattigan to assist. Would you stop fidgeting and let me hug you?"

"That's nearly impossible in my shape." But Zora yielded happily as he wedged her against him. How strong he was, yet he held her with a tenderness that almost overwhelmed her.

Zora became acutely aware of his quick breathing. The discovery that she excited him spurred her passion. She floated in the heady scent of his citrus cologne, her nerve endings coming alive.

When Lucky's mouth brushed Zora's, her lips parted. The flick of his tongue sent rivulets of desire streaming through her, and an answering moan burst from him.

She grabbed his shoulders and lightly rubbed her breasts over his hard chest. The sensations flaring through her were almost painfully intense. Lucky angled her tighter, his hands closing over her derriere.

The urge to bring him inside her, to merge with him, proved irresistible. "Let's find a place to be alone," she began, and then, shifting position, he stumbled.

"Oh, hell!" Lucky caught his balance against the counter, anchoring her against his hip. "Are you all right?"

"Delirious," she murmured.

Drawing in a ragged breath, he studied her in confusion. "We shouldn't be doing this."

"You're right. It's a terrible idea." Clinging to him,

Zora didn't mean a word of it. "But as long as we've gone this far…"

"I never expected to get carried away." His thoughts seemed to turn inward. "What's wrong with me?"

"Wrong?" Zora bristled.

"I never lose control this way," Lucky said. "Considering your condition and our situations, I apologize."

"For what?" Oh, why was she torturing herself by prolonging this conversation? Zora wondered. She'd acted impulsively, and clearly Lucky didn't like the way he'd reacted. What a control freak! "Never mind. Forget the whole thing."

"That's a good idea." He sounded as if he was struggling for composure. "That wasn't how a gentleman behaves."

"If you apologize again, I'll slug you."

He laughed, an unexpected rumble that rolled right into her heart. "That's my Zora." A bout of hard breathing reawakened her hope, but he sucked in a lungful of air and held it. "Okay. Better."

"Than what?"

He ignored the question. "Since I inveigled you into working today, let me buy you lunch to celebrate."

Was that his interpretation of what they'd been doing—celebrating? Slapping him would have been totally satisfying. Still, she was starving. Why reject a good meal? "Where did you have in mind?"

"There's a new vegetarian Chinese restaurant I've been meaning to check out."

Zora loved Chinese food. "Do they serve anything besides tofu?"

"Kung pao mushrooms, according to the online

menu. Deep fried, with a tangy sauce. And more, I'm sure."

"You're on." The heat in her body hadn't exactly dissipated, but it had faded to her normal pregnancy-enhanced high temperature. As for Lucky, he'd evidently banished whatever desire he'd experienced.

I guess I'm nowhere near close enough to perfection to suit him.

As common sense reasserted itself, Zora recalled his previous comment about her babies. Never mind Lucky's withdrawal from her—he didn't, couldn't and never would accept these babies as his own.

She was glad they'd stopped. Going any further would have been yet another in a long line of mistakes she'd made with men.

Gathering her possessions, she waited until Lucky locked up, and they sauntered out together. Friends again, nothing more.

Which was obviously how they both preferred it.

Chapter 9

Lucky enjoyed the Sunday meet-ups at Casa Wiggins. He'd learned from his parents, who'd run a small business, that organization was the key to controlling your destiny. In the eight months since the household had formed, the gatherings had enabled the group to stay on track through changes in occupants and in individual situations.

This afternoon, despite his awareness that the future was more of a meandering path with speed bumps than a superhighway, he felt optimistic about his plans. Thanks to whatever diplomacy Zora had exercised toward the Adamses yesterday, all systems appeared to be a go.

Relaxing in his favorite armchair in the den, he sipped white grape juice from a glass. As usual, Rod and Karen had chosen the couch, with their sock-covered feet propped on the worn coffee table. Zora preferred the straight chair, which was easier for a pregnant woman to get in and out of. That left newcomer Keely, who clomped down the staircase to join them.

"Am I late?" she asked. "I had trouble finding the laundry room."

"It's the narrow door next to the garage," Zora said.

"I thought that was a closet."

"Everybody assumes that," Karen assured her. "Don't hesitate to ask where things are."

"You're running laundry already?" Rod fingered his short, graying beard. "You just moved in."

Karen nudged him. "Not our business, dear."

"It's a harmless question."

"I'm a strong believer in hygiene." Crossing the den, Keely lowered her sturdy frame onto the remaining armchair. "How often do we clean and who does what? With a pregnant woman on the premises, we must be vigilant about germs."

Don't tell me she's a germophobe. Lucky rolled his eyes, then caught Zora's stern gaze and subsided.

"We have a rotating schedule. I'll give you a copy," Karen promised. "Feel free to swap chores with anyone who's willing."

"Surely Zora doesn't have to handle chemicals or do heavy work." Keely slid to the edge of her seat, no doubt having discovered that otherwise she sank into the depths of the chair. Lucky decided to ask Karen about replacing the cushion. They maintained a household fund for that sort of thing.

"We have a great system," Rod said. "We chain pregnant women to a wheel in the basement so they generate electrical power."

Keely's jaw dropped.

Zora, who was seated closest to her, murmured,

"There is no basement. I handle dusting and other light chores."

Their newest housemate nodded. "I forgot that Dr. Vintner is famous for joking."

"Dr. Vintner? Anytime you see me with my shoes off, you can call me by my first name." Rod wiggled his sock-clad toes on the coffee table.

Karen presented a few more house rules, such as putting snack plates and cups in the dishwasher rather than accumulating them in the sink. "And no sticking them in the oven because you're in a hurry," she tossed in Zora's direction.

"Anya and I only did that once," she replied cheerfully. "It's not our fault someone turned on the oven without checking if there was anything inside."

"Oh, dear." Keely clutched her hands together. "What if I do things wrong?"

"We'll toss you out," Rod replied.

"Where would I go?" To Lucky's astonishment, Keely regarded Rod in dismay. The woman needed to develop a sense of humor.

Zora reached over to pat the newcomer's hand. "You'll get used to our silliness. Are you still upset about what happened on Tuesday? That must have thrown you off balance."

The older nurse's head bobbed. What had happened on Tuesday? Lucky had to search his memory before he dredged it up. "You mean that nasty prank with your tires? What's the connection?"

"She was bullied in school," Zora said fiercely. "I understand what it's like to be an outsider. Keely, nobody will bully you in this house. If they do, we'll toss *them* out."

"You bet," Karen affirmed.

"I'll cheer while Lucky does the physical tossing," Rod said.

"No problem." Lucky was pleased when Keely responded with a smile.

What a spirited defense Zora had mounted, he thought. As for that outsider business, he bore a share of the responsibility for being tough on Zora. When she first arrived at the house, he'd considered her a heartless predator who'd hurt Stacy. Gradually, he'd forgiven her, and since she'd stood up to Andrew, he'd come to respect her. As for her empathy toward Keely, that demonstrated her kind heart.

The doorbell rang. "I'll get it." With unaccustomed speed, Rod hurried to the door. Lucky heard low voices and then caught a heavenly whiff of garlic, tomato sauce and cheese.

Rod returned toting three large pizzas. "My treat. This will be my atonement for cracking jokes at Keely's expense."

"Three pizzas?" the nurse replied in astonishment. "That's too much for five people."

"Don't you like leftovers?" Lucky asked.

"And it *is* Sunday," Karen said. "People might drop by."

"I'll set out the paper plates and stuff." Rod was definitely acting out of character today—for a reason, as Lucky knew.

To distract Keely, and also because he cared about the answer, Lucky said, "I've been wondering about the timetable for the in vitro process. It's not a situation Dr. Rattigan and I usually deal with. We have a patient who might be affected."

"I'm happy to answer, but are we finished discussing house rules?" The dark-haired woman glanced from him to Zora to Karen.

"Yes, unless you have more questions," Karen said. "Don't let Lucky rush you."

"I'm fine. Is everyone interested in hearing about in vitro?"

"I am," Zora said. She, too, was probably wondering how long it might take before Portia and Vince saw results.

Keely launched into a spiel that she must have heard Dr. Brennan deliver to patients a hundred times. "Depending on the phase of the woman's cycle when you begin, the whole process can take about a month."

"Fantastic." Noting her puzzled reaction, Lucky quickly added, "Go on."

With increasing confidence, she complied.

Zora listened attentively, though that was partly for Keely's sake—the other woman obviously craved reassurance that she belonged here. The subject matter was familiar to her, but she wanted a clearer picture of how things might progress for the Adamses.

The first stage, Keely noted, was the administration of medication to stimulate the ovaries, almond-size glands that flanked the uterus. Normally, only one or two eggs matured each month, but drugs could produce the simultaneous maturing of multiple eggs. This improved the chances of harvesting and fertilizing enough viable eggs.

Keely was explaining step two, harvesting, when the doorbell rang again. From the table at the farthest part of the den, Rod plummeted toward the front door.

No one attempted to rise; if they had, he'd have bowled them over.

A creak of the door, and excited, girlish voices filled the air.

"Daddy!"

"Grandma Helen, give Daddy the cake before you drop it."

"I'm not that decrepit," responded the dry voice of their grandmother.

"I'll get it." Lucky, who'd ordered the cake, went to join the new arrivals.

Until yesterday, the plan had been for the Adamses to return to San Diego that same day. However, Portia had been lobbying to stay over at a hotel so she and Vince could attend an exclusive charity concert and reception tonight, and in his expansive mood, he'd agreed. Helen Pepper had promptly called her former son-in-law to inform Rod that she and the girls could join the household for dinner tonight.

As long as they were having guests, Lucky had decided this was a good chance to show their new roommate what a great group she'd joined. Zora couldn't wait to see her reaction to the cake honoring Keely's birthday.

"I smell pizza!" cried thirteen-year-old Tiffany Adams, her red braids bouncing on her shoulders. "Ooh, where are my manners? Hi, everybody. Zora, you're *huge*!"

"The twins have grown since August." Last summer, Rod's daughters had visited often, since their parents had rented a beach house nearby while Vince underwent surgery.

Eleven-year-old Amber followed shyly. "Have you picked names?" she asked Zora.

"Not yet."

"Gee, they brought dessert." Grinning, Lucky carried in a castle-shaped pink box bearing the logo of the Cake Castle. "Is somebody having a birthday?" No one responded. "Or did someone have a birthday last weekend?" he asked with feigned innocence.

Keely shook her head. "You don't mean me, do you?"

"Hmm. Let's check."

As Lucky passed Zora, she studied his physique appreciatively. His tattoos and muscular build used to remind her of her stepfather, a foul-mouthed ex-gangbanger. Now, she knew that Lucky was nothing like that loser. In fact, as yesterday's encounter had proved, she found him tantalizingly attractive.

Last night, she'd lain awake, her brain defiantly replaying the incident. What if he hadn't stumbled? How far would they have gone? At this stage of pregnancy, making love wasn't wise. Just as importantly, if he'd repeated his insistence afterward on holding out for Ms. Perfect, she'd never have forgiven him.

It was fortunate for Zora's sanity and their friendship that they'd stopped. If only her dreams would quit defying her common sense. But then, where a man was concerned, this was familiar territory.

Carefully, Lucky opened the box to reveal the cake. "It says, 'Happy 50th Birthday, Kelly.' Doggone it! I spelled 'Keely' for them twice!"

The amazement on Keely's face touched Zora's heart. "It's for me?" She approached the table and stared at the icing inscription. "But being fifty isn't worth celebrating. I'm over the hill."

"You consider fifty old?" The girls' grandmother patted Keely's shoulder with an arthritic hand. "My fifties were my best years. Still, I don't mind growing older, not when it means watching these darling girls grow up."

When Zora reached fifty, she reflected, she'd have twenty-year-old twins. For a second, she visualized them with dark hair and smooth olive skin, like Lucky. But of course, they'd either have her reddish hair or Andrew's blond coloring.

Amber joined the small group around the cake. "It's beautiful. I want a rainbow on my next birthday cake, too."

Tiffany took out her cell phone. "I'll snap a picture so we don't forget."

"Hang on, honey." Rod caught his daughter's wrist. "You said Vince snoops through your stuff, right?"

"Oh, rats." The girl scowled. "He'll demand the details of who it was for and where we saw it."

"He's mean." Amber's frown mirrored her sister's.

Keely looked puzzled. "I don't understand."

"I'll explain while we eat," Rod said.

Over pizza, they filled in the story of how Vince had wrested his stepdaughters from the man who'd raised them and attempted to banish Rod from their lives.

"Surely the Adamses must suspect that they visit Dr. Vintner." Keely had chosen a tight spot at the table's corner, declining the place of honor toward which the others had tried to direct her.

"They sort of know but pretend they don't," Amber said. "I'm sure Mom has an idea."

"It's like a game," Tiffany put in.

"Despite the satisfaction of flipping them the bird, we shouldn't be forced to sneak around." Rod spoke from the head of the table, the seat Keely had bypassed. "I spent my life's savings fighting that man in court."

"If you run into Mr. or Mrs. Adams, please don't mention that you met their daughters," Karen told Keely.

The nurse swallowed a bite of food. "I won't. I promise."

Lucky met Zora's gaze. They were both thinking the same thing, she gathered: that it was fortunate Karen had issued the warning before Portia became Paige Brennan's patient. Keely would be running into her often.

"The girls might be in town more often now that my daughter's trying for another baby," Helen observed.

"Mom and Vince plan to rent a beach cottage again, closer to the medical center," Tiffany filled in.

"What about your education?" Rod asked. "You'll have to switch schools."

"I don't mind," Amber answered. "The kids at my school are snotty."

"Besides, private schools bend over backward to accommodate you if your parents give a big donation." Tiffany's cynical attitude bothered Zora until the girl said, "Oh, yeah, and Mom and Vince promised a gift to the animal shelter here, because it's our pet project."

"Pet project?" Rod waggled an eyebrow.

"Tiffany made a pun!" Amber giggled.

"And you volunteer there, Dad," his older daughter said. "It'll be cool for Vince to be funding *your* favorite charity without realizing it."

Zora wondered how Vince would treat his future genetic child or children. And how would he behave toward his stepdaughters? Perhaps he'd mellow out. She doubted it, though.

After wiping her hands on a napkin, Zora rested them on her bulge. Thinking about daddies reminded her that Andrew had had his blood drawn on Wednesday. The results might arrive by the end of the week, not that she had any doubts about them.

"Let's cut the cake." Tiffany jumped up to clear the table.

They'd polished off the better part of two pizzas, with leftovers to stock the fridge. Karen, with her usual efficiency, would jot on the cardboard box the number of slices allocated to each resident. Despite occasional carping in the early days—accustomed to living with other guys, Lucky had pushed for the first-come-first-served approach—they'd found that this method maintained the peace.

Karen produced birthday candles, which Lucky lit using a strand of spaghetti in lieu of the fireplace torch they'd misplaced. Then they sang, lustily if raggedly, a round of "Happy Birthday."

Keely stood with hands clasped and eyes sparkling. As they finished amid cheers, she sniffed. "I can't believe you guys did this."

"You're part of the family now," Karen said.

"Hurray for Keely!" added Tiffany, who hadn't had a clue to the woman's identity until today.

Amber sidled up to the newcomer and took her hand. "Being fifty sounds good. I bet nobody bosses you around."

Too choked up to speak, Keely nodded.

Rod did the honors, at Karen's request. "This is as close as I get to performing surgery," the anesthesiologist said as he divided the cake. "Keely, which piece do you prefer?"

"Take the one with the rainbow roses on it," Amber advised.

The nurse bestowed a quavering smile on the youngster. "If you recommend it."

"I do."

Across from her, Zora watched Lucky beam at the cozy tableau. He was deriving as much joy from the situation as if they'd thrown *him* a surprise birthday party. What a natural father he'd make.

Whenever he found the perfect time and the perfect woman.

That week, Keely, Karen and Lucky alternated providing rides for Zora. Since Rod's unreliable car was in the shop, he tagged along, too. That led to hilariously nonsensical discussions, and kept Zora from feeling that she was imposing too heavily on her friends.

On Friday, the radiology scheduler assigned her to the same-day surgery unit on the fourth floor of the hospital. Busy with clients, Zora only glanced at her phone in rare free moments in case of urgent voice messages or texts. There was one asking her to call Keely, which she presumed meant a change in whoever was driving home from work.

During her break that afternoon, Zora headed for the fourth-floor staff lounge, eager to put her feet up and answer messages. Waddling around a corner, she nearly collided with her ex-mother-in-law. Her hand shot out to the wall for support.

"Sorry." Betsy braced as if preparing to catch her. "Are you okay?"

"Sure." Zora removed her hand. "I, uh, don't usually see you here." The nursing supervisor's office was on the fifth floor, although Betsy's duties might take her anywhere in the building.

"I was looking for you." The older woman walked with her toward the lounge. "Radiology said you were on this floor today. Can we talk?"

Zora occasionally chatted with Betsy about crocheting or mutual acquaintances when they ran into each other, but the older woman didn't usually single her out this way. "Is there a problem?"

"Hold on." Opening the lounge door, Betsy scanned the interior. It was empty, Zora saw. The vending machines and kitchenette appeared in pristine condition, no doubt tidied since lunch. "Good. We're alone."

Why was that good?

Zora settled on a couch. Without asking, the older woman brought her a cup of herbal tea from a machine. "You ought to stay hydrated," Betsy said from an adjacent chair. "In fact, you should be on maternity leave."

"I'm saving as much of my time as possible for after the twins are born." Zora hoped she could hold out another few weeks.

"You don't have to go through this alone." Betsy's green eyes, augmented by her spectacles, zeroed in on her. "I wish you'd felt comfortable confiding in me, although I understand your reluctance."

"Andrew told you that he's the father?" He must have received the lab results of the paternity test today.

"Yes, he did." Worry lines deepened in Betsy's square face. "That's why I wanted to talk with you. I believe you ought to hear his plans."

He was up to something already? With a sinking sensation, Zora conceded that she should have expected this. She sighed. "Hit me with it."

Chapter 10

Trying not to panic while Betsy gathered her thoughts, Zora stretched out along the couch. As usual, she'd been floating on what Lucky had once termed the river of denial. She hadn't bothered to consult her attorney to prepare for Andrew's stratagems, such as ducking child support payments. She'd let matters drift, while he'd apparently prepared a trap.

Betsy spread her hands in dismay. "There's no way to soften this. He might sue for custody."

"What?" Zora would have bolted to her feet except that she was long past the ability to bolt anywhere. "How ridiculous! He doesn't want the kids." More objections tumbled through her mind. "And since Lin walked out, who does he think would care for them on the wildly improbable chance that he won the court battle?"

"Me," her ex-mother-in-law said. "He asked me to

raise the babies. I guess he assumed I'd leap at the chance, because he knows how much I would love grandchildren."

Zora stared at her, stunned. Never in her most bizarre dreams could she have concocted such a scheme. Finally she found her voice. "You told him no, right?"

"Without a moment's hesitation."

"Can you please explain what he was thinking?"

Betsy rolled her eyes. Zora didn't recall ever seeing her ex-mother-in-law do that before. "I long ago gave up on understanding my son. Sadly, he takes after his father. In case you don't remember Rory very well, my ex is a total narcissist."

"He seemed distant." As a teenager, Zora didn't recall exchanging more than superficial greetings with Andrew's father. When she and her old flame reconnected ten years later, his parents had divorced.

Rory hadn't attended their wedding, a lovely ceremony followed by a reception she'd rather forget. Zora's mother had drunk too much, waxed maudlin about her baby girl, then vomited on the buffet table.

"I asked Andrew why the hell—excuse me, heck— he'd sue for custody," Betsy said. "He claimed you'd tricked him into fathering kids just so you could hit him up for support, and he doesn't plan to let you win. His words, not mine."

The man had incredible nerve. "He lied to me about reconciling so he could seduce me. That's how I got pregnant." Embarrassment heated Zora's cheeks. "I was naive. The fact that he didn't bother with protection struck me as a sign that he was serious, because we'd been trying to have kids. I had no idea until later that he'd had a vasectomy and believed he was sterile."

Then she realized what she'd revealed. "I'm sorry to drop that on you."

"Oh, my son already did," Betsy said wryly. "He was almost gleeful as he informed me these are the only grandchildren I'll ever have. He failed to grasp that I can be their grandmother without depriving them of their mom."

Betsy was running a risk by bringing Zora the truth—she might offend her son and she had no guarantee Zora would grant her access to the kids. "Of course you're their grandmother. I'd love for you to be part of my children's lives, and mine, too."

The other woman glowed with relief. "I've always felt as if you were my daughter."

"Me, too." In high school, Zora had often relied on Betsy for comfort and advice, since she couldn't trust her own mom. A rush of happiness ran through her, to be on intimate terms with Betsy again.

"I doubt any court in California would hand my son sole custody," Betsy added. "If you need me to testify about how unfit he is, just say the word."

Zora swallowed hard. "You're a saint."

"Oh, I have my faults." With a quirk of the eyebrow, the grandmother-to-be inquired, "To change the subject, I've been wondering—have you picked names?"

Suddenly, Zora had an answer. Half of one, anyway. "The girl will be Elizabeth."

Betsy's eyes widened. "For me?"

"Absolutely." Also, Zora liked that name.

"Count on me as your number one babysitter." The nursing supervisor appeared about to explode with joy. "Do me a favor, would you?"

"Sure. What?"

"Don't name the boy Andrew." Quickly, Betsy added, "Not to deprive my son. It's because being a junior can cause confusion."

"Understood." The reason scarcely mattered; Zora wouldn't name her little boy Andrew for a million dollars. Well, maybe a million. And then she'd use a nickname.

Outside in the hall, she heard light footsteps approaching. In midafternoon, there hadn't been much traffic in this wing. Same-day surgeries were conducted early enough for patients to recover by late afternoon, and most were still recuperating at this hour.

Zora glanced at her watch. "Sounds like we're about to have company, and I'm due to see a patient."

"If you need help arranging for leave, let me know."

"Thanks, but..."

The door opened and a woman peered in, reddish-brown hair rioting around her head. "Excuse me. I'm supposed to be interviewing with Dr. Davis on the fourth floor but I can't find his..."

Utter and total silence fell over the lounge. Because the face looking back at Zora was her own.

For Lucky, Friday afternoons could be crammed with last-minute patients or, like today, extremely light. Cole had accepted several extra surgeries and ordered him to reschedule office appointments.

Since Keely had to work late, Lucky was happy to switch their arrangement and drive Zora home, but she wasn't answering her phone. Not unusual—she might be with patients. After determining that she'd been assigned to the same-day surgery unit, he decided to grab a snack at the cafeteria and stop by the fourth floor to try to catch her in a free moment.

Emerging from the stairs, he had a moment of disorientation when he spotted her down the hall. Why was Zora wearing street clothes, and— Wait a minute— what had happened to her pregnancy?

Then he remembered that Dr. Davis was in town to interview nurse candidates and find a place to live. He'd be joining the staff at the beginning of November, a few weeks from now. Zady, one of the nurses slated for an interview, must have been confused about which fourth floor was involved—she'd gone to the hospital instead of the office next door.

"Miss Moore?" Lucky didn't like to shout, but she failed to hear him. Instead, with no nurses' station in sight, she headed for the next best thing, the staff lounge.

After opening the door, she stood frozen, her shoulders rigid. A warning bell rang in Lucky's head.

Standing behind the slender figure with hair a shade lighter than Zora's, he peered inside. Sure enough, staring at Zady with her mouth open was the shocked face of his housemate.

From the recesses of his suddenly sluggish brain, Lucky dredged up the words, "I can explain." But before they reached his vocal cords, a third woman spoke from the side.

"What a pleasure to run into you, Zady." Betsy Raditch, he realized, must have met Zora's twin when the girls were teens.

While she and Zady exchanged greetings, Lucky tried wafting apologetic vibes in Zora's direction, but she ignored him. It hadn't occurred to him the sisters might come face-to-face today. In the event that Zady landed the job, he'd assumed there'd be plenty of time for him to break the news once it was no longer a matter of confidence.

He wondered what issues had separated the sisters. If someone unexpectedly threw him together with his brother, there'd be hell to pay. But their split had occurred under unusually traumatic circumstances.

He snapped to attention, hearing Zady say she was in search of Dr. Davis's office. "That's on the fourth floor of the building next door," he said.

"Dr. Davis?" Betsy's forehead wrinkled. "Oh, the new urologist. I heard you were vetting the nurse candidates, Lucky."

Two pairs of large gray eyes fixed on him. "You must be Mr. Mendez," Zady said.

Zora mouthed the formal name—*Mr. Mendez?*—and grimaced.

He'd have to wait until later to provide the details of his involvement. "I'll escort you," he told Zady, adding for Zora's benefit, "I'm driving you home today. Keely has to stay late."

"Fine," she growled. Since he'd brought her in this morning, she knew where he'd parked his car.

The twins regarded each other hesitantly. "I don't understand why—" Zady began.

"What're you doing—" Zora started.

They paused, radiating mistrust. But something else too, Lucky thought. Hope, perhaps?

"You ladies should talk," Betsy said. "But right now, I gather there are people waiting. Do you have each other's phone numbers?"

Both heads shook. While they input the numbers in their mobiles, Zady said, "I'm staying at the Harbor Suites. Let's meet when you finish work." She provided her room number.

"I don't mind driving you over there," Lucky put in, although he didn't expect to receive any thanks.

"Okay." To her twin, Zora said, "Good luck with the interview, I guess."

"Yeah, thanks. I guess."

Lucky accompanied Zady to the elevator. In answer to her query, he said he was one of Zora's housemates, which seemed to puzzle her even more.

She had a lot of questions, including why Zora was renting a room in a house instead of living with her husband. Lucky told her he'd leave that for her sister to answer.

How strange that Zady didn't know her twin was divorced. But then, he had no idea whether his brother was married or had kids, or what Matthew had been doing these past sixteen years. The only cousin with whom Lucky kept in touch diplomatically avoided the subject.

Occasionally, Lucky had considered searching online to scope out Matthew's status, but that risked arousing old fury and resentment. Better to let sleeping dogs lie. He'd fought hard to regain his equilibrium after his brother lined up the rest of the family against him. Now that he'd found a second home among friends, why revisit the past?

Unlike Lucky, these sisters had a mother with whom Zora was in contact, and Zady probably was, too. Why hadn't she passed along vital information such as Zora's marital status?

Lucky expected to learn more in due time. Although he might catch a scolding from Zora during the drive, it would be worth it.

After Zady departed, Zora struggled with a wave of bewilderment and regret. Had it really been nine years since they'd fought? Her outrage had long ago dissipated. But according to Mom, Zady did nothing but boast about her happy marriage and loving children while dropping snide remarks about Zora. Yet if Zady was content, why did she want to leave Santa Barbara? And why apply for a job at the medical center where Zora worked?

Betsy broke the silence. "I know you two are estranged, but I've never heard why. Granted, it's none of my business. Still, I noticed during high school that whenever I saw the two of you laughing and having fun together, the next thing I heard, you were fighting. I hope you've outgrown that."

Zady used to play nasty tricks on Zora, after which she not only feigned innocence but leveled accusations at *her*. It would be childish to dredge that up, however. "A lot of siblings fight."

"I can't speak from experience. My brother was much older, more like an uncle, and I only had one child." Betsy arose. "You have a patient scheduled?"

"Oh, that's right!" She'd forgotten to watch the clock.

"I hope you'll talk to your attorney about Andrew," Betsy added.

"I will." After a quick hug, Zora departed, her mind buzzing with the latest developments.

Good thing she'd have Lucky to review them with after work. Right after she read him the riot act.

* * *

On the second level of the garage, Zora approached the familiar black sedan where Lucky was comfortably ensconced, apparently listening to music. On the sloped ramp, she paused to observe him.

With his dark coloring and dramatic cheekbones, Lucky had drawn her attention as soon as he'd started working at Safe Harbor, about a year after she had. While she'd considered him handsome, he wasn't her type, and she'd been married to Andrew.

Later, when Cole fell in love with Stacy, loyalty to his doctor—although Cole had never indicated any animosity toward Zora—had turned Lucky into her fiercest critic. She'd refused to let him scare her out of moving into Karen's house, however, and over the past months, he'd changed.

When he'd reviewed the nurses' applications for Dr. Davis, why had he chosen her twin as a finalist—to create trouble? Surely he hadn't eliminated more qualified applicants for Zady's sake, though. Perhaps she simply deserved to be considered.

"Oh, good, I caught you." Rod's voice yanked her from her reflections. "My transmission's on the fritz again. Blast that car. I'm definitely trading it in."

"Hi, Rod." He must have received Lucky's permission to join them—how else would he know the car's location? Zora mused as they strolled side by side to the car. "We have a stop en route," she informed the anesthesiologist. "My sister and I are having a, well, touchy reunion."

"Fine with me." He opened the rear door for her. Inside, the blare of country music cut off. "I'd offer to sit in the back but it's safer for you to be there."

"Thanks." Zora hefted her body inside.

"I'll drop you at the Harbor Suites," Lucky said from the front. The one-bedroom suites rented by the day or week. "I'll pick you up again after I take Rod home."

"That's a lot of driving," Zora said.

"It's ten minutes in each direction." Rod closed her door and hopped into the front, adjusting his fedora to avoid it bumping the roof.

Lucky put the car into reverse. Although tempted to ask why he'd approved her sister as a potential colleague, Zora wasn't keen on reviewing the whole business in front of Rod.

Fortunately, he was preoccupied with the latest developments concerning his daughters. Helen had reported that the girls were starting at their new school next week, and that Vince had insisted both of them play soccer, which Tiffany hated.

When the youngster begged to study dance instead, her stepfather had said he was tired of her complaints. He planned to send her to boarding school in Switzerland when she entered high school the following autumn.

"Her mother doesn't bother to defend her," Rod said angrily. "If the girls are too much trouble to have around, they should let me raise them."

"Not much chance of that, is there?" Lucky observed.

"I wish there were. Karen would welcome them. They can have my room." Rod and Karen had begun spending nights together in her master suite.

Vince would never let go of anything he considered his, Zora reflected. The thought of the billionaire sent a shiver through her. The memory of him groping her abdomen repulsed her. Well, he'd accomplished his goal of arousing his wife's jealousy, and hopefully that was the end of that.

They pulled into the parking lot in front of the Harbor Suites. Among the vehicles, she spotted license plates from neighboring states: Arizona, Oregon, Utah, Nevada. Patients undergoing fertility treatments often rented rooms here.

Lucky halted in front of the office. "You want me to stay? If you're worried, I will."

What a sweet offer. "I'll be fine."

"If we hear screaming, we'll turn around," Rod joked.

After Zora got out, Lucky lowered his window. "I'll pick up food on my way back."

Why was he acting so nice? In self-defense, Zora supposed. "Chinese would be good. Or Italian."

"Okay."

Despite her brave words, dread filled Zora as the car drove off. Years of silence between her and Zady loomed in front of her like an abyss.

Still, she was curious about her sister's situation, she conceded as she followed a sidewalk between the one-story buildings. And if Zady ended up at Safe Harbor, they'd have to reach an accord sooner or later.

Halfway across the grassy courtyard, past a few squatty palm trees, Zora spotted the room number Zady had given her earlier. Taking a deep breath, she knocked on her sister's door.

Chapter 11

Inside, footsteps rushed across the carpet. Zora's pulse sped up as the door opened and she stared into a face at the same height as hers, a face that mirrored hers, from the freckles to the wary expression.

A memory sprang up. For their senior prom, they'd accidentally bought the same dress and, after a horrified moment, they'd dissolved into laughter. Rather than quibble about who should return the gown, they'd coordinated the rest of their outfits, as well. Their classmates had assumed they'd deliberately picked matching dresses and shoes, while they'd confounded their mother. It had been rare fun.

"Hi." Zady moved aside, admitting her to an austere living room furnished with a nondescript sofa and reproductions of seascapes on the walls.

Zora noted a can of soup in the kitchenette next to

the microwave. If that was her sister's idea of dinner, Zady was either on a diet or short of money. Well, according to their mother, her sister had three children, enough to strain any budget.

"Let's get one thing straight." Zady's words sounded rehearsed.

"What's that?"

"If Dr. Davis offers the job, I'm accepting it."

It hadn't occurred to Zora to suggest otherwise. "That's fine. I won't beat around the bush, either."

"Okay." Hands clenched, Zady waited by the couch.

Ignoring the sofa, Zora chose a hard chair. "Regardless of what Mom may have claimed, here are the facts. Right before Andrew and I finalized our divorce, I slept with him because I believed he still loved me. Then he married his new girlfriend. Now I'm pregnant with twins, which I plan to keep."

Zady dropped onto the couch, eyes wide. "You're divorced? Mom said your husband dotes on you. Takes you on luxury cruises, showers you with jewelry—I'll admit, it didn't sound like the Andrew I remember from high school, but—you're carrying twins? Are they identical?"

"No. A boy and a girl."

"That's good. Maybe they won't hate each other."

The remark brought an unexpected pang. "Do you hate me?" Zora asked.

"No, I assumed…" Zady broke off.

Although Zora was dying to learn more about her sister's feelings, first things first. "Why did you apply to Safe Harbor? What about your husband and kids— are they moving here?"

"Dwayne and I never married." Zady kicked off her

low-heeled pumps. "And I don't have kids, unless you count his three obnoxious children who treat me as their personal maid."

The world was shifting on its axis. "Are you still living with him?"

"No." Her twin didn't look up, apparently fascinated by her stocking-clad feet. "He's like Dad, forever cheating."

"So is Andrew!"

"And I was too stubborn and proud to admit it until he forced my hand."

"Me, too."

They regarded each other across the coffee table. Zora could almost have laughed, except the situation was pathetic.

"You didn't finish your story," Zady said. "Since Mom obviously lied about everything, I'd like to hear the truth. She said Andrew sought you out during his first marriage because he'd never stopped loving you. Is that right?"

"No. We bumped into each other at our high school reunion. Wish you'd been there."

"Are you kidding? I was too embarrassed about my situation with Dwayne. Go on."

Zora poured out the tale of how Andrew had dumped Stacy, then cheated on Zora. "In high school, you told me he sneaked around with other girls," she recalled. "I'm sorry I accused you of being jealous."

"And I'm sorry I didn't listen when you warned me that Dwayne was a jerk."

"I guess I did." With all that had happened since, Zora had forgotten that she'd tried to steer her sister away from him. She'd had more sense about Zady's choices than her own.

"You were right not to trust him." Zady waved her hands in a gesture Zora recognized, because she did it herself when agitated. "Not only didn't he marry me, Dwayne refused to have kids. He stuck me with his unholy brood during their vacations, claiming I should learn to love my 'stepchildren.' He used the free time to play around. I closed my eyes to it, until his new girl-friend got pregnant."

"How did he react to that?"

"Oh, he's excited about being a proud papa again." Bitterness laced Zady's voice. "I wouldn't count on it lasting, if I were her."

"Andrew didn't refuse to have children with me," Zora said. "We were trying for a pregnancy before he met, well, *her.* I stopped taking birth control pills during our last year together, but nothing happened until after we separated."

"Hmm...that timing is weird." Zady frowned.

"I agree, but it's not as if he tricked me while we were married. I'd have noticed if he was wearing a condom."

"If I've learned anything, it's that a manipulative jerk will do stuff you'd never dream of."

"Maybe, but I can't imagine how..." Zora stopped. "Oh, Lord, you're right. I may have just figured it out."

"What?" Her sister leaned forward.

Zora smacked herself in the forehead. "After I stopped taking the birth control pills, he claimed he threw them out. I was touched. But what if he crushed them into my food?"

"For an entire year?"

"There was a three-month supply in the drawer."

He'd become solicitous about her diet, preparing breakfast to be sure she ate properly for their future children. "As my husband, he'd have had no problem refilling the prescription."

"But a year's a long time." Zady appeared both disgusted and fascinated.

"He went out of town on occasion," Zora conceded. "But we weren't having sex during his absences, either. And I marked our wall calendar with what I assumed were my most fertile days. I was frustrated when he always claimed to be exhausted after he got back from a trip right when we should have been making love. I should have suspected something."

"What a lot of trouble. He could have sneaked off and had a vasectomy without telling you," Zady said. "The scar's usually very small."

Zora threw up her hands—just as her sister had done moments earlier, she realized. "Why be straightforward when you can be manipulative? Andrew enjoyed playing games and tricking people. Or I could be wrong about this."

"I'm sure it must be illegal to dose a person with prescription medication without her consent," Zady added.

"That wouldn't bother Andrew." Nothing could be proven now, Zora supposed, even though the scenario explained a lot about Andrew's behavior. "Well, eventually he did have a vasectomy, but he assumed his sperm count was zero after a month. Now he's attempting to punish me for demanding child support."

"How?"

She described the plot to sue for custody and persuade his mother to raise the kids. "Betsy gave me all the details earlier today."

"That's what you were discussing in the lounge?" Zady slapped the coffee table. "How could we have fallen for such jerks? Why didn't we tell them to go to hell a whole lot sooner?"

"Gullibility. Love," Zora assessed. "And pride. Mom kept bragging about how perfect your life was."

"I cried on her shoulder practically every week. And she regaled me with stories of how happy you were." Zady blushed. "I couldn't give up on Dwayne because I refused to let you win."

"I felt the same way." Zora winced at how easily they'd been maneuvered. "How long do you think she's been lying to us?"

"Since we were born?"

Zora recalled Betsy's observation. "You're right. Whenever we had fun together, you could count on something happening to mess it up."

"Such as you borrowing my new sweater and ruining it." That incident had triggered their final blowup while they were in college. The squabble over a minor transgression had deteriorated into cross accusations and name calling. Soon afterward, Zady had left town with Dwayne.

"I didn't touch your sweater," Zora said. Had their mother really stooped that low? Obviously, yes. "You didn't borrow my earrings and lose one, either, did you?"

"No." Zady buried her face in her hands, then peeked between her fingers. "How sick, that she was jealous of her own children being close."

"Mom destroyed your sweater and my earrings so we'd fight." Zora struggled to grasp how cruel that had been.

"She always had to be the center of attention," Zady noted.

"That's why we were sitting ducks for Andrew and Dwayne," Zady said. "We grew up being manipulated."

"Imagine how she'll react when she learns we're on good terms again." Zady blew out a long breath. "She'll do anything to split us up."

"Let's not tell her." As she spoke, Zora could almost hear Lucky coaching her in the background, urging her to avoid her old traps by changing her behavior.

"How can we avoid it?"

"If we confront her, she'll start scheming," Zora pointed out. "We should say as little as possible to her."

A smile lit Zady's face. "That'll drive her crazy."

"Exactly."

"But if I land the job at Safe Harbor, she'll realize we must be talking," Zady said.

"We can say we only see each other around the building. End of story."

"She'll interrogate her old friends who live here."

"If she has any, they won't know anything." Zora's only contact from her mother's generation was Betsy, who was too smart to play those games.

"Wow." Zady regarded her in admiration. "That's both simple and diabolical."

"Let's function as a team. Full disclosure about everything."

"Done!"

Across the coffee table, they high-fived each other. For nearly ten years, Zora had been missing part of herself. "I'm only sorry it took us this long to come together. I'm glad my kids will have an aunt."

"Me, too." Zady regarded Zora's bulge wistfully. "How will you raise them alone? If I'm living here, I'll pitch in, but I'll be working all day, too."

"There's day care at the hospital. And I have friends." Zora would be lost without her supportive household. "They've already raised money for a part-time nanny." Her phone buzzed with a text. Glancing down, she saw Lucky's message. "And there's my ride, waiting out front."

"Is that Mr. Mendez?" Longing shaded Zady's expression. "He's very kind. And he admires you, I can tell."

This was interesting news. "Did he say so?"

Her sister shook her head. "Not specifically. It's the way he looks at you, and how he avoided revealing too much about your situation while he walked me to the office building. He was protecting you."

"As a friend." Yet what if it meant more? Was it possible Lucky was falling in love with her, too? But he'd never abandon his ideal scenario, let alone agree to raise Andrew's children. "I shouldn't keep him waiting."

"Of course not."

Rising, Zady held out her hand to boost Zora. Then they flung their arms around each other.

"We're back," Zady crowed. "Twins forever!"

No more allowing others to separate them. "I hope, hope, hope you get the job."

"Me, too."

Amazement filled Zora as she eased out of the suite and along the path. How wonderful it would be to have family in town, especially the person who ought to be closest to her.

She couldn't wait to share their conversation with Lucky.

As the October darkness gathered, Lucky drummed his fingers on the steering wheel. He had no idea what to expect from Zora—complaints? Fury? But his tension also derived from another matter.

Rod's complaints on the drive home had reminded him that Vince and Portia were barreling ahead on their pregnancy project. Once his wife had yielded, the billionaire hadn't wasted a moment. Since his treatment needed to be coordinated with hers, Lucky was able to follow their efforts.

After reviewing Portia's up-to-date medical records and confirming that she was in excellent health, Dr. Brennan had started her on medication to adjust her cycle. Once her eggs ripened, Dr. Rattigan would remove sperm from Vince's testes. Then her eggs would be harvested and injected with her husband's sperm.

Despite the most advanced treatments available, there were no guarantees. The average pregnancy rate per cycle was in the 20 to 35 percent range, but Portia's age lowered her chances. It was likely to take more than one cycle for the implantation to be successful.

But the men's program had to win Vince's support sooner than that. Cole had informed Lucky yesterday that the bankruptcy court was expected to approve the vacant dental building going on sale by mid-November. Several doctors' groups had expressed interest in the space.

Without that building, expansion of Lucky's program would be difficult. No comparable facility with offices and labs existed in Safe Harbor. As for constructing a new one, the logistics of acquiring land and receiving government approvals made that option prohibitive.

So if Vince delayed too long, Lucky might have to choose between using the degree he'd worked so hard for and leaving his friends. Friends who, as he'd become keenly aware, filled the lonely places in his soul.

The creak of the car door jerked Lucky from his reverie. Zora swung onto the seat beside him. "Have you met Dr. Davis? Is he a nice guy? Do you think he'll hire Zady?"

She sounded excited rather than angry, thankfully. "You're in favor of her landing the job?" Lucky switched on the ignition.

"Yes!" She drew the seat belt across her body. "It would be fantastic to have my sister here. My kids could grow up with their aunt, and besides, we belong together."

Things had gone well, then. Lucky smiled. "I was afraid you'd take my head off."

"For keeping her interview a secret?" Zora issued a growly noise. "You deserve it! But no."

"Her application was private." Moot point, now that Zady had revealed the facts to her sister. "I only met Dr. Davis briefly, but I like him. As for who he'll choose, the other candidates are also excellent. Tell me, what did you and Zady discuss?"

"Everything! It's incredible." Any concern that she'd keep Lucky in the dark vanished as she described Zady's selfish boyfriend and the similarities in their romantic experiences. The revelation about Andrew's possible abuse of her birth control pills was outrageous, but, unfortunately, in character for the louse.

Navigating along Coast Highway toward their house, Lucky maintained a leisurely speed to prolong the conversation. Beside him, Zora radiated an almost sexual intensity. The curve of her cheek invited his hand to stroke it, but he gripped the wheel tightly.

It wasn't safe to get distracted while driving. And once he touched her, he might not be able to stop there. He'd recognized his susceptibility to her that day in the office, when they'd nearly gone too far.

If it were only a question of the two of them, maybe... but he refused to risk giving his whole heart to a family that he couldn't be sure he could provide for. And what if Andrew decided he wanted to be a father to the twins? How he could be sure he'd never let Zora or the children down when, ultimately, control could be snatched out of his hands?

He'd made a workable plan for the future, one he could live with and sustain, and right now that plan did not allow for a wife and kids. No matter how he felt about Zora, ultimately he'd have to move past it.

"I understand better now why we fell for Mom's crap." She adjusted the seat belt, which tended to creep up on her abdomen. "Our mother pulled stunts to pit us against each other, and we bought it. She's been lying to us for years, convincing each of us that we were in competition."

She'd never told him that before, only that her mother was an alcoholic and her stepfather a bully. Lucky hadn't pressed for details, partly because he and Zora hadn't been close until recently, and partly because he resented it when people probed his own past. "I had no idea she was fomenting trouble for you."

"Neither did I. It's because of her that Zady and I had our last big blowup." She outlined how their mother had destroyed their property and tricked them into blaming each other. "It was cruel. We've lost nearly a decade. Our mother must be a— Who was that Greek guy that fell in love with his own reflection?"

"Narcissus."

"That's it! She's a narcissist."

"You should cut her off," Lucky said. "It's what she deserves."

"We're putting up a united front," Zora responded. "Keeping her at arm's length will drive her nuts."

"Don't play games." Zora's assertiveness was new and likely fragile. She could easily be sucked back into self-defeating behavioral patterns if she continued to speak to her mother. "You should have nothing further to do with her."

In the faint light as they passed a streetlamp, he saw frown lines pucker her forehead. "She's our mother."

"To feed her ego, she groomed you to be patsies," he retorted. "Don't let Zady persuade you to stay involved with your mother. It's great that you've reconnected with your twin, but not if she's a bad influence."

"My sister isn't a bad influence!" Zora's shoulders stiffened. "And how we handle our mother is none of your business."

"It is if you spiral back into codependency," he said. "Because I have to live with you."

She appeared about to argue, but curiosity won. "What's codependency?"

"Codependents try to save loved ones from the consequences of their own actions because of a misguided sense of loyalty." After reading about the subject in a class on substance abusers and their families, Lucky had been astonished at how often he spotted the behavior in acquaintances and patients. "They feel guilty and trapped and blame themselves for the other person's faults, as you did with Andrew. You're a raging codependent, Zora."

"Now you're claiming I have a mental defect?"

"I'm helping you keep your life on track." To him, it seemed obvious.

"Wow, and I thought you'd changed." Far from heeding his warning, she was working up a head of steam. "Mr. Judgmental."

"It's for your own good." Lucky winced at the banality of his words. "That may be a cliché but in this instance, it's true."

"You expect me to abandon my mother and my sister because that's what you did with your brother when he crossed you."

Anger flared. Her situation didn't remotely compare to Lucky's. "You have no idea what separated Matthew and me."

"I know you're estranged from your entire family," Zora snapped. "He offended you, so Mr. High and Mighty Luke Mendez rejected him and everyone who stood by him."

"I had very valid reasons."

"What reasons?"

"He said vicious things no one could forgive, and obviously he doesn't regret it, since he never apologized."

"What did he say that was so terrible?"

"I have no intention of repeating it." Although Lucky had been only eighteen, his older brother's cruel words remained seared into his brain. *It's your fault our parents are dead, and you cheated me of my inheritance. You should be in prison.*

Matthew had repeated the lies to their aunts and uncles, who had barred Lucky from family gatherings. After several attempts to reason with them, he'd decided to cut himself off from them entirely.

True, he'd messed up, badly. He'd never forgive himself for the mistakes that had hurt their parents. But he hadn't caused their deaths and he would never, ever cheat anyone.

"Maybe he's changed," Zora suggested.

"I've led a fulfilling life without my brother's destructive influence," Lucky replied tautly. "You should do the same with your mother."

"I'm not you." As they entered the driveway, Zora said, "Thank heaven."

"I agree."

"You do?"

"If you were like me, you'd be the first pregnant man in history."

She didn't laugh. Too bad. Lucky had been aiming to lighten the mood.

He supposed she believed that his promise not to nag her over Andrew also applied to the rest of her behavior. But to him, she'd come so far in the last couple of weeks, he didn't want to see her lose her newfound confidence and self-esteem.

If he'd annoyed her, it was worth it.

Chapter 12

Angered by Lucky's arrogance, Zora avoided him over the weekend. She kept busy exchanging photos and messages with Zady, and went grocery shopping with Keely, although the nurse's insistence that she buy organic foods ran up the bill.

It was more than Lucky's haughty attitude that disturbed her, she realized after a second night of troubled sleep. In her dreams, her angry father raged at her, Zady and their mom. After his sudden death from a heart attack when she was twenty-two, Zora had pushed those ugly memories aside, preferring to dwell on her father's kinder, more loving moments. But the discovery of this rigid, unforgiving side of Lucky's nature had reawakened them.

Not that she hadn't expected this, at some level. After all, he insisted on the perfect family situation, including, presumably, a wife who arrived without baggage. No messy old relationships, and no children.

Yet, foolishly, she'd allowed herself to count on Lucky, to venture close to loving him, as if he might find it in his heart to change.

Why do I keep falling for the wrong guy?

If she entered another intimate relationship, Zora vowed to do it with her eyes open. Until then, once she discovered a man's fatal flaw, she'd distance herself from him, no matter how much her heart ached. And Lucky's fatal flaw was his intolerance for other people's flaws.

On Monday, she consulted Edmond regarding child support. He promised to file for half of Zora's unreimbursed medical and other maternity expenses.

"Once the babies are born, their father will be entitled to visitation and possibly shared custody," Edmond advised from behind the desk in his fifth-floor office. "That doesn't necessarily mean he gets physical custody half the time, but he will have an equal say in decisions about their care."

Much as she would hate sharing the children with their unworthy father, Zora supposed that she could hardly refuse contact. "He can't take them away from me, though, can he?"

"That would be extremely unusual," Edmond assured her. "He would have to prove that being around you endangers the children, such as if you were using drugs."

"I'd have to prove that for him, too, to block shared custody?"

"That's right." He adjusted his glasses. "In a case like this, it's tempting to try to cut him out. However, the courts have ruled that it's in a child's best interest for him or her to have a relationship with both parents."

Privately, Zora doubted it. However, she understood

that laws and legal rulings had to apply to a wide range of cases.

When Lucky drove her home that evening, she suppressed the instinct to spill out what she'd learned from Edmond. She hadn't shared Betsy's confidence about Andrew's latest ploy, either.

He's judgmental and pitiless. The words played through her mind on a repeating loop, warning her to maintain a distance.

So when the silence weighed too heavily, she broached the merits of organic foods, a topic that interested him. Lucky explained that he was vegetarian more for health reasons than for philosophical ones, although sparing animals' lives was a bonus. The man didn't appear to notice that she was withholding any information of a personal nature.

On Tuesday morning, Zora was assigned to perform sonograms at Dr. Brennan's office. Her obstetrician urged her to stay off her feet as much as possible, and Keely brought enough cups of tea to double her already frequent trips to the restroom.

While every patient was important and required her focus, Zora sensed an undercurrent of excitement building among the staff in the late morning. The reason became clear when she wheeled her cart into an exam room where Portia Adams lay on the table. Her auburn hair highlighted with chestnut and gold strands, she wore a hot-pink hospital gown that she must have brought with her. The only other person present was the doctor.

Lips pressed into a thin line, Portia watched Zora with a flare of the nostrils. Was the woman still jealous? *How sad*, Zora thought as she readied her equipment.

She was thankful for Dr. Brennan's narrative during the sonogram. "Everything's right on target." Seated on a stool, the doctor crossed her long legs. "We may be ready to harvest your eggs by the end of next week. Are you experiencing mood swings?"

"No more than usual," Portia said tartly. "How soon will my pregnancy start to show? I'm on the committee of a Christmas charity ball for the animal shelter and I must be sure my dress will fit."

Dr. Brennan blinked. She must have heard a lot of odd questions, Zora mused as she removed the probe, but this one evidently caught her by surprise.

"If you become pregnant on the first try, you'd still only be a few months along by Christmas," she said. "Maternity clothes probably won't be necessary. However, for comfort, I recommend a loose-fitting style."

"That's what I meant," Portia said. "I just want to buy the right style."

When Keely entered the room, Zora started to wheel her equipment out. As she opened the door, she heard the nurse say to Dr. Brennan, "Mr. Adams has arrived. Shall I send him in?"

"Wait till I straighten my gown," Portia responded. "How's my hair?"

It was too late for her to retreat, Zora realized as the door closed behind her, leaving her alone in the hallway. And there he was, his large frame nearly filling the corridor and forcing her to halt.

"Well, well." Despite the expensive cologne and expertly cut hair, Vince had a sleazy air. "If it isn't the lady with the earth-goddess body."

"Your wife's waiting for you, Mr. Adams." Zora

peered past him, hoping to spot another staff member. No such luck.

"Has anybody told you lately how sexy you are?" The man's low voice might not carry into the closed examining room, but Zora wished it would. Then surely Dr. Brennan or Keely would respond.

"Thank you." She rattled the cart. "Excuse me."

Vince's expression hardened. "I'm an important man around here. You should consider the advantages of keeping me happy."

What nerve! "That's hardly appropriate for a woman in my condition." *Or any woman in any condition.*

"There are other ways of pleasing a man," he muttered close to her ear.

Zora's stomach churned. "I have a patient waiting." Not true, but she didn't care. And neither, she gathered from Vince's unmoving stance, did he.

Mercifully, noises from inside the examining room finally penetrated his awareness. From his pocket, he produced a business card and scribbled a phone number on the reverse. "My cell." He stepped aside. "Call me."

Zora stuck the card in her pocket and hurried away. As she stored her equipment, her hands were trembling.

What was she going to do? The only way to be sure of avoiding the man in the future was to complain about his disgusting behavior. Sexual harassment violated hospital policy, but it was his word against hers.

No, not entirely. She'd attended a talk by the hospital's staff attorney, Tony Franco, highlighting the seriousness with which such claims were regarded.

But if the hospital hassled Vince, that ended any chance of a donation. His wife could transfer to a doctor in San Diego. Was it worth it? The man hadn't tried to *force* Zora to do anything against her will. He'd merely been unpleasant.

Still shaky, she headed for the elevators. In her pocket, she imagined the card covered with slime. Best to discard it immediately. Except, what if she needed to prove that he'd propositioned her? Zora resolved to let her emotions settle before reaching a decision.

After washing her hands—it was impractical to take a shower, despite the icky emotional residue left by her encounter—she went to the cafeteria. In her present mood, she'd rather avoid Lucky, and was glad to see no sign of him. Instead, she spotted Betsy at a table with Lin. The third Mrs. Raditch must have had her follow-up appointment with Dr. T this morning.

With her tray of food, Zora joined them. At nearby tables, heads swiveled and voices murmured. Didn't these people have anything more substantial on their minds?

Betsy pulled out a chair. "I'm glad you're here."

"Me, too, Grandma," Zora said lightly. "Lin, how are you?"

"Dr. Tartikoff found nothing suspicious," the young woman replied.

"That's wonderful." Zora hesitated to raise another sensitive topic. Lin's next comment spared her that.

"I have talked to the attorney you recommended." Lin placed her dirty tableware neatly atop her empty plate. "He suggests an annulment on the grounds that Andrew defrauded me."

"By pretending to be a human being?" Embarrassed at her bluntness, Zora glanced apologetically at Betsy. "Sorry."

"No offense taken." Her ex-mother-in-law's mouth quirked.

"He lied about the vasectomy," Lin answered. "He claimed he had it during your marriage and promised to reverse it for me."

"Instead, he had the vasectomy *after* you got engaged." Which meant he didn't intend to reverse it, in Zora's opinion.

"Mr. Everhart called me after he contacted Andrew's attorney. It appears he will agree to the annulment," Lin said. "It will be as if the marriage never occurred."

How strange that, a month ago, this was what Zora had dreamed of, she mused as she ate. No more third wife. Instead, her sympathies now lay with Lin. "Will you stay in America?"

The other woman sighed. "I called my parents and they are eager for me to return."

"I wish you all the best," Betsy told her. "I hope you meet a man who deserves you."

"I doubt I will have as nice a mother-in-law," Lin said.

"How sweet." Betsy gazed at her pensively before turning to Zora. "If I may ask, what's the latest on your sister?"

Zora sketched the situation to her rapt audience. When she finished, she spotted Lucky standing with his tray, gazing around. A tremor ran through her at the reminder of the difficult choice she faced about Vince.

If she told him what Vince had done, how would he respond? Was it possible he'd think Zora had invited the other man's attention? Or, with his rigid insistence on propriety, would he pressure her to report Vince's harassment?

"You look pained," Betsy said. "Are you okay?"

"It's heartburn." Zora didn't dare reveal the truth. As nursing supervisor, Betsy would be obligated to inform the administrator.

"I must go." Lin stood, and Betsy, who'd finished her meal, did the same. "It is good to meet you again, Zora."

"Congratulations on your annulment." Zora almost regretted that Lin was returning to Hong Kong. She'd grown fond of her fellow sufferer.

How had Andrew managed to trick three intelligent women into loving him? Zora recalled Lucky describing her as a raging codependent. It must be a common condition.

He strode over, nodding to Betsy as she departed. Keely headed in their direction as well, her strong-boned face alight.

As the housemates settled, Keely spoke first. "I have great news! Mr. Adams plans to announce his donation soon."

Lucky gave a start. "He told *you*?"

"Dr. Brennan and me." The nurse transferred her dishes from the tray to the table. "He said the hospital is arranging a press conference. They're rushing the announcement because the dental building is going on sale."

Lucky slapped his thighs. "Fantastic!"

"He won't be able to jerk us around anymore," Zora burst out.

"Absolutely." Lucky's dark eyes sparkled. "Once he donates the money, we can stop worrying."

"That's right." This development reinforced Zora's resolve to keep quiet. Losing the billionaire's support at this point would be devastating, and unnecessary.

But what a relief that she only had to hold out for a little while longer.

"He and his wife were joking about whose name will go on the building," Keely added. "Just his, or both of theirs."

"I can guess which side Vince was on." It wouldn't surprise Zora if the man's monstrous ego required the hospital to paint an enormous portrait of him covering the front of the structure as well. She wondered how hard it would be to sneak out and ornament it with a large mustache, blackened tooth and eye patch.

"They can put their daughters' names on it, too, as far as I'm concerned." Lucky popped open his carton of milk. "We can call it the Everybody Who's Ever Been Named Adams Medical Building."

Zora tucked into her tapioca pudding, relishing the creamy texture and vanilla flavoring. The rest of her meal had gone down almost untasted.

Idly, she wondered why a number of other diners were sneaking glances at them. Betsy and Lin had left, and Keely hadn't spoken loudly enough for her disclosure to carry above the general chatter. Lucky's enthusiastic reaction might have drawn attention briefly, but the staring seemed to be increasing.

"What do you suppose Laird's up to?" Lucky indicated a compact male figure perched triumphantly on a chair while the listeners at his table leaned toward him attentively.

Keely stiffened. "He keeps smirking at me."

"That's the third table he's bestowed his noxious presence on." Lucky didn't miss much. "The man already took his petty revenge on you for beating him to the rental. What more does he expect to gain?"

A lull fell across the room as a group of prominent physicians—Dr. Tartikoff, Cole Rattigan and hospital administrator Mark Rayburn—entered from the patio dining area. Into the quiet, Laird's words—*her own mother*—jangled like an old-fashioned telephone. The administrator frowned at him before glancing in Keely's direction with a troubled look.

The nurse paled. "Oh, my gosh! How did Laird find out?"

"Find out what?" Lucky asked.

As Zora tracked the path of the doctors toward the exit, the answer hit her. "He must have heard Keely and me talking in the garage. He was lurking in his car to watch her discover the flat tires."

"What were you discussing?" Lucky queried.

"It's…personal." Keely closed her eyes, her face a study in anguish. Fury rose in Zora at the jerk who'd inflicted this on her.

Or could she be mistaken? "That was two weeks ago. I don't understand why Laird would wait till now to attack you."

Keely's shoulders slumped. "I do."

"Would somebody please enlighten me?" Lucky said, clearly growing frustrated.

"I'll start at the beginning." Keely described her mother's death and the false allegation of elder abuse made against her that she'd eventually been able to disprove. "On Monday, Dr. Brennan asked if I was involved in any legal proceedings. I told her I wasn't. She apologized for jumping to a conclusion."

"I don't follow." What did Dr. Brennan have to do with Keely *or* Laird?

"Neither did I, but it worried me," Keely admitted.

"When I pressed her, she said her husband had asked if I was still her nurse. That's all, but it reminded me that he's a private detective."

"Laird must have hired him to dig into your background." Unbelievable. To go that far, the psychologist had to be deadly serious about driving Keely away.

"I'm sure the detective informed him that the charges had been dropped." Lucky scowled in Laird's direction.

"People already dislike me." Keely shuddered. "Did you notice Dr. Rayburn's expression? Laird must have gone to him."

"You haven't done anything wrong," Lucky insisted.

"When the old community hospital was sold, we all went through a rehiring process and background check." Keely's thick eyebrows formed an almost straight line. "They asked if we'd ever been charged with a crime. I put down 'No.'"

"Well, you weren't," Zora protested.

"But I was arrested," the older nurse said. "Some people assume that's the same thing."

"Let's call an emergency house meeting tonight," Zora said. "We'll help you deal with this. Okay?"

Keely nodded. Lucky tilted his head in agreement, but in view of his judgmental tendencies, Zora was prepared to stand up to him tonight. She might not be able to take on Vince Adams, but Lucky Mendez was another story.

Chapter 13

Due to schedules and commitments, it was nine o'clock before the household assembled in the den. Lucky had filled in Karen and Rod, who were ready for action.

"I'll chip in for an attorney." As usual, Rod shared the couch with Karen. "Legal costs can grind you under. That might be part of Laird's agenda."

Lucky assumed the anesthesiologist's view was colored by his own experience with the legal system.

In her chair beside Zora, Keely twisted her hands. "Do I *have* to get a lawyer?"

"It might be premature. Has anyone from Human Resources spoken to you about this?" Karen asked.

Keely's straight dark hair slashed the air as she shook her head.

"Edmond offers a free consultation." Lucky studied Zora's reaction, and was disappointed that she gave no sign of how she felt. He'd been hoping to learn that she'd met with Edmond herself to set the wheels rolling against Andrew.

How frustrating that she'd barely spoken to him since their disagreement on Friday. When Lucky had urged her to shut out her mother and, if necessary, her sister, he'd never expected her to shut *him* out instead. He had to admit, he might have gone overboard where her sister was concerned. Although he didn't entirely trust Zady's influence, she meant a lot to Zora. And family was precious—unless they performed a demolition act on your happiness.

But he hadn't had a chance to soften his position in the face of Zora's stonewalling. Talk about driving a person crazy.

Talk to me. Not this instant, of course, but he wished she'd stop avoiding his gaze.

This afternoon, he'd confirmed that the hospital had scheduled a press conference for a week from Thursday to announce a major donation. Lucky should have been exultant, but his emotions refused to cooperate because he couldn't share his happiness with Zora. After all, expanding the program would allow him to stay in Safe Harbor. It angered him that she seemed willing to forgive Andrew almost anything, and him nothing.

However, they had a more immediate matter on the floor. Lucky seized the initiative. "We should advise Dr. Rayburn about Laird's behavior. Don't forget he let the air out of Keely's tires—"

"We can't prove that," Zora interrupted.

"You saw his car at the scene." Lucky had checked, and her description, including the bumper sticker, fit

Laird's vehicle. "He also hired a private detective to snoop into a staff member's background for revenge."

"We can't prove that, either," Rod observed. "And if there was a hospital policy forbidding nosiness, we'd all be out of a job."

Keely hunkered down, arms crossed protectively. Zora scooted her chair closer to Keely's as an indication of solidarity.

"Laird's an embarrassment to the hospital." Lucky had developed a disgust for the man since witnessing his drunken, lecherous behavior more than a year earlier during Elvis Presley night at the Suncrest Saloon. "I'm willing to march into Dr. Rayburn's office and demand he put a stop to this bullying. Who's with me?"

Zora laid a hand on her bulge, which was rippling beneath her maternity top. "Before we start painting protest signs, let's hear Keely's opinion."

"Fine." From his easy chair, Lucky fixed his attention on the older nurse.

She cleared her throat. "I'd like to run this by Dr. Brennan."

"Tomorrow?" Lucky urged.

"She's busy on Thursdays," Keely said. "She has surgeries scheduled."

"She can spare five minutes." The doctor had already showed concern for her nurse when she mentioned her husband's question, hadn't she? "Get her on your side."

"I don't want to drag her into my personal business."

"Don't let Laird intimidate you." With adrenaline pumping through his system, Lucky felt the urge to jump to his feet and pace.

"Oh, quit pressuring her," Zora snapped. "Keely has a right to handle this however she chooses."

"You mean through avoidance?"

Karen raised her hands. "Peace, everybody. As Zora said, this is Keely's decision. We're the backup team."

"Yeah, okay." How had this conversation become an argument between him and Zora, anyway?

Keely released a breath. "I'll talk to my doctor tomorrow."

"Good for you," Zora said.

How come she didn't give Lucky any credit? He'd pushed Keely to do exactly that.

"Are we finished?" Rod asked. Everyone nodded. "Before we break up, you'll all be pleased to hear that I plan to replace my broken-down junkmobile. Any suggestions?"

"A hybrid," Zora said. "You'll save a fortune on gas."

"Consult the online ratings," Keely contributed.

"I'm considering a sports car," Rod added. "Possibly red."

"Watch out. The cops will ticket you every time you edge a few miles over the speed limit." Lucky had heard that from officers who'd chatted with him during his stint as an ambulance driver.

"I should drive a gray SUV instead?" Rod demanded. *"Boring."*

"Buy a car that seats five or six," Karen recommended. "So you can transport the girls and their friends."

"If only."

"Speaking of guests, that brings us to the topic of Thanksgiving," their landlady said, deftly seizing control of the discussion. "How about cooking our dinner a day or two after the holiday? There'll be more chance your daughters can join us."

They speculated on how next week's announcement might affect Vince and Portia's holiday plans but weren't able to reach a conclusion. As for the dinner, scheduling it on a Saturday was fine with Lucky. He usually volunteered to serve food at a homeless shelter on the holiday.

Amid yawns—they were an early-rising bunch—the meeting dispersed. Aware that Zora customarily drank a glass of milk before bed, Lucky watched for his chance and slipped into the kitchen when she was alone.

He noted her cute freckled nose, red hair that frizzed by day's end and legs propped up on a nearby chair. Choosing a chair around the corner of the small table, he reached for her nearest foot.

"Hey!" Zora attempted a glare that bore a strong resemblance to a squint.

"Tired?" Lucky drew his thumb along her instep.

"It's been a busy day." She patted her belly for emphasis.

She should go on maternity leave before she collapsed and delivered in a hall. However, Lucky was trying to reconnect with her, not irritate her. "How're things with Betsy and the third Mrs. Raditch?" he ventured.

"Fine."

He gritted his teeth. As he lifted her other foot and massaged it, her body relaxed. Progress! "Any word from your sister about the job?"

"No." She sank lower in her chair, eyelids drooping.

As Lucky stroked her feet, he noted they were puffy. It must be agony for her to stand all day. *None of your business.* Great—he didn't have to speak any longer; her responses sprang up automatically in his thoughts.

"It must be interesting, working in a different department each day," he said.

"Oh, there are a lot of repeats," she murmured, and fell silent.

"Doggone it!" Oops, he hadn't meant to speak out loud.

Her eyes flew open and her muscles tightened. "What's your problem?"

"You never talk to me anymore." Had he really said that? He sounded like an old married woman. *Or man. Don't be sexist.*

"Why should I? So you can critique my behavior and complain about how stupid I am?" she demanded.

"Of course not." Resentment flared at this unfair description of his statements. "I'd merely advise and counsel you."

"Same difference." Her feet vanished from his hands. Lucky felt like the prince, caught on his knees, rejected by Cinderella.

"What happened to our truce?" He realized he'd entered dangerous territory, since their pact had required him to refrain from criticizing her. But their agreement had been specifically about Andrew. It was unreasonable of her to extend that to a blanket ban on all helpful comments.

"Don't pretend we're teammates," Zora grumped. "We agreed to collaborate to secure the Adamses' donation, and apparently we succeeded."

"There's still a week to go." Lucky was grasping at straws. But surely they could resume their camaraderie.

"I promise not to screw things up before then. Satisfied?" An unfamiliar tightness transformed her into a woman he scarcely recognized, older and more guarded.

This was what he'd been trying to prevent by steering Zora past her poor choices. Before he could assess what it meant or frame another question, the tension vanished and she was once again his peppery little friend.

"I'm off to bed." She handed him her empty glass. "Do something useful. Put this in the dishwasher."

"Not the oven?"

"Whatever." Thrusting her feet into her slippers, she padded off.

Well, at least she'd addressed him directly, Lucky mused as he carried the glass to its destination. He'd count that as a victory.

How fortunate that Lucky had the male clueless gene, Zora reflected tartly while she prepared for bed. He'd mentioned nothing was certain for another week, and at the prospect of facing another week in which she might be exposed to Vince's obnoxious behavior, she'd suffered a wave of revulsion. She'd schooled her features quickly, though, and was fairly sure Lucky hadn't noticed.

She was unclear about the precise mechanism of the donation, but she assumed the billionaire would hand over a check or sign a document when he announced his gift. After that, she doubted he'd withdraw it merely because an ultrasound tech refused to service his needs.

Wrenching her mind away from the whole awful situation, Zora climbed into bed for the night. Mercifully, maternal hormones zapped her into an instant deep sleep.

Over the next few days, the housemates did everything in their power to counter the spread of the rumors about Keely. They told others the true circumstances, including that the charges had been dropped. They pointed to examples of the older woman's kindness, which were often overlooked due to her downbeat personality. They also cited Laird's unscrupulous motives, although by now he must realize they'd never let him move into their house.

It was an uphill battle. Gossip spread madly and either distorted Laird's account even further, or else he embellished it himself. According to one version that reached Zora, Keely had gotten off murder charges on a technicality. By another, she'd been suspected in the deaths of several elderly patients. Many workers, having consulted Laird about their personal problems in the past, were inclined to trust him implicitly.

Keely declined to mount a defense. "I should have stayed home with my mom that day," she told Zora. "I deserve my share of blame."

"Stop acting like a codependent," Zora replied, and, for clarification, displayed the definition on her cell phone. Keely just shrugged.

As they'd expected, Dr. Brennan supported her nurse. Although a few of her patients who were staffers at the medical center claimed to feel uncomfortable around Keely due to her history, no one requested a change of doctors.

But rather than fading, the opposition was growing. In the corridors, people avoided Keely. Zora had been ostracized to an extent for stealing Stacy's husband, but it had never sunk to this level.

Human Resources had contacted Keely and reviewed her history, but there'd been no attempt to fire her. Nevertheless, on Thursday she informed her housemates that she was tired of being a pariah and planned to search for another job. Shoulders hunched, she brushed off their objections.

"She feels guilty," Karen observed after Keely left the room. "The hardest person to forgive is yourself."

"That's ridiculous," Lucky growled. "The past is the past and we should leave it there."

Zora didn't bother to point out that he ought to leave his quarrel with his brother in the past. She was too worried about Keely to waste her energy bickering.

On Friday at lunch, a lab technician deliberately bumped Keely as she walked to their table. Fortunately, Keely kept a tight grip on her tray. Her stoic air didn't fool Zora, though. She knew her friend was close to tears.

"Don't you dare leave without eating," she told the nurse, and walked beside her to their seats. Karen, Rod and Lucky closed ranks with them.

Once they were settled, Zora dared to hope they could eat in peace. Then a tall woman of about fifty, with short brown hair and weathered skin, stalked over and stood over Keely, scowling until the chatter quieted.

"What's on your mind, Orla?" Rod demanded.

The name prodded Zora's memory. Orla Baker was a circulating nurse, which explained how Rod knew her—circulating nurses set up the operating room and checked the stock of instruments and disposable items, which they refreshed during the procedure. They played a key role in protecting patients from mistakes by verifying their identities and reviewing the site and nature of the operation with the surgeon.

"It's disgusting that she left her mother to die." She spat out the words as if it had been *her* mother who'd perished. "The DA may not have charged her, but what kind of person does that? She should be ashamed."

In the stillness, Zora spotted Laird leaning against a wall, arms folded and a smile playing around his mouth. If she'd had a rubber band, she'd have shot it at him to wipe the smirk off his face.

Rising, Lucky pointed at the psychologist. "Orla, *you* should be ashamed for allowing that man to manipulate you into bullying her. He's trying to drive her away because of petty resentment."

Zora had never admired anyone more in her life. Awkwardly, she rose, too. "Laird Maclaine played a mean prank on Keely by letting the air out of her tires. What is this, high school?" Her voice rang out with a touch of shrillness. "He also hired a detective to dig up dirt that he then distorted for his smear campaign. How can any decent person be a party to that?"

Karen sprang up. "Keely may not be slick and persuasive, but she has a kind heart and I'm with her one hundred percent."

Rod stood beside her. "That goes double for me, Orla."

The circulating nurse wavered. "My mother has Alzheimer's. I understand the stresses involved, but there's no excuse for abandoning her mother."

Keely sat silent, unwilling to speak on her own behalf. Zora feared others would take that as an indication of guilt.

Across the cafeteria, a six-foot-tall woman with a commanding air uncoiled. All attention fixed on Dr. Paige Brennan, whose eyes flashed with anger.

"This situation has been discussed at the highest levels and the case is closed," she declared. "If anyone continues creating a hostile work environment for my nurse, I will ensure that disciplinary measures are taken against them. And that is the last I or any of us had better hear about this."

The other obstetricians at her table burst into applause. With a spurt of amusement, Zora registered that the loudest clapping came from Dr. Tartikoff. Apparently he'd forgiven Keely for their long-ago dispute, or else he had zero tolerance for bullying.

Orla spoke directly to Keely. "I apologize. I shouldn't have listened to gossip."

"Have a seat." Karen waved her over. "I'm sorry about your mom, Orla. How're you holding up?"

After a brief hesitation, the circulating nurse sank into a chair. "Some days are better than others."

As the conversation flowed, Zora noted that Dr. Brennan's declaration had restored the color to Keely's face. Orla's apology appeared to have helped, too.

But best of all was watching Laird slink from the cafeteria. Paige Brennan's scorching setdown must have impressed on him that his campaign against Keely had not only failed, it had also damaged his own reputation with the top staff.

A wise person would take a long, hard look in the mirror. She didn't credit Laird with wisdom, however.

That night, Casa Wiggins celebrated the victory with meatless burgers and fizzy apple juice. There was no more talk of Keely changing jobs.

Still, it was too soon to let all her anxiety go. In less than a week, the future of the men's program would be secure, Zora hoped, and prayed silently for nothing to go wrong.

Chapter 14

"I produced fifteen eggs?" From the examining table, Portia stared in dismay at Dr. Brennan. "You must be kidding!"

"That's an excellent number to ripen," the doctor assured her as Zora carefully adjusted the position of her ultrasound wand. "We'll select those in the best condition, fertilize them and choose the healthiest embryos to implant. If we have more than three, we can freeze the rest for later."

"Three? Surely two is plenty!" Portia's fingers curled, as if she longed for someone to hold her hand. Vince, who'd positioned himself in front of the ultrasound monitor, didn't appear to notice.

He'd barely glanced at Zora, either. She'd been disturbed on discovering she'd been assigned to Portia, but the scheduler had insisted.

"I'd prefer four," Vince announced. His wife gasped. Zora might not like her, but she empathized with the woman.

"That would violate hospital policy," Dr. Brennan said. "Portia, if you don't want more than two, we'll respect your wishes."

After a tense pause, the patient said, "Three will be fine."

"You're sure?"

Vince blew out an impatient breath.

Tautly, Portia said, "Yes."

Dr. Brennan jotted a note in the computer. To Zora, the doctor appeared concerned, but didn't press the point. "Now that the eggs are mature, timing is crucial. As I explained, you'll need an injection of HCG—human chorionic gonadotropin—to prepare for ovulation. Harvesting should take place thirty-six hours later."

As Zora finished her work, she half listened to the details. Normally, the patient's husband, after being shown how to give the shots, would have injected her with hormones for the past week or so, and would administer HCG at ten o'clock tonight. Instead, the Adamses had hired a visiting nurse.

"We'll set the egg retrieval for Wednesday morning," Dr. Brennan continued. "Mr. Adams, we'll coordinate with Dr. Rattigan to be sure he collects your sperm before then."

"I can attend the egg harvesting, I presume." The billionaire shifted from one foot to the other as if cramped by the confines of the examining room.

"Absolutely," the doctor said.

"We'll use the same sonographer, as per my instructions?"

Zora's stomach tightened. Today's assignment hadn't been by chance. Did the billionaire simply enjoy throwing his weight around or was there more to it?

Dr. Brennan looked startled. "The egg retrieval is a specialized procedure. We'll have a team in place."

"It's good luck to have a pregnant woman nearby. Maternal hormones and all that." Vince gestured toward Zora. "The process has gone smoothly so far with her present, hasn't it, Doctor?"

If Portia had had a death ray, Zora didn't doubt she'd have used it. *On me.*

"That's true." Dr. Brennan smiled. "However, I'm not sure we can credit Zora's maternal hormones." Without further comment about the sonographer request, she provided them directions to the hospital's retrieval room on the second floor, where the procedure would take place. "Don't eat or drink anything after midnight Tuesday, Mrs. Adams, and be sure to arrive an hour early."

"I'll be asleep for it, I hope," Portia grumbled as she sat up, finally receiving her husband's hand in assistance.

"You'll be sedated, and in recovery for two to three hours afterward," the doctor said. "We'll let you know later the same day how many eggs were retrieved. They'll be examined by an embryologist, and by Thursday we'll inform you of how many we were able to fertilize."

Thursday was the day of the press conference. Of course, the embryos wouldn't be implanted into Portia's womb for a few more days to give them time to grow in the lab. Was Vince also going to demand that Zora be present for the implantation?

He wasn't likely to succeed; as Dr. Brennan had indicated, the fertility team worked with its own techs.

However, to be sure of preventing any further contact with the man, Zora could schedule her maternity leave. She had to admit that, with her ankles swollen and her abdomen sore, she was overdue.

When Keely entered the room, Zora rolled out her cart. Her knees weak with relief at having weathered the encounter with Vince, she headed around a corner toward the storage closet.

She'd just stowed the equipment when heavy male footsteps jolted her pulse into high gear. Turning, she spotted Vince Adams at a bend in the hall.

This late in the afternoon, there was no one else in view. Before she could exit, the heavyset man blocked her escape.

"What're you doing?" Zora demanded.

"You should have called me." He reached for the nearest door and shoved it open to reveal an empty examining room. "Let's talk inside."

"I'm fine right here." The words emerged breathlessly.

"This is a private conversation."

"Forget it." Zora tried to dodge past, lost her balance and stumbled. He caught her arm as if to assist, but instead pulled her into the room.

"Listen, I'm donating twenty million dollars to this hospital. And I'll spend money on you, too, if you make it worth my while." This close, she caught the scent of alcohol on his breath. Zora knew all too well what effect that had on the wrong kind of man.

"Leave me alone." She pressed her palms against his chest, but that only seemed to amuse him.

"Be nice to me, honey," he slurred.

She flashed on stories she'd heard about Vince's past:

that he'd gotten his start through gang connections in a rough part of Phoenix and that a former business rival had disappeared under mysterious circumstances. Yet she'd never imagined he'd dare to assault her.

The door flew open. There stood Keely, aghast. "What is this?"

Vince glanced over his shoulder. "If you know what's good for you, Nurse, you'll keep your mouth shut."

Instead, Keely commanded, "Get your hands off her!"

"Shut up, you…"

While he was distracted, Zora grabbed a pair of scissors from a drawer. "Let go of me!"

Startled, the hulking man released her. "Neither of you says a word to anyone or you're both out of a job."

Angry breathing filled the room. No one spoke, and finally, he left. Heart pounding, Zora clutched the scissors, ready to fight if he returned.

"Are you all right?" Keely asked.

The adrenaline seeping out of her, Zora set the instrument on the counter. "Thank goodness you showed up." How far would that monster have gone?

"Has he done anything like this before?"

It was on the tip of her tongue to deny it. *Keep the secret, don't cause problems.* But Zora had kept his secret once, and this was where it had led. "Yes, although it wasn't this bad."

"We have to report him."

Despite her outrage, Zora hesitated. "If we raise a fuss, there goes the donation. Think what that will do to the hospital, and to Lucky."

"Men like Vince Adams depend on their victims

keeping silent," Keely growled. "That's how they get away with it."

"I don't want to involve the police." Zora had no idea how this situation would appear to an officer.

"You might have to," Keely said. "But you can start with Dr. Rayburn if you prefer. I'll come with you."

How brave of her, and what a great friend. Tearfully, Zora nodded. "Okay."

"First, let's settle your nerves," the nurse advised. "How about tea and peanut-butter crackers?"

"Thanks."

Twenty minutes later, after a snack in the lounge, Zora could speak without trembling. Her brain still skipped from objection to objection, however. What if her complaint smashed Lucky's dreams? What if the administrators believed she'd encouraged Vince? But she had to do this, for other potential victims as much as for herself.

It was nearly five o'clock when they reached the hospital's fifth floor. What if Dr. Rayburn had left for the day? If Zora had to wait until tomorrow, she wouldn't be able to sleep.

As they approached the executive suite, she heard movement inside. Then the last two people on earth she'd expected to see emerged into the corridor.

Vince and Portia Adams. He regarded Zora with a superior smirk. His wife gave a start, her face pale.

With the sensation of falling into an abyss, Zora realized that her tormenter had performed an end run around her. Whatever story he'd concocted, it would make her sound like a liar—and possibly end her career.

Lucky knew something was wrong when Keely texted that she'd drive Zora home instead of him. Why the last-minute change? Keely had added that she was calling a house meeting as soon as everyone arrived.

When he tried to call Zora, her phone went to voice mail. Was she in labor? But if she was, why would Keely be bringing her home?

Perhaps Laird had pulled another stunt and the women wanted to talk about it in private. Or maybe Dr. Brennan had discovered something worrisome about Zora's pregnancy.

Adrenaline pounded through Lucky's system. If Zora was in danger, he should be there to protect her.

In the garage, he cruised up along the ramp in search of Keely's car. With most of the staff gone and few outpatients or visitors on hand, he should have been able to spot it, but no luck.

Cursing himself for wasting time, Lucky headed home. He had to fight the tendency to stomp on the gas pedal.

Why was he reacting so strongly? It was silly and useless. But he kept imagining Zora's emotions in turmoil and longing to reassure her.

At the house, he was glad when he spotted Keely's car in the driveway. Just ahead of him, Karen pulled into the remaining open spot, with Rod beside her.

Lucky parked at the curb and broke into a lope. "What gives?" he asked when he came within earshot.

"No idea." Karen straightened her blazer. "I haven't heard any gossip from our receptionist." That young woman, Caroline Carter, reputedly had the keenest radar in the hospital.

Rod's fedora shadowed his face as the three of them followed the walkway. "I haven't picked up anything in the doctors' lounge, either."

Inside, Lucky barreled into the den, grateful that neither Karen nor Rod objected when he bypassed them. He felt a spurt of relief when he saw Zora in her usual chair, sipping a cup of juice. Keely paced nearby, unable to contain her restlessness.

Just like me. "Are you okay?" Lucky demanded.

Zora didn't answer.

"Sit down." No sign of Keely's customary reticence. "Everyone."

He took his favorite chair, while Karen and Rod slid onto the couch, not bothering to remove their shoes or hats or jackets. "Don't keep us in suspense," Rod said.

"This afternoon, I walked in on Vince Adams assaulting Zora." Disgust emphasized the deep lines in Keely's face.

"He did what?" Lucky sprang up, prepared to find the man and pummel him. "Were you hurt? You should go to the police."

"Let us finish, please." When he subsided, Keely described the scene she'd interrupted in an examining room. Thank goodness she'd arrived when she had, although Lucky would have paid a fair amount of money to watch Zora stab that jerk with scissors.

But before they could take the matter to Dr. Rayburn, Vince had beaten them to the punch, claiming Zora had tried to extort money by threatening to accuse him of harassing her.

"Mark can't believe that," Karen protested when Keely paused for breath. "It's ridiculous."

"Still, I'm glad to have Keely as a witness." Zora's voice trembled. "And I showed Dr. Rayburn the business card Vince gave me with his private number scrawled on the back. He pressed it on me the last time he cornered me."

"He's done this before?" The revelation sickened Lucky. "Why didn't you report it?"

"It didn't go this far," she told him. "And I was worried it might have an impact on the men's program."

"The program isn't your responsibility," Karen said.

"But I care about—about the rest of the staff," Zora replied.

"You were protecting me?" Lucky would never allow her to put her safety at risk. "I didn't ask you to do that."

"You were happy enough when Portia agreed to in vitro," Zora shot back. "He all but said he'd leave her for some 'earth mother,' as he described me, if she didn't agree to in vitro instead of insisting on surrogacy."

Stunned, Lucky recalled the scene outside Dr. Rattigan's examining room. He'd never known the details of how Portia had made her decision. And all this while, she'd kept Vince's mistreatment a secret?

Once, long ago, Lucky had vowed never again to let down anyone he loved the way he'd let down his parents. Yet now he had. Worse, by scheduling Zora to work that first morning because he valued her insight, he'd put her in harm's way.

Wordlessly, he listened as the conversation moved on around him. In the administrator's office, Mark had been accompanied by attorney Tony Franco. They'd assured Zora that her job was safe and that she had every right to contact the police.

"Great idea." Lucky would love to see Vince hauled off in handcuffs.

"As if I'd have any chance against a billionaire and his legal team," Zora said miserably.

"We have honest cops in Safe Harbor," Karen responded. "Tony Franco's brother is a police detective."

"Vince will just repeat his claim that I tried to extort money from him," Zora said. "How can I prove I didn't? And if he sues me for slander, I can't afford to fight."

It was unfair that his wealth enabled a man like Vince to crush people, as he'd already done with Rod. If only Lucky had been the one to discover that scene today, he'd have taught the bastard a lesson on the spot.

And probably lost his job, not to mention being locked up for assault. But it would have felt good to smash his fists into the man's oily face.

"Dr. Rayburn seemed worried about the emotional and physical effects on Zora," Keely put in. "He offered her an extra two months of paid maternity leave, not in lieu of anything else, just for health reasons."

"He suggested I go on leave immediately while he sorts this out," Zora added. "I refuse to slink away as if I did anything wrong, but I am going to start my leave on Monday, because I already had that in mind."

"Extra paid leave—that's a positive thing, anyway," Karen said.

"How does Dr. Rayburn intend to sort this out?" Lucky persisted. Zora had been attacked at work, and other staffers could be at risk, too. If only Vince weren't so rich, and the hospital staff so eager for his donation.

Including me. It revolted Lucky to think of how hard he'd worked to keep Vince involved with Safe Harbor.

"Dr. Rayburn said there are complicating issues." Having practically worn a path in the carpet with her pacing, Keely plopped into an armchair.

"Like what? Vince's money?" Rod grumbled.

"He and Portia are patients, so disrupting their care

would be unethical if no wrongdoing is proved." Zora clasped her hands atop her baby bump. "It's a crucial week for them."

"The hospital should cancel that damn press conference." No matter what the donation meant for Lucky or his doctor, he'd never sacrifice an innocent person's well-being. Especially Zora's.

"Dr. Rayburn has to discuss it with the hospital corporation," Keely said. "They'll make the final decision. Except he was very clear that he will not allow any repercussions against Zora or me."

"Dr. Brennan would be up in arms if he did, I'm sure," Karen said.

"Along with the rest of the medical staff," Rod added. "No one would believe Vince's story."

Zora set her empty cup on the table. "Keely and I aren't exactly the most popular members of the staff."

"You've seen what our household can do," Lucky reminded her. "If you need us, we're here."

Both women nodded. "Oh, we aren't supposed to discuss this," Zora added. "Please don't tell anyone else."

Despite an eagerness to rally the troops behind Zora, Lucky supposed he had to respect her decision. "All right." *For now.*

"How about dinner?" Karen got to her feet. "I'll bet the mommy-to-be is starving."

Rod stood also. "My cooking skills may be notoriously bad, but Jack taught me how to cook angel-hair pasta with wine and onions. It doesn't take long. And the alcohol in the wine evaporates."

"I'll fix a salad," Lucky volunteered.

The dinner went well, but he continued to be frustrated for the rest of the evening. He should be the person Zora turned to, but instead she remained glued to Keely's side. Lucky tried in vain to catch her alone so he could massage her tense little shoulders. Or fetch her ice cream—why didn't she send him on errands anymore?

How ironic that he'd criticized her for leading a messy life. Now she'd landed in her biggest crisis yet, and the person most to blame—after Vince, of course—was Lucky himself.

Yet again, he'd been responsible for causing pain to someone he cared about. And yet again, there didn't seem to be any way to make up for his mistakes.

Chapter 15

Catching sweet, sympathetic glances from Lucky all evening, Zora yearned to fly to him. Temporary though the respite might be, she longed to curl up in his arms and enjoy the illusion of safety.

But it *was* an illusion. She understood Lucky too well. Their relationship could only progress to a certain point before he'd slam the door on her. She and her babies would never fit his requirements for a perfect family.

How ironic that, while she failed to measure up to Lucky's standards, his influence had helped her shake free of her old codependent habits. She'd told off Andrew, stood up to Vince Adams and marched into Dr. Rayburn's office when her instincts screamed at her to flee.

It had been terrifying to confront two such powerful men in the meeting. Dr. Rayburn had towered over her dauntingly when they'd shaken hands. As for Tony

Franco, beneath his reserved manner lurked a brain capable of raising who-knew-what legal complications against which an ordinary mortal was defenseless.

Zora had been grateful that Keely was there, and for the strength that she was beginning to realize had been within her all along. She'd managed not to break down in tears when the administrator repeated the lie Vince had told them. She'd stuck doggedly to the facts, painful as they were. There'd been two previous incidents, and she had the business card to prove it. Not much evidence, but it helped, as did Keely's testimony.

Tossing and turning in bed that night, she searched without success for a solution. If the Adamses canceled their planned donation, the whole hospital would suffer and Lucky might have to go elsewhere to build his career. But if the grant went forward, how could Zora stay? The vengeful billionaire would find a way to destroy her.

In the morning, she received a message from her sister: Got the job! Start in 3 weeks!

Under other circumstances, that would have been fantastic news. Now, Zora worried that if Vince saw her identical twin, he'd target Zady, too.

She arrived at the medical center on Tuesday with her senses on high alert. As the day progressed, no one mentioned Vince's accusations, but the news spread about Zora starting maternity leave on Monday. The hospital's public relations director, Jennifer Serra Martin, presented Zora with a pair of adorable teddy bears that played lullabies. Dr. T's nurse, Ned Norwalk, slipped Zora a gift card to Kitchens, Cooks and Linens.

"I'm not sure whether you're short of pots and pans, but you can always use more knives." He whisked off before she could ask what he meant. Had that been a veiled reference to her scissors wielding?

By Tuesday's end, the press conference hadn't been canceled, nor, apparently, had the next day's egg retrieval. And she learned that Vince had undergone the procedure to collect his sperm. The only change Zora observed was that the billionaire was now accompanied everywhere by a male patient care coordinator, supposedly to ensure his comfort.

And to protect me and the other women on staff?

On Wednesday morning, Zora was again assigned to Dr. Brennan's patients. No danger of running into the Adamses, whose egg retrieval was taking place in the hospital. Dr. Brennan, Zora discovered, had arranged for Dr. Zack Sargent to perform the procedure on the grounds that he performed more of them.

The moment she spotted Zora, Dr. Brennan zeroed in on her. "I'm sorry that you were assaulted."

"I'm fine."

"It was an unforgivable act, and I'm furious that it took place on my watch," the tall woman said. "If you need me to go to bat for you, just say the word."

Zora thanked her, pleased to have another person on her side.

At lunch, aware of prying ears, Zora and her housemates were careful not to discuss what was foremost on everyone's minds. She had almost finished eating when a call came from Dr. Rayburn's assistant, asking Zora to meet with him.

"I'll go with you," Keely announced.

"You have patients," Lucky reminded her.

"You can't let them down," Zora echoed. Despite her words, Zora shivered to think of what lay ahead. What if the corporation insisted on firing her? What if... Her brain wouldn't stretch further than that.

"Dr. Rattigan's in surgery for another hour, so I'll go with you." Lucky piled her dishes onto his tray. "No arguments."

"I didn't plan to raise any."

On the elevator ride to the fifth floor, Zora held Lucky's hand. Tension rippled across the muscles in his neck and arms, with the ironic effect that the dragon protruding from beneath his navy blue sleeve appeared to be winking at her.

"I hope I don't break down." She released her grip as they stepped into the empty hallway. "I've always been terrified that someday everything would fall apart and I'd be alone."

He touched her shoulder gently. "You aren't alone."

Zora blinked back tears. Impulsively, she asked, "What's *your* biggest fear?"

"Failing the people I love," Lucky said without hesitation. "And I'm not about to do that again."

Did he include her among the people he loved? Zora cautioned herself against leaping to conclusions. She had a bad habit of hearing only what she wished to hear.

"Don't go out on a limb for my sake," she told him.

"My integrity isn't for sale," Lucky answered. "Cole's isn't, either. He has opportunities elsewhere, although before he leaves Safe Harbor, I'm sure he'll consider the impact on Stacy."

"Oh, great." Zora hadn't considered how wide the fallout might be from the loss of Vince's donation. "As if I haven't done Stacy enough harm already."

"You did her a favor, taking Andrew away," Lucky returned. "I should have realized that sooner."

In the administrative suite, the assistant regarded Lucky in surprise. "I'm here for moral support," he said.

"Hold on." She picked up her phone.

From one of several inner rooms, Tony Franco appeared, his rust-brown hair rumpled as if he'd been running his fingers through it. After introducing himself to Lucky, he shook hands with them both. "Dr. Rayburn and I would like to speak to Mrs. Raditch alone."

"Without her lawyer?" Lucky demanded.

Tony gave a start. "If she wishes…"

"Lucky, that isn't necessary." How could she afford it? Also, since Edmond worked as a consultant for the hospital, he had a conflict of interest. Where would she find another lawyer on short notice?

"Then I'm sitting in," Lucky responded firmly. "I'll keep quiet, I promise."

To Zora's surprise, the attorney acquiesced. "Very well."

Tony's expression remained opaque. Did they learn how to do that in law school? she wondered, and pictured a classroom full of law students training their features to remain flat.

When they entered Dr. Rayburn's office, the administrator rose to shake their hands, and it was obvious he hadn't mastered the same art. In his face, she read unease, a touch of surprise at Lucky's presence and regret.

Oh, damn.

True to his statement, Lucky took a seat in a corner of the large office. Dr. Rayburn, whom she'd expected to retreat behind the desk, instead positioned himself in a chair beside hers. "I'll get straight to the point. The corporation insists we accept the Adamses' sponsorship of the men's program and move forward with tomorrow's press conference."

Zora swallowed. She hadn't seriously expected the hospital to reject millions of dollars simply to spare the feelings of one ultrasound tech, had she?

"They would have preferred that I not talk to you directly about this, but that's bull," he continued.

"Mark," the attorney warned.

"Hey, Tony, you're the guy who recommends our doctors apologize to patients when they've made a mistake." Dr. Rayburn's thick eyebrows rose in emphasis. "Isn't it your opinion that honesty and contrition cut the risk of lawsuits?"

"Mark!" Tony said more forcefully. The reference to lawsuits must have set off alarm bells in the man's head.

Dr. Rayburn returned his attention to Zora. "I disagree with this decision, but I've done all I can. I've negotiated for you to receive six months of paid parental leave." Normally, staffers received two months. "Afterward, you can resume your job if you wish, with a guarantee that you won't be assigned to attend to either of the Adamses."

Relief warred with an awareness of how touchy the situation would be, in numerous respects. "What about my sister?"

"Your sister?" Dr. Rayburn asked blankly.

"My identical twin sister is joining the staff." *Please don't let this mess things up for Zady.* "She'll be assisting the new urologist, Dr. Davis."

The administrator regarded the attorney, who fielded the question. "That's tricky, since Mr. Adams is a patient in the men's program. However, we can take precautions so she won't be put at risk."

But what about other women who might be subjected to Vince? Then Zora remembered the patient care coordinator shadowing the billionaire. Apparently, safeguards were already in place. "Okay."

"To bring you up to date, the corporate vice president will be flying in for tomorrow's events," Dr. Rayburn said. "There'll be a gala reception beforehand at the yacht club. The press conference will be at 5:00 p.m. in the auditorium. The staff is invited."

"I plan to skip it." Zora had no interest in watching the billionaire gloat.

"That's your choice." Dr. Rayburn still sounded dissatisfied. "You've undergone a traumatic experience. The hospital will be happy to provide sessions with a therapist."

With Laird? Zora's fists clenched. "No, thanks."

"We can arrange outside counseling with a woman." Tony must have noticed her reaction.

"I don't think that will be necessary. But I'll let you know if I change my mind." Despite her anxiety, Zora hadn't suffered nightmares about the incident. Still, she respected the value of professional help. If she'd received it during her divorce, she might not have clung to her foolish delusions for so long.

Neither she nor Lucky had any more questions, and the meeting ended. She still disliked the situation, but not enough to consider leaving Safe Harbor.

In the hall, Lucky kept pace with her. "Are you okay? I'm glad you mentioned Zady. I was wondering whether to bring her up, but you beat me to it."

"I appreciate the backup," she said. "Having someone who was in my corner there was important."

How had she failed for so long to realize what a strong, kind man he was? Of course, his previous antagonism toward her might have had something to do with that, Zora reflected.

And now? Circumstances had thrown them onto the same team, their loyalties more or less aligned. But was she really destined to remain nothing more than friends with him?

Now that she'd summoned the courage to confront her problems, maybe she ought to call Lucky to task for ignoring how much they meant to each other. But standing up for herself at work was one thing. Relationships were an entirely different matter. Where men were concerned, Zora still didn't trust her instincts.

That afternoon, the gossip mill at the hospital focused on possible developments at tomorrow's press conference, and she heard no mention of Vince's misconduct. On the drive home, Lucky agreed with Zora's observations.

"Dr. Rattigan doesn't seem to have any idea what happened between you and that jerk or that there was any question about accepting the donation," he told her as they headed south. "He was singing to himself in French this afternoon, which means he's excited."

"Why in French?" Zora asked.

"His father's French," Lucky said. "They aren't close, but Cole has an affinity for the language."

"At least he's happy." She sighed. "And this means he and Stacy won't have to consider moving." *Nor you, either.*

"I only wish the circumstances were different."

Stopped at a red light, Lucky drummed his hands on the wheel. "When I threw myself into winning Vince's support for the program, I had no idea he'd harm someone I care about."

"Even me?" Zora teased.

"Especially you!" But his next words disappointed her. "Or anyone." The light changed and he tapped the gas pedal. "If the men's program does expand and I land a management post, I'll stand by my nurses. That man better leave them alone."

"After he donates the money, surely he won't continue meddling." Zora assumed that was the case. "If he and Portia have children, there'll be no reason for further treatment."

"I suspect he'll find a way to keep us dancing on his strings." Lucky's jaw tightened.

Reluctantly, Zora agreed. Then she decided not to worry about matters beyond her control. For once, her practice in denial stood her in good stead.

A lot of stomping shook the two-story house that night. Rod stomped to and from the kitchen, complaining about the upbeat conversations he'd overheard in the operating room. "Everyone thinks Vince's generosity is fantastic. Don't they realize they're bringing in a monster?"

Lucky did his share of stomping as he carted a pair of cribs upstairs and assembled them in Zora's oversize closet-turned-nursery, which had a small window. To accommodate her displaced clothes, he also hauled a rack to the second-floor alcove.

While he was happy to help, he mused that Andrew ought to be chipping in so the new mom could afford the larger downstairs suite. Fond as Lucky was of his quarters, he would willingly swap.

Did Zora plan to let her ex continue to ignore his financial obligations? Surely she didn't maintain the fantasy that he'd return to her after the babies' birth. Yet in spite of everything, she might.

Lucky feared that in her mind, the twins would always be Andrew's babies. And with his current marriage dissolving, the man might decide to toy with her emotions again, just to feed his ego. Until he found another wide-eyed young woman to fall for his manipulations, and broke Zora's heart all over again.

Lucky went downstairs for a snack. "You going to the press conference tomorrow?" he asked Rod, who'd taken the next-to-last slice of apple pie left over from dinner.

"You bet. I never miss a chance to see my girls." The slender man tugged at his short beard, which, like his hair, was going gray. Rod was only in his early forties, but stress from his long custody battle might have played a role in giving him more gray hairs. "I'm sure he'll require Tiff and Amber to show up, since it's scheduled after school hours."

"I'm not sure I should attend," Lucky admitted. "My opinion of Vince might show on my face."

"I doubt he'll care," Rod said.

In the den, a phone rang. Lucky heard Karen answer. "Edmond? What...?" Then her tone grew urgent. "Of course. I'll meet you at the hospital. No problem!"

Lucky's brain leaped to the likeliest conclusion: Melissa was having her triplets. In their haste to talk to Karen, he and Rod collided in the doorway. "Sorry!"

"Ow, damn it!" Rod snapped. "I mean, I'm sorry, too."

"Anyone need medical attention?" Karen inquired dryly. "No? Great. Rod, want to ride with me to pick up Dawn? She's spending the night with us." Karen occasionally babysat the seven-year-old, who always proved good company.

"Sure." Rod plucked his fedora from a coat rack. "Melissa's in labor?"

"Her water broke. She's at thirty weeks, earlier than they were hoping for but not bad for a multiple birth. They're assembling a team."

"I'll notify Zora and Keely." There were others who should be informed, too, Lucky thought. "Also Anya and Jack. Should I make up one of the couches for Dawn?"

"She can sleep with me," Karen assured him.

Rod sighed. "Guess I'm alone in my bed tonight."

She punched his arm. "Discretion!"

He grinned.

"Please tell Melissa and Edmond I'm rooting for them," Lucky said. Despite the skill of the hospital's doctors and nurses, the birth of triplets would pose a challenge.

"I will." Karen headed out with Rod behind her.

If all went well, this would be a joyous event, Lucky reflected on his way upstairs to spread the news. What a timely reminder of the miracles wrought at Safe Harbor.

Although his gut churned at the prospect of tomorrow's press conference, the donation would enable the staff to perform even more miracles. Too bad the price tag included putting up with a preening, triumphant Vince Adams. At Zora's expense.

Chapter 16

"We had a devil of a time agreeing on names for three girls," Edmond remarked to Zora at midday as they viewed the triplets in the intermediate care nursery.

Weighing over three pounds and with mature lungs, little Simone, Jamie and Lily were in excellent shape. Nevertheless, they had to be observed for signs of infection or other potential problems.

Wrapped in pink and attached to monitors, the trio were adorable. Zora's arms ached to reach through the viewing window and hold them. A tiny yawn from one—was that Jamie?—was almost too cute to be real.

"I still don't have a name for my son." Zora rested her hand on her by-now enormous bulge. "My daughter's name will be Elizabeth."

"After her grandmother?" The attorney knew Betsy, of course.

She nodded. "I read that the first Queen Elizabeth was named after *her* grandmother."

"Here's a bit of trivia—both her grandmothers were called Elizabeth." Edmond adjusted his glasses.

"I'm impressed that you know that."

"History fascinates me. Melissa and I used to travel and tour historic sites as often as we could." He gazed dreamily at the babies. "Someday we'll take the kids abroad."

"I'm envious." Since there was no one else nearby, Zora added, "Any further word from my charming ex?"

"His attorney indicated he'll comply with the law," Edmond said. "I did forward your list of expenses, but I've heard nothing since."

"Thanks, and I'm sorry to bring this up when you must be exhausted." Zora had spoken without thinking.

"I took a nap this morning." The new father grinned. "I went home and crashed after dropping Dawn at school." The excited seven-year-old had visited the hospital early to meet her new cousins, after spending the night with Karen.

"You've adjusted well to fatherhood." As Melissa's former housemate, Zora recalled that her friend's marriage had broken up over Edmond's refusal to have children.

"I'm grateful for the second chance. I had no idea what I was missing." Joy shone from his face.

A lot of events had changed Edmond, from accepting custody of his niece after his sister went to prison for robbery to the discovery that Melissa had "adopted" three embryos. Parenting Dawn had awakened Edmond's suppressed instincts, and his renewed love for his once and future wife had filled in the rest.

Once, Zora had believed Andrew might undergo a similar change of heart. Witnessing his cruelty to Lin had erased the last of her delusions, however. That, and being around Lucky. He demonstrated how a man ought to behave, in contrast to her father, her stepfather and her ex-husband.

A touch of heartburn roused Zora with a reminder that she ought to eat. "I'm going to the cafeteria," she told Edmond. "Please assure Melissa I'll visit her later."

"I'll do that," he said. "And soon she'll be visiting you in the maternity ward, too."

"That's true, isn't it?" When Lucky installed the cribs last night, it had emphasized to Zora that soon her babies would emerge into the world. Despite an eagerness to lighten her physical load, she wasn't sure she was ready to cope. But then, what single mother *was* ready to cope with twins?

On the ground floor, receptionist Caroline Carter waved her to a halt. "I have something for you. Can you hang on a minute?"

"Sure."

The young woman darted into her nearby office, returning with a children's book. "Sorry it's not wrapped, but I wanted to catch you before your leave starts."

"How beautiful!" Zora traced a finger over the stunning cover photograph of a butterfly. The book described how to study nature in your backyard, a topic she found especially relevant in view of the fact that her home was located next to an estuary.

"Nurse Harper Gladstone took the photos," Caroline said. "And her husband wrote the text."

Harper, a widow with a young daughter, had married a biology teacher. "It's perfect. Thank you."

"Enjoy your lunch. Oh!" With a confidential air, Caroline leaned closer, her brown eyes alight with her favorite subject: gossip. "Did you hear that Vince Adams assaulted a woman?"

Zora couldn't breathe. Apparently, the news had spread. Yet Caroline didn't seem to realize she was addressing the target of that assault. "Who told you that?"

"Laird," the receptionist said.

Since he had an office near Dr. Rayburn's, he must have caught wind of the confidential discussions. What a creep to shoot his mouth off! "He isn't always truthful." That was the best Zora could do.

"Yes, but he usually has reliable sources." Caroline shrugged. "Do you suppose it will spoil the press conference?"

"The less we talk about it, the better." Zora hoped the other woman would heed her warning.

"You're right." Caroline wrinkled her nose. "I keep swearing I'm going to stop spreading rumors. It's addictive, though."

"Thanks for the book. I'm sure the twins and I will enjoy it." On that note, Zora beelined for the cafeteria.

If word of what Vince had done reached the media, how would that affect the billionaire's donation? And if her name became attached to the rumor, there was no predicting what the reporters would say. The notion of the press camping out on Karen's lawn horrified her. Whiffs of swamp gas might discourage them, but she doubted it.

Zora decided not to mention the story to her friends. As she'd said to Caroline, the more discreet they were, the less risk the press conference would be disrupted.

* * *

The staff, reporters and VIPs filled the auditorium, leaving Lucky and a scattering of press to line the edges. Standing in the back above the steeply raked rows, he studied the scene uneasily.

Seated on the stage with the administrator, the public relations director, the corporate vice president and the Adamses, Cole appeared relaxed and cheerful. He evidently didn't notice what Lucky considered warning signs that something was going to go wrong.

Vince's ruddy complexion was flushed and, judging by his gait when mounting the steps, he'd imbibed more than he should have at the reception. While he sprawled on his chair with his legs apart, Portia's shoulders were painfully stiff beneath her ivory suit jacket. Her gaze traveled frequently to her daughters, who fidgeted in the front row beside their grandmother.

Around Lucky, more members of the press squeezed in, with cameras bearing the logos of LA news teams and a couple of national networks. He hadn't seen this much media since Cole presented a speech on men's declining sperm rates, sparking a furor that had blown the matter wildly out of proportion. Surely Dr. Rattigan's involvement couldn't account for this much interest, but what did?

Next to him, a reporter murmured to a photographer, "Wonder if Adams can keep his hands to himself on stage? That PR lady's awfully pretty."

"And he's well oiled," the other man responded. "Hey, it's a slow news day. We can always hope."

Anxiety churned in Lucky's stomach. What had these guys heard? He was grateful that Keely had driven Zora home earlier, sparing her any immediate fallout.

On the stage, Jennifer Martin took the microphone. After a brief greeting, she introduced Medical Center Management Vice President Chandra Yashimoto.

The dark-haired executive, whose striking black-and-white suit rivaled Portia's for elegance, glided to center stage. With a practiced smile, she sketched the history of the medical center's transformation from a community hospital to a national center for fertility and maternity care.

When she cited the importance of Dr. Cole Rattigan, Lucky braced for an audience reaction. If reporters planned to revive their silly stories terming him Dr. Baby Crisis, they'd start lobbing questions now. But no one reacted.

They seemed to be waiting. For what?

Ms. Yashimoto didn't call on Dr. Rayburn, whose furrowed brow reflected a less than enthusiastic attitude, nor did she ask Cole to speak. Instead, she cut to the announcement: Safe Harbor was poised to become an international center for the treatment of and research into men's fertility, thanks to a twenty-million-dollar gift from San Diego financier Vincent Adams and his wife, both of whom were—according to Chandra—well-known philanthropists.

Lights flashed and lenses clicked as Vince strode to the front and shook hands with the vice president. A staff photographer captured the moment, but to Lucky it seemed that others snapped only perfunctory shots.

"Thank you, Chandra." Vince beamed, in his element as the center of attention. "This program means more to me than merely putting my name on a building. It means leaving a legacy of children, mine and other men's, that will last until the end of time."

"There's modesty for you," the nearby reporter observed in a low tone.

"This week, my wife and I moved forward in our quest to expand our family," Vince continued. "My wife prefers that I not go into detail, but thanks to Dr. Rattigan, we expect to have a blessed event of our own by next year."

Portia's eyes narrowed. No doubt she'd asked him to keep that private, too, especially since they hadn't implanted the embryos yet.

The reporter murmured, "I wonder if she'll be the only woman popping out his offspring."

Was the man referring to Zora? Lucky wouldn't put it past the more irresponsible members of the press to imply that her pregnancy was the result of a liaison with Vince. Never mind facts or her DNA test—they'd drag her name through the mud.

When Vince paused for breath, a man in a central row scrambled to his feet. "Mr. Adams, this morning your former personal assistant Geneva Gabriel filed a five-million-dollar lawsuit against you in San Diego Superior Court, alleging sexual assault. We understand the district attorney is investigating. Care to comment?"

That explained the reporters' snide exchanges! Lucky experienced a spurt of relief, then immediately regretted it. He was sorry that Ms. Gabriel had suffered, too.

"She's just out for my money." Vince spluttered with fury. "I fired that witch because she's stupid and incompetent."

Chandra Yashimoto stood frozen. Cole's face registered his confusion, while Lucky could have sworn Mark Rayburn was barely suppressing a smile.

Jennifer rose to the occasion, literally. Crossing the

stage to seize the microphone again, she said, "I'm sure Mr. Adams will have his attorney respond to your questions. My assistant is handing out a press release with the details of Mr. and Mrs. Adams' generous gift. Thank you for joining us."

After a few inaudible words to Vince, she steered him and Portia toward a side door. Shaking with anger, the billionaire gestured at the front row, summoning his daughters. Tiffany might have stood her ground, but when Amber raced up the steps, the older girl followed.

Cole and the others left the stage via a second exit. Unable to reach them as the crowd filled the aisles, Lucky shuffled out with the rest of the audience.

In the corridor, he passed Laird, who'd shanghaied a couple of puzzled reporters. "I'm embarrassed to be associated with a hospital that would accept money from a man like Vince Adams," the man announced. "That's why I'm handing in my notice and joining a private practice in Newport Beach. My name is Laird Maclaine."

A listener thrust out a small mic. "Are you a doctor in the men's fertility program?"

"I'm the staff psychologist."

"You're the staff opportunist," Lucky called, and dodged away. He wove through the milling assemblage, in case his doctor had been hemmed in by the press. He'd learned from experience that a show of muscle could prove handy.

Rounding a corner, he spotted a small group bunched near the staff entrance—the Adamses and the public relations director. All Lucky could see of the man blocking their escape was his fedora.

"You're in no condition to drive." Rod's voice was shrill with emotion. "The girls stay here."

"Get out of my way, Vintner." The bigger man towered over his opponent.

"Rod, you're making things worse." That was Portia, hovering beside her daughters. Jennifer, the only non-family member of the group, regarded the scene with uncertainty.

Where was Mark? The administrator, a former football player, was a physical match for Vince, but he must be occupied whisking Cole and Chandra out of harm's way.

"You're drunk," Rod persisted. "I'll take the girls to their grandmother." They'd left Helen behind in their rush, Lucky saw.

"Out of our way!" Vince shoved Rod, hard. The girls gasped as the smaller man staggered and fell against the wall. When blood spurted from his nose, Vince raised his fists in a victory gesture.

Rage surged in Lucky at the man's brutality. His fury mounted when the billionaire clamped onto Amber's wrist. "Let's go."

His younger daughter wriggled fruitlessly. "We're not supposed to get in a car with a drunk driver."

"Shut up." Vince yanked the girl toward the exit.

"Leave her alone!" Tiffany screamed.

As their stepfather wrenched open the door, Lucky barreled forward. The others parted, leaving him a clear shot at the distracted billionaire, who half turned to gape at him.

Lucky's kick hit its target: Vince's knee. With a cry of pain, the big man released Amber and stumbled out into the parking area reserved for administrators.

"Let's get out of here." Tiffany gestured to her sister. "Dad needs a doctor." Clearly, she meant Rod.

"Never mind him. You're both coming with us," their mother snapped.

"No." Tiffany slid an arm around the dazed Rod, who had a tissue pressed to his nose. "Thank you, Lucky."

"My pleasure."

Portia flinched as, outside, her husband bellowed for her. "He's too impaired to drive," Lucky warned, following her through the door. "Please stop him before he injures someone."

She glared. "Mind your own business."

"Where are the girls?" Vince roared, standing between his high-performance sports coupe and Dr. Rayburn's sedan.

"They're staying," Lucky retorted.

"I'll have you fired for this," the billionaire snarled.

"You planning to push me around, too?" Lucky demanded. "Or do you only attack people smaller than you?"

He could see Vince weighing the urge to punch him out. The man might have tried, but a shift of position put too much weight on his injured knee and he stumbled and then produced a deep groan. Regaining his balance with a hand on the sedan, the man snarled at his wife, "In the car. Now!"

"Let her drive," Lucky said. "For both your sakes."

"Shut up, you punk."

Mouth pressed into a thin line, Portia slid into the passenger seat while Vince got behind the wheel. How sad that she'd thrown in her lot with her husband, willing to sacrifice her safety to maintain her wealth and status. Worse, she'd been ready to risk her daughters' safety, too.

A hand on Lucky's arm alerted him to Jennifer's presence. Holding her phone in the other hand, she said, "Thanks for intervening. I arranged with Mark to make sure Rod gets medical treatment and the girls stay with their grandmother."

"Watch out!"

They beat a quick retreat as the sports car shot in reverse. After scraping the bumper of another car, Vince twisted the wheel, hit the gas and zoomed forward. He and Portia disappeared around the building.

"I'm calling the cops." Lucky took out his cell. "That's a hit-and-run. Also, he shouldn't be driving in his condition."

"Good." Jennifer straightened her spine. "I'd better corral the press. I don't want them harassing the staff."

Lucky thought of Laird. "Nor do we want the staff taking advantage of this mess."

Despite a puzzled glance, she didn't request an explanation. Duty was calling, and she hurried inside.

He dialed 911 and explained the situation to the dispatcher. Although Lucky hadn't observed which direction Vince took, the Adamses' beach cottage lay south of here. The most direct route would be along Pacific Coast Highway.

The dispatcher thanked him and said she'd alert patrol officers to be on the lookout. One would stop by to take a report about the hit-and-run, as well.

Bathed in October sunlight, Lucky eased his breathing. He'd never imagined such a devastating outcome of today's announcement. There was nothing anyone could have done to prevent this, he supposed. The lawsuit filing had changed everything.

Damn Vince and his arrogance. But at least the girls were safe. As for Rod's injury, the man had every right to report the assault and to sue for damages. However, he'd learned a hard lesson about the difficulties of fighting Vince in court.

Checking his phone, Lucky saw he'd missed a call from Zora. He returned it, and after two rings, her excited voice said, "Lucky! Keely's driving me to the hospital."

"Why?"

"I'm in labor!" she said happily.

"Everything's okay?"

"Yes—the pains aren't bad yet," she said. "I called ahead and they're setting up a C-section. Honestly, I was surprised what a relief it is. And the day after Melissa! Must be fate."

He gave a low chuckle. "Well, if that doesn't put the cap on an already over-the-top day."

"What happened?" She must not have been following the news. He presumed that radio reporters were already describing the brouhaha on the air.

"Vince's former assistant is suing him for sexual assault," Lucky told her. "He stalked out in a huff. Guess you're not the only one he's victimized."

"I hope she nails him to the wall."

"Five million dollars' worth of wall," he agreed.

"Yay for her." Then Zora gasped, "Watch out!"

"What...?"

The call went dead.

Inside Lucky, fear tightened into a knot. Had there been an accident? Surely not, yet...

The shortest route from Karen's house to the hospital was via Pacific Coast Highway—directly in Vince's path. His heart nearly stopped.

Don't be ridiculous.

On his phone, Lucky pressed Zora's number. He listened, struggling for calm, as it rang and rang, then went to voice mail.

He heard a siren in the distance. Then another. They sounded as if they were heading for Coast Highway.

Lucky began to pray.

Chapter 17

The sports car appeared out of nowhere, weaving madly across lanes, and only Keely's swift veer to the right prevented a crash. Overcorrecting, the other car swerved, hit the curb and went airborne.

With a horrifying crunch, it landed on its roof. Shaken, Zora realized that she'd recognized the occupants as they sped past: Vince and Portia.

A siren shrilled almost instantly. Within seconds, a patrol cruiser and a fire truck swarmed in, followed by paramedics. An officer stopped behind Keely's brown sedan, which was parked on the right shoulder.

The police had been watching for Vince's car, he explained while examining Keely's license. After asking whether the two women were injured—neither was—he prepared to take their statements.

Zora cried out as another pain gripped her. "She's in labor," Keely explained.

"I'll call for another ambulance."

"We're only two miles from the hospital. It'll be faster if I drive," Keely said. "Don't worry. I'm a nurse."

After radioing the dispatcher, the officer offered to follow them in case they required aid, and they accepted. As they drove, Zora and Keely listened to a news station's account of billionaire Vince Adams facing a harassment lawsuit. There was no mention of the crash yet.

As the initial shock wore off, Zora recalled Vince's puffy face behind the windshield and Portia's terrified expression. How weird that the Adamses had nearly hit them. Since she hadn't observed any reporters in pursuit, Vince had no one but his arrogance to blame for his speeding.

However, he was probably in no condition to blame anyone. And what about Portia?

Zora regarded Keely, who'd remained stoic throughout the incident. "That was awful. Do you suppose they're…?"

"Badly injured or worse, unless they had their seat belts fastened." Swinging onto Hospital Way ahead of the cruiser, the nurse said, "I don't believe there was anyone else in the car."

The girls. How could Zora have forgotten them? "I sure hope not."

They stopped at the maternity entrance. Staffers rushed out with a gurney to assist them.

Keely checked a message on her phone. "Dr. Brennan's on site. She'll do the surgery."

"Fantastic." That was reassuring.

"They have the pediatricians prepping, too." There'd be one for each twin, the doctor had said earlier.

"Okay." After the near miss on the road, Zora had no strength left. Fortunately, she could simply lie back and entrust her care to the experts.

Her thoughts returned to the Adamses. Vince might be a repulsive man, but she'd never wished him dead. And certainly not Portia. How badly were they hurt? How would this affect their daughters?

As Zora was transferred onto the gurney, Lucky raced to her, breathing hard. "Is she okay? Zora?"

"I'm fine. Sorry I left you dangling." In the heat of the moment, she'd forgotten their interrupted conversation. Later, she'd been vaguely aware of her cell ringing, but had been too overwrought to answer.

He stared down, desperately drinking in the sight of her. She'd never seen him so shaken.

"The Adamses nearly hit us." Zora stroked his arm, yearning to take away his tormented expression. "Keely steered out of their path."

"What about Vince and Portia?"

"We saw their car flip over," Keely said, joining them after conferring with the officer. "Beyond that, I have no idea."

Lucky swept the older nurse into a hug. "Bless you!"

"I didn't sneeze," she said tartly.

"You kept a cool head, from what I hear," Lucky responded.

Keely extricated herself from the hug. "Anyone else would have done the same."

"Not necessarily." Lucky turned to Zora. "How's my sweetheart?"

"Still trembling." Lying on the gurney, Zora was glad when he took her hand, his strength flowing into her.

She wished *he* was the babies' father. Then he could stay with her, comfort her and share her joy.

An orderly moved the gurney forward, toward the entrance. "I'll stay with her after I answer a few questions for the police," Keely told Lucky.

"So will I."

"If you wish, but how is Dr. Rattigan handling all this?" the older woman asked.

"I have no idea."

Reminded that their plans for the future might have been crushed today, Zora felt a twinge of concern. "You should check on him."

"I'll text you when she goes into surgery," Keely volunteered. "They won't let you in, anyway."

Another spasm seized Zora. "Ow!" A curse word slipped out. How did women bear this for hours and hours? She was very glad she was having a C-section and the doctor would give her something to stop the labor.

As the contraction eased, she wished Lucky would stay. But when he excused himself to attend to his doctor, Zora merely nodded.

"Later," she whispered into the air.

Zora was safe. Yes, there were risks in surgery and childbirth, but nothing like what Lucky had feared: a head-on smashup at high speed, pieces of car scattered across the highway, horrifying injuries to the occupants.

He'd witnessed the aftermath of such tragedies as an ambulance driver and a paramedic. The fact that Safe Harbor Medical didn't have an emergency room had added to its appeal when he'd joined the staff, because he didn't have to witness the arrival of trauma patients and relive those terrible memories. But today they'd hit him full force.

I love her, Lucky acknowledged as the gurney vanished into admitting. It was foolish and irrational and inescapable. He had no idea when he'd fallen in love with Zora, or what to do about it.

He'd clung to his ideals of perfection since his parents' deaths. If they had a family at the ideal time and in the ideal circumstances, money problems didn't force parents to neglect their children's internal struggles and teenagers didn't have to work such long hours that they rebelled—or so he'd rationalized.

He'd been trying to control the future, to prevent a repeat of his family's tragedies. But danger could strike without warning, as it had today. How stubbornly blind he'd been to his own flaws, criticizing Zora's illusions while harboring his own.

Yet she was still having another man's babies. Even a slug like Andrew would surely visit them, and there remained a possibility—remote, but real—that she would reconcile with her ex. Lucky might love her so hard and deep that his entire soul throbbed with it, only to have her torn away from him.

He could do nothing about it while she was in surgery. Frustrated, he decided to make himself useful elsewhere.

Since people gathered in a central location in a crisis, Lucky set out for the cafeteria. En route, he passed the elevators, one of which opened to reveal a welcome pair: Karen, her expression worried, and Rod, holding a cold pack to his nose.

Lucky halted. "I hope it's not broken."

"No, fortunately," Karen said. "They X-rayed him and gave him pain pills."

"Hurts to talk," Rod muttered.

Lucky didn't doubt that. "Zora's having the twins. Keely's with her." He filled them in on the details.

"I'm so glad they're okay," Karen said.

"The girls." Rod peered down the hall. "Where are they?"

"Helen said she was going to get them something to eat. Let's try the cafeteria."

Sure enough, they spotted Tiffany and Amber huddled with their grandmother at a table. Doctors, nurses and other staffers were sprinkled around the large room. Although some were eating dinner, most appeared to be waiting for news. Cole looked tense but composed, drinking coffee alongside Dr. Tartikoff.

From the food service area, Jennifer greeted them and asked Rod how he was feeling. Her dark hair was rumpled and her mascara had smeared. Today's events must be a PR director's nightmare.

"Thank you," she said after her questions had been answered. "Now I'm sure you're eager to join your daughters."

Rod agreed, and off he went with Karen. Lucky lingered, unsure where he could help the most.

"Any word about the Adamses?" he asked.

"So far, only that the police are on the scene."

"Well, I have a little more info than that."

She listened intently to the account of Zora and Keely's close call. "Thank heaven they escaped," she said, then raised a hand for silence. "Hang on. I'm monitoring news reports." She listened on her earpiece before saying, "No updates."

"Where's the press?" Lucky had expected to find them crowding the hallways.

"They went haring off to the crash scene," she said. "The police public information officer is handling them, although I'm also receiving calls for our reaction."

"What kind of reaction?" How could anyone respond to such a complex situation?

"Our official position is that our thoughts and prayers are with their family," Jennifer said.

"That sounds right." Lucky admired the publicist more than ever.

"Keep on the alert for stray reporters, will you?" she asked. "We can't let them eavesdrop or hassle people."

"Agreed." While he respected the job of the media, this was a traumatic enough situation without the press breaching people's privacy.

"There should be a counselor on hand. For some reason, I can't reach Laird," Jennifer fretted.

"He's leaving for private practice." Lucky repeated what he'd heard the psychologist announce.

She groaned. "Great timing. I'll arrange for an outside crisis counselor."

A murmur ran through the room. Tony and Mark had just entered. The attorney strode over to the girls' table and spoke in a low voice. The group, including Rod and Karen, got up and accompanied him out.

Lucky's chest clenched. This couldn't be good.

Once the girls and their entourage had departed and Jennifer gave the all clear from the hall, Mark took a position in full view of everyone. Thanks to his height and deep baritone, he had no trouble commanding attention.

"I'm sure you've heard that Mr. and Mrs. Adams were involved in a single-car crash on Coast Highway," he said. "I've just received word from the police chief that both of them died at the scene."

Gasps and a few sobs rose from the crowd. Even Lucky, angry as he'd been at Vince, was shocked by their deaths. Yet this could have been worse, much worse. Tiff and Amber might have died, too, if he and Rod hadn't prevented the girls' parents from forcing them into the car.

Mark resumed addressing the staff. "For those of you wondering how this will affect the men's fertility program, I'm afraid we don't have an answer on that yet. Any other questions?"

There were a few, which the director fielded with complete frankness. Then a buzz of conversation broke out as staffers shared their grief with each other.

At a tap on his arm, Lucky swung around to meet Betsy Raditch's solemn gaze. "I heard Zora's having her babies," she said. "Have you talked to her?"

"Yes. Did you know she and Keely had a near miss on the road?"

"What do you mean?"

He repeated the story. The nursing supervisor clamped her hand over her mouth. "That was close!"

"She should be in surgery now," Lucky added.

"I'll tell Andrew," Betsy said. "And, Lucky, I heard what you did, keeping Rod's daughters safe. That was heroic."

"Thanks, but I don't deserve that," Lucky responded. "Heroes are people who risk their safety, like Rod. I knew I was a match for that—" in view of Vince's demise, he decided against using a harsh term "—that man."

"You and Rod both deserve credit," the nursing supervisor said. "Well, I'd better get moving. Some of my nurses are in shock, and we have a hospital to run."

"Absolutely right." If Lucky had a supervisory position like hers, he'd be eager to support his nurses, too.

Outside the cafeteria, Cole caught up with him. "We're holding a strategy session in Dr. Tartikoff's office. You should be part of it."

"I'd like that." Lucky joined his doctor and a handful of others. To be included with this prestigious group was an honor, and his future might depend on what they devised.

All the same, en route to the fifth floor, his thoughts were mostly on Zora. She'd been his collaborator this past month, as invested as he was in trying to ensure the billionaire's gift. All she'd requested was for him to stop nagging her.

She'd kept Vince's hateful harassment a secret, no doubt to prevent this type of blowup. What had she gained by it? Her position and her advancement didn't depend on the program's expansion.

She did it for me. From simple generosity, or because she hadn't been able to bear the prospect of Lucky leaving? Had Zora started loving him, too, perhaps without realizing it?

If Andrew reached her first, would she still fail to recognize that her heart belonged to Lucky?

Suddenly he couldn't wait to be with her. But Dr. Rattigan was counting on Lucky's input.

He steeled himself to have patience. In view of Andrew's track record, there was no reason to assume he'd show up promptly.

The distinguished group of top staffers, including several whom Owen Tartikoff had brought with him

from his Boston practice, gathered around the conference table in the fertility director's office. They included Alec Denny, the director of laboratories, and
Jan Garcia Sargent, head of the egg donor program.

For the next hour, they brainstormed, tossing out
the names of distinguished foundations, government
grant programs and Silicon Valley billionaires. Could or
would any of them respond—let alone quickly enough
to purchase the dental building?

Just as they were about to call it a night, the administrator entered. Dr. Rayburn's dark eyes were rimmed
with red.

"Have a seat." Lucky vacated his chair, since all the
others were taken.

The big man accepted the offer. "Considering you're
a hero, I shouldn't, but I've had a rough day. As we all
have."

Lucky decided not to bother arguing about the hero
designation. No one questioned it, so apparently they'd
all heard the tale.

"On such a terrible day, I'm pleased to bring good
news." When Mark coughed, Lucky fetched him a glass
of water from the sideboard. The administrator swallowed a few gulps before continuing. "Portia's mother,
Helen Pepper, is a very kind woman. In the midst of
her grief, she informed me that her daughter and son-
in-law placed their estate in a living trust. They des-
ignated her as the successor trustee on behalf of the
couple's children."

Lucky had assumed Vince's money would be tied
up for a year or more as the estate was settled. Without
a living trust, probate in California could be a lengthy,
expensive and complicated process.

"She and her granddaughters intend to carry out the Adamses' wishes to donate twenty million dollars to our program." A smile broke through Mark's weariness. "And a million dollars to the Oahu Lane Animal Shelter, which appears to be a favorite of the girls."

Around the table, the others expressed relief and gratitude. "I hate to raise the question, but how soon can this happen?" Cole asked. "That building will be snapped up quickly."

"Helen plans to talk to an attorney tomorrow." Mark downed more water. "She's agreed to let Jennifer Martin and Ms. Yashimoto arrange the funeral while she looks into setting up a foundation to underwrite the men's program. She said that having her daughter and son-in-law's names on the building will be a fitting tribute."

Lucky was pleased that they'd include Portia's name. She deserved it.

The news buoyed the exhausted participants, though no one was happy about the circumstances. The impact of today's events would play out in everyone's emotions for a long time, including Lucky's.

A glance at his watch sent his heart speeding off. Several hours had passed since he'd last seen Zora. He'd received texts from Keely, indicating the C-section had gone well. By now, the new mom should be out of the recovery room, which meant he'd finally be able to visit.

After excusing himself, he hurried down to the third floor. Despite his eagerness to reach Zora, the window of the intermediate care nursery drew him irresistibly.

He spotted Melissa and Edmond's triplets—had it really been only two nights since their birth?—and a sprinkling of other newborns. Among the half dozen babies in clear isolettes, he wasn't sure which were Zora's, but if he had to bet, he'd put his money on a red-haired little girl and the blond boy beside her. Both appeared alert and healthy.

At the nurses' station, Lucky obtained Zora's room number. "Mr. Raditch is with her," a nurse advised him.

A lump stuck in Lucky's throat. He hadn't thought Andrew would arrive so fast.

Why was he here? To stake his claim? He *was* the babies' father. But it was his claim on *Zora* that worried Lucky most.

It was up to her whether she would reconcile with Andrew, but Lucky didn't intend to let her go without a fight. He'd waited too long already to realize that she was the perfect woman for him.

Chapter 18

The first thing that occurred to Zora when her ex-husband entered was, *You're the wrong man*.

She longed for Lucky's honest, caring presence. Why hadn't she told him she wanted him to stay with her, that he was the most important person in her life? Sure, it meant taking a big emotional risk. Maybe he'd never accept her, flaws and all, but something about the way he gazed at her said otherwise. She'd taken leaps of faith, over and over, with the unworthy Andrew. Now she'd let Lucky go off without asking for what meant the most to her—keeping him close.

He must be busy, though, with the hospital in an uproar. Keely had brought news of Vince and Portia's deaths, and the two women had shared their turbulent reactions. Zora supposed the aftermath would affect her for a long while. Her heart went out to Tiffany and

Amber on the loss of their mother, but mostly she was thankful she and Keely had escaped injury.

After Keely left for dinner, Edmond had peeked in. He'd been visiting his wife and triplets, and stayed just long enough to express his best wishes and present a gorgeous bouquet that perfumed the room.

And now here was her ex-husband. "So you had the babies." Andrew hovered near the exit as if fearing a giant clamp might drop from the ceiling to hold him in place, forcing him to—what?—take responsibility? "They look, uh, cute."

That was the sum of his reaction? When Zora had cradled the babies after their delivery, their delicate scent and wonder-filled faces had instantly become engraved on her heart. Elizabeth had a tumble of reddish-brown hair and inquisitive gray eyes, while the boy was blond with bright blue eyes. As she crooned to each of them, she'd been rewarded with a gaze of pure devotion.

She'd have died for them. Their father thought they were, *uh, cute.*

Andrew shifted from one foot to the other. "Have you picked names?"

"The girl's Elizabeth."

"Like my mother."

"That's right." She waited, wondering if he had ideas about the boy's name. What a silly fantasy she'd harbored, that he would leap at the chance, yet the moment had played through her mind so often that it almost seemed real: Andrew declaring that he'd always loved the name something-or-other, or that he couldn't wait to take Elizabeth and what's-his-name to the zoo. When he didn't speak, she blurted, "I might call the boy Luke." That ought to get his attention.

"Okay." Obviously, Andrew hadn't connected the name to Lucky. Maybe he was too busy preparing his next revelation, which was: "I'm transferring to New York."

He was moving out of state? That seemed sudden. "When?"

"Next month."

"Permanently?"

"That's the idea."

Once, this news would have arrowed pain deep into Zora's gut. Now, she experienced relief tinged with sadness for this self-absorbed man. He would never do anything more important than fathering these children, yet clearly he didn't intend to play much of a role in their upbringing. As she'd suspected, his bid for custody had been merely an attempt to one-up her.

"Good luck with that." She didn't bother to point out that states enforced each other's child-support requirements. Her lawyer could take care of the details.

"Do me a favor, would you?" Andrew muttered.

Warily, she asked, "What?"

"Let my mom play with the kids once in a while. She's into this grandmother thing."

He'd been around Zora since they were teenagers, yet he believed she might exclude Betsy? "You don't know me at all," she said.

"Is that a yes?" He sounded like a sales agent impatient to conclude a deal.

Zora lifted her head from the pillow for a better view of the man who used to dominate her world. Yep, he'd definitely shrunk. "Okay," she said. "Thanks for stopping by."

Andrew regarded her with a shade of disappointment. "That's it?"

He must have expected her to plead for him to stay in Safe Harbor. After Lin's rejection, his ego was hungry to be fed. "That's it. Sayonara."

He glared at her. "Whatever," he said, and stalked out.

The air smelled suddenly fresher, and the colors of the flowers intensified. Then the best thing of all happened.

Lucky peered in. Although his face could use a splash of water and his navy blue uniform had picked up bits of lint, he was the handsomest man in the world.

The dismay on Andrew's face as he stomped down the hall thrilled Lucky. "You knocked him down to size," he told Zora admiringly as he entered her room. "You're such a tiny thing but wow, you pack a punch."

She lifted an eyebrow. "You're just figuring that out?"

Careful to avoid jostling her, Lucky sat on the edge of the bed. "Among other things. A lot of them."

Including that his image of a perfect wife and kids had been nothing more than a defense mechanism to protect against the kind of devastation that had torn his family apart. That his delusion about controlling the future was as self-defeating as anything he'd accused her of. That he didn't see how he could go through life without this delightful, maddening woman.

"Did you figure out yet that you're in love with me?" As soon as the words flew out, blood rushed to her cheeks. "Oops. I didn't mean to say that aloud."

Lucky nearly bounced off the bed in glee. "Yes, I'm

in love with you. Now tell me you're in love with me, too."

"Um… I have to think about it."

"Zora!" He could barely tolerate the delay.

She folded her arms. "What other things did you figure out today, smart guy?"

"That you have the most precious children in the world." Lucky visualized the babies again. "Your twins are the red-headed girl and the blond boy, right? I couldn't read the names on the isolettes."

Her face remained adorably flushed, this time with pride rather than embarrassment, he guessed. "Elizabeth and Luke."

Lucky couldn't have heard correctly. "You're giving him my name?"

"I'm trying it on for size." Zora shifted against the pillow.

Much as Lucky cherished the idea, it wouldn't be fair to the boy. "He should have his own name," he said. "How about Orlando?"

"Like the city in Florida?"

"Like my father." He'd meant to reserve that honor for his firstborn son. Well, this little guy had taken over that spot in Lucky's heart.

"I might go for that," Zora responded. "But if you name him, you might have to claim him."

"I'm claiming both of them." Lucky smiled at the dear, freckled person studying him expectantly.

"You don't still consider them Andrew's children?"

Her question startled him. "I consider them *your* children. I meant that *you* considered them Andrew's children."

"Really?"

"I believed you might forgive him for past sins if he, shall we say, embraced the miracle of fatherhood."

Zora's nose wrinkled. "I was an idiot. I believed love could conquer all, but it can't conquer heartlessness. Or a weak character. Or—should I go on abusing him, or is that enough?"

"For now, because I have something important to say." Lucky gathered his courage. "Let's get back to the part where I confess I'm in love with you."

Why didn't she respond in kind? But perhaps she was waiting for him to lay out the whole picture. Well, he'd better start by being cautious. Although it appeared Lucky might be able to stay in Safe Harbor, there was no guarantee he'd be hired in the new program. He might not be as hung up on financial security as before, but he couldn't ask for a commitment from Zora without pointing out that his situation was still unsettled.

"Another thing I discovered today was that I couldn't bear to leave Safe Harbor unless you go with me," he blurted. "Will you?"

"You have to go?" Her joy dimmed. "But…that means leaving our friends."

"I'll make it worth your while."

"I'd go with you in a heartbeat," Zora answered. "Except…"

"What?" His breath caught.

"My sister did that and ended up unmarried and un-loved." She stared down at her hands.

"Such trust," he murmured.

She folded her arms and hunkered down.

His impatience nearly exploded. But what did he expect, reassurance before he popped the question? *Put it out there, fella. Quit stalling.*

From the zipper compartment in his wallet, Lucky produced a gold ring set with diamonds and emeralds. Then he slid off the bed and onto one knee. "Zora, will you marry me?"

She stared at him in astonishment. "What about your perfect family?"

He pushed past the lump in his throat. "You are my perfect family. You, Elizabeth and Orlando."

"But your plans…saving for a house…"

"I nearly lost you today," he said. "That put everything into perspective. I want you today, and tomorrow, and forever. Marry me, Zora."

"Yes."

"Yes?" He couldn't quite believe she'd said it so simply and plainly. "No ifs, ands or buts?"

"Don't be silly. I love you."

"I love you, too!" Hoisting himself onto the bed again, he showered kisses on her forehead and cheeks and mouth.

Chuckling, she held up the ring. "Let me put this on."

He straightened. "Of course."

As she angled it toward her finger, her forehead creased. "Where did you… This looks familiar."

"I borrowed it from Betsy." Lucky had run into the nursing supervisor in the hall and shared his plans. When he mentioned that he wished he had a token ring to present until he had a chance to buy a new one, Betsy had removed the heirloom from her finger and loaned it to him.

"Did she mention that I wore this ring during my marriage to Andrew?" Zora asked, laughing.

"She left out that part." Lucky sighed, sorry that he'd

screwed up such an important detail. "I was planning for us to choose our rings together later."

Zora studied it fondly. "It's beautiful and it means a lot to Betsy. How sweet of her to loan it to us."

"This doesn't change your answer, does it? We *are* engaged, right?"

"You bet."

Sliding his arms around Zora, he leaned down for a long, tender kiss. She smelled of babies and happiness. Lucky's heart swelled as her arms closed around him and the two of them hung there, happily suspended in a private world.

A world they would share with their little guys. A world that would be full of bumps and twists and imperfections, exactly as it ought to be.

"For the record, I came to the conclusion that we loved each other long before you did," she whispered in his ear. "It didn't occur to you until today? Slow, slow."

Lucky grinned. "Guess I am. By the way, there's an excellent chance we won't have to leave Safe Harbor." Releasing her, he explained about Helen's proposal to fund the expansion.

"That's fantastic." Zora tapped her fingers together restlessly.

"What?" he asked.

"Maybe I shouldn't bring this up now."

"Let it out," Lucky told her. "If you have reservations, now's your chance to air them."

"It's not exactly a reservation."

"What is it?" He stroked her hair. Whatever the problem was, they'd deal with it.

"Your brother," Zora said.

Lucky blinked. He hadn't been expecting *that*. "What about him?"

"Do you still reject him for whatever he did?" she said earnestly. "Are you still so rigid?"

Despite an urge to protest that he could never forgive what Matthew had done, Lucky paused to reflect. This past month, he'd learned a lot from Zora's generous nature. While her weakness for Andrew had infuriated him, she'd also befriended Lin Lee, mended fences with Zady and regained her closeness with Betsy. He could use some of her grace.

"I'd like to tell you what happened," he said.

Zora gripped his hands. "Please do."

As Lucky began, the hospital faded around him and he was once more in his parents' convenience store in LA. He could hear the street traffic and smell the salty temptation of potato chips. When he looked up, a security mirror revealed a bulging image of shelves crammed with the odds and ends of a neighborhood market.

"My brother Matthew joined the navy at eighteen," he said. "I was proud of him, but that left me to juggle attending high school and helping my folks keep the store afloat." He'd unloaded supplies, stocked shelves, carried receipts to the bank and fetched change. He'd also operated the cash register many evenings late into the night.

"It must have been hard, missing school activities," Zora said.

"Yes, and I longed for the occasional evening to hang out with my friends." Lucky felt a twinge of his old resentment. "I rebelled in small ways. Sneaking a cigarette, showing up late or leaving early. Mom used to scowl and Dad complained that I was letting down the family while my brother risked his life for his country."

"How did you feel about that?" she asked.

"Guilty, but angry, too." In retrospect, his selfishness haunted him. Still, he owed her the whole truth. "One evening, we were supposed to close at nine, but my mother insisted on staying open late because customers kept drifting in. While she worked the register, she sent me into the storage room to open boxes of supplies we'd received that day and catalog the contents. I was furious."

"Where was your father?"

"He'd put in twelve hours and gone home exhausted." Lucky's gut twisted. "If I smoked on the premises, my mom would smell it. So I sneaked out the rear door into the alley."

Strange—he'd relived that night repeatedly in nightmares, yet now he had trouble dredging up the details. *Get it over with.*

"While I was outside, a junkie entered the store and demanded cash from my mother," he said. "The store surveillance tape showed he had a bulge in his jacket, but not whether it was a gun."

"How terrifying." Zora's gaze never strayed from Lucky's face. "What happened?"

"My mom collapsed." Lucky swallowed. "Later, the coroner said she died from stress cardiomyopathy, which is a response to overwhelming fear. A huge jolt of adrenaline can cause the heart to develop ventricular fibrillation—abnormal rhythms. She literally dropped dead."

Zora shivered. "I'm sorry. But you weren't at fault."

"If I'd been inside, I might have heard the robbery,

rushed in and scared the creep away," Lucky said. "Maybe before Mom succumbed."

"If he did have a gun, he'd have killed you," she countered.

"I doubt he did." Lucky refused to let himself off that easily. "Anyway, he snatched a handful of cash and ran."

"Did they catch him?"

"More or less." His jaw tightened. "He was a meth addict—a couple of days later the police found him dead of an overdose, probably with drugs he bought at my mother's expense."

"And that didn't bring her back," she observed sympathetically.

"No, it didn't." The discovery of his mother lying on the floor, the sirens, the arrival of police and paramedics had blurred into a montage of pain. Worst of all had been accompanying the police to inform his sleepy, disbelieving father.

Lucky had feared his father might collapse, too. Instead, Orlando Mendez had thrown himself into his work. "He gave his all to that store. I offered to postpone college and put in longer hours, but he refused. Instead, he hired an assistant. Nearly a year later, we discovered the assistant was embezzling from us."

"That's terrible." Zora stroked his arm.

Lucky had had trouble believing anyone could take advantage of people who were already suffering. Sadly, he and his father had learned otherwise.

"The guy fled to South America and we never recovered the money. A month after that, Dad died of an aneurysm," Lucky said grimly. "Literally, of a broken heart. I had to sell the store. There was barely enough to cover the debts and the funeral expenses."

That brought him to the bitter quarrel with Matthew. When his brother had attended their mother's funeral, he'd scarcely spoken. After their father's death, Matthew had blown up at Lucky.

"He accused me of contributing to our parents' deaths." Although the years had lessened his outrage, the memory stung. "He claimed I cheated him of his inheritance, that I'd used the profits from the sale of the store to pay for college. He even filed a theft report with the police. After they cleared me, Matthew informed our relatives I'd hidden the money and gotten away with it."

"Wow," Zora said. "That puts my quarrel with Zady in the shade."

As she spoke, guilt and regret flooded through Lucky. "If I hadn't been such an immature jerk, we might have avoided the argument. In a way, he was right. I let everyone down with my irresponsible actions the night my mother died. And I vowed that I'd never do that again to anyone I cared about, yet I let you down with Vince."

"What?" Astonishment filled Zora's face.

To his dismay, a sob shook Lucky. He never cried. He was the strong one, the tough guy. But the idea that Zora had put up with that man's groping in order to protect Lucky's career was intolerable. "I'm glad he's dead. I'm sorry about his wife, but…" His hands formed fists. "I messed up. And I had the nerve to rag on you about *your* mistakes."

"Yeah, that was the worst thing. I mean, death and destruction and being estranged from your brother hardly count compared to your nagging."

Her mischievous tone had the desired effect of banishing his self-pity. "You little goof."

Zora reached out to cup his cheek. "You're a wonderful man, Lucky. You've carried this burden for too long. I don't think you need to forgive your brother as much as you need to forgive yourself."

"I let everyone down. I can't undo that." Her touch soothed him, though.

"How many people did you save as a paramedic?" she asked. "And according to what I heard, if not for you, Rod's daughters might have died today. You were a kid when you sneaked out for a smoke. I don't know if you can mend the rift with Matthew, but as for the rest, let it go, Lucky."

Relief spread through him, a healing balm. "When did you get so smart?"

"When I fell in love with the right man," she said.

Lucky hugged her again, careful of her surgical wound. "You don't mind sharing a house with Karen and Rod? We could rent an apartment."

"I'd rather stay there, if it's okay with you," she said. "It's like having a big family."

"I agree." While it might not be possible for that family to include his brother, Lucky intended to try.

They were starting fresh, a man and woman who'd stumbled and screwed up plenty. Yet the future gleamed ahead of them in rainbow colors, because together they were stronger and wiser than separately.

They'd have a lot more fun, too.

Chapter 19

The adobe house had neatly trimmed bushes and a red tile roof, with striped woven curtains tied back at the windows. Mounting the porch steps, Lucky rubbed his damp palms on his jeans.

In response to his inquiry, a cousin had emailed that Matthew was stationed here in Point Hueneme, a few hours' drive to the north of Safe Harbor. Lucky hadn't even been sure how to say the town's name, which he'd learned on the internet was pronounced WY-nee-mee.

When he'd phoned, Matthew had cautiously agreed to meet with him. He'd suggested meeting at his house today while his wife and school-age children were attending a birthday party.

It might have been more sensible to choose a public place, Lucky mused. What if his brother threw a punch at him?

Well, he hadn't slammed down the phone or insulted Lucky. Although his tone had been wary, Lucky's mood was cautious, too.

Not finding a bell, he knocked, then wiped his palms on his pants again. Had Zora been this nervous when she'd prepared herself to see her sister? She must have waited like this, uncertain, anxious...

The door opened. Sixteen years had matured Matthew's olive face. He was, surprisingly, a couple of inches shorter than Lucky— *I must have grown.* Yet in every other respect, despite the passage of time, Matthew was incredibly familiar. In a rush, Lucky realized how much he'd missed the pal who'd taught him to play baseball when their dad was too busy and had advised him on which classes to choose in high school.

"Thanks for agreeing to meet me," Lucky said.

Matthew extended a strong, callused hand. They shook, and then his brother pulled him close and clapped his shoulder. "I'm glad you had the guts to make the first move."

"Damn," Lucky said. "If I start to cry, I'll be embarrassed."

"Nothing to be ashamed of." Releasing him, his brother moved aside to let him enter.

A couch and comfortable chairs, along with a bookshelf, TV and game system, filled the living room. On the wall hung a red, black and buff ceramic Aztec calendar almost identical to Lucky's. "Hey, we have the same interior decorator."

Matthew followed his gaze to the plaque. "It's like the one Grandpa and Grandma used to have."

"I'd forgotten."

"Aunt Maria and Uncle Carlos own it now. Man, I'm

sorry." Matthew stood squarely balanced on both feet, his khaki T-shirt emphasizing the breadth of his chest and shoulders. "You should have been at those family gatherings all these years."

Their grandparents had died before their parents, so Lucky hadn't been denied the chance to say goodbye to them at least. As for the aunts and uncles, it had been their decision to exclude him without hearing his side. "I'm fine. Just got engaged, in fact."

"Fantastic!" Matt raised his hands to signal he had more to say. "Let me get this out. I nursed my anger at you for years, until gradually it dawned on me that I was angry about a lot of things that had nothing to do with you. At myself for not being there when our parents needed me. Also at leaving you to carry the burden. I worked such long hours that I ran off to join the navy to get away from the store."

Lucky had never suspected that his brother's motives in enlisting had included escape. Not that he blamed Matthew. "I resented working so hard, too. That's why I sneaked out for cigarettes, which was totally irresponsible. I should have been there with Mom that night."

"I wasn't there, either. Even though I'm proud to serve my country, I signed up partly for the wrong reasons." His brother shook his head. "The other day, looking at some new recruits, I noticed how young they were, and it hit me you were about that age when our parents died."

"Eighteen," Lucky recalled. "Grown-up."

Matt tilted his head. "A baby."

"So were you when you enlisted."

"That's no excuse for my behavior." A crooked smile

brightened his brother's face. "Enough beating ourselves up. Can we put this in the past?"

"That's why I'm here," Lucky said.

"Tell me about this fiancée of yours," his brother said.

"I'll show you a picture." He took out his phone.

Soon they were lounging on the furniture, downing soft drinks and catching up on everything they'd missed.

"You've never been able to fix a pie crust as beautiful as mine." Playfully, Zady indicated the luscious apple pie on a side table reserved for Thanksgiving desserts. "I admit, your pecan pie looks yummy, but your crust isn't as shiny. The secret is to brush the unbaked crust with an egg mixed with a couple of tablespoons of cream."

Zora gave her sister a poke. They'd turned their old rivalry into friendly teasing since Zady had moved to town a few weeks earlier. "Insult it all you like. Lucky bought the pecan pie at the supermarket."

"You're kidding! You didn't bake your own pie?" Zady chuckled. "Mom would have a cow."

"Feel free to tell her."

"I doubt she's speaking to either of us since we informed her of your wedding after the fact."

At the reminder, Zora gazed happily down at the ring Lucky had placed there a week earlier. Although he'd offered to buy a more expensive one, she preferred this simple, classic design in gold. "I'm not sure which bothered her most, that I didn't invite her or that you served as my maid of honor."

She'd been a little saddened not to be able to include

her mother. But after Mom's drunken behavior at Zora's first wedding and her cruel manipulations with Zady, Zora had stuck to her resolve to keep some distance between them. Afterward, she'd written her mother informing her of her marriage and asking for her blessing. There'd been no reply.

The wedding at the county's picturesque Old Courthouse had been modest but magical, thanks to the love flowing between the bride and groom. And they'd been surrounded by friends and family. While Betsy and Keely held the twins, Zady had served as maid of honor and Matthew as best man. Zora had immediately liked Matthew, as well as his dark-haired wife and children. They planned to hold another reunion at Christmas.

"Are you ladies squabbling?" Lucky's arm around Zora's waist restored her to the present. "You'll set a bad example for our children."

"It'll teach them to stick up for themselves," she countered, and rested her cheek on his shoulder. "Besides, Zady and I don't fight any more. Just a little sisterly competition."

"That's okay, then."

What a wonderful man she'd married, she thought, nestling against Lucky.

As for a honeymoon, that was on hold until the babies were old enough to wean and leave with others. When she and her husband took a trip, there'd be no interruptions, however cute.

"These little guys are ready for their nap." From the den, Betsy brought Orlando into the kitchen, yawning in his hand-crocheted blanket. On her finger glittered the ring that would always remind Zora of their close connection.

"Elizabeth's dozing, too." Keely cradled her precious charge.

"Much as I adore them, thank goodness they're asleep." Breast-feeding two babies consumed more energy than Zora had imagined, and she was grateful for the help. "I'm starving."

The aroma of roast turkey and stuffing had been wafting from the kitchen all afternoon. Tiffany and Amber had insisted on pitching in to help Karen cook, while Rod and Grandma Helen arranged the dining room.

"Upstairs we go," Betsy said. "Keely?"

The nurse gave a start. "Of course." Head lowered, she hurried after the older woman.

Keely had been acting distracted since the wedding. Guiltily, Zora reflected that she hadn't been paying much attention to her friend.

For a while, Keely had been upbeat, buoyed by the news of Laird's departure. As his replacement, the hospital had hired a family and child counselor named Franca Brightman, whom Edmond had recommended. Already, she was helping the Adams girls adjust to their loss.

But since the wedding, Keely had retreated into long silences. Now that Zora was on leave and no longer required rides to work, they had less chance to speak privately.

Today was hardly the occasion for a tête-à-tête, but Zora resolved to find a moment alone with Keely later. Perhaps she was suffering a posttraumatic reaction to their brush with death, or struggling to adjust to the many changes at the hospital.

With the purchase of the dental building, buzz filled

the halls about the planned renovations and new staff to be hired. Exciting though it was, Zora remembered all the disruptions over the past few years as the hospital had been transformed. Perhaps that had contributed to Keely's downcast mood.

Her stomach growled as Tiffany and Amber paraded in and set hot dishes on the breakfast table, which would be used for serving. "I wish we lived here instead of at Grandma's," Amber said as she placed a casserole carefully on the tablecloth.

Tiffany glanced around. No sign of Helen. "I love Grandma, but honestly, we're underfoot in her house." Helen owned a two-bedroom cottage a few miles away.

"Especially with her arthritis," the younger girl added. "She's always cleaning up after us. I try to be neat but hey, I'm a kid."

Although newfound wealth had enabled Helen to hire a housekeeper to shop, cook and handle major cleaning, hosting a pair of active granddaughters was taking its toll, Zora had noted from the older woman's increasingly stiff movements. However, she respected that Helen chose not to buy a mansion or invest in more staff. She insisted on keeping the girls in touch with reality. In addition to sharing a bedroom, they would be transferring to public school next year.

Also, Tiff had enrolled in a dance class. Amber, who had loved to swim competitively until Vince turned every meet into a do-or-die situation, was easing into the sport again.

Partly to assist Helen, Rod had offered to relinquish his room to them and move in with Karen. The grandmother had replied firmly that she couldn't let the girls grow up in a home with a pair of unmarried adults sharing a bed.

Karen brought out a bowl of mashed potatoes, and Rod followed with a platter of sliced turkey. His daughters hurried into the kitchen to collect the salad and stuffing.

Helen joined them, along with Betsy and Keely. That was the whole group for today—Melissa, Edmond, Dawn and the triplets were dining with his parents, while Jack, Anya and their baby had flown to Colorado to share the holiday with her large family.

"I put the monitor by my place in the dining room," Keely told Zora. "That way, if the babies fuss, I can check on them. If you don't mind."

"Mind?" Zora repeated. "You're doing me a favor!"

"No problem." Keely avoided her eyes.

Before Zora could question her friend, she felt Lucky's hand on her spine, propelling her toward the food. "Serve yourself first. You're a nursing mommy."

Amid a chorus of agreement, she complied. Soon they were all seated, and after a prayer of gratitude for this special gathering, they dug into their heaped-high plates.

What a year it had been, Zora thought as she took in the beloved faces around the table. When a group of friends had moved into this house last February, they'd had no idea that by the end of November, there would be six babies born and three marriages.

"Have you found an apartment yet, Zady?" Betsy asked amid the chatter. Zora's sister was staying in a small unit at the Harbor Suites.

"Nothing I really love," Zady admitted.

Keely toyed with her food. In contrast to the others, she appeared to have little appetite for her meal.

Zora shot her a concerned glance. Keely ignored it.

"Can we have dessert?" Amber indicated the plate she'd cleaned at top speed.

"Where are your manners?" reproved her grandmother. "Not till everyone's finished."

"How about the pumpkin bread?" Amber persisted. "That isn't really dessert, is it, Grandma?"

"I suppose not." Seated between her granddaughters, Helen acquiesced fondly. "Why don't you bring in the plate for everyone?"

"I'll get it." To Zora's surprise, Rod sprang up. Usually the anesthesiologist moved at a slower pace than everyone else, and he'd milked his injured nose for sympathy until the bruising faded. He whisked out of the room, and Zora heard a cabinet open and shut in the kitchen.

"What's Dad doing?" Amber asked.

"I guess we'll find out," Tiffany said.

The slightly built man returned, jauntily hoisting the plate of pumpkin bread. When he set it in front of Karen, Zora saw a miniature van displayed in the center.

"What's this?" Their landlady lifted the little vehicle to inspect it.

"It's the first part of my surprise." Rod stood next to her, bouncing with anticipation. "That's a stand-in for the van I'm buying. I'll be taking delivery of it next week. It carries eight, so we can drive the girls and their friends. Helen, I made sure it was accessible for you to get in and out of."

"That's lovely." She sounded puzzled, though, and

Zora suspected they all were. Why display this in the middle of Thanksgiving dinner?

"The doors and hood open," Rod prompted.

"It would be hard to drive it otherwise." Beside Zora, Lucky smirked at the other man.

Instead of riposting as he usually would, Rod cleared his throat. "I mean the miniature. Open the hood."

With a bemused expression, their landlady tipped it open and gasped. "Oh, Rod!"

"What is it? What is it?" The girls crowded around.

Karen held up a diamond engagement ring. "My gosh."

Rod dipped, suggestive of lowering himself to one knee, although he never quite touched the floor. "Will you make an honest man of me?"

Karen's mouth hung open. Then she gathered her wits. "Of course I will, you crazy man!" To the girls' cheers, she kissed him.

Zora could have sworn Helen's smile revealed a hint of relief. This meant the girls could move in with their father and new stepmother, while living only a few miles from their grandma.

"Congratulations." Betsy seemed as thrilled as the rest of them.

A soft sob on Zora's far side riveted her gaze to Keely. The woman appeared to be fighting tears.

"What's wrong?" Surely the nurse hadn't fallen in love with Rod. Zora had seen no sign of it.

"I don't mean to spoil the happy occasion." She sucked in air.

"Calm down and share what's bothering you," Zora urged. "Please."

Glumly, Keely answered. "You're all families now. Of course your sister should live here, too."

"Why?" Zady asked.

Keely didn't have to answer, because Zora understood. "You've been expecting us to ask you to leave?"

The older nurse nodded.

"No way," Lucky said.

"You belong here," Karen chimed in.

"She's your twin," Keely said doggedly. "It's only right."

Zora wished she'd addressed this issue long ago. It simply hadn't occurred to her. "You saved my life. The twins' lives, too."

Zady spoke up, too. "Keely, my sister and I have been feuding for years. Yeah, we love each other and we're friends again, but share a house? We'd be at each other's throats in five seconds."

"Blood on the floor," Lucky said calmly.

"No, you wouldn't." Keely refused to be comforted. "You're a member of her family, and I'm not."

"I can fix that," Zora said. "I hereby dub you the babies' honorary aunt. You are therefore a relative. And we love you."

There was a chorus of agreement. "Including me," Rod put in. "Don't tell anybody at work."

Keely joined in the ripple of laughter that greeted this remark. "Really?"

"Really," Zora said.

"Will you help me plan my wedding?" Karen asked. "Since my mother died last year, I've been wishing I had more family."

"You have?" Keely sniffled.

Their landlady gazed dreamily around the table. "Growing up, I wished I had a houseful of brothers and sisters, and other relatives to celebrate holidays.

My wish has come true. Keely, you have a home here as long as you want it."

The nurse appeared too choked up to speak.

"Can we eat dessert now?" Amber asked.

"That's the best idea I've heard all day," Lucky said. "Aside from Rod and Karen getting married, and Keely becoming an honorary aunt to our children."

Zora couldn't have agreed more.

* * * * *

Carrie Nichols grew up in New England but moved south and traded snow for central AC. She loves to travel, is addicted to British crime dramas and knows a *Seinfeld* quote appropriate for every occasion.

A 2016 RWA Golden Heart® Award winner and two-time Maggie Award for Excellence winner, she has one tolerant husband, two grown sons and two critical cats. To her dismay, Carrie's characters—like her family—often ignore the wisdom and guidance she offers.

Books by Carrie Nichols

Harlequin Special Edition

Small-Town Sweethearts

The Marine's Secret Daughter
The Sergeant's Unexpected Family
His Unexpected Twins
The Scrooge of Loon Lake
The Sergeant's Matchmaking Dog
The Hero Next Door

Visit the Author Profile page at Harlequin.com for more titles.

Chapter 1

"How about that new guy from—"

"No." Ellie Harding paused mid-slice in the sheet cake she was dividing into equal squares to scowl at her friend's attempts at matchmaking.

Meg McBride Cooper stood on the opposite side of the rectangular table, a stack of plain white dessert plates cradled against her chest. Ellie and Meg were volunteering at the payment-optional luncheon held weekly in the basement of the whitewashed clapboard church on the town square in Loon Lake, Vermont.

"I don't need or want help finding a date," Ellie said, and considering what she'd survived in her twenty-seven years, going solo to a friend's wedding shouldn't even be a blip on her radar. Did her friends think she couldn't find a date on her own? Memories surfaced of how she'd sometimes been treated after her cancer diagnosis. She knew her friends didn't pity her, but experiencing being pitied behind her back as well as to her face as a child had made her more sensitive as an adult.

Ellie pushed aside memories and went back to slicing the chocolate frosted cake with vigorous strokes. Heck, guys called her. Yep. They called all the time. *Slice*. They called when they needed a shortstop for a pickup softball game or a bowling partner. *Slice*. One even called last month, asking if she had a phone number for that new X-ray tech. *Slice*.

Meg plopped the plates onto the table with a *thunk* and gnawed on her bottom lip as she gazed at Ellie. Yeah, Meg was feeling guilty and wanted to confess something.

"Spill it," Ellie ordered.

"Now, don't get mad, but…" Meg sighed. "I asked Riley if he knew anyone who might be interested in being your date for the wedding."

"Uh-oh. Is Meg trying to set you up with arrestees…again?" A fellow volunteer, Mary Carter, came to stand shoulder to shoulder with Ellie, another sheet pan clutched in her hands. Mary was the future bride in question and a transplant to their close-knit central Vermont community, but she had jumped into town life and activities with enthusiasm. "Really, Meg, don't you think Ellie can do better than a felon? I'm sure if I asked, Brody could contact one of his old army buddies. I'll tell him to only choose ones that have never been arrested."

Meg rolled her eyes. "I'm sure asking Brody won't be necessary, Mary."

"Just in case…" Mary set the cake next to the stack

of plates. "Ellie, what are your feelings on speeding tickets, because—"

"Oh, for heaven's sake," Meg interrupted and made an impatient sound with her tongue.

Ellie stifled a giggle at their antics but couldn't decide if she was grateful or annoyed. Now that her two besties had found happily-ever-afters, they seemed to think it their sworn duty to get her settled, too. So what if she hadn't found Mr. Right yet? Between long shifts as a nurse in the ER and studying for a more advanced degree, she led a full, busy life, thank you very much.

Mary winked at Ellie. "At least *I'm* not trying to set her up with someone who's been arrested."

"As I've told both of you already, that guy wasn't under arrest." Meg planted her hands on her hips. "He just happened to be in the building and Riley recruited him for a police lineup, that's all there was to it. No crime. No arrest."

Ellie continued to slice the cake. "If there was no crime, why was there a police lineup?"

"I meant *he* didn't commit a crime."

Mary slanted a look at Ellie. "Please correct me if I'm wrong, but didn't the witness identify him?"

"Mary," Meg huffed. "You're not helping."

"Sorry," Mary said, but her grin told a different story.

Ellie sucked on her cheeks to stifle a laugh, grateful to be off the hot seat, even temporarily. She appreciated her friends' concern but she wasn't a project. At times like this, Meg conveniently forgot she hadn't dated anyone for five years until Riley Cooper came back to town after serving in the marines in Afghanistan. Ellie decided not to point that out because her friends meant well. And she didn't want to turn their attention—and matchmaking attempts—back to her.

Meg blew her breath out noisily, disturbing the wisps of curly red hair that had escaped her messy ponytail. "I've explained this to you guys like a thousand times already. It was a case of mistaken identity. I swear."

"Uh-huh, sure." Mary laughed and elbowed Ellie. "Ooh, maybe Riley can get the sheriff's department to start an eligible bachelor catch-and-release program."

"You guys are the worst," Meg grumbled, and began laying out the plates.

"Yup, the absolute worst, but you love us, anyway." Ellie grinned as she plated cake slices.

"Yeah, it's a good thing— Ooh, Ellie, how about that oh-my-God-he's-so-gorgeous guy coming down the stairs? If I wasn't hopelessly in love with Brody..." Mary bumped shoulders with Ellie and motioned with head.

Ellie's gaze followed Mary's and her heart stuttered. *Liam McBride*. What was he doing at the luncheon? She'd had a serious crush on Meg's brother since...well, since forever. At four years older, Liam had seen her as an annoying kid and had treated her accordingly. By the time she'd matured enough for him to notice, she'd been "his kid sister's friend" for so long she doubted it registered that she was a grown woman.

"What? Who? Where?" Meg whirled around and made a sound with her tongue against her teeth. "That's Liam."

"Liam?" Mary's eyes widened. "You mean that's—"

"Ellie's date for the wedding." Meg swiveled back, clapping her hands together, her mouth in a wide smile. "It's perfect."

"What? No." Ellie took a step back, shaking her head and holding up the knife as if warding off marauding zombies. She could accept matchmaking between friends. Even being relegated to Liam's friend zone would be acceptable, but begging for a pity date? *Nuh-uh.* Not gonna happen. No way. "Absolutely not."

"No... *No?*" Mary glanced at Liam again and snapped back to Ellie, looking at her as if she were insane for refusing. "I don't know why you wouldn't want—"

"Because he's Meg's brother." Ellie sneaked another glance at the sexy six-foot-two hunk of firefighter strutting toward them.

From his chronically disheveled dark brown hair and broad shoulders to his slim hips, long legs and that touch of confident swagger, Liam McBride oozed pheromones. And Ellie longed to answer their alluring call by throwing herself at his feet, but good sense, not to mention strong self-preservation instincts, prevailed. Thank God, because she didn't relish getting stepped on by those size 13 Oakley assault boots. To him, she was his little sister's friend. The girl who used to make moon eyes at him, the teen who blushed and stuttered every time he talked to her. When she'd been diagnosed with cancer in her teens, one of her first thoughts had been that she might never get to kiss Liam McBride.

"Be right back," Meg threw over her shoulder and rushed to meet her brother as he crossed the room.

"Oh, my. I mean, I had no idea," Mary whispered, leaning closer to Ellie. "Whenever she mentioned her brother, I was picturing a male version of Meg. You know...vertically challenged, wild red hair, freckles."

Ellie burst out laughing, but drew in a sharp breath

when Liam's head snapped up. His gaze captured hers and his lips quirked into an irresistible half grin. The air she'd sucked in got caught in her chest. Why did he have to be so damn sexy? As if handsomeness had been handed out unchecked on the day he received his looks.

"Liam takes after their dad," she whispered to Mary. And not just in physical appearance.

Ellie knew Liam and his dad had buried themselves in work when Bridget McBride got sick. Firefighting was an admirable profession, but relationships needed care and feeding, too. All Ellie had to do was look at her parents to understand the cost when one partner checked out emotionally during a life-threatening situation. She might have survived the cancer that had plagued her childhood, but her parents' close relationship hadn't. As an adult she knew the guilt she'd carried throughout her teen years was irrational, but that didn't stop it from gnawing at her whenever she saw her parents together. What happened to them proved no relationship was immune to life's challenges.

So she'd admire the sexy firefighter, and if given the chance, she'd take that secret Make-A-Wish kiss, but she'd keep her heart and hopes for the future far, far away from Liam McBride.

"Heart? You listening?" she asked sotto voce before sneaking another longing glance at Liam.

Liam's footsteps had faltered at that distinctive laugh. *Ellie Harding.* Her laughter, like her honey-brown eyes, sparkled and drew him in whenever she was close. Today, her long, shiny dark hair was pulled back and secured with one of those rubber band thingies his sister and niece favored. He shook his head and tried to force his thoughts into safer territory. As his sister's friend, Ellie was off-limits, a permanent resident of the no-dating zone. It was a good thing they lived three hours apart so he wasn't faced with temptation on a regular basis. The last time he'd seen her was at his nephew's christening, nearly nine months ago.

The fact that she'd had cancer as a child and could have died had nothing to do with his resistance to her charms. Nothing at all. He'd hate to think he was that shallow, despite knowing the destruction illness left in its wake.

No. His reluctance was because messing with a sibling's friend could have nasty consequences. He and his best friend, Riley Cooper, were just patching up a huge rift in their friendship. Riley had broken the bro code and Liam's trust by getting Meg pregnant before deploying to Afghanistan and disappearing from her life. But all that was in the past. His sister was crazy in love with Riley, who'd come back, taken responsibility for his daughter and convinced Meg to marry him. Riley was also the reason for the glow of happiness in his sister's eyes these days.

So he'd buried the hatchet, and not in Riley's privates as he'd longed to do once upon a time. He was even spending saved vacation time in Loon Lake to help his brother-in-law renovate. Meg and Riley were outgrowing their modest cottage-style home after the birth of their second child, James.

His gaze met Ellie's and objections scattered like ashes. Damn, but off-limits would be a lot easier if she weren't so appealing. Why some guy hadn't scooped her up by now was a mystery. He almost wished one had and removed temptation. *Almost.* Something he kept buried deep and refused to explore railed against the picture of Ellie married to a random dude, forever out of reach. Except out of reach was where she needed to stay, because he'd filled his quota of losing people. From here on out, his heart belonged to his job. *Stay back three hundred feet, Ellie Harding.*

"Liam, what are you doing here?" Meg asked.

"I'm here to help Riley with your addition, remember?"

"I mean here…at the luncheon."

"When you weren't home, I remembered you volunteered here on Thursdays." He shrugged. "So, here I am."

She grinned and looped her arm through his. "You have no idea what perfect timing you have."

Then she began guiding—yeah, more like frog-marching—him across the church basement toward Ellie of the twinkling eyes and engaging laugh.

Liam's indrawn breath hissed through his teeth. "Uh-oh."

"You're the answer to our problem," Meg said in a too-bright tone, and squeezed his arm.

"Huh, that's new." He gave her a side-eye look. "Usually you're accusing me of being or causing the problem."

Meg's expression was calculating, as if sizing him up for something. *Crap.* He knew that look and nothing good ever came from it. Now that she was happily married, she seemed to think everyone should be. Living three hours away, he'd managed to avoid her less-than-subtle hints that it was time he settled down. He loved his sister and was happy to help with the interior finishing work on her new home addition, but he wasn't about to let her manipulate him into any sort of permanent relationship. Even if the intended target had the most beautiful golden eyes he'd ever seen.

He made a show of looking around. "Where's Riley? Why isn't your husband here solving your problems? Isn't that what he's for?"

"Nah, he can't help with this one, so enjoy being the solution for once, brother dear." Meg stopped at the table where Ellie and an attractive dark-haired woman about the same age were dishing out slices of chocolate cake.

"Meg tells me you need me to sample that cake." He winked at Ellie, who blushed. His breath quickened at her flushed features. *Friend zone*, he repeated to himself, but his mind kept conjuring up unique and enjoyable ways of keeping that pretty pink color on her face.

Meg tugged on his am, acting like her seven-year-old daughter, Fiona. "First, agree to our proposition, then you can have cake."

Ellie was shaking her head and mouthing the word *no*. Obviously whatever Meg had in mind involved her. Despite his wariness, he was intrigued.

Meg was nodding her head as vigorously as Ellie was shaking hers. "Ellie needs a date for Mary's wedding."

"I do not. Don't listen to her. This was all your sister's harebrained idea." Ellie dumped a piece of cake onto a plate and it landed frosting side down. She cursed and he cleared his throat to disguise his laugh.

"But Liam is going to be in town, so it's perfect," Meg said.

He winced. Tenacious was Meg's middle name. Another reason to keep Ellie in that friend zone. He'd have to live with the fallout into eternity.

"Hi, I'm Mary. The bride." The raven-haired woman

set aside the slice with the frosting side down and thrust out her hand. "And you're welcome to come to my wedding with—" she glanced at Ellie "—or without a date."

He untangled his arm from Meg's and shook hands. "Thanks, I—"

"Oh, look. They need help at the pay station," Meg said, and scooted away.

"Nice meeting you, Liam. I'd love to stay and chat, but I promised to help in the kitchen." Mary disappeared as quickly and efficiently as his sister.

"Cowards," Ellie muttered, and shook her head. "Look, I'm not hitting you up to be my date for the wedding. I'm fine going by myself."

He nodded. Ellie was smart and independent, but that didn't mean she wanted to go to a wedding alone if everyone else was paired up. They could go as friends. And if he happened to hold her close as they danced... He shook his head, but the image of Ellie in his arms wouldn't go away. Huh, Meg wasn't the only tenacious person today. And damn if Meg hadn't once again manipulated him. "Are you saying you don't want to go with me? I've been known to behave myself in public."

Ellie raised her eyebrows, but her eyes glinted with mischief. "That's not what I've heard."

"Lies and exaggerations. Don't believe a word you hear and only half of what you see." He pulled a face.

"Uh-huh, sure." She laughed and went back to dishing out cake.

Her laugh washed over him and he arranged the plates so the empty ones were closer to her. People had begun lining up at the other end of the string of tables, but no one had reached the dessert station yet. He took advantage and hurried to Ellie's side of the table. He could help hand out the cake. Yeah, he was a regular do-gooder and it had nothing to do with standing next to Ellie and breathing in her light, flowery scent. "Why don't you want to go to this wedding with me?"

Ellie shook her head. "I'm not looking for a pity date."

He sighed. If she knew where his thoughts had been, she wouldn't be saying that. Besides, it wasn't like a real date because they'd be friends hanging out together. As simple as that. "So how do I appeal to your better nature and get you to take pity on me?"

"What? No. I meant…" she sputtered, her face turning pink again. She made what sounded like an impatient noise and put the last slice of cake on a plate.

He shouldn't, but he enjoyed seeing her flustered and if he was the cause, all the better, because she certainly had that effect on him. "How did you do that?"

She looked up and frowned. "Do what?"

He could get lost in those eyes. *Focus, McBride.* He cleared his throat and pointed to the last cake square on the plate. "You made those come out even."

A smile spread across her face and she glanced around before leaning close. "It's my superpower."

"I'm intrigued," he whispered, but he wasn't referring to cake or plates.

She straightened and turned her attention to a woman who appeared in front of them. "Hello, Mrs. Canterbury. Cake?"

After the woman had taken her cake and left, he bumped his hip against Ellie's. "Whaddaya say, Harding, help a guy out. Do your good deed for the month and come to this wedding with me?"

She narrowed her eyes at him. "Why? So I can perform CPR on the women who faint at your feet?"

Liam threw his head back and laughed. He spotted Meg watching them, a smug expression on her face. He'd deal with his sister later. Maybe he could interest Fiona in a drum set or buy James, who would be walking soon, a pair of those annoying sneakers that squeaked.

Except he was intrigued by the idea of going with Ellie, so he gave her what he hoped was his best puppy-dog face. "Please. I hear it's the social event of the season."

"Oh, brother," she muttered and rolled her eyes.

Why had it suddenly become so important for her to say yes? He should be running the other way. Ellie didn't strike him as the sort of woman who did casual, and that's all he was looking for—with Ellie or anyone. Keep it light. No more wrenching losses. But that damn image of holding her while dancing, their bodies in sync, sometimes touching, wouldn't go away.

"How long are you staying in Loon Lake?"

Her question dragged him away from his thoughts and he frowned. "Exactly when is this wedding?"

"You missed the point. That was my attempt at changing the subject," she said, and greeted an elderly woman shuffling past.

Liam smiled at the woman and tried to hand her a dessert.

The woman shook her head and held up a plate loaded with meat loaf, potatoes and green beans. "Gotta eat this first, son."

Liam nodded, put the dessert back on the table and turned his head to Ellie. "I'll be here for a month."

"Goodness gracious, son, it won't take me that long to eat," the woman said before meandering off to find a seat.

Ellie giggled, her eyes sparkling with amusement, and he couldn't look away. *She's Meg's friend. Are you forgetting about cancer and how much it hurts to lose someone?* Sure, she was in remission, but there was a reason that term was used instead of *cured.* In his mother's case, the remission didn't last. Ellie was off-limits for so many reasons. But that message was getting drowned out. "So, you'll go with me to this wedding?"

"Look, Liam, I appreciate the offer, but—"

He leaned closer, dragging in her scent, and tilted his head in the direction of his sister. "It might shut her up for a bit. Let her think she got her way."

"Hmm." Ellie sucked on her lower lip for a second, then shook her head. "Nah. It'll just encourage her."

"It'll throw her off the scent if we hang out for a bit. We'll know that's all we'd be doing, but she won't." He'd lost his ever-lovin' mind. Yup, that must be the explanation for pursuing such an idiotic suggestion.

Ellie smiled and continued to hand out the cake. Although she had fewer freckles than she had as a kid, she still had a sprinkling of them high on her cheekbones and the bridge of her nose. He wouldn't have thought freckles could be sexy, but on Ellie they were, and he had to fight the urge to count them by pressing his fingertips to each one. Or better yet, his tongue.

"But we won't really be dating?" she asked during a lull in the line of people.

"Did you want to date?" What the hell was he doing asking such a loaded question? He handed out the last piece of cake to an elderly man in a Red Sox baseball cap.

"Meg means well, but it might be nice to take a break

from her matchmaking efforts." She picked up the plate with the frosting-side-down slice and held it up. "Split?"

"Sure." He reached for the fork she offered. His fingers brushed hers as he took the utensil and their gazes met. "Thanks. Looks delicious."

Her cheeks turned pink, making the tiny freckles stand out even more. As if they were begging for someone—him—to run their tongue along them. He cleared his throat and jabbed his fork in the cake.

"So, whaddaya say, Harding, do we have a deal?"

She shrugged. "Sure, McBride, why not?" Someone called her name and she turned away to leave but said over her shoulder, "We'll talk."

He set the fork on the empty plate and watched her disappear into the kitchen. She never did answer his question about wanting to date. Not that it mattered, because they would be hanging out. No dating. No relationship. Nice and safe: the way he preferred it.

Chapter 2

"Check out the guy who just walked in." Stacy, the triage nurse on duty, elbowed Ellie.

Ellie looked up from the notes she'd been studying to glance out the large glass window into the emergency waiting area. Her heart sped at the sight of Liam dressed in jeans and a dark blue Red Sox championship T-shirt approaching them. She hadn't seen him since the community luncheon two days prior, but he hadn't been far from her thoughts. If Stacy hadn't spotted him first, Ellie might have wondered if he was figment of her overactive imagination.

Ignoring Stacy's obvious curiosity, Ellie opened the door to the triage area. "Hey, what are you doing here?"

"Hey, yourself." He gave her that sexy half grin that threatened to leave her in a puddle.

Janitorial, mop up triage, please.

She clutched the clipboard across her chest as if it could protect her vital organs like a lead apron during X-rays. "Everything okay?"

"Heard you'd be getting off soon." He shrugged. "Thought you might like to grab some supper with me."

In the little office, Stacy cleared her throat, but Ellie ignored her.

Was he asking her on a date? "And where did you hear my shift was ending?"

"I asked Meg." He put his hands into his front pockets and hunched his shoulders forward. "So, how about some supper?"

A pen dropped, followed by a sigh. Stacy was probably memorizing every word and detail of the encounter to pass along later in the cafeteria.

Ellie shuffled her feet. Was she going to do this? *Repeat after me: "not a real date."* "Sure. I've got some extra clothes in my locker. If you don't mind waiting while I change."

From the sound of it, Stacy was rearranging files on her desk, and evidently, they were fighting back.

Ellie grinned and turned around. "Stacy, have you met my friend Meg Cooper's brother, Liam?"

Stacy stepped forward and stuck out her hand. "Pleased to meet you, Liam."

"Let me get changed. I'll be right back," Ellie said while Stacy and Liam shook hands.

Stacy laughed. "Don't rush on my account."

Despite Stacy's comment, Ellie hurried to her locker. Had this been Liam's idea or was Meg somehow behind this? After changing into jeans and a short-sleeved cotton sweater, she undid her hair from the braid and brushed it out. Even if this wasn't an honest-to-goodness date, she wanted to look her best. She fluffed her hair around her shoulders and applied some cherry lip gloss and went in search of Liam.

Hands shoved in his back pockets, Liam stood in front of the muted television in the waiting area. He turned as she approached and smiled broadly. "I gotta say, Harding, you clean up nicely."

"Not so bad yourself, McBride." She put her purse strap over her shoulder and waved to Stacy through the window. The triage nurse was with a patient but glanced at Liam and back to Ellie with a grin and a thumbs-up.

"I thought we'd take my truck and I can bring you back here for your car," Liam said as the automatic doors slid open with an electronic *whoosh*.

A light breeze was blowing the leaves on the trees surrounding the parking lot. A thunderstorm earlier in the day had broken the heat and humidity, making the evening warm but comfortable.

"Sounds good." *Sounds like a date.*

Using his key fob to unlock his truck, he approached the passenger side and opened the door for her. "Riley says that new hard cider microbrewery on the town square has great food."

"They do. Best burgers in town, if you ask me." She sucked on her bottom lip as she climbed into his truck. Everyone in Loon Lake knew Hennen's Microbrewery was the place to hang out with friends, while Angelo's was the restaurant you brought your date to. So, not a date. *At least we cleared that up.*

Once she was in the passenger seat, he shut the door and strolled around the hood of the truck. He climbed in and settled himself behind the wheel.

"Yeah, Meg mentioned that Angelo's has added a

dining patio but—" He started the truck and music from the Dropkick Murphys blasted from the speakers. Leaning over, he adjusted the volume. "Sorry about that."

His movements filled the front seat with his signature scent. She was able to pick out notes of salty sea air, driftwood and sage. Thinking about his aftershave was better than trying to figure out what he'd been about to say about Angelo's. Okay, color her curious. "You were saying something about Angelo's new patio."

He checked the mirrors and the backup camera before leaving the parking spot. "Hmm…oh, yeah. Meg said during the winter you can see across the lake to their house from the patio."

Serves you right for asking. "That's cool."

He cleared his throat. "She was going on and on about how romantic the new patio was with something called fairy lights."

Not exactly subtle, Meg. Ellie fiddled with the strap of her purse. "Yeah, they've got small trees in ceramic pots scattered around with tiny LED lights strung around the trunks and branches. Very pretty, with lots of atmosphere."

The air in the confined space felt supercharged with something…awareness? Chemistry? She couldn't be sure, couldn't even be sure that he felt it, too. Maybe this was all in her head. All one-sided, like it had been in her childhood.

He glanced at her for a second before bringing his attention back to the road. "So, you've been to Angelo's patio?"

Was he trying to get information on her social life or lack thereof? "No, but Mary and Meg have both been."

She huffed out her breath. "Believe me, I've heard all about it."

He reached over and laid his hand over hers. "Sounds like I may have to take up the challenge to be sure you get to experience this patio, too."

Her heart did a little bump, but she laughed, hoping to brazen through. "You signing me up as their new janitor, McBride?"

He squeezed her hand and brought it to his chest. "You wound me, Harding. I was thinking more along the lines of the waitstaff. I can see you in a white blouse and a cute little black skirt."

"Glad we cleared that up." She laughed for real this time. Date or not, there was no reason she couldn't enjoy being with Liam. Even if anything that could happen with Liam had nowhere to go. They didn't live in the same town. And then there was the whole thing with Liam having used his job to avoid dealing with his emotions. Even his sister couldn't deny that truth. But that didn't mean she couldn't enjoy hanging out with him while he was here. Having a life-threatening illness like lymphoma had taught her she didn't want to die with regrets if she could help it. After enduring chemo coupled with radiation, she'd been in remission for almost nine years, a good chunk of time, and her oncologist was optimistic but the experience had changed her outlook on life.

"How are the renovations coming?" she asked.

He squeezed her hand and put it back on her lap. "Is this you changing the subject?"

"So you *can* take a hint."

He jokingly muttered something about respect for her elders but launched into an amusing story about framing out the new master bedroom closet at Meg and Riley's place.

"That house is going to be awesome once the addition is finished."

He made a hum of agreement. "Yeah, I guess she made the right choice moving here."

"She said you had tried to get her to move into one of your rentals." She hadn't seen Liam's place, but she knew he owned one of those iconic Boston three-family homes commonly referred to as "three-deckers" by the locals. He'd purchased it as a bank foreclosure and had been remodeling it ever since, according to Meg. Ellie knew it was Liam's pride and joy.

"I did, but she's always loved this town and that vacation home. Even all the repairs it needed didn't deter her. My sister can be stubborn."

Ellie laughed. "Yeah, so I noticed."

"But I gotta say, she made the right choice for her." He stopped for a red light.

"What about you?" The words were out before she could prevent them.

He turned his head to look at her. "Me? I'm exactly where I belong."

Yeah, that's what she thought. And like Meg, he was happy where he lived.

Swallowing, she pointed out the windshield. "Green light."

She glanced at Liam's strong profile. Could *she* be happy in Boston? "No regrets" included trying new things, new places.

Hey, Ellie, aren't you getting a little ahead of yourself? This wasn't even a real date.

The route along Main Street took them past a few

rectangular, early-nineteenth-century gable-roofed houses gathered around the town green. Some of the stately homes had been repurposed as doctors' offices, an insurance agency and an attorney's office, but some were still single-family residences.

The manicured common space boasted a restored white gazebo that doubled as a bandstand for concerts and picnics in the summer. Homes soon gave way to brick-fronted businesses, and the white Greek Revival church where they held the weekly lunches. With its black shutters and steeple bell tower, the church anchored the green at one end.

No doubt the town was picturesque, but she recalled how, when she was sick, the women of Loon Lake had worked year-round to keep the Hardings' refrigerator full of casseroles and sandwich fixings. In the summer, the men had made sure their lawn was mowed. In the winter, the men plowing for the town had been careful to keep the end of their driveway relatively clear.

He pulled the truck into one of the angled parking spots in front of the pub-style restaurant. "I'm assuming you've been here before, since you said you liked the burgers."

"Yeah, I've been a few times with some of the people from work."

He turned the engine off and opened his door. Ellie opened hers and was getting out when he came around to her side. He put his hand under her elbow to steady her as she scrambled out. His touch sent sparks up her arm…straight to her core.

You'd better be listening, she cautioned her heart. *Liam and I are hanging out, nothing more.* Unlike Angelo's, this wasn't a romantic date place. Since this wasn't a date, she had no right to feel disappointed. And she certainly had no right to be using or thinking the word *romantic* in context with anything she and Liam did.

They strolled across the sidewalk to the entrance, his hand hovering over the small of her back, not quite touching. How was she supposed to read the mixed signals he was sending? Maybe it was all her fault for trying to read things into his actions and words that weren't there. *Your fault because you wanted this to be a date and it's a let's-hang-out night.* She swallowed the sigh that bubbled up.

He turned his head toward her as they made their way toward the restaurant. "Something wrong with Hennen's?"

Had he picked up on her confusion? She shook her head. "No. It's fine."

"Hey, I'm not such a guy that I don't know what 'fine' in that tone of voice means." He held the glass entry door open.

After stepping inside, she glanced up at him, her eyebrows raised. "And what does 'fine' mean?"

The outer door shut, leaving them alone in the restaurant's vestibule. A small table with a bowl of wrapped mints and stack of takeout menus stood off to one side. Muffled sounds—music, conversations and clinking of dishware—came from beyond the inner door.

"I'm thinking it means there's something wrong and I'm expected to figure it out." His light blue eyes darkened.

Lost in those eyes, she had to swallow before she could speak. "And have you figured it out?"

"No, but I have an idea how to fix it." He took a step toward her, his intense gaze on her lips.

"Oh? You can fix it without even knowing what it is?" All thoughts of why she was even upset flew out of her head. Liam's sexy and oh-so-kissable lips took up all available space.

"Uh-huh," he said, and lowered his head. "I was thinking of kissing it and making it all better."

She noisily sucked in her breath. Were they really going to do this? Here of all places?

"Are you in?" His voice was hoarse, his expression hopeful as his gaze searched hers.

She rose on her tiptoes, placed her hands on either side of his face, pulling him close enough she smelled breath mints. "Does this answer your question?"

He dipped his head until his lips latched onto hers. The kiss was gentle, probing but firm. Her sigh parted her lips and his tongue slipped inside. The kiss she'd been waiting for her entire life was even better than she'd thought possible. It was sexy enough to send heat to her most sensitive areas and yet sweet enough to bring tears to her eyes. *Make-A-Wish, eat your heart out.*

She wanted it to last forever, but cooled air and noise from the restaurant blasted them as the inner door opened. Someone cleared their throat and Liam pulled away so quickly she swayed. His hands darted out, coming to rest around each side of her waist and lingering for a moment before dropping away.

"Ellie?" a familiar voice inquired.

Liam stepped aside and she came face-to-face with Brody Wilson. She groaned inwardly. As if getting caught kissing in public wasn't embarrassing enough, it had to be by someone she knew, someone who would tell his fiancée, Mary, who would tell Meg. Trying to salvage the situation, Ellie plastered a smile on her face, which was probably as red as the ketchup on the tables inside.

"This is, uh…a surprise." She turned toward Liam. "Have you two met?"

Brody juggled a large white paper bag into the other hand, then reached out to shake. "We met very briefly at Meg and Riley's wedding."

"Speaking of weddings, you must be the groom." Liam shook hands. "I met the bride a couple days ago."

"Yes, Mary mentioned that." Brody nodded, his assessing gaze darting between them.

"Are Mary and Elliott with you tonight?" Ellie glanced through the glass door to the restaurant.

"No. They're at home." He held up the bag. "I stopped to grab burgers on my way back from checking in on Kevin Thompson."

"Checking on Kevin?" Ellie touched Brody's arm. "Did something happen?"

Kevin Thompson was a local youth who could have headed down the wrong path if not for Loon Lake's caring residents. Ellie knew Riley and Meg had encouraged Kevin to stay in school, and Brody and Mary had boosted his self-confidence by having him interact with the kids at their summer camp for children in foster care.

The camp had been Mary's dream. When she and Brody became a couple, they'd started a nonprofit and made her dream a reality. Their farm on the edge of town was the perfect spot.

Brody nodded. "Yeah, he sprained his wrist yesterday."

"Oh, no. Wasn't he your helper for the carnival preparations?"

Brody sighed. "With Riley working on their house and picking up overtime hours, I hate to ask him, but I may have to if we're going to be ready on time."

Liam quirked an eyebrow at her. "What's this about a carnival?"

"I help out with a childhood cancer survivor group," Ellie said. "We counsel survivors and those going through treatment. Plus, every year we put on a carnival as a fun activity for the kids." She enjoyed giving back to a group that had been so helpful when she'd needed it. "We have as much fun as the kids and it's important for them to see they can get through sometimes grueling treatments and enjoy life."

"What sort of help do you need?" Liam asked Brody.

Brody stroked his chin with his free hand. "Mostly muscle and someone to assemble wooden booths. You good with a hammer?"

Liam bobbed his head once. "Sure. I'd be happy to help out."

The inner door opened and Brody stepped aside to let a couple pass through. "Ellie, why don't I give you a call later and we can make arrangements."

"That sounds good. You might want to get home before those burgers get cold or you'll be in trouble with Mary."

"Yeah, we don't want that." Brody laughed and winked.

Liam's hand found the small of Ellie's back as if magnetized. He licked his lips at the cherry taste that lingered on them. What had he been thinking, kissing her like that in public? Yeah, no thinking involved. Ellie's presence tended to scramble his thought process.

A hostess inside the restaurant greeted them and led them to a booth.

"Thank you for offering to help out with the carnival," Ellie said as she slid into the seat. "You're here working with Riley and now spending off-time working some more. Hardly seems fair."

He sat across from her. "Are you going to be there?"

"Yeah. I always help out," she said, and picked up the colorful menu.

Normally he'd run a mile from reminders of the disease that claimed his ma. Just thinking about cancer made his skin crawl, but he could man up and do this. For Ellie. "Then I'm in."

She gave him a big smile and flipped open the menu. Yeah, that smile was worth giving up a few hours to help some kids. He should regret the kiss but he didn't, couldn't regret something that felt so damn good. With that kiss, tonight felt more like a date, despite him being careful not to turn it into one.

He'd decided to keep things casual with Ellie because being in remission was no guarantee the cancer couldn't return. Nothing like wanting his cake and eating it, too, or in this case, wanting his Ellie and none of the burdens of a real relationship. How the hell was he going to make this work?

"Do you want to?"

Ellie's question brought him back with a jolt. Had he said any of that aloud? "Huh?"

She *tsk*ed. "I asked if you wanted to split an appetizer."

Before he could answer, someone called her name. Two men in EMT uniforms approached their booth. Liam frowned at the way they strutted over to Ellie's side. The tall one appeared to be around Ellie's age, while the shorter, dark-skinned one was older.

"Sorry, Ellie, we didn't mean to interrupt your date," said the older one.

She glanced over at Liam. "Oh, we're just—"

"On a date but it's no problem." What the hell prompted him to say that? He was still striving for control, for keeping his feelings casual. If they'd run into two of Ellie's female friends, would he have made the same claim? If he were a better man he'd know the answer. Since he didn't, that put him in the "not a better man" category.

"We're not staying, just picking up our supper, and noticed you in here while we were waiting," said the younger guy.

"I'm glad you came to say hi," Ellie said. "This is my friend Liam. Liam, this is Mike and Colton. As you can plainly see by their uniforms, they're EMTs. It just so happens Liam is a firefighter."

Liam shook hands with both men, applying a bit of pressure with the younger one, Colton, whose intense gaze had been on Ellie since they'd come over to the table. Yeah, more juvenile than a better man would behave, that's for sure.

"We missed you at the softball game last weekend," Colton said to Ellie, but gave Liam the once-over as he said it, as if Liam had prevented Ellie from playing.

Ellie rested her elbows on the table, lightly clasping her hands together. "Sorry I missed it. Did you win?"

"No. We got clobbered." Colton shook his head and scowled. "That's why we need you."

Mike backhanded his partner on the arm. "Looks like our order's up."

Colton nodded but didn't take his eyes off Ellie. "The cops challenged us to another game to raise money for a K-9 unit. You in?"

"Sure." Ellie smiled and nodded. "Give me a call when you get a time and place."

Liam bit down on the urge to tell the guy to get lost already. If Colton was interested, why hadn't *he* taken her to the new patio at Angelo's? *Pot? Kettle. You brought her here instead of trying to get reservations at Angelo's.*

"Some of the guys were talking about getting a bowling night together." Colton mimed holding a phone. "I'll give you call."

"Hey, man, you can't pick her up while she's on a date with someone else," Mike said, and attempted to pull his partner away from the table.

"Sheesh, I wasn't picking her up, just asking if she was interested in bowling. It's for charity," he grumbled, but turned back and grinned at Ellie. "See ya, Els."

Els? What the…? Liam ground his back teeth as the two EMTs walked away. "He was definitely trying to pick you up."

Ellie rolled her eyes. "Yeah, right. Colton called a couple months ago asking if I had the number of the new X-ray tech."

So this Colton was a player? Well, he could go play in someone else's sandbox. He and Ellie were…what? Hanging out to get Meg off their case did not a relationship make.

"Believe me, he was hitting on you," Liam insisted.

She glanced over at the two men leaving the restaurant.

"Maybe it didn't work out with the X-ray tech," Liam muttered, and shook the menu open with a snap.

"Maybe." She shrugged and set her menu down.

Did she have feelings for this Colton? He pretended to be interested in the menu's offerings. "That Mike guy—"

"Stop right there. You're not going to try to tell me he was hitting on me." She heaved a deep sigh. "Mike's happily married. He has a beautiful wife and two sweet daughters, all of whom he adores."

Before he could say anything more about either EMT, a petite waitress with a short blond bob and an eyebrow piercing came over to the table.

"Hi, I'm Ashley, and I'll be your server tonight," she said, and rested her hand on the table near his.

"I'll have a bacon cheeseburger and onion rings," Ellie told the waitress.

Ashley nodded and scribbled on her pad without taking her eyes off him. He echoed Ellie's order because he'd been too busy fending off her would-be suitor to read the menu.

"*Now* who is getting hit on?" Ellie said in a dry tone as she watched the perky blonde sashay across the room.

"Who? The waitress? She looks barely old enough to be serving drinks." He sipped his water. "And we were talking about you. Colton was definitely hitting on you."

She made a derisive sound blowing her breath through her lips. "I find that hard to believe."

He shook his head. Did she not know the effect she had on guys? That megawatt smile that made her eyes sparkle created a pull, one he couldn't deny. So why wouldn't any other guy feel the same? "What? Why would you say that?"

"Because guys don't see me like that. All they see is a shortstop for their softball team or a bowler for charity."

"I don't know who put that idea in your head, but it's simply not true. And I'm a guy, so I should know." Damn. Why did he say that? If she liked this Colton dude, saying things like that might give her ideas.

She snorted. "I don't see you putting the moves on me."

"What if I were to put a move on you?"

"Yeah, right," she sputtered, and shook her head.

He let it drop, but began calculating how many moves he could make in thirty days.

Chapter 3

Several times during the day on Friday, Liam considered excuses to get out of helping Ellie with her carnival. Last weekend had been the anniversary of his mother's death from stage 3 breast cancer that had spread. The years had muted the pain, but he wasn't looking forward to all the reminders because it also reminded him of his friend and mentor, Sean McMahan. During Liam's year as a probationary firefighter, Sean had taken him under his wing and they'd become close. Cancer had claimed Sean eighteen months after Bridget McBride. And yet he couldn't—wouldn't—let Ellie down, so that evening, he accompanied her to the church where they were setting up for the carnival. He'd insisted on giving her a ride when she mentioned meeting him there. Generosity didn't enter into his offer; ulterior motives did. He wanted to see if she'd planned on coming or going with that EMT Colton, but her eager acceptance of his offer reassured him.

Liam resisted reaching for Ellie's hand as they descended the stairs to the brightly lit basement. The place buzzed with the sounds of hammering, chatter and laughter. The scent of raw wood and paint permeated the air.

"I promised to paint some of the signs and to help Mary corral some of the younger kids. We're providing nursery services to our volunteers," Ellie said with a touch on his arm. "I'll talk to you later."

Brody waved Liam over and wasted no time putting him to work constructing a booth for one of the carnival games. Brody gave him a rough sketch of what it was supposed to look like. After helping with Meg and Riley's renovations, this would be a cinch.

As Liam got busy laying out the precut wood Brody had supplied, a towheaded boy of around ten came to stand next to him. The boy shuffled his feet but didn't speak.

Liam picked up the first pieces. "Hey, there, I'm Liam. What's your name?"

"Craig." The boy glanced at his paint-stained sneakers. "Are you Miss Ellie's fireman?"

The pencil in Liam's hand jumped and messed up the line he'd been marking. *Calm down. He's a kid asking a question, not making an observational statement.* "I'm a fireman."

The boy's gaze rested on Liam. "I always wanted to be one."

Liam's heart turned over at the look of wistfulness on the boy's face. Did this kid have cancer? Or was he one of the survivors? The boy's choice of words hadn't gone unnoticed. "Have you changed your mind about it?"

Craig shook his head. "Nah. But my mom gets a worried look on her face when I talk about becoming a fireman…like she wants me to pick something else. She's been like that ever since my cancer."

"You still have lots of time to decide what you want to be when you grow up." What the heck was he supposed to tell the kid? Liam glanced around but everyone was busy building or shooing young ones back into one of the side rooms being used as a nursery.

The boy shrugged. "Yeah, the doctors say I'm in remission, but my mom still worries."

Liam knew how the kid's mom felt. He worried about losing more people to cancer, including Ellie, but he couldn't say that to the boy. "Do you think you could help me get this put together? I could use the extra hands."

Craig's face lit up as he vigorously nodded his head. "I sure would."

"Okay." Liam handed him a peanut butter jar full of nails. "You can hand me the nails when I ask."

The kid looked disappointed so Liam rushed to explain. "That way, I don't have to stop and grab one each time. This will go a lot faster with your help. And I'll be happy to answer any questions you have about firefighting as we work."

Craig seemed to consider it. "I just wish my mom wouldn't get that scared look when I talk about being a fireman."

"Well, you're still a little young to join. Maybe by the time you're old enough, your mom will feel better about you becoming a firefighter."

"I hope so. Does your mom worry?"

Had Bridget McBride worried when he joined the fire department? If she had, she'd kept it hidden. Of course, following in his dad's footsteps may have made a difference. He honestly didn't know if she worried because she'd never said so. "She might have."

"My mom says it's dangerous." The boy pulled his mouth in on one side.

Liam put his hand out for a nail. "I won't lie and say it isn't, but that's why you attend the fire academy for rigorous training and learn all you can about the job before getting hired. Even after you get hired, you're on probation."

"Huh?"

Liam resisted the urge to ruffle Craig's hair. Chances are the kid would be insulted. "It means you're still learning from the older guys."

Craig carefully laid a nail on Liam's outstretched palm. "You gotta go to school to be a fireman?"

"You sure do. Lots to learn about fires and staying safe." He hammered the boards together. At least with firefighting you had training and were in control of the equipment. It wasn't as if you could train for cancer. And doctors and others were in charge of the equipment to fight it, leaving you helpless. "We do all that training so we know exactly what to do to make it less dangerous. I can talk to the crew here in Loon Lake and see about taking you on a tour of the fire station. Maybe see what it's like to sit in one of the rigs."

Craig pulled out another nail. "That would be awesome. Thanks."

Liam nodded. "Sure thing. I'll talk to some of the guys."

"Miss Ellie says you're in Boston." Craig scrunched up his face. "How come?"

Liam took the nail. "That where I live, and my dad and his dad before him were on the Boston Fire Department. That's why I joined up."

"My dad's a lawyer. Is your dad still a fireman?"

"No, he's retired." Even after several years, it still felt weird to say that. Liam always thought Mac would be one of those guys who stayed until they carried him out the door. Had his dad let Doris talk him into retirement? He liked his dad's new wife. It had been awkward at first, seeing him with someone other than his mom, but now he was glad they'd found happiness together.

"What about your mom? Can you ask her? Maybe she can talk to mine and tell her it's okay."

Liam shook his head and swallowed. "I'm afraid not, buddy. My mom died."

"Cancer?"

"Yeah."

The boy nodded, looking much older than he should have. "That's a—" He broke off and glanced around. "That sucks."

"It does." Liam bit back a laugh. What had the kid been about to say? He caught that because he'd had to watch his language around his niece, Fiona.

"But Miss Ellie says you can't live your life afraid because you had cancer or you wouldn't have a life."

Liam began cleaning up after Craig left. He'd have to track down some of the guys at the Loon Lake station and see if they could arrange something for Craig. Maybe even something for the boy's mom to set her mind at ease. Ellie had said how she'd had to fight her

parents' need to smother and hover even after she'd
been in remission for the golden five-year mark. Her
words, as repeated by Craig, kept coming back to him.
*You can't live your life afraid because you had cancer
or you wouldn't have a life.*

"I wanted to thank you for pitching in." A deep voice
behind him caught Liam's attention.

He turned to Brody Wilson. "Hey, man, no problem.
Glad to help."

Brody chuckled. "And earning Ellie's gratitude probably doesn't hurt, either."

Liam couldn't deny he liked putting that light in Ellie's golden eyes. "Looks like you have your hands full."
Liam tipped his chin toward the curly-haired toddler
chasing another boy around under Mary's watchful eye.
Earlier, Brody had been chasing after his active son.

"Yeah, Elliott's a handful. When he's not sleeping,
he's full speed ahead. He has no neutral." Brody's love
and pride were evident in his voice and the expression
on his face as he watched his son.

Liam knew from Ellie that Brody had adopted
Mary's young son from her previous relationship with
his half brother, Roger, who had wanted nothing to do
with the baby. Elliott may have been rejected by his
biological father, but Brody's love for the boy was obvious. "He's got lots of space to work off that energy.
Meg tells me you've got a lot going on out at your farm.
Some sort of camp for foster kids to come and enjoy
fresh air and animals."

Brody laughed. "Yeah, believe it or not, I had picked
that particular place thinking I wanted quiet and iso-
lation."

Liam didn't know much about Brody except what

he'd heard from Meg or Ellie. But the guy had been through some nasty stuff during his time in the army, so his wanting someplace to nurse wounds, even the unseen kind, was understandable. "Funny how that sometimes works. What happened?"

"Mary and Elliott happened." Brody's expression went all soft. "I know it sounds corny, but they made me want to do what I could to make this a better world."

Brody had that same look Riley got when he talked about Meg. Ha, maybe it was something in the Loon Lake water. "And so you started the camp?"

"Camp Life Launch started as Mary's idea, but I guess you could say I took it and ran with it. Some of the guys I served with in the army are pitching in and we've even talked about doing something for returning veterans who might want to help with the kids or simply be surrounded by nature. You'd be surprised how calming watching the night sky or a pair of alpacas snacking on carrots and enjoying the sunshine can be."

Liam nodded and an idea struck him. Something Craig had said. "Sounds like something these kids might benefit from, too. Ellie says it can be hard for them to just be children, even after the cancer is under control."

Brody wiped a hand over his mouth. "You might have something there. The older ones might even enjoy volunteering as counselors to younger ones, show 'em life-after-cancer stuff. Kevin and Danny, those two boys your sister and brother-in-law were helping out, have turned into a valuable resource helping with some of our youth campers. I'll definitely talk to Mary about it."

Just then, Brody's curly-haired boy toddled up to

Liam. "Alley-oop," he said, thrusting his arms up and balancing on his toes.

"Alley-oop?" Liam shook his head and looked to Brody for help.

Brody chuckled and ruffled his son's hair. "Sorry, big guy, I don't think Liam understands Elliott Speak."

The boy bounced on his toes. "Alley-oop, alley-oop."

Brody glanced at Liam and laughed. "He's saying 'Elliott, up.' He's asking you to pick him up."

"Oh, okay, that I can do." Liam bent down and picked up the smiling toddler. He settled Elliott on his hip. "Have you been trying to keep up with the other kids? I think James is more your speed since he's still new to this whole walking gig."

"Won't be long before James will be running around, too." Brody laughed as he leaned over and chucked his son's chin. "Mary and I have started discussing giving this guy a brother or sister. We've been immersed in getting Camp Life Launch going this past year but things are settling down."

"Alley Daddy." The boy bounced up and down in Liam's arms.

"Yeah, that's your dad." Liam hung on to the agile toddler. Warmth spread across his chest at the feel of the toddler's sturdy weight in his arms. Holding Elliott had him thinking of what it would be like to have his own family. "You want to go back to him now?"

Elliott gave Liam a grin and pointed. "Alley Daddy."

Liam handed him over to Brody and the toddler threw his arms around Brody's neck.

"Alley Daddy." The toddler rubbed his face on Brody's shirt.

"I sure am, big guy." Brody rubbed the boy's back and turned to Liam. "He hasn't mastered his name yet."

Liam laughed. "I just got Fiona to say Liam and now James is calling me Meem."

"Meg is practically glowing these days. I'm so glad to see her happily settled."

"Yeah, I guess Riley has been good for her."

"Well, I know Mary and Elliott are the best thing that's ever happened to me." Brody shook his head as if in wonderment. "And I have a feeling this camp will be, too. If you ever want to stop by, feel free. Although I can't promise we won't put you to work."

"I may just do that," Liam said. Brody had the same glow of happiness as Meg. Would he ever be so lucky as to find such contentment? An image of Ellie came to mind and even the specter of her cancer returning couldn't chase it away.

"Thanks again for all the help. You should come back on carnival night and see everyone enjoying all your hard work."

Brody strolled over to Mary, who waved to Liam. Brody said something to her and leaned down and gave her a kiss.

"Hey, I see you're fitting right in." Ellie came to stand next to him.

"Fitting in?"

"Talking to Craig. He's been wanting to meet you ever since I told him I knew a real live fireman." Ellie hooked her arm through his. "Of course I was referring to your dad, but I guess you'll do."

"Hey." He drew his brows together and scowled, but his lips twitched with the need to grin.

"Did he ask about the job?"

"Yeah. He said his mom was trying to talk him out of it, but he's kinda young for her to be worried already." Liam leaned down and filled his nose with her scent.

"Things change when kids get cancer, and his mom has had a tendency to hover since his diagnosis. Fire-fighting can be considered a dangerous job."

Sure, but unlike cancer, *he* was in charge. "Yeah, I told him about all the training and safety equipment. I'd love to try to set something up locally if he wanted to visit the firehouse."

"That's really sweet of you. Thanks." She squeezed his arm. "What were you and Brody talking about?"

"He was telling me about the summer camp they've set up at their farm. When he said they had youths who'd turned their lives around act as counselors, I suggested kids like Craig might be interested in something like that, too. Maybe even act as advisers or counselors to children still going through that."

Her eyes widened. "You did that?"

"Yeah, why?" He tried to shrug it off, but the fact that she seemed pleased made his stomach swoop like it had on the day he'd shed his probie status with the department.

"I think that's a great idea. Thanks so much for suggesting it to Brody." She gave him a strangely amused smile.

Warmth rose in his face. How could he have been so oblivious? "You've already suggested it to him?"

She patted his chest. "Doesn't mean it's not a great idea, and I appreciate you taking an interest."

He grunted. "Are you patronizing me?"

She looked genuinely hurt and he regretted his accusation.

"Absolutely not," she said before he could apologize. "Mary and Brody offered to give me a ride home so you won't have to go out of your way to take me back. Your sister's place is in the other direction."

"I brought you. I take you home," he said, and scowled.

"Okay." She checked her watch. "It's still early. How about if I make some popcorn and we watch a movie? That is, if…if you want to."

He draped an arm over her shoulder. "I'd love to."

Ellie tried to contain her excitement as Liam drove them to her place from the church. How was Liam supposed to see her as an adult if she acted and sounded like her teen self around him? She'd even been sitting on the steps to her place waiting for him when he picked her up. *Way to go*, she scolded herself. Except he'd said yes to popcorn and a movie. And now she probably had a big goofy grin on her face.

They pulled into her driveway and drove past a rambling log home more suited to *Architectural Digest* than Loon Lake. Although she hadn't been inside she knew the floor-to-ceiling windows in the back offered a breathtaking view of the lake. The motion-sensitive lights came on as Liam's truck approached the three-car garage where she rented the upstairs apartment. Despite living here for six months, she had yet to meet the absent owner of the impressive main house. Her rental was handled through a management company.

Liam pulled his truck next to her car. "Am I blocking anyone if I park here?"

"No. It's fine. The log home's owner is still absent."

He hopped out of his truck. "Who owns it?"

"That's the big Loon Lake mystery." She started up the stairs to her apartment. Partway up, she turned to him. "There's a rumor it belongs to Thayer Jones, that ex-hockey player who grew up here. But no one really knows. Even Tavie Whatley doesn't know for sure."

Liam laughed. "Then it really is a mystery."

Warmth flowed through her at his laugh. "Yeah, I didn't think it was possible to do anything in this town without Tavie knowing all the details."

Seventysomething Tavie Whatley ran Loon Lake General Store and much of the town from her perch behind the cash register. She and her husband, Ogle, were not only fixtures in the community but the force behind many of its charitable endeavors. Brody jokingly called Tavie Loon Lake's benevolent dictator.

She unlocked her door and they entered her small but efficient kitchen. She loved the light gray bottom cabinets, porcelain farmhouse-style sink and open shelving above a wooden countertop. A breakfast bar divided the kitchen from the living area. Off the living room was a short hall leading to her bedroom and the bathroom.

"I'd give you a tour, but this is really it—other than the bedroom…" She cleared her throat. Why did showing Liam her bedroom feel so awkward? Her bed was made and there wasn't a stuffed animal in sight: an adult bedroom. Huh, did she want to avoid reminders she was an adult and old enough to be sexually active? "How about some popcorn?"

"Sounds good. Need help?"

"Thanks. I got it covered." She handed him the remote. "You pick something while I get it." She pulled out her glass microwave popcorn maker, glancing at him sprawled on her sofa. *Don't get any ideas*, she cautioned herself. They were hanging out, sitting together and watching a movie. She set the microwave timer and looked over at him again. She swallowed. When had her couch gotten so small?

Liam was flipping through the movies on her paid streaming subscription. "What do you feel like watching?"

"How about that new action movie with what's-his-name?"

He turned his head to give her one of his sexy half grins. "Are you psychic? That's the one I've been wanting to see."

She laughed. "Just another example of my super-powers."

The timer on the microwave dinged and she removed the glass popper. She poured the popcorn in the bowl and salted it. Handing Liam the bowl, she plopped down next to him.

"How about this one?" He clicked on a movie selection. "It's got what's-his-name in it."

She tossed a popped kernel at him, but he caught it in his mouth and grinned as he chewed. He set the bowl on the coffee table and leaned closer.

She couldn't be sure who moved first, but their lips found each other in a sweet kiss that held the promise of more. All thoughts of movies and actors flew out of her head. He angled his face closer and she—

The music for the movie startled her and she abruptly pulled away. "Sorry."

"I'm not," he said, brushing her hair off her cheek and tucking it behind her ear.

He leaned back on the couch and pulled her into his side. She cuddled next to him and tried to concentrate on the movie, but it wasn't easy with his body warm against hers and his luscious scent surrounding her.

As the credits rolled he set the empty popcorn bowl on the end table next to the couch and picked up a book that had been on the table.

"This looks like a textbook."

"Yeah, working on my advanced nursing degree."

He nodded. "So you can finally move away from Loon Lake?"

"What? Absolutely not." She wasn't about to abandon the people who'd been there for her and her family when they'd needed it. "I like living in Loon Lake."

He flipped through some of the pages. "Will you be able to use the new degree at the hospital?"

"I suppose I could, but they'll be breaking ground soon on a skilled nursing facility and I'm hoping to work as a nurse practitioner there. If I time it right, I will have my gerontology degree when they finish construction."

"Skilled nursing facility?"

Ellie grinned. "A nursing home."

"Is that nurse speak?" he asked and wiggled his eyebrows.

She rolled her eyes. "C'mon, you're not turned on by nurse speak, are you?"

"Only if you're the one speaking it." He put the book back and settled against the cushions. "Sounds like you have it planned out."

"I want to help the people I've grown up with. Give back to a community that gave so much to me. I haven't forgotten how everyone rallied around when I was sick." Damn. She hadn't meant to bring up the past like that. She glanced at him out of the corner of her eye.

When he didn't comment but put an arm around her shoulder, she relaxed against him. "What about you? I heard you're determined to follow in your dad's footsteps at the fire department."

He nodded. "That's the plan. I should hear if I made captain soon. My dad was one of the youngest captains and I'm hoping to follow suit."

"So we haven't convinced you yet that Loon Lake is a great place to live?" She tried to keep her tone light, but she needed to hear him say it so maybe her stupid heart would get the message.

"Are you kidding?" He shook his head as he toyed with her hair. "The Loon Lake firehouse is part time. If not for guys who are willing to work in the department on their days off from full-time jobs, Loon Lake FD would be an all-volunteer one."

"And that's bad why?" Her body tensed on behalf of the guys she knew who worked for the town.

"It's not bad. It's how most small towns are able to afford full-time protection," he said. "But it's not what I want."

She swallowed. Yeah, that's what she thought. Riley Cooper and Brody Wilson might have embraced small-town life, but Liam evidently didn't feel like he could do the same.

Chapter 4

Liam turned off his truck and grabbed a pizza box off the passenger seat before climbing out. It had been three days since he'd helped with her carnival. He glanced up at a curtain blowing in an open window in the upstairs apartment and inhaled a deep, satisfied breath. Ellie was in there.

Ellie had texted to thank him for arranging for Craig's visit to the firehouse in Loon Lake. When he replied, he'd suggested supper and she'd offered to cook for him. He'd responded that he knew she'd been on her feet all day in the ER and offered to bring pizza.

He was halfway up the stairs when her door opened and she stood silhouetted in the doorway. As if she'd been waiting for him, as if she'd been as eager to see him.

Don't make this more than it is, he cautioned himself. They were simply friends hanging out. Nothing more.

"Hey, there," she said, and grinned.

Dressed in a T-shirt and shorts that showcased her long, slender legs, she got his blood pumping.

He reached the small landing at the top of the stairs. She was barefoot and for some reason that had him struggling to drag in air. Who knew bare feet were sexy? To him, they'd previously only been necessary for walking. He stood mute in front of her, thinking about her purple-painted toenails until her welcoming smile slipped and her brows gathered into a frown.

Mentally kicking himself, he forced words past his dry lips. "Hey, yourself."

Yeah, a real smooth talker, McBride.

She held out her hands for the box. He passed it over but didn't let go of his end. Tugging the cardboard toward him brought her closer. He leaned over and gently brushed his lips against hers. After thinking about her all day, he couldn't resist and the kiss couldn't get out of hand with the box between them. He had this whole situation under control.

She sucked in air when they pulled apart. "Wha-what was that for?"

Yeah, what was that for? "It was meant as a greeting between two friends."

Something passed over her face, something he couldn't interpret and only noticed because he'd been staring at her.

"Well then, c'mon in...friend." She took the pizza and went inside.

He wiped his feet on her welcome mat before entering the kitchen. She set the pizza on the counter next to a bottle of wine and stood on her toes to reach up to grab plates from the open shelving. Her T-shirt rode up and revealed a swath of creamy skin above her butt. He picked up the bottle of wine to keep from reaching out and running his fingers along that exposed skin to see if it was as soft and smooth as it looked.

"I have beer in the fridge. If you prefer that over wine." She came down flat on her feet and tilted her head toward the stainless steel refrigerator.

"Thanks. I prefer beer." He forced himself to look away.

She set the plates on the counter and pulled her shirt back down. "A cheap date. Nice to know."

"Me, cheap?" He picked up the wine again. "Ellie, this is two-buck Chuck."

"But it was such a good month." She set napkins on the plates.

He bumped shoulders. "We talkin' last month?"

"Pfft. And you're such a connoisseur?" She pushed back.

"Hey, I've been down the wine aisle at Whole Foods."

When she rolled her eyes, he leaned down and gave her a quick kiss on the end of her nose.

"Wha-what was that one for?"

"For being so impertinent." He licked his lips before continuing. "Now that we've gotten that out of the way, let's eat. I'm starved."

To hide the color he was certain had blossomed on his cheeks, he buried his head in her refrigerator and pretended to look for the beer. He grabbed a longneck bottle.

"Yes, um…well…" She cleared her throat. "The breakfast bar or the couch? Your choice."

"Is this like Angelo's, where I can pick inside or patio dining?" What was that kiss all about? He twisted the cap off his beer and tossed the top into her recycling bin. This was Ellie and they were hanging out. He wasn't supposed to be thinking about her exposed skin or those tiny freckles or how shiny her hair looked. Or how he wanted to keep on kissing her until she was breathless.

"Exactly like Angelo's…if you don't count the lack of fairy lights, table service or cannoli." She nodded her head several times. "Couch or kitchen?"

"Couch sounds okay. That's what I do at home." He picked up the box and she trailed behind with the plates and napkins. "And what's this no-cannoli business?"

She set the stuff on the coffee table and snapped her fingers. "Actually, I do have some. Let me take them out of the freezer so they can defrost while we eat the pizza."

He set the box down next to the plates. "Frozen cannoli?"

She huffed out a breath. "Really? You gonna be a cannoli snob, too?"

He lifted his hands up as if surrendering, the beer dangling from his fingers. "I'll allow it since you haven't had Mike's."

"Mike's?" She went back to the kitchen area and took the cannoli out of the freezer, setting the package on the counter with a *clunk*.

"It's a bakery in the North End of Boston and totally worth fighting wicked traffic to get there." He took a sip of beer and set the bottle down. "I'll bring you some real cannoli the next time I come back."

"Thanks, but in the meantime we'll have to make do with Trader Joe's." She came back and sat on the couch.

He lowered himself onto the cushion next to her, close but not enough to crowd her. Or to tempt him into doing something he might regret. But she'd been into that vestibule kiss, his inner voice reminded him.

She flipped open the cover on the pizza, filling the room with the scent of fresh dough and pepperoni. Grabbing a plate, she set a slice on it and handed it to him.

"And you said there wouldn't be any table service," he said as he folded the piece in half and took a bite.

"I haven't had a chance to talk to Craig, but I hear he was on cloud nine after his visit to the fire station. Thank you again for arranging it."

"Happy to do it." Especially since it had given him another excuse to hang out with Ellie. He set his plate down. "Almost forgot. Craig made me promise to show this to you."

He pulled his phone out of a pocket and thumbed through his pictures until he came to the one of the youngster fitted out in bunker gear and handed it to her.

"Will you look at that. How did you manage this?"

He shrugged, but he loved making her eyes shine like a freshly polished fire engine. "I remembered the guys talking about another house getting their hands on reasonably authentic bunker gear in miniature for a Make-A-Wish recipient. I contacted the firehouse that arranged it and they put me in touch with the people they'd used."

She leaned over and kissed his cheek. "Thank you."

"Sure. My pleasure. He seemed like a nice kid." Damn but he wanted to turn his head so his lips were on hers.

She took another slice and put it on her plate but left it on the low table in front of them.

"Where'd the remote go? I always keep it here on the

coffee table." She pointed to the exact spot where it had been until he'd picked it up.

"Were you referring to this?" He held up the remote, trying not to laugh at her expression.

She tried to grab it, but he managed to keep it out of reach. Her shirt pulled up when she lifted her arm, exposing her stomach. Once again, his body tightened at the sight. He did his best to temper his reaction. If he wasn't careful, she'd know *exactly* what she was doing to him.

"I just want to see what's on your watch list," he told her, pointing the remote and chuckling, hoping to cool his rioting hormones. "Let's see what we've got here. Wait a sec, what's all this sappy romance— Oomfff."

She'd blindsided him by making a dive for the remote, but he reacted by pulling it farther out of reach, and she landed across his lap and chest. She struggled to sit up but he put his arm around her, trapping her where she was. Her honey eyes darkened as he lowered his head. He felt her tense, but then she melted against him once his lips touched hers. Her lips tasted like cherry. He kissed his way across her jawline, nipped her earlobe and touched his tongue to the spot where her neck and shoulder met.

Suddenly, "Bohemian Rhapsody" began blaring from the kitchen.

He lifted his head. "What the…?"

"My phone," she said in a breathless tone.

He pulled away, feeling equal measures of relief and annoyance. What was he doing messing with Ellie? She was Meg's friend…*his* friend. *Way to screw up friendships, dumbass.*

The air in the room suddenly felt thick. It was hard

to breathe, as if the oxygen had been vacuumed out. The phone continued to blast the unmistakable tune.

He managed to suck in some air. "Going with a classic?"

That was so not what he'd wanted to say, but the things he wanted to say were probably best left unsaid.

"It's a classic for a reason," she shot back, using her hands and elbow to scramble off his lap. Thankfully that elbow missed his important bits.

He shifted and adjusted his jeans. *That was a close call...*

Ellie went into the kitchen, arguing with herself whether the interruption was a good thing. It wasn't as if she'd ever aspired to be a booty call. And he'd pulled back in a hurry, so maybe it had been a good thing that he'd gotten freaked out. She grabbed her phone and checked the caller ID. Craig's mom. Was she calling to thank her for introducing her son to Liam? Talk about irony.

Ellie listened to the woman on the other end, but her gaze and her attention was on Liam, whose attention was on the television. Had he, like her, gotten caught up in the moment?

After accepting the gratitude and telling her she'd pass that on to Liam, Ellie disconnected the call. She tugged on the hem of her T-shirt and went back into the living area.

"That was Craig's mom. She said she can't thank you enough for arranging everything for him. The kid-sized bunker gear was the icing on the cake. She said she's having trouble getting him to take it off." She picked up her plate and sank back against the cushions. "We should finish the pizza before it gets cold."

He cleared his throat and picked up the remote again. "I see you've got *Seinfeld* on your list. Wanna watch some of those episodes?"

"Sounds like a plan. Have—have you ever seen the show?"

"No, but I've heard a lot about it. Another classic for a reason?"

"Probably." Were they going to ignore what happened? "Do we need to...uh, talk about..."

When he frowned, she waved her hand back and forth between them.

He sat forward a little, resting his elbows on his knees. "Do *you* need to?"

She shrugged. Did she want to discuss it or ignore it?

He straightened up and touched her shoulder. "This wasn't a booty call, if that's what you're worried about."

Worried or hoping? She huffed out a laugh. "If it was, it would've been a first."

"C'mere." He pulled her next to him and draped an arm over her shoulder. "Let's see what this show is all about."

"Sounds like a plan." She smiled and snuggled against him. "Catching up on our pop culture knowledge. There's talk about Hennen's starting a trivia night."

"We'll be an unstoppable force."

She liked the way he used "we" so casually. Tonight might be eating pizza and cannoli while watching classic television, but she would cherish this time spent with Liam. It wasn't what they were doing but being together that mattered.

When the episode ended, he turned his head. "Is there a path to the lake?"

"Yes, and not only a nice path, there's a small gazebo with a swing. I sometimes go down there in the evenings to unwind. Letting nature surround me is calming."

He rubbed his chin. "Yeah, that's what I was thinking...a nice night to be surrounded by...uh, nature."

She bumped his shoulder. "You are so full of it."

"Is it working?" He wiggled his eyebrows.

She heaved a sigh, but she loved that the awkwardness after the kiss had dissolved. "Let me get my shoes on and grab a sweater."

"A sweater? Ellie, it's August."

"For your information, I don't have the same amount of body mass that you do to keep me warm and sometimes it gets cool down by the water...even in August."

"Then go bundle up." He tilted his head toward the mess on the coffee table. "I'll pick this stuff up and put the leftovers in the refrigerator."

"A sweater is not bundling up," she muttered as she scooted off the couch but turned back. "Thanks for cleaning up."

In the bedroom, she pulled on her sneakers and grabbed a cardigan sweater from her bureau drawer.

"Do you have your key?" He touched her arm as she started to pull the door shut.

"We're only going down to the lake."

"But it's—"

"Loon Lake," she interrupted.

He gave her a look. "Please tell me you don't do this when you're alone."

"I don't usually go alone to the lake after dark. I love

listening to the loons, but if I open my windows I can hear them from the safety of my bedroom since those windows face the lake."

Landscape lights lit the crushed shell path and the dog-day cicadas serenaded them from the surrounding trees.

"Meg loves listening to the loons at night as they settle in and call for their mates to join them," Ellie said as they made their way toward the water.

"Yeah, my mom was the same. She used to drag us kids down to the water's edge in the evenings."

Ellie reached for his hand and squeezed. "I know you both miss her."

When she would have pulled her hand away, he held on.

"Yeah, as a kid I grumbled when she insisted on boring stuff like walks to the lake to stand around and listen. She said we were making memories and that someday I would understand. I would give anything now to tell her I understand." He sighed. "I never told her."

"I don't think your mother expected you to thank her, Liam. She probably didn't thank hers, either. But she passed on that experience by giving you a happy, secure childhood. Just as you'll do for your kids."

"Pfft. I know I disappointed her by choosing the fire academy over college."

"I'm sure she wanted you happy in your career." Her heart went out to him, reacting to the sadness in his tone. How could he not know this?

When he made a disparaging sound, she stopped and turned toward him. Most of his face was in the shadows but she didn't need to see his expression to feel his skepticism. "It's true. She told my mom how proud she was of how much you helped with Meg and Fiona."

He shrugged. "It isn't hard to love Fiona."

"But you put your life on hold to help out so Meg could finish her degree." She longed to make him understand, wipe away the self-reproach she heard in his voice.

"Put my life on hold?" He huffed out a mirthless laugh. "All I did was move out of a sparsely furnished apartment to move back home. Not exactly a big sacrifice."

"You did it to help. That meant a lot."

"When Meg finally confessed about the pregnancy, my mom had it all worked out that she'd babysit while Meg finished college. But then Ma got sick and Meg was ready to drop out. I couldn't let that happen. Mom had already been disappointed when I joined the department before completing my degree."

"So why can't you believe how proud she was of you for doing that for your sister?" Her hand still in his, she tugged on his arm.

He sighed. "It's not so much believing as wishing I had done more for her."

"As someone who has had cancer, take it from me—it eased her mind about Meg and Fiona. That means a lot."

"Yeah?"

"Yeah."

They came to the small gazebo and sat side by side on the wooden swing that hung from the rafters of the ceiling. He still had her hand in his. Using his feet, he set the swing in motion.

"You have a sweet deal here. How did you find out about the apartment?" he asked.

"I was on duty when an estate agent passed through the ER. He heard me talking with some of the other nurses about trying to find a rental apartment. He gave me his card and said to call him. At first I thought it might be a scam but Meg and Riley came with me to check it out. Other than being a bit farther out of town than I'd like, it's perfect."

He glanced around. "It's quiet. Has the owner ever shown up?"

"Not yet. They were still doing the interior work on the main house when I moved in. So it honestly hasn't been completed for all that long."

"Have you been inside?"

"Before they finished up, some of the workmen let me take a tour."

"Do you think you'll stay here for a while?"

"For now, yeah. When I was growing up we lived next door to my cousins and I loved it. Especially as an only child, it was nice to have playmates. My cousins and I are still very close today. If I ever get married and have kids, I'd love to live close to family, let our kids grow up together." She left out the part of dreaming about living with him and a couple of kids next door to Meg.

Jeez, live in your head much? No wonder you don't have an active dating life.

"If?" He turned to look at her. "What's this 'if' business? You planning to dedicate yourself to your career?"

"No. I'd love to get married, but first someone has to ask me, and I'm still not convinced I'll be able to get pregnant." She hated to admit it, but that fact alone sometimes held her back. What if she met a nice guy who wanted kids and she wasn't able to give him that?

"Because of the cancer?"

"Because of the treatments but yeah…because of the cancer. The doctors say it's possible, but possible and probable are two different things."

"Then I hope it happens if that's what you want."

"I've learned not to dwell on things out of my control." She shrugged. "Besides, there's other ways. Since becoming friends with Mary, I've given a lot of thought to fostering or at least helping out with their summer camp once they get the cancer survivors part going."

"Yeah, that seems like a worthwhile project. Whoever thought that up must be a genius."

She laughed. "I thought so, too."

Chapter 5

"Hey, Els, got any plans for tonight?"

The day after sharing pizza with Liam, Ellie had been on her way out of the hospital after her shift, but turned as Colton caught up to her. He and Mike had brought in a suspected heart attack just as her shift ended. Luckily, her replacement was already on duty for the night and she was able to leave.

She raised her brow. "Why? Did you lose the X-ray tech's phone number?"

"Aw, c'mon, you're not holding that against me, are you?" He stopped in front of her with a sheepish grin.

"No, but aren't you working?" she asked. Colton was a great-looking guy. One most women would be happy to date. But he had one big flaw. He wasn't Liam.

"My shift ends in an hour. Maybe we could—"

He was interrupted by "Bohemian Rhapsody." For

once, she didn't mind the interruption when she saw her caller was Liam.

"Sorry." Ellie pulled the phone from the front pocket of her purse. "Excuse me but I need to get this."

She had a pang of guilt but reminded herself that Colton had asked her for another woman's phone number. "Hey."

"Glad I caught you. Have you left the hospital yet?"

"No. Is there something wrong?"

"Nothing wrong. I simply hoped to catch you before you got all the way home. My dad and Doris arrived this afternoon and we're having an impromptu family cookout. Whaddaya say, Ellie, will you come?"

"But if it's family…" She was acutely aware of Colton watching her.

"You're family. Just say yes. You know you want to."

She clutched the phone tighter. Of course she wanted to say yes, but feared she was opening herself to more heartache. She glanced down at her scrubs. They were clean but they were still scrubs. "I'm not dressed for—"

"Did I mention it's a cookout?"

Could she pass up spending time with Liam? "Okay. What can I bring?"

"Just your cute self."

Colton's radio squawked and he held up his hands as if in surrender. "Gotta run. Catch you later."

Ellie waved as the EMT trotted away.

"Who's that with you?" Liam asked.

"Colton."

"The EMT?"

She nodded, then realized Liam couldn't see her. "Yeah, they brought in a patient as my shift was ending."

"So I'll see you in a bit?"

"I'm on my way."

Liam pocketed his phone and walked across the yard to his sister's place. He glanced at his watch. How long would it take for Ellie to get here from the hospital? What if Colton distracted her? He stumbled over a small exposed root in Meg's yard.

Meg glanced up from putting condiments, utensils and plates on the picnic table. "Is Ellie coming?"

"Yeah. She was just leaving the hospital." He shoved his hands in his jeans.

Inviting Ellie had been Meg's idea. That's right. All Meg's idea. He had this thing with Ellie under control. Although she didn't say anything, Meg had a smug smile on her face.

Yeah, the joke was on her because he and Ellie were just hanging out, throwing her off the scent. "Got any cold beer, sis?"

Meg tilted her head toward the house. "In the refrigerator. Get me one while you're at it and don't shake it."

He rolled his eyes. "I'm not twelve."

She rolled her eyes right back at him. "No, you just act like it."

"Yeah, yeah. Keep it up and you can fetch your own beer."

"And you can get in your truck and drive to the store and get your own." She planted her hands on her hips.

A screen door banged shut.

Mac McBride stood on the porch, arms folded over his chest. "Exactly how old are you two?"

"She started it."

"He started it."

Doris emerged from the house and stopped beside Mac, who put his arm around her.

The looks they gave each other seemed to say broken hearts did mend. Liam shook his head at the thought. Avoiding all that pain in the first place sounded like a better course of action.

His dad's new wife—he had trouble thinking of Doris as a stepmother—had been a widow who'd lost both her husband and only child to a drunk driver. And yet she'd found happiness again with his dad, and showered Fiona and James with as much grandmotherly love as his own mother would have. For that, and for his sister's sake, he was glad his dad and Doris had taken another chance. Since Mac's retirement, they'd purchased a Class A motor home and spent months at a time traveling.

Doris handed James's baby monitor to Meg. "He's sound asleep. Since he had supper he may sleep through the night at this point."

"Thanks for helping." Meg hugged Doris.

"My pleasure. I need to finish my pasta salad. Want to help?" Doris turned to Mac.

"I'd love to help." Mac grinned. Turning to his kids, he scowled. "Can I count on you two to behave?"

"Tell him that."

"Tell her that."

Doris slipped her hand in Mac's. "Let's get while the getting is good."

After they'd gone into their motor home, which they had parked in the side yard, Meg set the baby monitor on the picnic table and sat down on the bench. "Whaddaya think? Don't come a-knockin' if this van's a-rockin'."

"Eww." Liam shuddered. That was one picture he didn't want in his head.

"You're welcome." Meg gave him a toothy grin. "Hey, I thought you were getting a beer."

"I—" He stopped as a Subaru pulled into the long driveway. "Ellie's here."

Instead of going into the house, he swerved and headed toward where Ellie was parking her car. Meg snorted a laugh and Liam slowed his steps. He was greeting a friend, that's all, like he might greet Nick Morretti, the engineer driver on his shift, or any one of the other guys. *And when was the last time you wanted to plant a kiss on Nick?*

He opened Ellie's car door. "Hey. Glad you could come."

"Thanks." She swung her legs out and stood.

Reaching down, he took Ellie's hand as she stepped out. He looked up in time to see Meg's smirk. Canting his head to one side, he crossed his eyes at her. Meg responded by sticking out her tongue.

"That your dad's?" Ellie pointed to the motor home parked off to the side.

"Yeah, that's Matilda."

"He named it?" She laughed. "I love it."

He could listen to that laugh for the rest of his life. He took a step back and cleared his throat. Where did that come from? They were hanging out while he was in Loon Lake. Friends. Period.

Meg wandered over. "Ellie, glad you could come. My brother was just getting us beers. Would you like one?"

He winked at Ellie. "Or how about some cheap wine?"

"Hey." Meg shook her head. "Have you no manners?"

Ellie laughed. "It's okay. It's an inside joke."

Liam frowned. *Inside joke*. Isn't that what couples shared?

Friends could share them, too, he assured himself.

Ellie turned around as tires crunched on the gravel. A county sheriff's vehicle drove up and parked behind her Subaru. She waved to Riley, who flashed the emergency vehicle lights in response.

"You didn't tell me the cops were hot on your tail." Liam draped an arm over her shoulder as they walked toward the picnic table. "You led them right to us."

Ellie grinned. "Hmm…maybe Riley came up with a few more felons for me to date."

"Am I ever going to live that down?" Meg groaned and walked past them, heading toward Riley.

"What have I missed here?" Liam demanded, his gaze bouncing between Ellie and Meg.

Meg turned back, shaking her head. "It's nothing. All a misunderstanding."

"Just before you showed up at the church luncheon, Meg was trying to fix me up with some guy Riley arrested," Ellie told him. "She seemed to think he'd make a great date for Mary's wedding."

Liam scowled. "What? Why would—"

"Like she said, a misunderstanding," Ellie said, and explained what they were talking about.

Riley had gotten out of the car and Meg threw her arms around his neck and kissed him.

"Guys. Could you save that, please? You have company." Liam waved his arms as if directing airliners to the gate.

Ellie shook her head. The man had no clue how fortunate he was to have a family so openly affectionate. Even her aunts, uncles and cousins were more subdued in her parents' company, perhaps because they remembered how much things had changed during the cancer treatments, especially when her future had been uncertain.

Riley glanced around. "Where is everyone? I was led to believe we were having a big family get-together."

Riley kept his arm around Meg's waist as they strolled over to stand next to the picnic table. Riley grabbed some chips out of the bag Meg had brought out earlier.

"James is napping after having a meltdown and your daughter has another—" Meg checked her watch "—five minutes of house arrest."

"Uh-oh." Riley grimaced. "Would I be wrong if I assumed those two things are related?"

"And now for the *Reader's Digest* version." Meg grabbed the last chip in Riley's hand. "Fiona yelled at James because he threw her brand-new Barbie into the toilet when she left the lid up. James lost his balance and fell on his butt, but I think the tears were because his beloved big sister was mad at him."

Riley winced as he reached into the bag for another handful of chips. "Please tell me he didn't flush."

"Thankfully, no. We sent in G.I. Joe to do a water rescue." Meg giggled and turned to Liam and Ellie. "See all the fun you guys are missing out on?"

Liam took a seat on the picnic bench. "I'm sure if Ellie and I were in charge, we'd have it all under control, sis."

Meg rolled her eyes. "You are so clueless, brother dear. Right, Ellie?"

Ellie smiled and nodded. What would it be like to be a permanent member of this affectionate family? She sat on the bench next to Liam. She had to keep reminding herself they were hanging out so Meg wouldn't continue her matchmaking.

"Hey, two against one." Liam gently squeezed Ellie's shoulder. "Riley, some help here."

"Don't look at me." Riley held his hands up in surrender and leaned over to kiss Meg again.

"Jeez, guys, please." Liam brought his open palm toward his face and turned his head.

Riley laughed, giving Meg a noisy, smacking kiss. "Where are Mac and Doris?"

"They're in the motor home. Preparing the pasta salad." Meg made air quotes as she said it.

Liam groaned and buried his head in his hands, his elbows on the picnic table. Riley snorted with laughter.

"What's so funny?" Ellie asked.

"Ever since catching his dad doing the morning-after walk of shame, Liam doesn't like thinking about what his dad and Doris might really be doing." Riley clapped Liam on his shoulder.

Liam lifted his head, giving Meg an accusing look. "You told him."

"Of course. He's my husband." Meg put her arm through Riley's.

"Well, no one's told me." Ellie tugged on Liam's arm.

Liam shot Meg a you're-so-gonna-pay-for-this look. "It was after I'd moved to my Dorchester place. Meg was still living with Dad and had asked to borrow something. I don't even remember now what she wanted— that's probably my attempt to block the whole incident from my memory. Anyway, I stopped by wicked early one morning before my shift to drop it off. I was in the kitchen when Dad was letting himself in the back door wearing the previous day's clothes and looking way too satisfied for my peace of mind."

Liam closed his eyes and shook his head. Ellie laughed, enjoying spending time with the McBrides and being reminded some families laughed and teased and loved openly. Her parents were still subdued, as if joking around and having fun was asking for trouble. They might not have always been as boisterous as some families, but enough that she missed the love and laughter when they disappeared.

Riley gave his shoulder a push. "Think of it this way, McBride—Mac's still got it at his age."

Liam looked appalled. "Why would I want to think about that?"

"Face it. We're gonna be that age someday." Riley leaned down and kissed Meg's forehead. "I need to change out of this uniform."

"Is Fiona allowed out of jail?" Riley asked on his way into the house.

"Yes, tell her she can come out but Mangy needs to stay in the house or he'll be pestering us while we eat."

"You left the dog with her?" Riley shook his head. "Not much of a punishment if she got to keep her dog with her."

Meg shrugged. "I felt bad about her new doll."

"Was it ruined?" Riley frowned.

"No, but now it's tainted. Forever destined to be Toilet Barbie."

Mac and Doris came out of the motor home and crossed the yard. Doris set a large covered Tupperware container on the picnic table.

"Ellie, I'm so glad you were able to join us," Doris said, and gave her a motherly hug.

Ellie returned the hug. "Thanks for including me."

"Of course, dear, why wouldn't we?"

Ellie caught Liam's frown in her peripheral vision. Had including her been Meg's doing? She needed to be careful, or she would find herself with a one-way ticket to Heartbreak Ridge.

Chapter 6

Ellie checked her watch. Liam would be arriving soon to pick her up for Brody and Mary's wedding. She'd spoken to him several times over the phone in the week since the family cookout, but they'd both been too busy working to get together. At least that was the excuse he'd used, and she'd accepted it.

A car door slammed and Ellie contorted herself into another unnatural position but still no luck. That damn zipper was unreachable, despite all her valiant efforts. Footsteps on the stairs signaled that Liam was getting closer. No getting around asking for his help. Sighing, she opened the door and stepped onto the landing.

Liam looked up and paused partway up the stairs, mouth open and feet on different steps. He wore a deep charcoal suit, white shirt and royal blue tie. She couldn't decide which was sexier—Liam in a suit and tie or Liam in his red suspenders and turnout pants. *How about Liam in nothing at all?* a little voice asked, but she quickly pushed that away.

With all the excess saliva, Ellie had to swallow twice to keep from drooling. "Liam…" Was that breathless croak coming from her?

"Wow, look at you." He shook his head and continued up the stairs.

She'd splurged on a cream-colored dress with a scoop neck, gathered waist and sheer organza overlay from the waist down. The bright blue embroidered flowers on the dress made a bold statement, but the royal blue peep-toe platform high heels screamed *sexy*.

He came to a halt in front of her. "Are you sure we need to go to this wedding?"

"Why do you think I bought this dress and these shoes?"

"To impress me?" His tone was hopeful.

You better know it. "Ha! You wish. Come in."

"Oh, I wish for a lot of things. Want to hear some of them?" His mouth quirked up on one side.

"I'd love nothing better, but I don't want to be late for Mary's wedding." She did her best to keep her tone light and teasing as she stepped back inside. "However, I do need a favor from you."

Once they were inside her kitchen, she pulled her hair over her shoulder on one side and presented him with her back. "Can you zip this up the rest of the way?"

He made a noise that sounded like it was part groan, part growl.

She glanced over her shoulder. "Problem?"

He shook his head and swallowed, his Adam's apple prominent. "I'm just not used to having wishes granted so quickly."

A low, pleasant hum warmed her blood. "Helping me zip up was on your list?"

He snapped his fingers and made a face. "That's right. You said 'up.' Every time you say 'up,' I hear 'down' in my head for some reason."

"And what is this? Opposite day?" Thinking about his easing her zipper down gave her sharp palpitations.

"A guy can hope." His fingers caressed the skin exposed by the gaping zipper.

She drew in her breath. Was she going to do this? "Of course, I will need help *after* the wedding."

His light blue eyes darkened and glinted. "Anytime you need help getting undressed I'm your man."

"Good to know." She cleared her throat. "Now could you zip me up? *U-P.* Up."

He complied and rearranged her hair, pressing a finger to a spot near her collarbone. "You have a freckle right there."

"I do?" She'd always disliked her freckles, but it didn't sound as if Liam felt the same.

She turned her head toward him as he leaned over her shoulder. He cupped her chin to angle her face closer and kissed her. The kiss was hot and yet sweet, full of unspoken promises, a combination that had her blinking back tears of happiness.

Though neither one mentioned the kiss during the ride to the church, Ellie couldn't help replaying it. After the simple wedding ceremony, they drove to the far end of the lake in Ellie's Subaru for the reception, so she wouldn't have to climb into his truck in her dress and heels.

"This place is gorgeous," Ellie remarked as she and Liam walked across the parking lot toward the covered outdoor pavilion overlooking the lake. Flickering chandeliers hung from the A-frame log ceiling, and the tables, draped in white cloths, had flower centerpieces surrounded by votive candles.

"Is this what you would call romantic?" Liam had his palm planted firmly on the small of her back as they entered the venue.

She laughed and looked up at him. "Yes. Brody said he wanted Mary to feel like a fairy princess on her wedding day."

He gave a low whistle. "You're telling me Brody planned all this?"

"What? You don't think guys can be romantic?" She enjoyed teasing him, especially when he took the bait. "That's like the ultimate aphrodisiac to a woman. She'll pick the romantic guy every time."

He scratched his scalp. "Huh…"

"Relax." She grinned. "Brody came to Meg and me, and we suggested trolling Pinterest for ideas and put him in touch with people who could make it happen."

"Who knew you could be such a tease?" His mouth crooked at the corner.

"It's the shoes." She angled her foot from one side to the other.

"Are they imbued with special powers?" His eyes glinted as he admired her heels.

"They must be because they're holding your interest."

"You've always held my interest, Ellie."

Ellie wanted to believe him, but thinking like that was going to get her heart broken for sure. They were just joking around talking like that. Weren't they?

"Hey, wait up, you two," Meg called as she and Riley crossed the parking lot toward them.

Ellie let go of their conversation as they fell into step with the other couple and entered the wedding reception. During the meal, Ellie did her best to ignore Meg's calculating grin every time she looked at them.

When the music started, Liam held out his hand and invited her to dance. Having him hold her as they danced was even better than she imagined…and she'd done copious amounts of imagining over the years. Her current fantasies regarding Liam were very adult.

"What you said back at your place…" he began, and tightened his hold on her as they swayed to the music, "about needing help getting undressed…"

"Whoa." Even with the shoes he was taller and she had to look up to meet his gaze. "When did unzipping my dress turn into undressing me?"

He wiggled his eyebrows. "Huh, I guess my brain was connecting the dots."

"It was connecting something, all right," she said, but cuddled closer to him until they were barely moving.

"Ellie?" he whispered, his breath tickling her ear. "You need to know I'll only be here for another week, maybe less. Riley and I are almost finished with the reno."

"I always knew you weren't staying in Loon Lake." It hurt, but it was the truth and she'd accepted that.

"I wanted to be totally up-front about that."

"I'm a big girl. I'm not expecting this every time I get involved with someone." She waved her hand around at the wedding reception. And that was true, but she hadn't exactly been involved with a lot of guys. "Sometimes I just want to have fun."

* * *

Ellie couldn't help thinking dancing with Liam at the reception was like a prelude to what was coming next. After seeing the happy couple off to their honeymoon, she and Liam held hands as they walked to Ellie's car.

They didn't talk much on the way back to her place but the sexual tension was palpable—at least on her end. She threw a couple furtive glances at Liam, but his concentration seemed to be on driving. What if he didn't want this? She hated the thought of throwing herself at him if—

"Ellie?" He reached for her hand and enclosed it in his much larger one.

Oh, God. Was he going to tell her he changed his mind? Was he thinking of a way to let her—

"I hear you all the way over here."

"But I didn't say anything."

"But you were busy thinking it."

"Guilty," she admitted.

He angled a glance at her. "Are you having second thoughts?"

"Are you?"

"No, but I will respect your wishes."

"Then I'm wishing you'd drive a little faster. Pretend you're on your way to a fire."

"Fire?" He lifted an eyebrow. "More like a conflagration." Liam pulled the car into her driveway and glanced over at her as he parked the car. "Still with me?"

"Absolutely."

He took her hand as they climbed the stairs. Once inside her apartment, he kicked the door shut and took her into his arms. He brushed the hair off her cheeks with his thumbs. "Sweet, sweet Ellie, I'm praying you want this as much as I do."

More than you could ever imagine. "Yes."

He rained kisses along her jaw and neck; when he got to her collarbone, he paused.

"I've been thinking about these freckles all damn day," he said, and pressed his lips along her skin, followed by his tongue.

She shivered, and with a low growl he swept her up into his arms and carried her into the bedroom, where he pulled her dress up and over her head, dropping it to the floor at his feet. Laying her gently on the white comforter, he spread her hair around her head.

Easing over her, he caressed the exposed skin on her hip. "Look at what we have here."

She lifted her head. "My surgery scar?"

"Nope. More freckles, but these were hiding from me all this time," he said, and bent down to kiss above her hip.

Her nipples hardened as his hand neared her breasts, making her shiver. She sucked her breath in when his fingers found her breast and kneaded the flesh. He rubbed his palm over her hardened nipple through the lace.

Wanting more, wanting his mouth where his hand was, she arched her back to press closer to him.

He ran his fingertips along the top of her bra and sent shivers along her nerve endings. She pressed closer and he pushed the bra down, freeing her breasts.

"Finally," she moaned.

He chuckled. "Is that what you wanted?"

"I was ready to do it myself."

He made a tutting noise with his tongue. "I never knew you were so impatient."

"Only with you."

"Then maybe you'll like this," he said, and lowered his head and covered her nipple with his mouth. His tongue made twirling motions around the bud. At her sharp intake of breath, he began to suck gently. The moist heat of his mouth made her tremble with need.

When he lifted his mouth and blew lightly on the wet nipple, she nearly shattered right then and there. With clumsy fingers, she unbuttoned his shirt, needing to touch his bare skin.

He lifted his gaze to hers, his eyes glittering with something raw and primitive. Something she'd never seen in him before, and it thrilled her. She hadn't finished unbuttoning his shirt, but he simply pulled it over his head and tossed it on the floor. Standing up, he shed his pants and boxer briefs, then slowly lowered himself back down on the bed.

She pressed her lips against the warm, smooth skin on his chest; he tasted tart and salty.

His mouth brushed over hers in a light, caressing kiss that had her wanting to plead for more. He slid a hand under her nape and drew her closer.

She closed her eyes as his lips moved in gentle urgency over hers. Her blood felt like high-octane fuel racing through her body. Every thudding beat of her heart had her wanting him more and more, until her desire rose to a feverish pitch. She could feel a tension building within her in a push-pull sensation, leaving her hot and moist in a need for the full possession of her body by his.

His tongue demanded entry to her mouth and she

opened with a moan of pleasure as it danced with hers, cavorting back and forth, sliding and caressing.

His hand covered one of her breasts and sent shock waves down to her toes. With his other hand behind her he unclasped her bra and tugged it aside. Once again his mouth claimed her breast, his mouth sucking the nipple and teasing it with his teeth. Her other breast begged for the same attention and she ground her hips against him.

When his mouth touched the other nipple she thought she would explode from the pleasure and the longing. He gave that one the same attention, licking, sucking and nipping at the rigid nipple. As he lifted his mouth and blew on the nipple again, her hips twitched and bucked toward his erection.

All her nerve endings humming and sizzling, she reached up and twined her arms around his neck. She pulled him down, reveling in the way his weight felt on top of her. He kissed her with a searing hunger, as if he'd been waiting for her all his life. He feasted on her mouth like a starving man.

His mouth left hers and he trailed sweet, tantalizing kisses over her shoulders, stopping to kiss the freckles on her collarbone, then moved again to her breasts. He drew his tongue lightly across the underside of her breasts and toward her belly button. He kissed a spot on her hip and let his tongue drift over the elastic waist of her cream lace bikinis. She arched her hips up and buried her hands in his disheveled hair.

His breath flowing over her created goose bumps on her flesh and a mind-numbing sensation in her pleasure-fogged brain. Just when she felt she couldn't stand it a moment longer, he touched the spot that had been begging for attention and she exploded.

She'd barely come back to earth when a foil packet rustled and she reached up to take the condom, saying, "Let me."

He handed the packet to her, his eyes dark with desire and gleaming with anticipation.

His gaze locked on hers and held her in an erotic embrace before he thrust into her. He withdrew and thrust again, more deeply this time, all the while watching her, his blue eyes blazing with a light that should have blinded her. The depth of their connection shocked her, heated her from the inside out each time he filled her.

The need began to spiral to life within her for a second time and all thought was lost; she could only feel, drowning in sensation. He increased the pace as she tried to reach for her release. They both fell into the abyss at the same time, their heavy breathing the only sound in the room.

Liam climbed back into bed after taking care of the condom and pulled Ellie into his arms. He was still processing what they'd just shared. Somehow it transcended mere sex. That fact should scare him, but he was feeling too boneless and satisfied to worry.

She sighed and snuggled closer, resting her head on his chest. "That was…"

"Yeah, it was." He kissed the top of her head and rubbed his hand up and down her arm.

"I never knew freckles could be sexy." She caressed his chest.

He twined his fingers through hers. "You better believe it."

"I always hated them."

"And now?"

She giggled. "I guess they aren't so bad."

"What was the scar from?"

"Surgery."

"For the cancer?"

"Indirectly. They moved my ovaries aside to decrease the chances of becoming infertile due to the treatments."

"I guess the treatments can be as destructive in their own way as the cancer." He squeezed her hand. "So did the operation work?"

"I won't know until I start trying, but like I said, it's possible. Why?" She moved her head back to look at him.

Her silky hair brushing against his chest wasn't helping his current condition. "I don't have any more condoms with me."

"And I don't have— Oh, wait!" She sat up. "Would glow-in-the-dark ones work?"

What was his Ellie doing with glow-in-the-dark condoms? Was there even such a thing? "Ellie, what the…"

She grinned. "Leftovers from Mary's bridal shower."

He shook his head. "Do I even want to know?"

She leaned over and kissed him. "Probably not."

His body won out over his good sense. "Where are these condoms?"

She reached into the nightstand and held up a foil-wrapped strand.

He rolled his eyes. "Ellie, this better not ever become a topic of conversation at a future family gathering, like my dad's morning-after walk of shame."

"I wouldn't dream of it," she told him as they came together again.

* * *

Liam awoke with Ellie pressed against him, her back to his front, his arm around her waist as if he'd been afraid of her escaping while he slept. Where the heck had such a crazy thought come from?

Glow-in-the-dark condoms aside, he couldn't remember the last time—if ever—he'd been this affected. He tried to tell himself it was because they had become friends. It wasn't as if he had developed deeper feelings.

He and Ellie were hanging out while he was here and if that involved some sex, so be it. They were adults. They'd acted responsibly. Yeah, okay, the condoms had been unique but they'd used them. Responsible. He could go back to Boston, to his regular life, with memories of their jaw-dropping sex. He—

His phone began to buzz. Not wanting to wake Ellie, he slipped out of bed and found it in his pants. Going into the kitchen area, he answered the call from Chief Harris.

Several minutes later, he ended the call. He puffed up his cheeks and slowly released the trapped air.

"Who was that?"

He turned to face Ellie. She wore a very unsexy fleece robe but knowing she was probably naked underneath threatened to send his blood pooling below his waist. He did his best to shove those thoughts aside. Unlike Ellie, he hadn't stopped to put anything on before answering the phone.

"Liam?"

"It was my chief. Some of the guys are out sick and he was asking if I could cut my vacation a few days short. Guys are reaching their max for working extra shifts."

She huddled deeper into her robe. "So you need to go back today?"

"Yeah." He rubbed his chest at the sudden restricting tightness from the thought of leaving Ellie behind. Of Ellie becoming involved with someone like Colton. A guy who had the temerity to call her asking for another woman's phone number. Surely Ellie was smarter than that. "I need to jump in the shower and collect my stuff and let my sister know."

She smiled but it didn't reach her honey-gold eyes. "While you're in the shower, I'll make some breakfast."

He went to her and kissed her forehead. "Thanks. I—"

She waved her hand and stepped back. "We both knew it was temporary."

Chapter 7

Finishing his twenty-four-hour shift, Liam checked his watch as he headed out of the redbrick firehouse located in a densely populated area of South Boston.

"Got a hot date waiting for you at home?" Nick Morretti, the driver engineer on Liam's shift, caught up to him.

"I have last night's episode of *Around the Horn* waiting for me on my DVR." Liam stopped and turned to hold the door open. He hadn't had a date in the two months he'd been home from Loon Lake. Two months since he'd last seen Ellie. Last held Ellie. It wasn't as if they'd broken up, because there was nothing to break. They'd had fantastic sex after the wedding; that's all. No regrets. No recriminations. It all sounded very civilized. So why did it feel so shabby? *We both knew it was temporary.*

"Thanks." Nick grabbed the door and followed Liam outside. "When you gonna take that plunge and settle down? You ain't gettin' any younger."

Liam shook his head. "Have you been talking to my sister?"

Nick laughed and fell into step beside Liam as they went into the early-morning October sunshine of the parking lot. "Don't want you missing out on all the good stuff that comes with marriage and kids."

"Face it, Morretti, you're just jealous because I get to go home and watch sports highlights in my undershorts." Yeah, the exciting life of a thirtysomething bachelor.

Nick laughed. "Is that what floats your boat these days, McBride?"

"It beats fishing a Barbie out of the toilet," he shot back. It did, didn't it?

Nick huffed out his breath. "Damn. When did Gina tell you about that?"

Liam barked out a laugh and tossed his gym bag into the bed of his pickup. "I was talking about my sister's kids, but do tell."

"And put you off marriage and kids? No way." Nick fished his keys out of his pocket. "Your sister, she's got what, two now?"

"And another on the way." Liam shook his head. "I swear all she and Riley have to do is look at each other and bam, I'm an uncle again. That's why I took all that vacation time up there in Vermont a couple months ago. I was helping Riley with an addition to their place. Only I didn't think they were going to need it quite this soon."

Nick opened the driver's door to a soccer mom–style SUV and climbed in. Sticking his head out the window, he wiggled his eyebrows. "And I suppose that attractive nurse I heard about was an entertaining perk."

Liam's fist tightened around his key fob and the truck's alarm beeped. Ellie wasn't a *perk*. She was... what? Some summer fun? Why did that have to sound so shabby? He wouldn't have thought that with anyone else.

He lifted his chin to acknowledge Nick's departing wave and climbed into his truck. He was bushed from taking extra shifts at a part-time station, but working had helped keep his mind off Ellie. That's the explanation he was going with. A decent few days of uninterrupted sleep and he'd be back to his old self, stop wondering what Ellie was doing. And he'd stop thinking about her honey-gold eyes, the way her hair smelled like flowers he didn't know the name of, and stop tasting the cherry flavor of her lip gloss on his tongue. Yeah, sports highlights, breakfast and stop mooning over Ellie sounded like a workable plan.

Ellie drew her knees up to her chest and bounced her feet on the concrete stoop of Liam's three-decker in the Dorchester section of Boston. A perfect example of the city's iconic multifamily housing units, the colorful home towered above her, looking like three small homes neatly stacked one on top of the other. The large bay windows curving around the right side of the building reminded her of a castle turret. No moat, but the roots from the lone tree in front of Liam's house had cracked and lifted the sidewalk as if trying to escape its concrete jungle. Poor tree.

God, first a car commercial last night and now a stupid tree. She swiped at a useless tear with the back of her hand. Damn her hormones for running amok and turning her into a crier. If this kept up much longer, she'd have to learn better coping skills. Not to mention perfecting those before Liam arrived home.

She inhaled and stretched her neck to glance up and down the quiet street. Why hadn't she called or texted first? Just because he was completing a twenty-four-hour shift this morning didn't mean he'd come straight home. He might stop off somewhere to eat or... She hugged her knees tighter. Or he might be with another woman at her place. She closed her eyes and swallowed against a fresh wave of nausea. What if he was bringing a woman home? After all, it had been eight weeks since their— Her chest tightened painfully as she searched for the right word to describe what they'd had. What had it been? A fling? An affair? Friendship with benefits?

Sighing deeply, she turned her head toward the glossy chestnut-stained front door behind her. What if there was a woman in there right now also waiting for Liam to come home? She made a choking sound before turning to face the street again.

No, there couldn't be, because if *she* saw a strange woman on her front porch for thirty minutes, she'd open the door and demand to know what was going on. However, it would serve her right for not calling ahead if there was another woman. She'd have to laugh it off and say something like, "I was in the neighborhood and..."

"Yeah, like he's gonna buy that," she muttered. Heck, Meg hadn't believed her lame excuse when Ellie had asked about Liam's work schedule. Curiosity had been evident in Meg's expression, but for once she didn't meddle. Not that it mattered, because Ellie wouldn't be able to hold Loon Lake gossip off for very much longer.

She could tell the people she worked with were already getting suspicious by the looks they gave her.

She sighed and rested her forehead on her knees. Short of abandoning her family, friends, job, future plans and everything she held dear in Loon Lake, swallowing her pride to confront Liam was inevitable. Of course, showing up with no prior notice might not be the best way to begin this particular conversation. Lately her head had been elsewhere, but she needed to do this in person. This wasn't something that could be handled in a text or even a phone call.

The low rumble of a truck engine alerted her and she sat up and braced her shoulders as a late-model gray pickup turned onto the street and slowed. *Liam.* And he was alone. Thanking whatever lucky stars she had left, she stood and shook her legs to straighten her jeans.

Liam maneuvered his truck into a parallel spot two houses away. She swallowed hard as he shut off the engine. The door slammed shut.

"Here goes nothing," she whispered, and stepped away from the front stoop.

He walked around the back of the truck and she drank in all six feet two inches. Still dressed in his uniform of navy blue pants and matching shirt with the red and bright yellow Boston Fire Department patch, he looked as though he'd just stepped off a beefcake charity calendar. The only things missing were his turnout pants with those sexy red suspenders. Her mouth watered at that seductive image. At least something other than nausea was making her mouth—

"Ellie?"

"It's me," she said with forced brightness and a fake smile.

He frowned. "Is something wrong? Meg, the kids... or you? You haven't—"

"No. No." She waved her hands in quick, jerky movements. *Scare the poor man, why don't you?* Yeah, she should've warned him of her visit but what would she have said if he'd asked why she was coming? For all she knew, he'd moved on from this summer. Unlike her. "Everyone is fine. Sorry. I should have called ahead but..."

He lifted his arms and embraced her in a welcoming hug. She threw her arms around him, gathering strength from his solid warmth. Wait...was he sniffing her hair? His arms dropped away before she could decide and she let go, despite the desire to hold tight. No clinging. She was an adult and could take care of herself. This trip was to deliver news. That's all.

She glanced back at the front door. No outraged woman bursting out demanding an explanation. One less thing to fret about. A small victory but she'd take it. "I, uh... I hope I'm not interrupting anything."

He draped an arm over her shoulder, gave her a quick shoulder hug and let go. "Nah, I just got off work."

"I know. I mean... I checked with Meg before I came." She scuffed the toe of one red Converse sneaker against the concrete. Doing this on his front porch was not an option. She sighed and motioned with her head toward the house. "You gonna invite me in, McBride?"

He pulled out his cell phone. "Sure, Harding, just let me tell the Playboy bunnies inside to exit through the back."

She rolled her eyes. "Yeah, right. Getting them to hide your porn stash is more like it."

"Ouch." He pocketed his phone with a devastating

grin, then motioned for her to go onto the porch ahead of him.

"I won't take up too much of your time." *Just long enough to change your whole life.*

On the porch, she stood to the side so he could unlock the door. He smelled faintly of garlic and tomato sauce. "You on kitchen duty?"

"Why? Do I smell like an Italian restaurant?" He lifted his arm, sniffed his sleeve and laughed, his eyes crinkling in the corners, the wide grin deepening those adorable grooves on either side of his mouth.

Ellie's toes curled. Score one for her newly heightened sense of smell. Except she didn't need to go where his sexy laugh and her rioting hormones wanted to take her. This trip wasn't about that. And once she told him why she'd come, he wouldn't be interested, either. "You never did bring me any cannoli from that Italian bakery you told me about."

"Mike's?" His light blue eyes flashed with mischief. "Sorry, Harding, but even if I'd gotten some, believe me, they would not have made it all the way to Vermont in the same truck as me."

God, but she'd missed him. She was such a sucker for that teasing glint in his eyes, but nevertheless she made a disparaging noise with her tongue. "McBride, it's a three-hour drive."

"Exactly," he said with a firm nod and a wink. "Sorry, but you'll have to make do with frozen."

She gave him a playful shoulder punch before following him into the inner hallway. A stairway led to the upper units on the left and the entrance to the ground floor unit was on the right. Liam unlocked his door and pushed it open, lifting his arm so she could scoot under.

No sexy heels today to add an extra three inches to her five feet three inches.

Flooded with morning sunlight from the large bay windows, the living room was standard, no-frills bachelor fare, with a brown distressed leather couch and matching recliner facing a giant flat-screen television with an elaborate sound system. Two empty beer bottles, a pizza box and wadded-up napkins littered the coffee table along with an array of remote controls. A sneaker peeked out from under the couch. The sunny room, even the clutter, was like a comforting arm around her shoulder and it warmed her. She could do this.

He cleared his throat. "Sorry about the mess."

"It's a wonderful space. I love these windows. They give you so much natural light." She set her purse on the couch.

"Thanks. Meg says if I had some taste, this place could be great." He tossed his keys on the coffee table and glanced around. "She calls my decorating style the 'under arrest' method…everything lined up against the walls as if waiting to be frisked and handcuffed."

Ellie laughed, picturing Meg chastising him. "Sisters."

A new and unfamiliar awkwardness rushed in to fill the silence. Had sex messed with their friendship? Had he moved on? It was not like they'd made any promises to each other or anything. Ellie rubbed the pad of her thumb over her fingers and swallowed another, more urgent, wave of nausea.

"I guess you're—"

"Would you like—"

Bitterness coated her tongue, making it curl in warning. If she didn't get to a bathroom—stat—she was going to throw up all over Liam's glossy wood floor. She covered her mouth with her hand, barely managing to gag the word, "Bathroom?"

His brow furrowed as he turned and pointed. "Down the hall. First door on the left."

She stumbled into the bathroom, slammed the door and dropped to her knees in front of the toilet. Hugging the bowl, she threw up the breakfast she'd convinced herself to eat before driving to Boston. Yuck. It would be a long time before she could eat oatmeal again...if ever.

Well, there was one bright spot to this whole debacle. At least he hadn't had a woman with him.

Pacing the hall outside the bathroom, Liam calculated ambulance response times against how quickly he could drive her to Brigham and Women's Hospital in midmorning traffic. Listening to Ellie being sick brought back memories of his ma spending hours puking in the bathroom after endless rounds of chemo. The word *cancer* blocked his field of vision like flashing neon. No, that was silly, Ellie had been in perfect health eight weeks ago. God forbid, but what if she was in Boston for an appointment at the Dana-Farber Cancer Institute? No, Meg would have said—

He flung the door open with such force it banged against the wall and bounced back, hitting his arm.

Ellie sat hunched over the bowl and he knelt down beside her. "My God, Ellie, what's wrong? Should I call paramedics? Or I could—"

She held up her hand and croaked out, "No," before the retching began again.

He pulled her hair away from the porcelain with one

hand and rubbed her back with the other. Things he could've—should've—done for his ma but hadn't because he was busy burying his head in the sand, convinced she would beat the cancer. His chest tightened, but with the ease born of practice, he shoved unwelcome emotions aside. He refused to fall apart. If he could run into a smoke-choked inferno, he could handle this. Right? "Tell me what's wrong."

She flushed the toilet, sat back and wiped her mouth with the back of her hand.

He reached up and grabbed a towel off the sink. "Here."

"Thanks." She wiped her mouth and hands before giving the towel back. "I'm okay now."

A chill ran through him and he searched her face as if he would find an answer there. "Are you sure?"

She nodded vigorously and began to rise. He tossed the towel aside, put his hand under her elbow and helped her up.

"May I?" She motioned toward the sink.

He sidestepped to give her a little more room to maneuver, but she was pale and sweating so he was going to be a jerk and stay close, even if he had to crowd her personal space. He didn't want her passing out on him. She turned on the faucet, captured water in her cupped hand and rinsed her mouth. He leaned past her for the discarded towel and mentally kicked himself for not going to Vermont to visit her. Why had he fought his own instincts to call or text her on a daily basis? Yeah, that wouldn't have made him look needy or anything.

She splashed water on her face and he handed her the towel. After she dried her face, he offered his bottle of mouthwash. She glanced from the uncapped plastic bottle in his hand and back to him, a frown creasing her brow.

He shrugged. "What? I lost the cap. Swig it."

"You're such a guy," she muttered.

"And I'm sure you meant that in the kindest possible way." He grinned, relaxing because the bantering was familiar, comfortable, easy to handle. That was his Ellie and— Wait. What was this "his Ellie" stuff about?

She rolled her eyes but raised the bottle to her lips.

Folding his arms across his chest, he watched while she rinsed her mouth and spit into the sink. Now that her skin had lost its previous pallor, she looked more like the Ellie he'd left in Vermont, the healthy one. His friend. The one he just happened to—

He shifted his stance and turned his thoughts away from Ellie's eyes and upturned nose with the light smattering of freckles. He'd put himself back out there in the dating world soon and life would return to normal. That's what he wanted, wasn't it?

"Do you mind?" She bumped him with her hip. "A little privacy, please."

She also had freckles on that hip. *What are you doing?* Thinking about Ellie's skin was not the first step in getting back to normal. "Can I get you something to eat?"

Those honey eyes widened. "Really? You're talking food after my little display?"

Damn she was right, but he needed something to do. Standing around feeling helpless was not something he enjoyed. He needed to be productive. "Hmph, coffee then."

She shuddered.

What the heck? Ellie loved her morning coffee. Now

she was scaring him. "Since when don't you like coffee?"

She glared at him. "Oh, I don't know, maybe since I just threw up what I had this morning."

Yeah, that was a lame question, but he hated not knowing what was wrong. "Fair enough. What would you like?"

"Got any decaf tea?"

Unfolding his arms, he stepped away. "I think I still have some from…"

"From who?"

"From Meg. The last time she was here she wanted decaf, so she bought a box." He frowned at her sharp tone. From the moment he'd seen her sitting on his front steps, she'd thrown him off-balance. "What, Ellie, do you think there's a woman in the closet waiting for you to leave?"

Her eyes narrowed but she didn't say anything. He ground his teeth. Damn, why couldn't he just keep his big mouth shut? Because she was hiding something from him. He just knew it and he didn't like it. Nor did he like the way he wanted to pull her into his embrace, bury his face in her soft hair and let her sweetness take his mind off the restlessness that had plagued him these past two months.

He sighed into the strained silence, regretting his remark. Maybe if he had visited her since their time in Loon Lake, he'd know what was going on with her and there wouldn't be this weird vibe between them. "I'll go check and see if I have any tea bags."

"Thanks. I'll be out in a minute." She shut the door behind him with a soft *snick*.

He found the tea in a cupboard and put some water on

to heat. While he waited for the water to boil, he stuck a pod in his coffee maker. Sleep was probably out of the question so he might as well enjoy some caffeine. Why she had come was a mystery, but something told him Ellie wasn't there to renew their friends-with-benefits arrangement. A morning filled with fantastic sex was looking less and less likely.

Ellie appeared in the doorway as he poured boiling water into a mug with her tea bag. As always when he saw her, his heartbeat sped up. It would appear her red sneakers had a similar effect on his libido as those sexy bright blue heels from the wedding. Like that wasn't messed up or anything.

His gaze rose to her face to take in the pink nose and shiny eyes. His stomach tumbled. Oh, Christ, had his tough-as-nails ER nurse Ellie been crying? Had he caused that with his thoughtless comment? What the hell was wrong with him saying stupid stuff like that, to Ellie of all people? She was the last person he wanted to hurt with a careless remark.

"Your tea." He handed her the hot mug, but what he really wanted was to shake her and demand she tell him what was going on. Or to grab her close and never let her go. Keep her safe forever. But keeping her safe was impossible because cancer didn't respect how much or how many people cared.

She wrapped her hands around the chipped ceramic as if warming them. "Thanks."

"I'm…uh…" What was wrong with *him*? This was Ellie and they'd talked endlessly for hours when they weren't—*hey, remember, we're not going there.* "I hope you like that kind. Meg bought it."

"This is fine." She jiggled the bag up and down. "Got any milk?"

"Let me check." He pulled the milk out of the refrigerator and sniffed the open carton. "Yeah, I do."

Her sudden laughter sent a tingle along his spine. He'd missed that laugh, her unique view of the world, her friendship. Okay, that's what was wrong with him. Ellie hadn't been just a sexual partner like others but a true friend. Relieved to find a reasonable explanation for the way he'd been feeling, he grinned. "We can go in the living room and sit."

"Yeah, that furniture looks more…comfortable."

His gaze landed on the wicked ugly collapsible card table and metal folding chairs from his dad's basement that doubled as a dining set. Not that he ever once dined on it. Eating takeout in front of the TV was more his style. Cooking for the guys while on shift was different from preparing something just for himself. "I haven't gotten around to doing much in here yet."

Her golden eyes sparkled. "Why? Did the couch or recliner resist arrest?"

"Took me a while to read them their rights." His mood was buoyed by the shared moment. Yeah, he'd missed that wacky humor of hers.

"You should get Meg to help with the decorating." She dropped her used tea bag into the wastebasket in the corner. "She's done a fantastic job with her kitchen and the new addition. The entire place really."

"I think she's got her hands full at the moment with being pregnant again. They didn't waste much time after James was born." He was happy for his sister, but seeing Meg so settled had him looking more closely at his own situation. And he didn't always like what he saw. But that was crazy, because as he'd told Nick, he was doing exactly what he pleased. He had a full life.

Ellie clucked her tongue. "She's happier than I've ever seen her. I hope you didn't say anything stupid like that to her face."

He picked up his coffee and followed her into the living room. "It wouldn't do any good if I did. As she's been telling me since she was five I'm not the boss of her."

"No, but she respects your opinion." She sat back on the couch but scooted forward when her feet dangled above the floor. "Besides, you like Riley."

He plopped down in the recliner. "I do as long as I don't have to think about what he and my sister get up to."

"Or your dad and Doris?"

He groaned and shook his head. "At least they're not popping out kids as proof."

She took a sip of her tea and set it on the table next to the couch. The sunshine streaming in through his uncovered windows made the highlights in her shiny hair glow, and he itched to run his fingers through all those dark and reddish strands. He tried to think of a word to describe it and couldn't. *Brown* was too plain a term to describe all that lustrous silk.

"What color is your hair?" Oh, man, had he actually asked that out loud? What was wrong with him?

"What?" She gave him a quizzical look.

He shrugged and hoped his face wasn't as flushed as it felt. "Meg has a thing about people calling her hair red and I, uh, just wondered if you had a name for your color like she does."

She ran a hand over her hair. "It's chestnut. Why?"

He nodded, but didn't answer her question. He'd embarrassed himself enough for one day. "Are you planning on telling me why you're here?"

She rubbed her hands on her thighs and drew in a deep breath. "I know we decided this summer was no strings attached, but—"

"About that, Ellie, I—"

"I'm pregnant."

Chapter 8

Ellie winced. She hadn't meant to blurt it out like that, but he'd been acting strangely. Not that she could blame him, considering her showing up unannounced and then madly dashing to the bathroom. She could imagine him thinking the worst but that question about her hair color... What was that about? She shifted in her seat and glanced over at him. "Liam?"

He stared at her, his eyes wide, his mouth open, his breathing shallow. She'd imagined all sorts of scenarios during the drive to Boston, including him being stunned and angry, surprised and excited. The latter one was the one she preferred but not the most reasonable. *You left out the one where he declares his undying love and proposes*. Yeah, pregnancy hormones might be messing with her, but she was still tethered to reality. She'd been flummoxed to learn she was pregnant. Imagine poor Liam.

At least she knew now the cancer treatments hadn't rendered her sterile. Of course this wasn't the way she would've planned starting her family. Did wanting to be happily married first make her a prude?

"Are you going to say anything?" she asked, unable to stand the silence a moment longer.

He sprang from his chair as if galvanized by the sound of her voice, and came to sit next to her on the couch, crowding her space. He took her hand in his and rubbed his free one over his face. "Are you sure? Did you take a test? See a doctor?"

She tilted her head, lowered her chin and gave him the *are you kidding me* look. "Hello? Nurse Ellie here."

"Oh. Right." He closed his eyes and pinched the bridge of his nose. "This is... I mean... We... I... You..."

"Yeah, we did, but nothing is one hundred percent. Not even glow-in-the-dark condoms." Maybe Liam was as fertile as his sister. Of course now might not be the best time to point out that observation. Maybe someday they'd be able to get a chuckle or two out of it.

"Have you been to a doctor yet?" he asked.

"Not yet. I wanted to tell you before I went. In case you wanted to...to be involved..." Her voice trailed off.

Then she drew in a breath and plunged in with her prepared speech. "Look, I get that this is a lot to take in, but I want you to know I'm not going to force you to do anything you don't want. I have a good job and a great support system with family and friends in Loon Lake and—"

"Have you told anyone yet?"

"What? Why? Tell me why you would ask me something like...like... Liam?" Her voice had risen with each word; blood rushed in her ears.

He lifted their entwined hands and pressed them close to his chest. "Christ, Ellie, don't look at me like that. I figure you must've already come to a decision or you wouldn't even be here now telling me about the baby." He pulled her closer so she was practically on his lap. "Besides, you know me better than that. I know the ability to have children has been a concern of yours, and knowing how much you love kids, I'm sure you want them."

Relief washed through her and she nodded against his chest, the faint garlic aroma making her empty stomach rumble. Really? Food at a time like this? *You'd rather be thinking about sex?* "So why did you ask if I'd told anyone?"

He rubbed his thumb over her palm. "I was there when it happened, so I should be there when you tell your parents. At least I assume you're planning to tell them."

For the first time since coming to Boston, she was able to take a deep breath and released it with a laugh. Relief, or maybe it was oxygen, making her giddy. "I know it's early to be telling people but what happened in your bathroom is only a part of what's been happening. I either avoid my family for another month or tell them why I'm so tired, dizzy and pale. I don't want my mom thinking the cancer has returned. And it's not something I will be able to hide for very long from my family."

"You'd be surprised. I remember Meg hid it for as long as she could." He squeezed her shoulder.

"Your sister's situation was different. Meg was nineteen, still living at home, and Riley had left town, possibly forever. I'm twenty-seven, employed and, if that's not enough, I happen to know where you live." Why in heaven's name was she arguing with him? She should be ecstatic and yet she was…what? Disappointed because he hadn't pledged his love? This was Liam. Over the summer he had become not just a lover but also a friend. Still, he wasn't the most emotionally available guy she knew. Supportive was good. Supportive worked.

"I don't know about your parents, but my dad has this tone of voice…" He leaned against the couch cushions, drawing her back with him. "Makes me feel twelve all over again when he uses it."

"My mom…she gets this look." She blinked. Damn, but she'd never been a crier. She was smart, practical Ellie, a cancer survivor. A survivor who decided she wanted a fling with the deliciously sexy fireman who also happened to be a friend. She'd wanted to experience something a little wild, maybe even a little wicked. Of course she should have known better than to fall for her temporary fling. "I guess I'm a total failure at this fling business. Not getting pregnant must be like, what, number one on the no-no list?"

"A rookie mistake." He brushed his knuckles across her back.

She blew the hair off her forehead. "A big one."

He gently tucked those stray hairs behind her ear. "I'm sure your dad will be more likely to lay the blame on me."

She sat up straighter and pulled away so she could look at him. "I'll talk to my dad, make him understand that forcing someone into ma—into something they don't want isn't a solution."

He untangled himself and stood up, looking at her with that little half grin. "Wanna explain that to Mac, too?"

"I'm sure your dad will be fine." She huffed out a

mirthless laugh. "He dotes on Fiona and James. He loves being Grampa Mac. And he has to know at your age that you're, uh, sexually active."

"Did you want to tell Mac while I'm here in Boston?"

"My dad and Doris are on another one of their jaunts in their motor home and not due back until next week." He stopped pacing and perched his butt against the windowsill. "I do need to tell Meg. If she finds out before I tell her, she'll never let me hear the end of it. What about you?"

"I'll tell my parents and since we'll be telling Meg, I'd like to tell Mary before she hears it from someone else. We've become good friends since she's moved to town. I can call her or stop by the farm."

Liam chuckled. "Meg likes to complain about Loon Lake gossip reaching me down here, but she's usually the one to call and tell me stuff. She claims that she's doing it before the chatter reaches me."

"You can still change your mind about coming with me to talk to my parents." She was giving him an out but prayed he wouldn't take it.

"No, I want them to know I'm not some random guy that got you—"

"Gee, McBride, thanks a lot." She wasn't about to confess to Liam how few guys she'd been intimate with…ever. And this wasn't how she'd imagined she'd feel when having a baby. Instead of celebrating with the man she loved, this was beginning to feel more like triage. She scooted off the sofa to go and stand in front of him.

"What? I only meant—"

"I know what you meant." She sighed but couldn't help leaning into his warmth. "That's the problem."

"I know you don't sleep around. What I'm saying is I need to face your dad. Apologize and—"

Her gaze clashed with his. "Liam? Zip it."

"Right."

"So, we need to break the news to my parents and Meg. Is…" She cleared her throat and took a step back, needing space before asking this next question. Correction, she needed space before receiving his answer. "Is there anyone else you might need to tell?"

"Like? Oh, you mean…" He straightened up and away from the windowsill and took a step, closing the distance she'd put between them. "There hasn't been another woman since…there's no other woman."

She released the breath she'd been holding. That tidbit warmed her more than she would've imagined. "Me, either."

"That's because I'm irreplaceable." He flashed her one of his devilish, intensely sexy smiles.

She gave him a backhanded slap on the arm, but she couldn't wipe the silly grin off her face. Or the relief from her heart.

Liam scrubbed his scalp vigorously as he lathered the shampoo and tried not to think, but Ellie's *I'm pregnant* was stuck on an endless loop in his head. No question he needed to step up and be there for Ellie and their child. He ducked his head under the shower spray and rinsed. Ellie would be a great mom. Exhibit one: she wasn't hiding in the bathroom using taking a quick shower as an excuse to build up much-needed defenses.

On a scale from an unplanned pregnancy to Ellie's cancer returning, the pregnancy was less scary every time, but that didn't mean he wasn't scared. Being a dad had been a nebulous idea for the future. Not on today's to-do list.

When he'd seen Ellie waiting for him on his steps, it had taken all his willpower to remain casual, to not confess how much he'd missed her, to not tell her how many times he'd thought about her. The hug he'd given her had been meant as platonic, two friends greeting each other, but the moment she'd been in his arms, he'd wanted her with an intense ache. And it hadn't been all physical. He could handle simple lust but this felt like more. More than he wanted to admit or accept.

Angry with himself for dwelling, he snapped the faucet off, grimacing when the building's ancient pipes rattled and groaned at his careless treatment. He stepped out of the shower, snatched a towel from the rack and dried off, dressing in jeans and a long-sleeve pullover shirt.

He grabbed a pair of socks and went back in his living room, where he found Ellie seated on the couch, watching television and looking relaxed. But the trash was gone from the coffee table, the remotes were lined up like soldiers, except for the one in her hand, and both of his sneakers sat by his recliner. Yeah, Ellie liked organization and structure.

"You didn't have to clean." He scooped up his sneakers and sank into the chair.

"I'd hardly call throwing a pizza box away cleaning." She waved her free hand in a dismissive gesture, but she was white-knuckling the remote in the other.

Before he could think of something to say, she prattled on. "Did you know that there's a nonprofit organization that studies and ranks tall buildings? Evidently they give out awards or something. Who would have thought to give awards to skyscrapers?"

She continued her one-sided discussion while he pulled the socks on.

"Isn't that interesting?" She peered at him, an expectant expression on her beautiful face.

"Uh-huh." He stuffed his feet into his beat-up running shoes, all the while trying to figure out where she was going with all this skyscraper talk.

She thrust out her lower lip. "You're not even listening."

He met her accusing glare and tried not to smile at her being indignant on behalf of inanimate objects. He longed to take that plump lower lip between his teeth and nip it so he could then soothe it with his tongue and then— Whoa. What happened to not going there?

"Liam?"

"I'm listening…honest…nonprofit…tall buildings… awards. See? But I fail to understand why you're sounding like the Discovery Channel all of a sudden." Where was all this going? Had he missed something?

"Would you prefer I sit here and cry?" She set the remote on the table and sniffed.

"God, no. Tell me more about these awards. They sound fascinating." He crowded beside her on the couch. When he put his arm around her, she leaned into his side and he rested his cheek on her hair. Her chestnut hair. Now he needed the name of the flowers it smelled like, but he damn sure wasn't going to ask her—at least not today. Her subtle scent surrounded him like whirling smoke. "I told you, I'm not going anywhere and I'm gainfully employed. That has to count for something."

She sniffed. "But you only wanted a short fling."

He tightened his embrace. Ellie would demand, and deserved, more than what he could give to this relationship, but he had to try if they were going to be parents. "But we're friends. We'll be friends having a baby."

"Have you forgotten you live here in Boston, and I live in Vermont?" She sighed, a sound filled with frustration.

Ellie wasn't a quitter and neither was he. It would take some adjusting, but they could work this out. "Now that you've mentioned it, there's plenty of room in—"

She pulled away. "Forget it. I'm not moving in with you."

Huh, that stung. Way more than he would've thought. And definitely more than he liked. Especially since that wasn't what he'd been suggesting. "I wasn't asking. My second-floor tenant is—"

"No, thanks. I wouldn't like the commute to work or the high city rents." She shot him a sour look.

"I haven't said anything about charging you rent."

"And I don't want to be responsible for putting you in a financial bind. Don't you need both rents to make the mortgage?"

Yeah, losing a rent would make it tough, but he wasn't about to admit that to her. "You let me worry about that."

How were they supposed to work things out if she kept throwing up roadblocks? He tried to pull her back against him, but she resisted. Was she upset because he hadn't asked her to move in with him? "In case you hadn't noticed, Boston has hospitals."

"Why do I have to be the one to move?" she sputtered. "Vermont has fire departments."

In Vermont, he wasn't in line for a promotion. In Vermont, he wasn't a fourth-generation firefighter. Loon Lake was a part-time house. He needed full time with benefits. And the smaller the battalion, the longer it took to rise in the ranks. "They're not the Boston Fire Department."

"Oh, excuse me." She scowled. "Vermont might not have the honor of having the first fire department in the nation, but they know how to fight fires in Vermont. Last I heard they'd traded in their horses for shiny red trucks."

"I'm a fourth-generation Boston firefighter. It's a tradition that might continue with…" He glanced at her still-flat stomach. Would there be a fifth generation?

She placed a hand over her abdomen as if protecting it from him. "And maybe she won't want to be a firefighter."

"She?" All thoughts of their argument flew out of his head. He swallowed hard. How could a simple pronoun make his stomach cramp? "You already know it's a girl?"

"No, but I couldn't continue to say 'it,' so I started saying she. I figure I have a fifty-fifty shot at being right." She leaned back against the cushions, her expression smug.

"I see." By next year at this time, there'd be a new little person in his life, one he'd be responsible for and— He pushed those thoughts aside. One problem at a time. "So, you'll think about moving here?"

"Nope," she said.

Argh. Why was she being so stubborn? That would be the perfect solution. *You mean perfect for you.* He blocked out the accusing voice in his head. "Why not?

Your skills would transfer to any of the emergency rooms here and you could probably earn more, too."

"But I wouldn't be happy. I like living in Loon Lake. I like where I am, the people I work with." She crossed her arms over her chest.

"But didn't you say you were looking for a new job?" He seized on what he could to convince her while trying to ignore the way her crossed arms pushed up her chest.

"Those plans are up in the air for now." She patted her stomach. "It may take me a bit longer to finish the degree."

Guilt jabbed him. Here he was, trying to get her to do what he wanted to make life easier for him, without giving any thought to how this affected her plans. Was he that selfish? "Is there anything I can do?"

"Not unless you want to carry this baby for a while." She raised her eyebrows at him.

"Would that I could." His gaze went to her stomach. "But if you were upstairs, I could feed you, help you study."

She shook her head. "And don't you think having us living right upstairs would cramp your style? It might be hard to explain to your dates."

"There won't be any dates. I already told you there hasn't been anyone since…well, there hasn't been anyone else." He hated admitting his self-imposed drought, but maybe the reassurance would help change her mind. *That's mighty big of you, McBride. When did you get to be such an—*

"But that doesn't mean there won't be. You're not planning on being celibate the rest of your life, are you?" She raised her eyebrows at him.

Hell no. Huh, might be best to keep that to himself

for now. He had better survival instincts than to continue any talk about sex, even if that's what he'd been hoping for when he'd spotted her on his front steps. And how had this conversation deteriorated into a discussion of his sex life? Ellie had an uncanny ability to know what he was thinking and…yeah, best not dwell on that. She might be ignoring their chemistry, but it still sparked, at least for him. Although this might not be the best time to point that out. "How about we just get through telling the necessary people our news for now?"

"Sounds like a plan. I drank the rest of your milk."

"Oh-*kaay*…" The abrupt change of topic was enough to give him whiplash, but he'd take it. "We can go to the corner store and get more."

Her face brightened. "How far is it? This looks like a nice neighborhood to take a walk."

She wanted to take a walk? Hey, it was better than sitting here, *not* talking about sex. "Speaking of walking, where's your car? I didn't notice it out front."

Her gaze bounced away. "That's because it's not exactly out front."

"Oh? There are usually spots this time of the day. For instance, there was the one I took." He knew where this was going and he was going to enjoy taking it there. Teasing Ellie and watching her eyes spark always made him want to lean over and—huh, maybe this wasn't such a good idea.

"Well…there was only one and I thought… I thought—"

"Are you telling me you can't parallel park?" He leaned closer.

She scooted off the couch and went toward the bay windows. "Hey, it's not my fault. It's genetics. I'm missing the parallel parking gene."

"Genetics?" He stood and followed, as if tethered by invisible rope. "So does that mean this deficiency can be passed on? Isn't that something you should have warned me about?"

"Sorry?" She sucked on her bottom lip.

"Eh." He bit the inside of his cheek, trapping a smile. "Too late now. C'mon. Let's go to the corner store for milk." He puffed out his chest. "And while we're at it, I'll pull your car closer if you want, since I'm in possession of this awesome gene."

"Oh, brother." She rolled her eyes. "This corner store wouldn't by any chance have sandwiches or a deli?"

Was she serious? "You're hungry?"

"Starved."

"But I thought…" Liam tried to remember what Meg had been like when she was pregnant with Fiona and James, but his sister had hidden it or he'd been too blind to notice. Yeah, he was good at ignoring the obvious. Like with his ma. "If you say you're hungry, then I'll feed you."

She shook her head. "Yeah, not with what you've got on hand. I checked."

"You rummaged through my cupboards?" Was she really that hungry?

She scrunched up her nose. "Yes, Mother Hubbard, and I hate to break it to you, but they're pretty bare."

Who cared about what his kitchen cabinets did or did not contain when that pert, freckled nose was begging to be kissed?

"McBride?"

"Huh?" He shook his head, trying to get back on topic. He blamed his self-imposed eight-week period of celibacy for his lack of concentration.

She pointed to her mouth. "Food?"

It was his turn to wrinkle his nose. "You're serious about wanting to eat?"

"Oh, you mean because of the…in the bathroom?" She tilted her head toward the hallway and pulled a face.

He needed to proceed with caution if he wanted to avoid an argument or, worse, hurting her feelings. "You snapped at me for even suggesting coffee."

She fiddled with the neck of her sweater. "Yeah, about that… I lied. Sorry. The smell turns my stomach. I haven't been able to drink it or smell it for the past few weeks."

He glanced at the mug he'd set on the floor next to his recliner. "Do you want me to get rid of mine?"

Her eyes widened. "You mean you'd do that for me?"

"Of course." The coffee was probably cold by now, anyway. No great loss. He could make another cup when they got back from the store.

"That's so sweet," she gushed. "I can't tell you how much that would mean…you giving up coffee for the next seven months."

Wait…what? He opened his mouth but was incapable of forming words.

She patted his chest and hooted with laughter. "Sucker."

Yeah, he'd walked right into that one, but Ellie's laugh was worth it. Ellie made a lot of things worth it. He couldn't imagine going through this with anyone but her.

Chapter 9

Ellie pondered the situation as they made their way to the corner store. His offer to be present when she broke the news to her parents had surprised and pleased her, and yet at the same time disappointed her. Had she expected more or were her hormones messing with her? Regardless, she had to admit she yearned for an admission that he'd missed her as much as she had him and that he regretted the no-strings-attached part of their arrangement. She needed to remember her vow to stay rooted in reality. *Learn to want what you have, not wish for what you don't.* Even if he'd proposed marriage, she wouldn't have accepted. She didn't want to end up like her mother with a kitchen table that had a lazy Susan but no one to use it. No shared meals or lively conversations. Now, her parents sat in front of the TV so they didn't have to talk and slept in separate bedrooms. They were like ghosts rattling around in the same house. Things hadn't been like that before her diagnosis and Ellie carried the burden of guilt. If she hadn't gotten cancer, would her mom and dad still be that loving, demonstrative couple she remembered from her pre-cancer days? The thought of doing something like that to her own child chilled her.

Instead of dwelling on a past she couldn't change, she pushed aside depressing thoughts to admire the differences and similarities in the homes lining the narrow street. Front porches and columns were common, although some had ornate railings and trim while many of the homeowners had boxed in the rococo trim using vinyl siding. She glanced back at Liam's and admired how his had only original details...except one. "How come yours is the only one with an external fire escape?"

"I'm the only fireman on the block."

Before she could comment, an elderly woman wearing a burgundy sweatshirt that said World's Greatest Grandma came toward them, dragging a fully loaded fold-up shopping cart.

Liam approached the woman. "Good morning, Mrs. Sullivan, looks like you could use some help getting that up your steps."

"Morning, Liam. I'm not the doddering old woman you seem to think, but since you're here..." She opened the gate on a chain-link fence surrounding a three-decker painted the same red and cream as Liam's.

"It's not your age but your beauty that attracts me, Mrs. Sullivan." He took the shopping cart from her.

"Oh, you are so full of it today, Liam McBride." She

leaned around him and smiled at Ellie. "Is that because you have this lovely young lady with you?"

"You wound me, Mrs. Sullivan, I assure you I'm totally sincere." He picked up the cart and set it on the wooden porch of the home.

Ellie's stomach tingled at Liam's solicitous behavior toward the older woman. It confirmed what she'd always known about his character.

"Aren't you going to introduce me?" The older woman clucked her tongue.

"Of course. Ellie Harding, this is Mrs. Sullivan." He motioned between the women.

"Fiddle faddle, I told you to call me Barbara." The woman poked him. "A pleasure to meet you, Ellie."

Ellie shook hands with the woman. "Same here."

"I haven't seen you around here before," the older woman said.

Ellie smiled at Barbara Sullivan. "That's because I live in Vermont. Loon Lake."

"Ah, that explains why Liam was gone so much this summer." The woman grinned and poked him again. "And here you were, telling me you were helping your sister."

He raised his hands, palms out. "I was. I helped them add a new master suite and family room."

"Why didn't you say something about Ellie when I tried to set you up with my granddaughter Chloe?"

He wanted her to live upstairs so he could take care of her? Yeah, right. And how would Chloe feel about a third or fourth wheel? Or maybe he wasn't interested in this Chloe because of their summer fling. Realistic? Maybe not, but it helped her to keep smiling at Chloe's grandmother.

"Shame on you for not telling me you already had someone in Vermont," the woman continued.

"That's because I—"

"We're not—"

Mrs. Sullivan looked from one to the other. "Uh-huh. Usually I see him and he's running or jogging or some such thing to keep fit for the ladies. You're not running today, Liam? But I guess if you've already been caught…"

"I'm not running because—" His brow knit and he hooked his thumb in Ellie's direction. "She's crap at keeping up."

"Apparently I'm crap at parallel parking, too," Ellie muttered. She didn't want to think about Liam and other women. And she certainly didn't want someone insinuating that she'd "caught" Liam as if she'd deliberately set a trap by getting pregnant.

"Don't worry about it, dear. I've lived on this street for fifty years and never learned to parallel park." Barbara Sullivan winked at Ellie.

"You don't own a car," Liam pointed out.

The woman shot him an affronted look. "What's that got to do with it?"

Liam heaved an exaggerated sigh. "Apparently nothing. Do you need help getting your shopping inside?"

"No, but thank you. Now you and your Ellie enjoy your walk." The older woman made a shooing motion.

"She seems nice," Ellie said as Liam shut the gate with a clang of metal.

Liam nodded. "Mmm, she is…for the most part."

"Sorry if she assumed that we were…well, that we were together." Good grief, why was she apologizing? This baby wasn't an immaculate conception—even if that's what she'd love to be able tell her dad. Not to mention all the elderly ladies at the church next time she volunteered at the weekly luncheon. *Oh, grow up, those women were all young once.* "But then, we're going to have a baby so I guess you can't get more together than that."

He frowned. "Are you saying—"

"I'm not saying anything. Like I said—huh, well, I guess I am saying *something*." *Damn hormones.* "But I'm not pressing you for anything."

"For God's sake, Ellie, I'll do my share."

The rational part of her brain, when it still worked, knew that expecting him to move would be as crazy as him expecting her to move. Offering her a place to live might solve the problem of distance for him, but being on the periphery of Liam's life was not what she wanted. She wanted to *be* Liam's life. She wanted what Meg and Riley, or Mary and Brody, had. Yeah, that right there was the problem. "That might be difficult since you'll be here and I'll be in Loon Lake."

"Careful." He placed a hand under her elbow and pointed to the uneven sidewalk.

"I'm pregnant, not blind." She cringed at her own waspish tone and blinked to hold back tears. Since when did she have the power to make people react or feel the way she wanted? If she had that power, she'd have put her parents' in-name-only marriage back together.

"But with my schedule, I can get ninety-six hours off, unless I take extra shifts. That's four days."

"I know how long ninety-six hours is." And she knew how long it took to drive from his place to hers. How involved could she honestly expect him to be? She might have regularly scheduled hours at her job but it wasn't as if she was always able to leave on time. Same for Liam if they got called out before quitting time; she knew he couldn't just leave.

He blew out his breath. "Are you trying to start a fight?"

"No." *Liar.* "Maybe."

He stopped, placed his hands on her shoulders and turned her to face him. His gaze scanned her face, his blue eyes full of concern. "What can I do to get your mind off fighting?"

An image popped into her head. Yeah, like she was going to suggest something like *that*. She chose option two. "You could try feeding me."

Was that disappointment on his face? Hmm, seems his mind had gone there, too. *Join the club.* But now was not a good time to muddle things with sex, her sensible half pointed out. But it could be so much fun, her daring half argued.

At the moment hunger was the deciding factor. Those cookies and milk she'd eaten while Liam was in the shower seemed like ages ago. "Is that pizza I smell?"

"There's a small place around the corner."

Her stomach growled. "Can we go there?"

"It's barely ten and that place is a grease pit." He frowned.

"And your point is?"

"Grease can't be good for…for—" his Adam's apple bobbed "—the baby."

"For your information, grease is a food group." Despite her insistence, a pizza didn't hold the same appeal as it had a few minutes ago. And yet a feeling of dissatisfaction made her persist. "Are you going to feed me or not?"

"Fine. We can go to there if you really want or we can go to the store and get milk, some stuff for sandwiches and maybe some fruit or salad."

She already regretted acting so disagreeable. Why did being with Liam again make her feel so contrary? She was blaming her body's reaction to his touch. "Fruit and salad? Who are you and what have you done with the Liam I know?"

"Smart aleck." He dropped his hands, but not before giving her shoulders a gentle squeeze and dropping a kiss on the end of her nose.

She fell into step beside him. "Actually, sandwiches sound better than pizza."

He draped an arm around her shoulders. "If you insist on empty calories after sandwiches, I have some snickerdoodles from Meg and—"

"Had," she interrupted.

"Huh?"

"Had, as in past tense. I…uh, found them while I was tidying up. Why do you think I drank the rest of your milk?"

"Huh." He rubbed his chin. "I guess my cupboards weren't as bare as you claimed."

"Don't push it, McBride."

"I wouldn't dream of it, Harding."

A bell dinged and a cashier greeted them when they entered the neighborhood store, reminding Ellie of the Whatleys' Loon Lake General Store; Liam's offer of an apartment in his building flashed through her mind, but she just as quickly discarded it. They'd muddle through somehow, especially since their work schedules gave them both stretches with days off.

The cashier who'd greeted Liam by name as they entered immediately engaged him in a discussion of the baseball playoffs. Listening to the two debate a controversial ruling at second base, Ellie wandered to the rear of the store and a well-stocked deli.

"Morning." A woman with short dark hair and a Red Sox baseball cap stood behind the deli counter. She hitched her chin toward the front of the store. "You a friend of Liam's?"

"Something like that." *Friends who just happen to be having a baby.* Being friends with Liam was easy; resisting his crooked smile and quick wit was a different matter. Sleeping with him again would only complicate things. *But it sure would be fun.*

"What can I get you?" the clerk prompted, tightening the ties on her bibbed apron.

"Hmm…" Ellie's gaze traveled up and down the display case. She never knew what her stomach was going to accept. One minute she craved something, the next it made her gag. Her appetite was as mercurial as her moods.

"Liam's partial to the honey ham," the clerk suggested.

"Okay, that sounds good." At least he could eat it if her stomach revolted. "And some provolone."

Liam approached carrying a loaf of white bread and Ellie shook her head. "I'm not eating that."

He held the package up and eyed it. "What? You don't like bread now?"

She liked bread but was trying to eat healthy, or at least healthier. She was going to be someone's mom and needed to set a good example. "Don't they have whole wheat or twelve grain? Did you learn nothing from me this summer?"

"Yeah, I learned to hide my junk food," he said, and rolled his eyes.

A suspicious snickering sound came from the other side of the counter and Ellie glanced over. The woman's back was to them but her shoulders were shaking.

"Glad you find my being forced to eat healthier funny, Mrs. O'Brien," Liam said in a dry tone.

The woman turned around. "It's about time you settled down with a woman who is interested in taking good care of you, Liam."

"We're not—"

"Oh, we're just—"

The woman winked as she handed over two packages wrapped in white butcher paper. "I sliced it the way you like."

Liam was still stuffing his wallet into his back pocket after paying when Ellie poked into the bag and pulled out a package of chocolate-covered graham crackers. What the hell? He shook his head. She'd given him grief over some stupid bread and she was chowing down on more cookies. He made a mental note to ask Riley if pregnancy made women unreasonable.

Ellie stuck the package of cookies under her arm and held out her hands. "I can carry some of that."

He lifted the bags out of reach as they exited the store. "I got it."

She glanced back as they turned the corner onto his street. "See? That's why I could never move in upstairs."

He turned his head. What was she seeing that he wasn't? The street looked the same as it had when they'd arrived. "I don't follow what you're getting at."

"They assumed we were together."

"Umm…we were."

She shook her head vigorously. "I mean *together* together."

Maybe he was the one losing his mind. He chose silence.

"Once my pregnancy starts showing, people would be asking all sorts of questions and making assumptions."

"Assumptions? Like that we'd had sex?" Damn his big mouth. "C'mon, they'll do all that in Loon Lake."

"Yes, but, judgment or not, they'll also be there for me if I ever need help." Her lower lip came out in a pout.

Ooh, what he wanted to do with that sexy lower lip. Even in a pout, that mouth called to him. "This is Dorchester today, not in the 1950s. No one is going to judge you."

"That's what you think. How come you never went out with Mrs. Sullivan's granddaughter?" she asked as they passed Barbara Sullivan's three-decker.

"Because I have to live on this street." Evidently they were done talking about moving. He'd bide his time, but he wasn't giving up. Huh…he should be relieved she wasn't demanding all sorts of concessions from him, but the idea of her being so far away from him, in Vermont, annoyed him.

"But you said you always part on friendly terms with women you date. No harm, no foul," Ellie said.

"You wanna try explaining that to Grandmother Sullivan?"

She nodded. "Good point."

"And for your information, I'm not some sort of serial dater." However, he'd had enough relationships to understand the signals leading to the point where women began uttering accusations like "emotionally unavailable" and ended things before that happened. He liked to end on good terms. If the relationship progressed to the point of using those phrases, the inevitable parting could become acrimonious. He never wanted anything like that for himself and Ellie. Is that why he'd hesitated getting involved with her in the past? Of course the no-strings-attached thing hadn't exactly worked in his favor. He glanced at Ellie. Or had it? Could a child keep them together?

"You have to admit, you've dated a lot of women," she was saying.

"True, but they've been spread out over sixteen years. Never two at once and I never poached." Why did he feel the need to defend his dating history? He never had in the past.

They were back at his house and he shifted the bags so he could reach his keys.

Ellie reached over and grabbed a bag. "Here, let me take one of those."

Their fingers brushed and there was that spark he'd remembered but had tried to deny for the past two months. He needed to ignore it if he was going to put Ellie back into the friend zone. That was where she needed to be if they were going to work on a partnership for the sake of their child.

After lunch in the living room, Ellie brought her empty plate into the kitchen and paused in the doorway. Liam's hair had flopped over his forehead as he bent over to load the dishwasher and her fingers twitched with the need to brush it back. Their summer fling was over, and pregnant or not, she didn't have the right to touch him with such tenderness, as much as she ached to do so.

"I should leave soon to beat the traffic." She handed him her plate and grabbed another chocolate-covered graham cracker from the bag on the counter.

"Leave? Already?" He glanced up and frowned. "Why don't you stay tonight? You look beat."

"I'll be fine. I didn't plan to stay, so I didn't bring anything with me." She contemplated her cookie before taking a bite. The thought of packing an overnight bag had occurred to her, but she didn't like the message that would send. Whether to Liam or to herself, she wasn't sure. Maybe both.

"We can go and get you whatever you need. Boston happens to be a very cosmopolitan city. Stores, restaurants, hospitals—"

"Don't start with me." While she believed in co-parenting, living in such proximity to him without sharing his life would be impossible. She wanted it all. She was sick of being in the friend zone with guys. Was it too much to want one who saw her as a friend and a lover, a life partner, a guy whose heart sped up at the sight of her? Someone who was interested in something other than her bowling score or batting average? One who wouldn't bury himself in work when life got tough?

Her father used work to bury his emotions brought on by the uncertainty of her cancer. But blocking out his emotions meant he couldn't deal with his wife's, either. Ellie couldn't blame it all on her dad. She understood not everyone could handle all those emotions surrounding such a diagnosis. Of course, she also understood her mother feeling abandoned by the man who was supposed to be there for her in sickness as well as health. Trying not to take sides meant her own relationship with her parents was strained and not as close as it had once been.

He slammed the dishwasher door shut. "If you insist on going back this afternoon, I'm driving. I don't want you falling asleep at the wheel."

"Hello? I'm an ER nurse. I know better than that." If a brisk walk around the block didn't work, she would think of something that made her spitting mad. Angry people tended to be more alert. If that failed, she'd pull into the first rest area.

He leaned against the counter, his arms folded over his chest, his feet crossed at the ankles. "Either stay here with me tonight or I drive you back to Vermont. That's the deal."

She grabbed another cookie. She could argue with him, but what would that accomplish? And she really was dead on her feet and not looking forward to the drive to Loon Lake. Now that she'd delivered her news the nervous energy was gone, replaced with the usual afternoon fatigue. "But how will you get back?"

"One of the guys can drive my truck to pick me up."

"Were you able to get enough sleep on your shift?"

He nodded. "Yeah, a couple callouts but not bad."

"Okay, you can drive me back." Spending more time together was important if they were going to co-parent.

His head jerked back as he studied her. That devilishly sexy grin appeared, the one that deepened the grooves bracketing his mouth. The one that threatened her resolve to not throw herself at him. The one she was powerless to resist.

When he opened his mouth, she pointed her cookie at him. "Don't crow. It's not attractive."

"Says you." He straightened up and pulled away from the counter, his light blue eyes gleaming with mischief. "Let me get some things so *I* won't get caught short spending the night."

"Fine, but if you stay at my place, you'll be sleeping on the couch," she called to his retreating back.

He turned and began walking backward. His low chuckle said he was remembering the things they'd done on her couch. Damn. Now she had all those images in her head.

Those pesky snippets were still playing like movie trailers in her head as they drove through the narrow, winding streets of Boston.

"What can I say to convince you to move here?" he asked.

Tell me you love me and can't live without me. Tell me I'm the most important person in your life. Tell me you're in this for the good times and *the tough ones.* "Nothing. It ain't gonna happen."

He glanced over at her as he took the on-ramp to the interstate and sped up to blend into traffic. "The upstairs apartments are just as nice as mine. You said you liked it and you could decorate any way you wanted."

"I'm sure it's very nice, but I want to stay in Loon Lake." There, she wouldn't have to watch Liam living his life with her on the periphery. In Boston, she'd be cut off from friends. If she were truly already a part of Liam's life, giving up Loon Lake wouldn't be that hard. But she wasn't and it mattered. "You said Meg picked Loon Lake to live in to raise Fiona. I want the same things for my child. I have nothing against where you live. Your street is very nice and if Mrs. Sullivan is anything to go by, the people are nice, too. But I enjoy small-town living for all its inherent problems."

"Okay, I won't press."

"Thanks," she said, but she had a feeling the subject wasn't dead, just dormant. But she'd enjoy the respite. "I love the idea of our child growing up close to Meg's kids."

He nodded and sighed. "There is that."

"Just think, another seven or eight years and Fiona will be able to babysit." Family ties were another reason to stay in Loon Lake. Her child would have ties to the town and its people the same way she did.

"Fiona babysitting. Lord help us all." He chuckled.

Ellie laughed and yawned. She settled back against the seat. It seemed like she ran out of steam every afternoon, no matter how much sleep she'd gotten the night before. And due to her pending trip, she hadn't gotten a whole lot last night.

Despite her pregnancy fatigue, her mind wouldn't turn off. Yes, she wanted to do what was best for her child and she was convinced Liam would be a wonderful father. Not to mention, the rest of the McBrides would surround her child with family and love.

Was it selfish to want some of that for herself, too?

Chapter 10

Liam had meant what he said. He wouldn't keep pressing her about moving, but he hated having two hundred miles between them. What was he supposed to do in an emergency? What if Ellie or his child needed him? He didn't want to be so far away from either of them.

He spared a quick glance over at his sleeping passenger and grinned. As much as he enjoyed Ellie's company, he was glad she was getting the rest she so obviously needed, judging by the circles under her eyes.

Yep, not letting her drive was the right decision. She'd make a great mother, and surely Ellie could undo anything he might inadvertently screw up. The enormity of the situation was sinking in and he must be getting used to the idea of being a father because he didn't panic each time the thought ran through his head. Well, that whole not-panicking thing was relative.

Before they'd left, he'd decided telling his sister right away made sense and Ellie had agreed. He'd hate for Meg to hear the news from someone else. Slowing Ellie's car, he turned onto the driveway to his sister's house.

The driveway leading to Meg and Riley's began as a shared driveway, then it forked off into two. Her home was set back about one hundred yards from the main road. The house was surrounded by towering trees on three sides, and if not for the other home across the front yard from theirs, Meg and Riley would be all alone in the woods. On the other side of the trees, the lake was visible only during winter.

A swing set, sandbox and bicycle leaning against the open porch announced this was a family home. At one time, Liam had urged Meg to go in with him to purchase the Boston three-decker, but she'd been adamant about wanting a real yard for Fiona and his wasn't much more than a postage stamp. He saw now that she'd made the right choice. Even before Riley returned to claim his small family, Meg had done the best thing for her and Fiona by moving here. Was that how Ellie felt?

He parked next to his sister's car and shut off the engine. Reaching over, he shook Ellie's shoulder. "Hey, sleepyhead, we're here."

Ellie blinked and sat up straight. She wiped a hand across her mouth and groaned. "Was I drooling?"

"Only the last hour or so." He took the key from the ignition.

"Why didn't you wake me?"

"Because then I couldn't razz you about drooling."

"Brat." She unbuckled her seat belt and scrambled out of the car. "Let's get this over with."

He got out and followed her onto the porch. Leaning down, he squeezed her hand and whispered, "Think of this as a practice run before we tell your parents."

Ellie had barely knocked when the front door was flung open and Meg, dressed in jeans and an oversize sweatshirt, greeted them.

"I thought I heard a car pull in." Meg gave Liam a questioning look as he hugged her and kissed her cheek. "This is a surprise."

"I hope we didn't come at a bad time," Ellie said. She was chewing her bottom lip.

"No, no. Come in." Meg waved them in and led them through the original cozy living room to the kitchen. "I hope you don't mind, but I have cookies in the oven and don't want them to burn."

Liam glanced around, surprised by the silence. With two kids and a dog, Meg and Riley's home was usually a lot more boisterous. "Where is everyone?"

"James is taking a nap and Riley had the day off, so he did the school run to get Fiona, and the dog jumped in the truck with him. He texted that they were going to stop at the lake to let Mangy and Fiona blow off some steam before coming home." Meg pulled out a cookie tin and set it on the table. "Sit."

Liam reached for the tin. "Snickerdoodles?"

"Manners much?" Meg swatted his arm. "Let Ellie have some first. These cookies are Riley and Fiona's favorites. They already gave me grief for taking half the batch to you last time I made them."

"I didn't forget, but *someone* got into my stash and ate the rest." He scowled at Ellie, doing his best to hide a grin.

Ellie glared back and pulled out a chair. "Hey, there weren't that many."

"Want some coffee to go with the cookies?" Meg asked, giving them quizzical looks.

"No," Liam practically shouted, remembering Ellie's aversion to the smell. Clearing his throat, he searched for a calmer tone. "No, thanks. Milk is fine."

Meg frowned but pulled a gallon of milk out of the refrigerator and reached into the cabinet for glasses.

Ellie sat down and grabbed a cookie while Liam poured milk for everyone.

Meg leaned toward Ellie. "I knew you were going to Boston, but you didn't tell me you were bringing trouble back with you."

Ellie broke a cookie in half and dipped it into her milk. "I didn't know he was coming. He insisted. You know how bossy he can get."

"You know I can hear you two," he grumbled before shoving a cookie in his mouth. Meg's body language told him she suspected something was up and they weren't going to be able to hold her off for much longer.

He swallowed his cookie and made eye contact with Ellie, checking to make sure she was ready. "We, uh, have something we need to tell you."

Meg did a fist pump. "What's up? I know how you clicked over the summer. You two getting married?"

Liam nearly choked on his milk. "No!"

"Ass." Meg punched his arm, sending milk sloshing over the top of his glass and onto his hand.

"Language?" Liam used a napkin to wipe off his hand and wet sleeve. He tried to act affronted but he regretted his knee-jerk answer. Looking at Ellie's face, he knew he shouldn't have said anything, even if that was his first reaction.

"You deserved it and the kids can't hear me." Meg turned to Ellie and shook her head. "I apologize for my—"

"It's okay," Ellie interrupted. "We don't have any plans like that."

Liam felt like the ass his sister had called him. Ellie was smiling, but her eyes were overly bright. Damn, he'd made her cry twice in one day. He reached across the table and touched Ellie's hand. "I didn't mean it the way it sounded."

"I know." Ellie cleared her throat. "I'm... That is, we're having a baby."

"A baby?" Meg's eyes grew wide. "Wow... Uh, I mean congratulations. That's...serious."

"Oh, we're not—"

"We aren't—"

"Uh, guys." Meg's gaze bounced from one to the other, shaking her head. "Having a baby together is pretty serious."

Seeing Ellie's flushed face, Liam sent his sister a nonverbal warning, hoping their sibling connection would say what he wasn't, even if he didn't know exactly what he was trying to say. "Yes, it's serious, but we're friends who will also happen to be parents together."

Meg nodded, but her expression screamed skepticism. "Does Dad know?"

Liam squeezed his eyes shut. "Not yet."

"At least you're in a better situation than I was when I had to confess," Meg said.

Liam groaned. "It's not like I can use my age as an excuse."

"He'll get over it. Doris has been a good influence on him and she'll be thrilled. She loves babies," Meg said, and turned her attention to Ellie. "I'm happy for both of you and excited to be an aunt. I never thought I'd have that honor. Riley's an only child and, well, Liam, he's—"

"Sitting right here, sister dear," he interrupted, raising his eyebrows.

Meg rolled her eyes. "I'm excited to be an aunt and for Fiona and James and this new baby to have a cousin."

Before Ellie could respond, Meg rushed on, "Too bad you won't be here in Loon Lake. We could be like pregnant sisters."

Ellie shook her head. "Oh, but I have no plans to move anywhere."

Liam ground his molars. Ellie's pregnancy wasn't planned but it was a reality and he didn't appreciate being shut out of major decisions, which might happen if Ellie stayed in Loon Lake. What other explanation was there for his caveman behavior around her?

Meg glanced at him with a *help me out here* look. He responded with a quick shake of his head.

"That's even better," Meg said. "We can be pregnant together. I think Mary and Brody are starting to think about giving Elliott a brother or sister. Wouldn't that be fun? Our kids could form their own play group."

Ellie pulled her hand free of Liam's. She leaned over and gave Meg a hug. "I'd love that. Our kids are going to be family and I want them to be close."

"Yeah, you're getting to be an old pro at this, sis," Liam said.

"Liam!" Ellie poked him with her elbow.

Meg laughed. "What can I say? Riley and I—"

"Riley and I what?" another voice came from the doorway to the kitchen.

Riley greeted Liam and Ellie as he walked over to Meg and leaned down to give her a kiss.

Meg put her arm around her husband's waist. "Where's Fiona?"

"Dang, I knew I forgot something." He leaned in for another kiss. When he finally pulled away, he said, "She's outside with the dog. Mangy's paws got all dirty and I didn't think you'd want muddy prints all over your floors."

"Mmm. Good call." Meg gave him a dreamy look.

Liam brought his hand up and covered his eyes. "Guys, company here."

Despite his joking complaints, something sharp poked him when he saw how happy his little sister was in her marriage. He was glad, he truly was, but seeing it made him realize what he was lacking. Could he and Ellie build that sort of life together? Whenever he imagined his future, Ellie was front and center.

"Oh, yes." Meg patted Riley's chest. "Wait until you hear Liam and Ellie's news. They're having a baby."

"Really? Congratulations." Riley clapped Liam on the back. "When's the big day?"

"Uh, we don't know yet… Ellie hasn't gone to the doctor." Liam looked to Ellie.

Riley shook his head. "I didn't mean the baby due date, I meant— Oomph."

Meg's jab to the ribs effectively silenced Riley, and she turned to explain. "Ellie and my brother are going to be…" She glanced at Liam but didn't wait for confirmation before saying, "They're going to be friends who have a baby together."

Before anyone could say anything else, Fiona burst into the kitchen. "Mommy, I taught Mangy to catch the Frisbee. 'Cept he won't bring it back to me."

"That can be lesson two," Meg said. "Did you tie him to the outdoor run before coming in?"

"Uh-huh, I tied him so he can't run away or run into the woods and get lost. Uncle Liam, I didn't know you were here. Where's your truck?" The redheaded dynamo, a mini Meg, barreled over to Liam and hugged him.

"I came with Nurse Ellie." He gave his niece a bear hug.

"Are you sick?" She tilted her head back and looked up at him.

He chucked her under her chin. "No, Ellie and I are friends, just like she and your mom are friends. We came in her car to visit you."

"How come you came to visit me?" she asked.

Liam laughed. "I meant—"

A baby's cry came from somewhere in the house.

"I'll go get him," Riley said.

"Thanks." Meg pulled him back with a hand on his shirt and gave him another kiss.

Fiona pointed at her parents. "Uh-oh, Mommy, you better be careful. Uncle Liam said all that kissing stuff is what leads to all our babies."

Liam groaned and rolled his eyes. The little blabbermouth. He just couldn't catch a break today.

"Oh, he did, did he?" Meg gave him a stern look. "Fiona, why don't you take Ellie outside and show her how you taught Mangy to catch the Frisbee. Maybe

Auntie Ellie knows how to make Mangy bring the Frisbee back."

Fiona scrunched up her face. "Aren't you and Uncle Liam coming?"

"Yes, we'll be out in just a minute."

Riley chuckled and clapped Liam on the shoulder before leaving the kitchen. "Good luck."

Liam watched Fiona take Ellie's hand as they went outside and wished like heck he was going with them.

Once the door shut behind them, he turned to his sister. "You gonna rip me a new one now?"

"Nope." Meg shook her head. "But I will say that how many kids Riley and I have is none of your business, just like whether or not you marry Ellie for the sake of *your* child is none of mine."

"Maybe we shouldn't have stayed for supper with my parents," Ellie said when Liam yawned as they drove to her apartment later that evening. He hadn't had the benefit of a nap as she had and he'd spent the better part of the afternoon chasing the dog to retrieve the Frisbee for Fiona to throw again. "I forgot you just came off a shift this morning."

After leaving Riley and Meg's, they'd stopped at her parents' home to break the news. Liam had suggested it, likening it to ripping off a bandage. Faster was better, he'd suggested. She would have preferred maybe another day to gather her courage but didn't want to take a chance they'd hear it from someone else.

But if she were honest, having to tell her parents she was pregnant hadn't been what bothered her the most about going to her childhood home. When they'd arrived, her father had been in his basement workshop, where he spent most of his time. As if he wasn't a part of what went on above those stairs. Her mom was in the stark white living room, where footprints didn't mar the carpet. Ellie could remember when the house was full of noise and clutter. No, it was the memories being dredged up. She could remember the laughter, the loving glances and tender touches between her parents before she'd gotten sick. She'd taken all of that for granted when she'd had it, thinking it would last forever. Now they were more like polite strangers. They'd remained married because her mother believed that's what you did. The marriage was in place but their relationship had withered and died.

"It's okay. Your mom's a good cook and I slept some last night. Plus, I have time to sleep before the extra shift I mentioned at supper." He glanced over at her and grinned. "Besides, I wasn't about to argue with your dad when he extended the invitation."

She picked at a hangnail. Despite her mom's initial concern over the fact that they had no marriage plans, she was looking forward to being a grandmother. Her dad had started to say something about the risk to her health but her mother shut him up with a stern look and a muttered "It's not our decision." When her dad had suggested Liam join him in the den while she helped her mom load the dishwasher she'd wanted to throw herself into the doorway to block their exit. And her objection wasn't solely because of her dad's sexist attitude toward chores. If she wanted to know something, she needed to ask. "What did my father say to you when you two went into the den?"

"Oh, you know…" He shrugged. "The usual guy talk."

She rubbed her chest. Had he already put her back into the *one of the guys* category? "You forget, I'm a woman." She managed a small laugh. "What's the usual guy talk?"

He took his eyes off the road to give her an assessing glance. "Whether or not the Patriots can go all the way again this year. You okay?"

"Fine." She glanced at the passing scenery as they drove across town. They might not be in any sort of committed relationship, but having a baby together was pretty important. Important enough to share things. "So you're going to tell me that you and my dad went into the den to talk about football?"

He blew out his breath. "It's all in the subtext."

Okay, so maybe they did talk sports. "So my dad didn't come right out and threaten your manhood?"

"Don't go there. Please." Liam winced and glanced down at his lap.

"Sorry," she said, and bit the inside of her cheek to keep from laughing.

"No, you're not." He huffed out his breath. "Your dad was subtle. He didn't drag out a shotgun to polish or anything like that. He did, however, stress that it was important for me to be an involved father and that included financial support. I assured him I'd do my share."

"My mother said maybe we should have started out a little slower, like maybe getting a dog first…see how that worked out." Her mother had been torn between rejoicing at having a grandchild and being concerned over her still-single status.

Liam chuckled. "There's still time…to get a dog, that is. I could check with Riley. I know he researched the one he got for Fiona so it wouldn't aggravate Meg's asthma."

"Yeah, Meg said he was careful before getting it."

"And then he went and spoiled it by letting Fiona name it Mangy."

She choked out a sob of half laughter. "How would we take care of it? With both our jobs, we—" She shifted in her seat. "Oh, God, Liam, how can we be parents if we can't even take care of a dog?"

He pulled into the driveway that led to her rental apartment, but didn't go all the way up to the place. Putting the car into Park, he grabbed her hand and gave it a supportive squeeze. "First of all, we don't have a dog, so quit worrying about a hypothetical situation. You're going to be a great mom. And we have plenty of time to work out the logistics."

"I'm going to be a single mother. Who knows if I'm going to be able to finish everything for my NP certification? That means I can't give up my current job." She hated that she sounded as if she were whining. Her job, while sometimes stressful, was something she enjoyed and it paid enough to support her and a baby; she had it a lot better than most. Plus Liam said he would be stepping up and she knew he was a man of his word. Poor Meg had had to do the single-mother thing for years before Riley came back into her life. Ellie knew Liam had done what he could to help Meg, but she'd still been alone at the end of the day.

"No one is asking you to give up your career goals. We'll work out our schedules."

She opened her mouth to ask how he could be so cavalier, but shut it without saying anything. He was being supportive and didn't need her finding fault. "You're right."

"What did you say?"

She huffed out a sigh. "I said you're right."

"Can I get that in writing?"

"Don't push it."

He laughed and squeezed her hand once more before letting go and driving the rest of the way to her place.

The motion-sensitive lights came on as they approached the three-car garage.

"Do you park in the garage?" Liam asked.

"I haven't been, because there's no inside access to the apartment. Of course, I may rethink that in the middle of winter if the owner of the main house still hasn't moved in."

Liam parked her Subaru and she led the way up the exterior stairs located on one side of the garage and unlocked the door. Her place was perfect for a single woman. But where would she put all the paraphernalia needed for a baby? Even a high chair would be a tight fit for the kitchen.

The *thump* of a duffel bag hitting the floor interrupted her thoughts, and hands came to rest on her shoulders as if he'd been able to follow her silent thoughts. She leaned back into Liam's warmth and strength.

"It's going to be okay," he said as his fingers massaged the kinks caused by the day's tension.

She tilted her head back and stared up at him. He had the beginnings of a five o'clock shadow. He'd let his facial hair grow out a bit on his four-day rotation, but he would have to be clean-shaven when he went back on duty to allow the secure suction his respirator needed.

She knew so many things about him and yet they now felt like mere details. "How come I'm the one freaking out and you're the voice of reason?"

His arms went around her and he leaned down and kissed the tip of her nose. "Just abiding by the rules."

"Rules?" She turned in the shelter of his arms. It felt so good to be there, to lean her head against his chest and listen to his steady heartbeat.

"I've decided only one of us is allowed to freak out at a time. I'm counting on you to be the voice of reason when I panic." He gave her a quick squeeze. "Whaddaya say? Deal?"

She hugged him but quickly stepped back, making sure the contact didn't last too long. Like ripping off a bandage. She didn't want him to think she was throwing herself at him—even if that was what she wanted to do. "Deal."

Chapter 11

Liam stooped to pick up his duffel from the kitchen floor. Ellie's message was clear that she'd put him back in the no-sex friend zone. But that was good...wasn't it? Friendship was what he'd been telling himself he wanted. Anything more than that meant opening up, making himself vulnerable, which he was pretty sure Ellie would demand, and he was just as sure he would refuse. How could he tell her his concerns about the threat of being left a single parent if the cancer returned? He'd look like a selfish chump saying something like that. Shaking his head at the thoughts dancing around in his head, he followed her into her living area.

Her apartment, around six hundred square feet, was half the size of his place. He remembered all the stuff his sister had needed for Fiona; there'd been baby gear everywhere in the traditional Cape Cod–style house he'd been sharing with his dad and sister. After his ma had been diagnosed, he'd moved back to his childhood home, ostensibly to help, but frankly he'd welcomed being closer to his family during that time. He'd bought his three-decker after his mother's death, hoping Meg would join him, but she'd insisted on moving to the family's vacation home in Loon Lake.

He glanced around. Where would Ellie put all the baby stuff? Ellie was compulsively neat and organized, even keeping her possessions to a minimum in the apartment to avoid clutter.

"Are you going to have enough room here?" If she intended to move, he and Riley could help, maybe even scrounge up a few other guys. She didn't need to be lifting things in her condition.

"You've stayed over before. It was never a—"

"No, I meant after the…" He swallowed. "After the baby comes."

"I told you already, I'm not moving into your upstairs apartment." She opened the linen closet next to the bathroom in the short hall leading to the bedroom.

"That's not why I said it." That was still his idea of the best scenario but he wasn't going to argue with her tonight. She looked tired and his conscience pricked him. Rest was what she needed. "If you decide to move to somewhere else in Loon Lake, Riley and I can help. I'm sure we can find plenty of people willing to do the heavy lifting for you."

She stepped back from the open closet, a stack of sheets and a blanket in her arms. "Right now, I'm not sure I have the energy to pack and move."

He lifted the bedding from her arms. Would the fact that she'd had cancer make a difference to the pregnancy? Could all that she'd gone through have an impact on her ability carry the baby safely to term? "Is that normal? Should we go to the doctor to be sure?"

"Fatigue is perfectly normal in the beginning."

"Like the throwing up?" He crushed the sheets in his grip.

"Yeah, I'm afraid that is, too." She frowned and snatched one of the sheets from his grasp. "Hopefully, both will improve in about a month. I understand the second trimester is actually rather pleasant. Don't you remember any of this from your sister?"

"Like I said, she was good at hiding it the first time and I didn't live with her the second time around." Or he was just that good at ignoring the obvious.

"Given the circumstances for her first pregnancy, I guess that makes sense." She reached for the sheet in his arms and began to put it on the couch. He set the rest of the bedding on the coffee table and began to help her.

"So you were serious when you said I had to sleep on the couch." He raised his eyebrows as he tucked the sheet between the cushions and the back of the couch.

"You can always sleep at your sister's, if she'll have you." Ellie slipped a pillowcase over the pillow.

Okay, she put him in his place. But hey, a guy could try. "I think it would get a little crowded."

"Crowded? I thought that's what the new addition was for." She punched the pillow.

He winced as he watched her treatment of his pillow. "I was thinking crowded more in terms of people and dog, rather than space."

Sighing, she fluffed the pillow out. "What do you think this place is gonna be like once we have a baby?"

"Why do you think I suggested moving into my upstairs apartment?" He regretted the words as soon as they found air. Pressing his point right now was counterproductive.

"Give it a rest, Liam." Ellie smoothed out a blanket over the sheet and arranged the pillow at one end of the sofa. "Well, good night. I hope you get a good night's sleep."

"So you're not going to take pity on me?" he called to her retreating back.

"That puppy-dog face of yours won't get you anywhere, McBride."

"Hey, you weren't even looking."

After she had shut the bedroom door, Liam stripped down to his boxer briefs and got between the covers on the sofa.

A short time later, he jackknifed into a sitting position and glanced around. He sat and listened to see what had awakened him up from a sound sleep. He was accustomed to sleeping around a dozen other guys during shifts at the fire station, so noises in the night didn't usually bother him.

"Are you okay?" he asked Ellie as she came down the short hall from her bedroom.

She nodded. "I got up to use the bathroom and decided to get a drink of water. I'm sorry if I woke you, but I'm not used to having someone here with me."

"It's okay. I just wanted to be sure you weren't sick again." And he wanted to say stuff, but he wasn't even sure what it was he wanted to say, let alone how to say it. And, man, wasn't that messed up?

She shook her head. "No. That's mostly in the mornings but that's not hard and fast."

He nodded. "That's good."

"Glad you think so." Her tone was dry.

Aw, man, could he not catch a break? "I didn't mean... I only meant—"

"You're making this way too easy." She thumped him on the shoulder and grinned.

"And yet you keep doing it," he grumbled, and rubbed his shoulder, but his actions were for effect. She wasn't angry and he was grateful. He certainly hadn't meant to piss her off. "I'm trying to be supportive."

"And I appreciate it, but you don't need to hover."

"I don't hover." And even if he did, who could blame him? Ellie was pregnant with his child. He was doing his best to hold it all together and not let his panic show.

"Well...good night. And sorry for waking you."

"Don't worry about it."

She went back into the bedroom and he sank down on the couch and punched the pillow. He had just stretched out when a noise had him opening his eyes. Ellie was standing next to the couch.

He sat up. "What's the matter?"

She chewed on her bottom lip. "Umm...that couch isn't very comfortable."

"I've had worse."

She reached out her hand toward him and he grabbed it. Still unsure of what was happening, he frowned. "Ellie?"

"I don't want to send the wrong signal but..." She tugged on his hand. She waved her free hand toward the bedroom. "We can share, right? I'm talking platonic."

Relief swept through him as he grabbed his pillow with his free hand and let her lead him to the bedroom. Spending the night in the same bed with Ellie, even in a platonic sense, was important. He couldn't pinpoint why. Too much had happened today to make sense of the jumble of emotions. He just knew he wanted to be as close as possible to her.

Ellie's first thought upon awakening was Liam. She lay in his arms and it wasn't a dream. Oh, yeah, she'd invited him to sleep in the bed. At the time she'd fallen asleep he'd been way over on his side of the bed and she on hers. Now they were huddled together in the middle as if their bodies had taken over while they slept.

Sighing, she burrowed closer, intent on enjoying the moment. This time of year, the mornings could be cool, so waking to warmth was unusual.

"Ellie?" he murmured near her ear.

"Mmm?" She huddled closer.

He cleared his throat. "Could you not do that?"

She moved again, shimmying closer, then scolding herself. What was she doing? She shouldn't tease unless she intended to follow through. Maybe sex wouldn't be a total disaster. After all, she couldn't get pregnant again. She shifted.

"Yeah, that," he groaned, his voice tight.

"Sorry." She scooted away and turned to face him. Did she want to do this? "Truly, I am sorry. That wasn't nice."

"Not unless you plan to—" His cell phone rang before he could finish. He heaved an exasperated sigh. "That's my dad's ringtone."

Ellie was already scooting to the other side of the bed. Interrupted or saved? She couldn't decide. "Then you'd better get it."

"Wait." Liam stopped her retreat to the other side of the bed with a hand on her arm.

She turned back to face him and he gave her a quick kiss. The mattress bounced a little as he got up. She got a good look at his broad back and fine butt encased in black cotton boxer briefs as he hurried into the living area.

Grabbing her robe and pulling it on, she followed him into the other room.

"Hey, Dad. What's up?" He listened and winced. "I should have known this would happen. We had planned to tell you when you got back. So we could do it in person."

Ellie couldn't hear the other end of the conversation but she imagined Mac being more hurt than angry if he'd heard the news from someone else.

Liam rolled his eyes when their gazes met and she smiled.

"Yeah, you did and I was but—" Liam nodded. "I will and yes, I was with her when we told her parents. Thanks. Talk to you soon."

He placed the phone back on the counter. Blowing out his breath, he rubbed a hand over his face.

"I take it your dad found out?"

He nodded and rubbed a hand across his face.

"Meg?"

"Fiona. Dad said at first he thought she was talking about Meg's pregnancy but Fiona clarified before Meg could get the phone away from her."

"Was he angry?" She felt bad that Mac had found out through someone else, but at least it was a family member.

Liam rubbed the back of his neck. "Not about us

not telling him. He understood the situation with them being out of town."

Yeah, Mac was a pretty reasonable guy. "Let me guess, he doesn't understand the friends-having-a-baby part."

Liam stabbed a finger in the air. "That would be the one."

She put her arms around his waist and gave him a loose hug. "Once the baby is here, he'll be thrilled."

"Yeah, I could hear Doris in the background saying congratulations." He hooked his arm around her waist, pulling her closer and kissing the top of her head.

His phone rang again. He dropped his arm and stepped away. "And that'll be my sister."

He picked up the phone and pointed the screen at her. "Told ya."

"Uh-oh." Ellie laughed.

Liam swiped his thumb and answered. "Well, if it isn't my blabbermouth sister."

Ellie was close enough to hear Meg apologizing on the other end.

"When has Fiona ever been able to keep a secret? She takes after someone else I know." He quirked a smile. "Yeah, you. As I've said before, it's like growing up with you all over again."

While he was talking with Meg, she pulled out ingredients to make breakfast. Most mornings she ate cereal but the thought didn't appeal, and since Liam was here, she decided on scrambled eggs and sausages.

Liam set his phone back down. "Do I have time for a quick shower before breakfast?"

"Sure."

After breakfast, he helped her clean up the kitchen.

"I noticed your tire pressure light was on so I thought I'd take your car to get some air in the tires and fill you up your gas tank."

"Okay." She found her purse and pulled out her wallet to reimburse him.

"Ellie." He shook his head. "Put that away."

"But…"

"No buts." He leaned over and kissed her forehead. "We're in this together."

Ellie stayed home to catch up on some studying for an upcoming exam. She wasn't sure if she'd be able to finish her degree requirements in time for her plans for getting a job at the proposed assisted living and nursing facility, but she still needed to keep up with the classes she was taking.

The money she'd been spending on school might be better spent on a bigger apartment. This one would be crowded with a baby. *There's always Liam's offer of one of his rentals*, an inner voice reminded her.

She frowned and rubbed her stomach, sending a silent apology to the new life growing inside. Was being stubborn going to mean her baby would ultimately suffer for her decisions? Or would getting involved with someone who coped with emotions by pulling away and burying himself in work be worse?

The apartment door opened and she slammed her book shut, realizing she hadn't really studied. "That took a while."

Liam closed the door behind him. "I got your oil changed, too."

"You didn't have to do that."

"Ogle insisted. Said it was time." Liam shrugged. "Who am I to argue?"

"Well, if Ogle wanted to do it."

"He's got some kid working for him that he said needed the experience."

"A kid? You and Ogle let a kid change my oil?" She frowned. Her tone carried a bit of annoyance, but she was touched by his actions on her behalf. It was the type of thing her dad did for her mom, even after the breakdown of their relationship; she suspected Mac had done it for Liam's mom and now for Doris. Ellie realized it was nice to have someone who had your back.

"Yeah, Kevin says hi." Liam chuckled and held up his hands in a self-protection stance.

She made a moue with her lips. "You shouldn't tease me when I'm hungry."

"Oh, no, do I have a hangry diva on my hands?" He put his arm around her shoulders and squeezed.

"Yes, you do. I slathered peanut butter on a banana for lunch, but it's worn off."

"Don't worry about it. I'm taking you out for…" Liam said and grinned. "An early supper."

"You are?" Her heart skipped a beat. *As in a date?* Here they were, having a baby and never actually been on a real date. That strange quasi-date at Hennen's when they'd run into Mike and Colton didn't count.

"I'm here, so we may as well hang out together."

Oh, but she yearned for more than hanging out. She wanted them to be a couple—a family—a real family. Maybe she should come right out and tell him what she wanted. How could you get something if you didn't ask for it? "Liam, I—"

"Maybe if we'd gone out more, we might not be in this situation," he interrupted.

Maybe now wasn't the time for confessions. She managed a little laugh. "You think?"

His blue eyes twinkled as he regarded her. "Nah, not really. I think it's payback from the universe for all the comments I make about Meg and Riley."

"I think it was a little more than that."

"Really?" He raised his eyebrows. "Maybe you need to show me...just so I'll know better in the future."

"Nice try, but you promised to take me out to supper and I'm starving." Not that she didn't want to explore that chemistry again, but hunger took precedence.

He sighed. "If I feed you, maybe we can revisit this discussion?"

She tilted her head from side to side as if sizing him up. "Perhaps."

"There's nothing more appealing than a decisive woman." He draped an arm around her shoulders and laughed. "So, when you're not tossing your cookies, you're hungry. Have I got that right?"

"It's not funny. Sometimes I feel as though I'm all over the map. One minute happy, the next crying. And food I used to love makes me sick just to think about it."

"I hate to disagree...especially with a pregnant woman but..." He gently rubbed his knuckles across the top of her head. "It's a bit funny from where I'm standing, but I will take you out to eat."

"Ha, you weren't exactly Mr. Calm-and-Collected when I was losing it in your bathroom."

He sighed. "You had me scared to death."

She knew he was probably thinking of his mother, so she didn't tease. "Sorry."

He gave her a smile that melted her heart. "Let's get some food in you before you become unbearable."

Scooting out from under his arm—even though it felt heavenly—she said, "Sounds like a plan."

He reached behind him and scooped up her car keys from the kitchen counter. "Ready?"

"You're driving?"

He jangled her keys and tilted his head. "No?"

"Fine, but quit messing with the presets on my radio."

"If you had decent music, I wouldn't be forced to listen to the radio." He shook his head, looking at her as if he pitied her.

She pushed him toward the door. "We won't listen to anything then. I'll serenade you."

"Oh, good Lord." He stopped dead in his tracks.

She plowed into him and swatted his freaking broad shoulders. "Hey!"

He chuckled and captured her hand and threaded his fingers through hers. "C'mon, let's go."

Chapter 12

Ellie hummed to herself the next morning as she pulled out a carton of eggs from the refrigerator. Liam had gotten out of bed and brought her saltine crackers to settle her stomach before jumping into the shower.

Having breakfast ready for him was a good way to repay the favor. She was dicing peppers and onions when her cell phone rang. She wiped her hands on the kitchen towel hanging over the oven handle before answering.

"Ellie, so glad I caught you." Meg sounded a little breathless.

"What's up?" Ellie frowned.

"I really hate to bother you on your day off, but do you think you could watch James for a couple hours today? Riley got called in to work and I'd already promised to help chaperone Fiona's class trip to the pumpkin patch."

"Sure." Ellie glanced at the clock on the stove. "Do I have time to shower and get dressed?"

"Of course. Thanks, I really appreciate this."

"No problem. I'll be there as soon as I can."

Liam appeared in the in the living area, his jeans unbuttoned and riding low on his hips, the band from his boxer briefs visible. He was shirtless, a towel thrown over his shoulder. "Did you get called in to work or something?"

"No. That was Meg. She asked if I could help her out." She swallowed as her gaze took in his gloriously bare chest, remembering how those muscles reacted to her touch.

"What does Meg need help with?"

Of course if he was on one of those calendars, then all women would be drooling over the six-pack abs and the dusting of hair that formed a V and disappeared under the waistband of his jeans. His dark hair was more disheveled than normal.

"Ellie? My sister?"

She forced her gaze upward and her thoughts on the conversation, but it wasn't easy. Liam wasn't muscle-bound like a weight lifter, but he was fit. Oh, boy, was he ever.

Clearing her throat, she explained, "Meg asked if I could watch James while she helps chaperone Fiona's class trip to the pumpkin patch."

He tossed the towel over the back of the chair and picked up a gray waffle-weave henley draped over the back of the couch. "What time does she need you?"

"As soon as I shower and dress." She checked her watch.

"Do you want some breakfast before we head over?" he said and pulled the shirt over his head.

Her heart rate kicked up. "Oh, you're coming with me?"

"Is that okay with you?" He grabbed his sneakers and sat on the sofa.

"Sure. I had already started on breakfast but I'd better jump in the shower instead."

He stuffed his feet into his sneakers. "What were you making?"

"The ingredients for omelets are on the counter."

He finished tying his laces and came to stand next to her. "Go get in the shower. I can handle omelets."

Liam drank a quick cup of coffee while Ellie was in the shower and rinsed the cup in the sink. He finished chopping the peppers and onions and set about making omelets. He was putting the plates on the breakfast bar when she came back from her shower. They ate quickly and Liam stacked the plates in the sink before they left.

Meg met them at the door, holding James on her hip, the dog at her side. The baby had a piece of a banana clutched in his fist. "Ooh, two for the price of one."

Liam bumped shoulders with Ellie. "You didn't say you were getting paid. Trying to get out of sharing with me?"

Meg led them through the small original living room into the new, expansive family room with large windows and patio doors looking into the woods at the back of the house. They didn't have a deck or patio yet, but Riley hoped to put one in soon.

"Yeah, good luck getting to those snickerdoodles before me," Ellie said, and smiled at James and gave him a kiss on the top of his head. "Hello there, little man."

He waved the banana around and showed her a toothy grin. The dog, an Aussiedoodle with reddish-brown curls, whined, his intent gaze on the fruit.

Meg wiped a piece of banana off his cheek. "He was just finishing his morning snack. I haven't had a chance to get him washed yet."

The baby thrust the smashed banana toward Liam. "Meem."

"Thanks, buddy, but I just ate."

"I can get him cleaned up." Ellie reached out and took James in her arms. "Looks like you're enjoying that nanner, bud."

Meg nodded. "Bananas are his new favorite snack."

He offered it to Ellie, but she shook her head, her lips clamped firmly together. James, imitating her by vigorously shaking his head, opened his fist and let the banana piece fall, but Mangy scooped it up in midair.

Meg laughed. "You guys might want to consider getting a dog."

Remembering how upset Ellie had gotten over the thought of taking care of a pet, Liam winced. He glared at his sister, shaking his head, but Meg threw him a puzzled look. His gaze went to Ellie, but evidently she was too busy talking to James to be upset.

Meg kissed James before Ellie took him to wash his hands and face. She turned to Liam. "What was that all about? Ellie likes dogs. So do you."

He swiped a hand over his face. "It's a long story."

"And I'm in a hurry. Any questions before I leave?"

Liam glanced at the flat screen he and Riley had

mounted to the wall. "As a matter of fact I do. Tell me again the channel number for ESPN on your television."

"I don't know." Meg picked up her purse and keys.

"How can you not know something that important?"

"Yeah, like I have time to watch television. By the time I get Fiona and James down for the night, I'm ready to crawl into bed myself, especially with Riley on nights." Meg patted her still-flat stomach. "At least by the time this one comes, he'll have enough seniority to get a day shift when one becomes available."

"Okay. Jeez. Sorry I asked." He threw up his hands in a defensive gesture but laughed when Meg held up a fist. "I'm sure I can find it."

Meg lowered her arm. "You'll have to find the remote first. It's James's new favorite thing now that he can lift up against the coffee table."

"Not exactly running a tight ship, are we, sis?" As soon as he said it, he realized his mistake. Meg would have plenty of opportunities to point out parenting errors to him in the near future.

She gave him a big, evil smile. "Oh, I am so going to enjoy picking on you when you have one running around."

"Ellie and I will have it all under control." *Nothing like compounding your mistakes.*

"Ha! I love it." Meg laughed and rubbed her palms together. "You are so clueless. I'd help you look for the remote, but I'm already running late."

"So much for sitting around watching sports high-lights in my underwear," he muttered as he lifted couch cushions in his search for the remote. Each time he lifted a cushion Mangy stuck his shaggy head under it. He patted the dog's head as he pushed it out of the way so he could replace the cushion. "What you looking for, boy?"

The dog whined and stuck his nose in the space between the arm and the cushion, grabbing something.

Liam latched onto the dog's collar before he could scamper off with his treasure. He pried a set of plastic keys from the animal's mouth.

"What are you two doing?" Ellie stood in the doorway to the large family room, James perched on her hip. The baby spotted the dog and grunted and lunged, but Ellie managed to hang on.

"Mangy and I were looking for the remote and he found these." The dog sat and whined as his gaze followed Liam's hand. "Sorry, boy, I doubt these are yours."

"Here, you take James and I'll wash those keys off."

He shook his head. "If I set them down, the dog is going to run off with them."

She leaned down and put James on the floor. "You stay here with Uncle Meem while I take care of this."

"Don't start with that Meem stuff. I just got Fiona to say it correctly."

"Meem... Meem... Meem," James babbled as he crawled to the coffee table and pulled himself up. One hand rested on the table and the other stretched toward Liam.

Liam tossed the keys to Ellie and reached down to ruffle his nephew's hair. "Hey, buddy, not sure what you're talking about. Can you say 'Liam'?"

"Sorry, but I think you're going to be Uncle Leem or Meem for the foreseeable future. At least you won't have to worry about that with ours."

Liam looked up from his search for the remote. "Why not?"

Ellie clicked her teeth. "Because she will be calling you Daddy."

"Oh, yeah." He scratched his scalp and frowned.

"What?"

"That's a scary thought, but I guess if my baby sister and Riley can do it, so can we." Had his dad gotten a mini panic attack thinking about being a parent before Liam was born?

"Can we?"

"You certainly can, you're an ER nurse. Of course you're qualified." Ellie was going to be great. He wished he had as much confidence in himself as he did her.

"Bet they wouldn't let me take home a baby if they knew how scattered I've been lately."

"I find that hard to believe." He jammed his fingers in the back of the couch. That damn remote had to be here somewhere.

She sank down next to James as he slapped his palm on the coffee table. "Believe it. I poured orange juice on my cornflakes last week."

"Run out of milk?" His searching fingers found something and he pulled out a tiny pink plastic hardhat. What the…?

"No, I didn't run out of milk. I pulled out the OJ by mistake."

"What did you do?" He started to set the tiny toy on the coffee table but looked at James and decided against it.

"I threw them out and started over, but what's that got to do with it?"

"It proves you're good at problem solving, because I would have eaten them."

"You are such a guy."

He wiggled his eyebrows. "Glad you finally noticed. Aha, here's the remote."

Ellie rolled her eyes. "Give that hat to me and I'll put it in Fiona's room. It belongs to her Barbie Builder set."

"How do you know these things?" He put the cushions back on the sofa.

"It's a girl thing."

"Hey, James, how about we watch some sports? Make sure that father of yours is teaching you the right teams to root for." He scooped his nephew off the floor and sat down on the sofa with him.

"I think he's wet. Let me go get a fresh diaper."

Liam held James up in the air. "Now she tells me. Are you wet?"

The boy let out a string of baby giggles.

Ellie came back with a diaper and tub of wipes. "Want me to take him?"

"It's okay. I've changed Fiona's. May as well get some more practice in." He truly did want to be involved.

He put James on the blanket on the floor and unsnapped the baby's pants to get at the diaper. At least he remembered how to do that much from when Fiona was a baby. He removed the soggy diaper.

"Liam, wait! Put this over…"

He glanced up as Ellie launched what looked like a washcloth at him.

What the heck was she on about? He knew how to— Something wet and warm squirted all over the front of his shirt.

He glanced down at his giggling nephew. "Why did he do that?"

Ellie had her fist pressed against her mouth and her shoulders were shaking. She cleared her throat. "It's something baby boys do."

"Why didn't you warn me?" After getting over being grossed out, he could appreciate the humor in it. And he couldn't be angry with an innocent—he glanced down at his giggling nephew. Huh, maybe not quite so innocent.

"I thought you knew. You said you'd changed diapers before," Ellie said.

"I changed Fiona's diaper a time or two and nothing like this ever happened." He shook his head.

"Girls are different but it can still happen."

"So, is there a trick to not getting wet?"

"I think the trick is to keep something over him like the old diaper or a cloth."

"Why would I know something like this?"

"You've never changed James's diaper before?" He shook his head and she continued, "Well, now you know. Look on the bright side, at least your face wasn't in the line of fire."

James began laughing and Liam put his palm over the baby's belly and tickled him. "You think that's funny? Now I'm going to have to wear one of your daddy's shirts and I'll make your mommy wash mine."

The baby giggled. "Meem."

He shook his head at James. There was so much he didn't know about babies and kids despite having spent a lot of time around his niece and nephew. Had his dad been nervous and clueless in the beginning? Maybe by the time his child was old enough to form memories of his or her childhood, he'd have a better handle on the whole parenting thing.

Once again, Ellie awoke to a cold, empty bed. She'd been doing that ever since Liam's friend Nick had picked him up three days earlier. She rolled over and rubbed her hand over the cool sheets. Liam had only slept over for a few nights, but she'd gotten used to having him here.

She had no idea when she'd see him again. He'd told her that during his time off he was taking an extra shift at one of the part-time stations. He apologized and explained that this had been planned for a while.

Sighing, she got up and pulled on her pink fleece robe against the apartment's early-morning chill. She paused to see if this was a morning sickness day. It wasn't. At least not yet. Of course her nausea didn't just strike first thing; sometimes it lasted all day or hit unexpectedly. Smells could trigger it, too.

The nausea had been getting worse but she knew the extra hormones that caused it kicked in around the eight-week mark, so it wasn't surprising.

Today was her first appointment with the obstetrician. She'd be going alone and part of that was her fault. She'd assured Liam that the checkup was just routine and it was, but now that she was faced with going alone, it felt…sad. It was still early in the pregnancy for the doctor to want an ultrasound. At least Liam wasn't missing out on something like that.

Buck up, Ellie, and quit your whining.

Liam had stepped up, but the fact that they lived three hours apart wasn't going to change unless she moved to Boston. Pulling up stakes, leaving everything she knew and had worked for to move so she could live on the periphery of Liam's life, held no appeal.

"But I'm reserving the right to revisit this decision," she told her reflection as she brushed her hair before dashing out the door.

At the doctor's office, Ellie flipped through old magazines, kicking herself for not remembering to bring a book. Not that it mattered since she doubted she'd be able to concentrate any better on the latest spy thriller than she could this three-month-old *People* magazine. Too many things running through her head. Being in the medical profession at times like this was not helpful.

The blood tests scheduled for today might be routine, but this was *her* baby they were running tests on. That changed everything. She was doing this so she could be prepared, not because she suspected something was wrong. Intellectually she knew her chances of a successful pregnancy were the same as anyone else's, but emotions didn't always operate on facts. But the situation gave her some perspective on what her parents must've gone through when her cancer was diagnosed.

Would she be faced one day with her child having a life-threatening illness? Her hand covered her still flat stomach as sympathy for her parents filled her.

She glanced around the waiting room at the other women in various stages of pregnancy, some with partners, others alone like her.

Heaving a sigh, she tossed the magazine aside just as the inner door opened and the nurse called her name.

Ellie jumped up. At least doing something would be better than just sitting and waiting.

The nurse smiled. "Ellie, it's so good to see you again."

Ellie recognized the woman from hospital rotations during nursing school. "Kim Smith, right?"

"It's Dawson now." The nurse led her down a hallway.

"Mine's still Harding, but I guess you could see that from the chart." Ellie hated the warmth in her cheeks. Plenty of single women had babies these days. Even in Loon Lake.

"It's been a while." Kim stopped in front of a balance beam scale. "How have you been?"

"Is that a professional question or making conversation?"

"Both, I guess." Kim laughed. "Okay, hop up on the scale."

"I hate this part." Ellie sighed and glanced at her red sneakers. "Can I take these off first?"

"Really? At your first appointment." Kim clicked her tongue but grinned. "This is only the beginning."

Ellie glanced at her feet and debated, but giggled and toed her shoes off.

Kim marked her weight on the chart. "Okay, take a seat and we'll get blood pressure next."

"You should've done that *before* you weighed me." Ellie motioned toward the scale. "Having to get on that thing probably raised it."

Kim chuckled. "So you're feeling okay? No complaints?"

"I'm doing good, if you don't count the morning sickness that pops up at all hours and crying over the stupidest things." Ellie sat in the chair and rolled up her sleeve.

"I hear that. I carried sandwich bags and tissues in

my purse." Kim set the chart on the table. "Take a seat and we'll get your pressure, then some labs, but I guess you know the drill."

Ellie nodded. "Yeah, I know all this stuff like getting a patient's blood pressure is standard procedure, but when it's being done to you, it doesn't feel routine at all."

So far there was no need for Liam to be here for these mundane things. So why did she feel so bereft?

"Yeah, we don't always make the best patients, do we?" Kim adjusted the blood pressure cuff on her upper left arm. "You still like working in the ER?"

"I do, but I've been thinking of a change." Ellie laid her other hand over her stomach. "Especially now. Do you like this kind of nursing?"

"I'm sure it's not as exciting or interesting as the ER but the hours are easier. Plus, holidays and weekends off is nice for family life." Kim made notes on the chart as the Dinamap displayed her blood pressure.

Ellie nodded. From now on, she'd have someone else to take into consideration. Working twelve-hour shifts might not be feasible. She put out her arm but cringed when Kim came at her with the needle. Being a nurse didn't make getting stuck any easier.

"We should have the results back in one to two weeks." Kim marked the vials of blood. "And we'll just take a quick look today to verify the pregnancy and check for iron and vitamin levels. We'll need to get you started on prenatal vitamins."

After a week of denying her suspicions, Ellie had decided she needed to be proactive. "Yeah, I took some over-the-counter ones, but they don't have the same folic acid levels."

"I've got everything I need. It was good seeing you again." Kim opened the door and dropped the chart in the holder on the door. "The doctor should be in shortly."

Ten minutes felt like an eternity and Ellie was starting to get antsy when the door opened and Kim popped her head in. "The doctor has decided he'd like you to have an ultrasound. Fortunately, we can do one on-site. The tech will be in in just a minute to escort you back there."

Ellie's stomach twisted into knots. Not since being diagnosed with cancer had she felt so helpless. "Tell me what's wrong. Why do they want to do an ultrasound now? What can't wait?"

"Ellie, you of all people know I can't say anything." Kim shook her head. "Let's keep the imagination reined in," she added with a smile before closing the door.

Ellie glared at the closed door Kim had escaped through and wrung her hands. Was she overreacting? The way she saw it, she was allowed to do so. This was *her* baby, maybe her only chance to be a mom.

She should have said yes when her mother had offered to come. But she would've had to take off work and Ellie hated for her to use her PTO to come to a routine first exam. She had assumed the most exciting part would be to hear the baby's heartbeat. Except being alone with only her thoughts for company wasn't a good idea. She sat on her hands trying to keep them warm and swung her legs.

There was a quick rap on the door.

"Finally," she muttered. At least they'd be getting this show on the road. Despite Kim's advice, she'd let her imagination run roughshod over her rational self.

The door opened but instead of the ultrasound tech or the doctor, the receptionist stood in the doorway. "Someone is insisting on seeing you, but we can't let anyone back here without your permission."

Had her mother come, anyway? Who else could it be? The receptionist cleared her throat and Ellie nodded. "Yes, that's fine."

Before she could react, Liam loomed in the doorway, still in his dark blue BFD uniform. She blinked, but he didn't disappear. Liam was here! Oh, God, the news was so bad they called him. No wait, that was crazy. They hadn't done anything yet and he couldn't have gotten here in such a short time even if he'd been in town. Nothing had been wrong ten minutes ago... but was it now?

Chapter 13

She straightened and pulled her hands from under her thighs. "What are you doing here? How did you get here? How did you find me?"

He shut the door and crossed the small room in two strides. "I'm here because I was serious when I said wanted to be involved. I hit the road as soon as I got off shift this morning and I called Meg to ask where you'd be," he said, ticking off his answers by holding up his fingers. "I think that covers all your questions."

"You don't know how glad I am to see you." Ellie swallowed several times, trying to keep it together, fiercely holding back the tears burning at the back of her eyes. "Something isn't right."

He stood directly in front of her, then nudged himself between her legs until his thighs rested against the table. "What is it? What's wrong?"

"I don't know. It was supposed to be just a routine exam and labs but then...then..." She waved her hands in front of her, fumbling for words.

Without a word, he pulled her into the shelter of his arms and held her close. *She loved him.* She was in love with Liam. Not a schoolgirl crush. Not lust for a sexy-as-sin fireman. But soul-deep, forever love.

She snuffled against his chest. "Oh, Liam, what if something's wrong with our baby?"

His arms tightened into a bear hug. "Then we'll deal with it."

"Did..." He cleared his throat and loosened his hold. "Did they say what could be wrong?"

She shook her head and eased away from him enough so she could speak. "No, but they test for Down syndrome. But they won't have those results for at least a week. I don't know what this means."

He rubbed her back. "The receptionist didn't act like anything was wrong."

"She probably doesn't know and even if she did, they're not allowed to say anything." Next time she was faced with an angry relative demanding answers, she'd have a lot more sympathy.

"Ellie?" Kim opened the door. Her eyes widened when she spotted Liam, her gaze taking in his uniform. "Oh, I didn't know anyone had come with you."

Liam stepped away from Ellie and held out his hand. "Liam McBride. I arrived a bit late. I came after getting off shift this morning."

"Off shift?" She glanced at the Boston patch on his shirt and lifted an eyebrow. "As in Boston off shift?"

Liam nodded. "That's the one."

Ellie leaned to the side so she could see around Liam. "Liam's the...uh, baby daddy."

What a silly thing to call him, but it was the easiest explanation.

"Nice meeting you, Liam. I'm Kim. Ellie and I went through nursing school at the same time." Kim shook his hand. "They've got the ultrasound ready for you. It's just down the hall. Ellie, you can leave your things in here."

Kim glanced at Liam. "Umm...if you'll—"

"I want him with me," Ellie said, and reached for his hand.

Kim nodded. "Of course, I just thought he might want to wait here while we get you ready."

Liam paced the small room, waiting for the nurse to come and get him. His gut churned with every step. Was something wrong with Ellie? Or the baby?

Every time the word *cancer* tried to invade his brain, he shoved it aside and slammed the door. *One worry at a time, McBride.*

"Wait until they tell us," he muttered, and glared at the closed door.

He wanted to fling it open and demand they tell them something. He wanted to run to Ellie and hold her and make everything okay.

Thank goodness he'd listened to his gut, not to mention his conscience, when it told him he should be with Ellie. She had needed him. How could he have thought she didn't? Her assertion that it was just a routine exam had rung false because this was *their* baby. Nothing would be just routine for either of them. But this...

He couldn't imagine leaving her to go through this

uncertainty alone. He remembered his promise to be strong when she needed him to be. It looked like it would be his turn to be the strong one today.

The door opened and he resisted the urge to pounce on Kim and demand answers.

"We're ready for you," she announced cheerfully.

He followed the nurse to a room with complicated-looking equipment and a monitor on a rolling stand. Ellie lay on her back on an exam table with her knees up and a sheet draped over the bottom half of her body.

"This is Liam," Kim said to a technician.

The technician looked up. "Hi, I'm Sherrie."

"I'll leave you to it," Kim said. "Sherrie will take good care of you."

Sherrie smiled as she got her equipment ready. "You know we won't be able to determine the baby's sex yet."

"Yeah, that's not why we're here," Ellie told her.

The other woman nodded. "I wanted to get that out of the way so you won't be disappointed."

Liam went to stand next to Ellie and she reached for his hand.

The technician got out what looked like a wand and rolled a rubber sheath on it. Ellie squeezed his hand. He winked at her and she grinned, some of the tension melting away. He leaned close to her ear.

"I think it's a little too late to give me pointers now," he whispered.

She choked on a laugh.

"Okay, if you could relax for me now, Ellie," the technician said, and scooted the stool to the end of the exam table.

He laced his fingers through Ellie's and pulled her hand against his chest. Watching the monitor, he tried to make sense of what he was seeing. The technician's face gave nothing away. He'd bet they were trained to not reveal anything.

"I'm just going to call the doctor in." Sherrie stood and scooted out the door.

"Liam?" Ellie looked from the closed door and back to him. "I thought I saw—but her face was blank."

"Hey, hey, calm down." Brushing the hair back from her cheek, he tucked it behind her ear and cupped his palm against her jaw. He pressed his lips against her forehead. "You know yourself, technicians aren't allowed to tell you anything."

"They tell you good stuff like 'Oh, look, there's your perfectly healthy baby.'" Ellie sniffed. "If she went to get the doctor, that means something is wrong. Oh, Liam, I'm scared."

"Look at me." He leaned over so his face was directly in front of hers. "Whatever it is, we'll handle it together. I'm not going anywhere."

Tough talk from a guy who'd rather be feeling his way through thick smoke in an unfamiliar structure in danger of collapsing than to be here right now. Ellie's fear gutted him and his belly clenched.

A man with a thick thatch of gray hair hustled in and introduced himself. Liam shook hands but he couldn't hear the man's name above the roaring in his ears.

"Let's take a look and see what we have." Dr. Stanley put on a pair of glasses and settled on a stool in front of the screen.

"What is it?" Ellie asked in a hoarse voice.

The doctor slid his glasses onto the top of his head. "It appears there are two embryos."

Liam cleared his throat. "T-two?"

Dr. Stanley nodded. "Congratulations. You're having twins."

The man's words caused all the air to swoosh out of Liam's lungs. Wait…what? Twins? Was that even possible? *Of course it's possible, dumbass.*

"Thank you… I don't know what to say. I'm so relieved. Thank you," Ellie was saying to Dr. What's-His-Name. "Isn't wonderful, Liam? Liam?"

The doctor jumped up and pushed the rolling stool toward Liam. "Son, I think you need this more than I do."

Liam sank down, still trying to digest the information. Of course he was ecstatic that nothing was wrong…but two babies? At the same time? "You're sure?"

"Most definitely. It's too early to determine the sex yet, but I can tell you they're fraternal." The doctor slipped his glasses back down onto his nose to look at the monitor again. "Everything looks normal for twins. Of course with multiples, we'll want to monitor you a bit more closely, especially toward the end, but I see no reason for concern."

"With fraternal, we could have one of each," Ellie said. "Meg will claim we're trying to keep up with her."

Dr. Stanley glanced between them. "Well, if you don't have any questions, I'll have Kim give you some pamphlets on multiples and a prescription for prenatal vitamins."

"Thank you, Doctor, I'm just relieved everything is okay," Ellie said.

"Sorry if you had some anxious moments, but rest assured, everything appears normal." With a quick nod

of his head, he stuck out his hand to Liam. "Congratulations again, son."

Liam shook hands with the other man, but if asked to
describe him after he left the room, he wouldn't have a
clue. It was as if he was experiencing the world through
his respirator…his breathing loud in his ears while everything else was muffled.

"You look a little shell-shocked," Kim observed as
she led him to the previous exam room while Ellie got
cleaned up and dressed.

"I was just wrapping my head around one and now
it's two…at once." His voice cracked on the last part.

Kim patted him on the shoulder. "Believe me, this
isn't the first time I've seen that look. Before you leave,
I'll put you in touch with the local support group for
multiples."

"Support group for multiples…" Liam shook his
head. "That's a thing?"

She chuckled. "Yup. Your reaction to the news is
quite typical."

"Ellie should be back in a moment," Kim added and
left.

He needed to hold it together for Ellie. Today's news
was unexpected but he could handle it and keep everything under control. Sitting hunched forward with his
elbows on his thighs, his mind raced at the thought of
two babies. Would having twins put more of a strain on
Ellie's body? Having her move to Boston seemed even
more urgent now, but he knew better than to confront
her. Ellie could be stubborn. He stared at his boots as
if they could supply him with answers. Maybe he'd talk
to Meg. This was a role reversal…asking his little sister for advice.

* * *

Standing next to Liam on Meg and Riley's porch, Ellie knocked on the door. Meg had insisted they come to supper while Liam was in Loon Lake. Ellie wasn't quite sure how she felt about Meg treating them as a couple. It wouldn't be long before the whole town was doing that, especially with Liam showing up in time for the ultrasound. The medical personnel couldn't say anything but that privacy didn't extend to the people in the waiting room. Liam showing up in his uniform hadn't gone unnoticed.

Waiting for Meg or Riley to answer, Ellie turned to Liam. "This feels like déjà vu."

He wiggled his eyebrows. "Yup. Déjà vu all over again."

She rolled her eyes but was glad he could joke. His face had drained of color when the doctor had told them she was expecting twins. He'd recovered quickly, but she could see he'd been putting on a happy face. Once the relief that nothing was wrong passed, the truth of her situation had started to sink in. She was going to be a single mother to twins. She wiped her clammy hands on the front of her jeans. Her initial relief that nothing was wrong had started to wear off and it was sinking in that the situation she thought she'd had under control this morning had done a one-eighty.

The door swung open and Riley greeted them with a sobbing James in his arms. "C'mon in. Sorry about this."

"Oh, no. What's wrong?" Ellie's heart ached for a now-hiccuping James. And for herself. She was going to have this, times two!

"He's crying because he's not allowed to play with Fiona's toys." Riley stood aside so they could enter.

"Worried about his masculinity?" Liam chuckled as he stepped into the living room.

Meg appeared and clucked her tongue at her brother. "It's a choking hazard. All those little pieces go in his mouth."

Liam glanced around. "Where is Fiona?"

"She had a half day of school and she went out to Brody and Mary's farm. She spent the afternoon entertaining Elliott so Mary could catch up on some paperwork. They'll bring her home later tonight."

James threw his arms toward Meg. "Mommy."

Riley ruffled his son's hair before handing him over to Meg. Turning his attention to his guests, he motioned with his head. "C'mon in and sit, you two. Supper isn't ready yet. We got a little behind with all the ruckus."

Ellie draped her jacket over the back of the sofa. "Can I help with anything?"

"Thanks, but I have it under control...for the moment." Meg laughed and tickled James's tummy and the baby burst into giggles. "But Riley can take my brother with him to help get the grill ready."

"Maybe we should give them our news first," Ellie said, and glanced at Liam.

Meg looked from one to the other. "More news? Does this mean you two are—"

"The news was from the doctor," Ellie interrupted. She didn't want Meg getting the wrong idea and starting a discussion she had no intention of engaging in.

"Is there something wrong?" Meg adjusted James on her hip. "Guys, you're scaring me."

"No, it's okay." Ellie put a hand over her stomach. "They said the babies are fine."

"Oh, well that's— Wait! Did you say *babies*? As in plural?" Eyes wide, Meg pointed to Ellie's stomach. "You mean…"

"Twins." Ellie couldn't help grinning. She was still riding high, grateful that nothing was wrong. At one point in her life she hadn't been sure she'd be able to have kids at all because of the cancer treatments. At the time of her treatment, being able to get pregnant didn't mean a whole lot but as she got older, having a baby became more important. Now to have two, while daunting, was a real blessing.

Meg shifted James and gave Ellie a one-armed hug. "I'm so happy for you. I know… Well, I just want you to know how happy I am."

When Meg pulled away, Riley gave Ellie a hug. "Congratulations."

"And you, too, bro." Meg gave Liam a quick hug. "Leave it to Liam to try to outdo me."

"I told you she would say that!" Liam scowled at his sister.

Meg sniffed and stuck her nose in the air. "Of course you'd have to be having triplets to catch up, or quad—"

"Bite your tongue," Liam grumbled.

Ellie raised her hand and waved it about. "Let's not forget I'm the one carrying these babies."

"Sorry." Meg laughed. "I'll settle for being an auntie twice over."

"Are there any twins in either of your families?" Riley asked.

"None that we know of. I asked my mom when I called to tell her the news," Ellie said.

"I'll bet she's excited," Meg said.

Ellie nodded. "She's already trying to decide what she wants to be called."

Meg laughed. "She may not get a choice. Fiona called Doris 'Mrs. Grampa Mac' for the longest time."

James pointed a finger at Liam. "Meem."

Everyone laughed and James bounced on Meg's hip, as if proud of having made everyone laugh.

Ellie's throat closed up and threatened to choke her. If, in the future, she and Liam weren't a couple, would he bring the children to McBride family gatherings without her? Would her kids come home and tell her how much fun they'd had? She blinked against the sudden burning in her eyes.

"Yeah, your kids seem to have a problem with names," Liam said, but the look he gave James made Ellie's insides feel all squishy. He might not believe it yet, but he was going to make a great dad.

"And I suppose yours won't?" Meg shot back. "You can call him anything you want, sweetie," she told James in a stage whisper. "Maybe when you get older, I can teach you a few other names."

Riley chuckled and clapped a hand over Liam's shoulder. "Maybe you'd better come help me get the steaks on the grill before you dig yourself an even deeper hole."

With the guys outside, Ellie helped Meg get James ready for bed.

"Pretty soon, we'll be doing this together to your kids," Meg remarked as she put pajamas on James.

"I have a feeling I'll be coming to you a lot for advice," Ellie told her.

Meg picked up her sleepy son and cuddled him. "I'll be here for you. You know that, right?"

"Of course, and I know Liam's going to be a great dad." And she did believe it.

"He will," Meg agreed, and gave James a small blanket with satin binding.

"Nigh-nigh." James hugged the ragged blanket to him and stuck his thumb in his mouth.

"Is it always this easy to get him to bed?"

Meg shook her head as she laid him in his crib. "I wish. No, he calls the security blanket his 'night-night.' I put him in his crib a few times when he was actually asking for his blanket."

Ellie went with Meg back to the kitchen to get the rest of the supper ready while the guys finished grilling the steaks.

Ellie was setting the bottles of salad dressing on the table when Liam came back in carrying a plate of foil-wrapped baked potatoes, Riley was behind him carrying a platter of grilled steaks.

"Hope you ladies are hungry," Riley said as he set the platter on the table.

Meg stepped behind Riley and put her arms around his waist. "For you, dear, always."

Liam made gagging sounds. "How are we supposed to eat now?"

"Can't you control him?" Meg asked Ellie.

Ellie shrugged it off with a grin, but her stomach clenched because she longed for what Meg had with Riley. Liam's pallor over having twins was fresh in her mind, along with the way he'd been fake-smiling on the porch. She needed a relationship that could withstand whatever life threw at them. Was that asking too much?

With a scrape of chairs, they all sat down and began dishing out the food.

"Will you be staying in your current apartment once the babies are born?" Meg asked as she passed the bowl of salad.

Ellie was hyperaware of Liam next to her. "For now. But twins changes things a bit. I had thought I could squeeze a crib into my place...but two?"

She was aware of him tensing and she rushed on, "I definitely want to look for a place in Loon Lake. Staying here is important to me."

In her peripheral vision she saw Liam press his lips together but didn't say anything.

Meg snagged a steak and put it on her plate. "Wouldn't it be awesome if you could buy that house next door?"

"But the property isn't for sale," Riley pointed out as he passed the platter of potatoes.

Meg nodded. "I know, but the owner has had trouble keeping it consistently rented. I'm not sure why."

"That's easy," Liam said. "It's because they have to live next to you, sister dear."

Meg pulled a face. "If you think you're safe because you're on the other side of the table, think again."

"Riley, have you no control over your wife?" Liam joked as he opened the foil on his baked potato.

Riley leaned over and kissed his wife. "Happy wife. Happy life. Right, dear?"

"Jeez, you've got him brainwashed," Liam grumbled, but he was grinning.

"Maybe he'd be interested in a long-term rental." Ellie put butter and sour cream on her potato. "Do you have his contact information?"

"I can call the agent. I think I still have her information somewhere from when I used to clean cottages between rentals," Meg told her.

"Thanks. I'd appreciate that." Ellie knew it was a long shot, but it was worth it to get in touch with the owner. Living next to Meg and Riley would be wonderful. Her children could grow up together with their cousins, as she had.

The table fell silent while everyone started eating.

"Are you here for three days now?" Riley looked across the table at Liam.

Liam shook his head. "Nah, I have to head back tonight."

"You do? Why?" Ellie chewed on her lower lip. She'd assumed Liam would be spending his off time with her. Didn't she have a right to expect that, after the news they'd just received? It wasn't every day you found out you were going to be parents to twins. She wanted to talk about it, maybe make some plans or even argue over names, something for him to show her he was in this with her. She blinked back tears. *Hormones*, she told herself.

His gaze searched hers. "Nick worked my part-time shift today and I promised to work his tomorrow."

She met his gaze and forced a smile. "I'm so glad you could come for the appointment today, but I hate that you have to drive back tonight already."

"It's okay. It was totally worth it." He touched her arm.

"Now who is making the googly eyes." Meg *tsk*ed. "But you're forgiven because finding out you're going to be a dad twice over doesn't happen every day."

Liam's knee was bouncing up and down under the table and Ellie gently laid her hand on it. When he looked at her, she whispered, "My turn to be the calm one. Remember we said we wouldn't both freak out at the same time?"

The wink he gave her said he understood what she was doing and he put his hand over hers and squeezed, but it was as if he'd had his hand around her heart.

She blinked to clear her vision. She'd fallen in love with Liam. Sure, she hadn't had far to go, but now it was like a neon sign blinking in her head.

She swallowed, glancing around the table. What would happen to her if she moved to Boston and left behind her support system? And if she stayed in Loon Lake, could her and Liam's tenuous relationship withstand the stress of long distance? What if her cancer returned? Her heart clenched. What would happen to her children? Would another fight for her life cast a pall over this family as it had hers? Or, unlike hers, would they rally around and wrap her and the twins in their warmth?

Chapter 14

Ellie rubbed her back as she left the ER after her shift. Three days had passed since she'd seen Liam and she missed him. Ever since he found out about the babies a few weeks ago, they had been spending more time together. But talking over the phone wasn't the same. She stretched her neck, trying to work out the kinks. If she was this tired and sore now, what was going to happen over the next few months? The exhaustion should ease up in the second trimester but carrying twins had to be tiring, regardless of the month. What did she have at home to make for supper? She had to eat and she had to eat right, but sometimes she was too tired to go home and do much more than make a peanut-butter-and-Marshmallow-Fluff sandwich.

She and Liam had spoken every night since he'd left. They made small talk, and every night she stopped short of admitting her love. If she said the words, put them out there, would he use them to get her to move to Boston? Would he think she said them to wrangle a proposal or him uprooting his life? She didn't know the answer so she bit her tongue and didn't say anything.

In the corridor, she looked up and saw Liam leaning against the nurses' station. Surprise had her halting mid-stride. He was chatting up the nurses, who looked enraptured by whatever story he was telling. Before she could decide if she should be jealous, he glanced over and a huge grin split his face when he spotted her. The smile, the glint in his eyes, were for her and that knowledge filled her. She felt lighter in spite of her exhaustion.

"Sorry, ladies, but it looks like my date has arrived," he said, and stepped toward her.

Ellie said goodbye to the nurses and fell into step beside Liam as they left the hospital.

"What's this about me being your date?" She asked, torn between the prospect of going out with Liam or putting her feet up in front of the television. At this time of year it was dark when she left the ER, and going home suited her.

"I was talking about feeding you," he said, and stopped under a humming sodium vapor lamp near her car.

She looked up at him in the yellowish glow from the lights. "That sounds lovely but I confess I was looking forward to going home and not moving for at least twenty-four hours."

Would he take that as a rejection? She shivered and pulled her light jacket closer around her. The temperature had dropped along with the sun.

He put his arm around her shoulders and pulled her against his chest. "No problem. I brought things with me. We can go to your place and I'll cook while you put your feet up."

"I can't tell you how amazing that sounds." She burrowed closer to his warmth and rubbed her cheek against the soft cotton of his sweatshirt. He smelled like clean laundry.

"What were you planning on having if I hadn't shown up?" he asked, his voice rumbling in his chest.

"My old standby. A Fluffernutter," she said, referring to her craving for a peanut-butter-and-marshmallow sandwich. She pulled away enough to look up at him.

He quirked an eyebrow and his lips twitched. "On the appropriate whole-grain bread?"

"Um…" She stared at her feet.

He clicked his tongue against his teeth. "Shame on you, Ellie Harding. After all that grief you gave me."

She shrugged. "I know, but it's not the same if it's not on white bread."

"Well, if you can see your way clear to eat healthy, I brought stuff to make a stir-fry."

"That sounds wonderful. Thank you."

"Don't thank me until you taste it." He cleared his throat. "And I brought something special but you gotta eat the healthier stuff first."

"What? Are you practicing saying dad stuff?"

He laughed. "I have to start somewhere."

"About this dessert. Did you buy it or—"

He held up a finger. "I'm not saying anything except maybe a certain bakery might be involved."

She cuffed him on the shoulder. "Don't tease if you can't deliver."

"Wouldn't dream of it." He kissed the top of her head. "And believe me when I say I can deliver."

She rubbed her slightly rounded stomach. "I know you can."

"C'mon. Let's get you home so you can relax while I make supper."

"You must be tired, too, if you just came off shift."

"Yeah, but I wasn't on my feet the entire time like you and I'm not carrying around two extra people."

"But at the moment your turnout gear weighs more than these two." She pointed to her stomach.

"True, but I get to take it off at some point."

"You got me there." She laughed and rubbed her belly. "If they're wearing me out now, I can't imagine what it'll be like once they're born. I watch Mary's Elliott running around and I can't imagine two doing that at the same time."

"Just remember, you're not in this alone." He met her gaze. "You know that right?"

"Yes, I know that." She did, but part of the time he'd be nearly two hundred miles away. She didn't voice her thoughts. A lot of women had it worse. Meg had been alone until Riley returned from Afghanistan, and Mary had been a single mother with no help until she'd met Brody and they fell in love. Unlike Riley, who hadn't even known about his daughter for years, or Roger, who had rejected Mary and his son, Liam was willing to be involved. Sure, she'd vowed to live her life out loud, but there was that sticky thing called pride. Their children would tie her to Liam for a lifetime, regardless of whether or not they were a couple. If she admitted her feelings and he didn't return them, he might pity her.

She'd had enough of being pitied to last her a lifetime. It was one of those things that eroded self-esteem.

"Okay, let's get you home, warmed up and fed."

Liam followed Ellie to her place, the bags from the Pic-N-Save on the passenger seat. Before going to the hospital, he'd stopped at the local supermarket for ingredients. He wasn't much of a cook but he could do a simple stir-fry and rice. Glancing at the white bakery box with its bright blue lettering on the passenger-side floor, he grinned.

He pulled in behind Ellie's car and cut the engine. Scooping up the box, he stuck it in one of the bags and got out. His chest tightened as he followed her up the stairs. Being back in Loon Lake with her felt comforting, secure. But that was crazy. Why would he need comforting?

Following her into her kitchen, he set the bags on the counter. "Before I forget, someone named Lorena at the Pic-N-Save said to say hi."

Ellie laughed. "Did you tell her you were cooking supper for me?"

"She gave me the third degree as she rang up the stuff. I got the feeling if I said I was cooking for someone else, I was going to be in trouble."

"Small-town life," she said as she took off her jacket. "Let me go change and I'll help."

"Take your time. I got this." He began pulling things out of the bags.

"There's beer in the fridge if you want. Help yourself, I can't drink it," she said, and disappeared down the hallway.

He pulled the rice cooker off the shelf and dumped in

rice and water before plugging it in. Sipping on a long-neck, he began chopping the vegetables. He was slicing the beef when she came back into the kitchen area; when he looked up, his breath hitched in his chest. A strange combination of feelings, a confusing mixture of lust and fierce protectiveness, filled him. He'd experienced both before but never at the same time. This was like a punch to the gut.

"Liam?"

He blinked. "Huh?"

"What can I do?" she asked, frowning when he didn't respond.

"Just stand there and look beautiful." He winced when the casual, teasing tone he was going for fell short.

She sighed and shook her head. "That's hardly productive."

"Then tell me about your day." He poured oil in a pan and adjusted the burner.

She got dishes down and utensils from the drawer, telling him how the EMTs brought in a man having a psychotic episode. "Luckily, Riley and another deputy came in with him."

"Damn." He paused in the middle of adding the vegetables to the pan. He'd heard stories from EMTs about how volatile those situations could get. The thought of Ellie—his Ellie and their babies—caught in the middle of something like that chilled him. "Do you think the ER is the best place for you?"

She set the plates and utensils on the counter with a clatter. "What's that supposed to mean?"

"I know how these situations can go bad. You could've been hurt trying to defuse it." He stirred the vegetables and removed them from the pan once they'd started to soften.

She put her hand over her stomach. "These babies are very well protected at the moment."

"I wasn't talking about them. I was talking about you. You, Ellie, *you*." He pointed at her to emphasize his point, adding the thinly sliced meat to the pan to brown.

"I'm an adult. I don't need someone hovering."

"Since when is being concerned about your safety hovering?" He recalled the time Meg told him how Ellie had gotten beaned by a foul ball during a game to raise money for new water and ice rescue equipment for the EMTs. He took a sip of his beer and put the vegetables back in the pan with the meat. "And should you be playing softball?"

"Softball? It's October. What are you on about it?" She planted her hands on her hips and glared at him. "Oh, wait, I get it. We wouldn't even be having this conversation if I wasn't pregnant, would we?"

The rice cooker clicked from Cook to Warm. He shook his head. "I can't answer that because you are pregnant."

"I assure you, pregnant or not, I can and do take care of myself. I don't need you—"

He turned the burner off and put the meat and vegetables on a platter. "Your supper is ready. We should eat before it gets cold."

She opened her mouth and closed it again. He set the hot pan in the sink where it sizzled when the faucet dripped. With a strangled sound she went to him and put her arms around his waist, pressing her front to his back.

He grabbed her hands in his and turned around, putting her hands back at his waist, and held them there.

She looked up at him. "Why are we arguing?"

He shook his head. "I'm sorry if I worry about you. And I mean *you*. I'm not saying I'm not concerned over the babies, but it's you I think about, Ellie."

"That's good because I think about you, too, Liam." She gave him a squeeze. "And I appreciate you making me a healthy supper."

"Better than a peanut-butter sandwich?"

"Much."

"You haven't tried it yet." He wasn't much of a cook, but stir-fry was pretty easy and healthy.

After eating seated side by side at the breakfast bar, Ellie insisted on cleaning up while he found them something to watch on TV. He decided not to argue with her. Since he didn't do much of the cooking at the firehouse, the guys usually put him on cleanup.

Taking a seat on the couch, he picked up Ellie's pregnancy book from the cushion next to him. He opened the book to the place she had bookmarked.

"Ellie?" His voice sounded strained to his own ears.

She had a bookmark on the chapter about engaging in sex during the different stages of pregnancy. Well, well, well. So, did Ellie have this on her mind? Or was she simply reading the book cover to cover and happened to stop there?

"Ellie?"

"Hold your horses. I'm coming." She came into the living area carrying the bakery box and napkins. Her gaze went to the book in his hand and she stopped short, eyes wide, cheeks pink.

He held up the book. "Interesting reading."

She put the box of cannoli on the coffee table and sat down next to him on the sofa. "I'll take that."

"But I'm not done reading this fascinating chapter yet," he said, and winked.

She tried to pry the book out of his hands, but he was holding on tight.

"I think it's important we read this together. You know, share *all* aspects."

"That's because you're reading the chapter about sex."

"We could read it together," he offered.

She narrowed her eyes. "Just this one? Or all of it?"

"I guess if I was there for the good stuff, I should be there for the…uh, other stuff. Huh?" Leaving Ellie alone to handle all of this would be unforgivable and he liked to think he was better than that.

"Well…" She canted her head to one side as she studied him. "We could start with this particular chapter and then move on to some of the others."

He tossed the book onto the coffee table and jumped up.

She lifted an eyebrow. "No book? Does this mean you're going to wing it?"

His gaze bounced between her and the book. "Is there something special I should know?"

"Not really. I'm not that far along."

That was all he needed to know, as he placed his arm behind her knees and swept her high up into his arms.

"Liam! You're going to hurt yourself."

He grunted and staggered but kept her close in a firm grip. "Now that you mention it…"

"Hey, I haven't gained that much weight, especially with all the nausea."

"If you say so," he teased. He was enjoying the way her eyes sparkled.

"Brat. Put me down," she said, then looped her arms around his neck.

He shook his head as he headed toward the bedroom. "Momentum is on my side."

"Why are you even doing this?" She tightened her hold on him.

"What? You saying you aren't impressed?"

"Maybe if you weren't grunting so much."

He stepped into the bedroom and set her down gently. Straightening up, he put his hands on his back and made an exaggerated groaning sound.

She studied him with a sly smile. "I guess this means you won't be able to—"

He put his hands around her waist to fit her snugly against him. "Does that seem like I'm incapacitated in any way?"

She put her arms around him and nuzzled his neck. "Hmm… I might need further convincing." She kissed him. "Just to be sure."

"Mmm." He nibbled on her earlobe. "Should we get some of these clothes off?"

"Sounds like a plan," she said and pulled her sweat-shirt over her head.

His gaze went to the small swell of her stomach. His babies were in there. Without conscious thought, he dropped to his knees and pressed his cheek against the taut skin.

Her hands were in his hair, her nails grazing his scalp as he put his arms around her. The moment might have started as sexy teasing but this was suddenly something more. He searched for words, but the tangle of emotions inside him prevented them from forming.

Her fingers tightened in his hair. "Liam?"

He might not have the words but he could show her what she meant to him.

Rising, he took her hand and led her to the bed, where he quickly disposed of the rest of her clothing.

He caressed her breasts and the areas around her nipples. "Have these gotten darker?"

"Yeah, it's increased pigmentation from…" She swallowed audibly. "Sorry, TMI?"

"You know I'm a sucker for nurse speak." He grinned, then sobered. "You're beautiful, Ellie."

She looked up at him. "And you have too many clothes on."

He reached around her and pulled the covers back. "Get in and I'll take care of that."

He left his clothes in a pile and slipped into bed, taking her into his arms.

Unlike the first time, when they'd both been so eager, he took this slow to demonstrate how much she meant to him. Even if he hadn't said the words.

Afterward, Liam settled her against him and rested his cheek against her silky hair. They worked as a couple and he dared to think about their future. Together.

Chapter 15

Ellie stepped out of the shower the next morning still glowing from the previous night's lovemaking. Dared she hope they had a future together? She smiled to herself as she grabbed a towel from the rack. He might not have come out with the words she longed to hear, but then neither had she.

Liam was taking her to Aunt Polly's, a local restaurant known for its pancakes. Maybe after that she'd—

All thoughts scattered as she felt a slight swelling under her left arm. She shook her head and swallowed back nausea. A swelling where the axillary lymph node was located wasn't good.

Of course there could be any number of non-lethal explanations but her mind insisted on taunting her with cancer. Fighting the urge to curl up in the fetal position on the floor, she wrapped herself in her ER nurse persona and called to Liam.

He popped his head in the doorway and his eyes widened and a grin spread across his face. His smile was her undoing and she choked back a sob.

"Ellie, my God, what is it? What's wrong?" He stepped inside her small bathroom.

"It's here." She lifted her left arm.

"What? What's there?" He stood in front of her.

"A lump...the axillary lymph node is enlarged," she whispered.

His gaze met hers. "Are you sure?"

"Of course I'm sure," she snapped.

He pulled her into his arms. "I only meant that we shouldn't panic. Maybe you bumped yourself."

"Don't you think I've been through all those excuses already? I think I would have remembered bumping myself under my arm. It's not sore or black and blue like a bruise." She buried her head in his chest while he rubbed her back.

They stood locked in the embrace, the only sound was that of a sports show coming from the television in the other room.

Sighing, she pulled away. "I'll need to get a biopsy."

Liam sucked in his breath. "Okay. Where and when do we get one?"

If only it was that easy... Well, it was, but those were the mechanics. The emotions that went along with it weren't. Especially now with her pregnancy. And Liam. Whatever they had was just beginning. She shook her head. Maybe her parents were right not to want— No! She refused to give in to defeatism. "You make it sound like ordering something off the internet."

His fingers were shaking when he reached out. Using

his thumbs, he wiped the moisture from her cheeks. "I'm sorry. I only meant—"

"No, I'm sorry. I shouldn't take my anger out on you." She sighed. "Let me get dressed and I'll make some calls."

Sometimes being an ER nurse, not to mention a resident of a small town like Loon Lake, paid off. Ellie was able to get a biopsy scheduled for that afternoon with her oncologist.

Liam insisted on taking her to breakfast as planned, telling her sitting around and brooding wasn't doing either one of them any good. She appreciated his attempts at proceeding as normal. At the same time they annoyed her. But she had to eat for the sake of the babies so she agreed.

After the restaurant, Liam drove them to the doctor's office. He was by her side and yet…

She clung to his hand in the waiting room, but thoughts of her parents clamored in her mind. Was this how it started for them?

The oncologist, a kindly man in his fifties, carefully examined a cut on her forearm. "This could be our culprit."

"But it doesn't appear to be infected," Ellie told him.

"And maybe your immune system is doing its job and fighting it off." The doctor pushed his glasses on top of his head as he looked at her. "We'll do some tests just to be certain, but I don't want you to worry. We'll have the official results early next week."

Back at home, Ellie tried to take the doctor's advice and remain optimistic. She pretended to read her textbook while Liam fixed her toilet that kept running.

She'd told him she'd put in a work order with the management company but he'd insisted. Not that she could blame him. Doing busywork was probably his coping strategy.

She heard him on his phone and soon he came out of the bedroom with his duffel bag: the one he used when going back and forth to Boston.

"What's going on?"

He looked up from his phone, a flush rising in his face. "I was asked to take an extra shift."

She'd heard him on the phone, though she hadn't heard it ring. Had he called looking for an excuse to escape? She immediately felt guilty for even thinking he'd do something like that.

He ran his hand through his hair, a muscle ticking in his cheek. "It's my job. Something I will need to support these babies."

"Are you sure you're not taking it to escape?" She hadn't meant to challenge him like that, but it hurt that he'd chosen work over her.

"Escape?" He scowled at her. "What the heck does that mean?"

She scuffed the toe of her sneaker on the rug. "Maybe it means that going to work is preferable to being trapped here with Cancer Girl?"

"Why would you even say something like that?"

"You see how my parents are. My dad used work to escape and look what it did to them."

"We're not your parents."

No, her parents were in a committed relationship.

When she didn't respond, he made an impatient motion with his hand. "The doctor said you won't have test results for three days at least. I'll be back once the shift is done. You make it sound like I'm deserting you."

You are! She swallowed and tried to remain calm but it was getting harder. Was this how her mom felt when her dad buried himself in work? Like he deserted her when she needed him? She resisted the urge to act childish by stamping her feet or using emotional blackmail by crying and carrying on. "You're absolutely right, Liam, but I also can't help feeling abandoned. I'm sorry and it might not be fair, but that's how I'm feeling right now. You didn't even consult me."

"I didn't realize I had to." He rubbed the back of his neck. "I'm going to work, not out partying, for crying out loud."

"I know it's irrational but feelings just are...they don't always subscribe to what's rational." It hurt to have him point out that they didn't even have enough of a relationship that he would consult her.

He heaved a deep sigh. "We're in this together."

She glanced at his duffel sitting by the door. "If you say so."

His gaze followed hers and he frowned.

"Could you have refused?"

"It's my job." He shook his head, his face a blank mask.

"My father had a job, too. I saw what my cancer did to my parents, to their relationship. For a while I blamed myself. I was convinced it was all my fault but now I know better. Cancer happened *to* me. I'm not my disease. And I'm sorry if you can't handle it, but that's not my fault."

"I'm not deserting you, Ellie," he said, and shook his head. "I need a little time and space to process all this."

"And that's fine. I understand that." She stuck out her chin. "I can give you time and space, but I refuse to be in a relationship with a ghost."

Three hours later, Liam walked into the station with Ellie's words echoing in his head. Leaving Ellie alone while she waited for the biopsy results was a cowardly move. But the emotions he'd been trying to deny had threatened to overcome him, so he'd run. He wouldn't blame Ellie if she hated him. He hated himself. By rules, the department couldn't force him to come back early but he hadn't said no. He hadn't said no because he'd panicked. From the moment he'd walked in on Ellie in the bathroom, he'd been unable to take a deep breath. His insides were a tangled black mass threatening to choke him. It was his ma, and to a lesser degree his friend and mentor Sean, all over again. He was going to lose Ellie and it was going to hurt more than the other two combined.

He went about his duties at the house by rote, his mind refusing to be calmed by the familiar routines.

Had he honestly believed being away from Ellie would make his black mass of emotions hurt less, make the panic disappear? Instead, being away increased the pain a thousand times over. He called to check in and they engaged in what could only be described as a stilted conversation.

Had he made the biggest mistake of his life by leaving?

He shook his head and threw the chamois cloth over his shoulder and stood back to check the shine on the engine he'd been polishing instead of watching a movie with the other guys.

"Chief wants to see you, McBride."

Liam nodded and tossed the chamois to the probie. "Have at it, Gilman."

What could the chief want? He hovered in the doorway to the office. "You wanted to see me?"

Al Harris stood up and held out his hand across the desk. "Let me be the first to congratulate you, Captain McBride."

It took a minute for the words to penetrate. Captain? Him? He'd done it. He made captain at a younger age than his dad.

He shook Chief Harris's hand and tried to feel something other than numb.

"You don't look like someone who has just accomplished a lifelong goal."

Yeah, why didn't he feel more? Sure, he was proud, but even that was fleeting.

"Okay, now, sit your ass down, McBride, and tell me what the hell is wrong."

The next morning, after his shift, Liam went straight to the white, Cape Cod–style home where he'd grown up and his dad still lived with Doris. He always had mixed feelings returning here. In the beginning, it was comforting because he felt his ma's presence. But that had faded and this was now as much Doris's home as it had been Bridget McBride's.

He rang the bell and waited. The rhododendrons his ma had loved so much needed trimming, but it was too late in the season to do it now. She had taught him they needed pruning immediately after they finished blossoming or you'd be cutting off next year's flower buds. Helping her trim them one day had actually been punishment for a transgression he no longer remembered. He rubbed his chest, recalling how, that same day, she'd bought him a treat from the ice-cream truck and let him eat it before supper. She'd winked and laughed as they sat on the front steps eating their ice cream.

Doris answered the door, surprise and pleasure evident in her expression. "Liam, it's good to see you. C'mon in."

"Hi, Doris, is my dad here?" He gave Doris a quick hug and she kissed his cheek.

"Yeah, he's out back if you want to go on through the house." She stepped aside. "Can I get you anything? We've already had breakfast but I can get you coffee or a muffin."

"I'm good. Thanks. I can't stay long."

"How's Ellie doing?" Doris asked as they went through the kitchen to the back deck.

"She's doing good." Other than a cancer scare and being left to face it alone, but he wasn't about to get into all that right now. "She's looking forward to the second trimester which is supposedly much easier."

"Normally, yes, it is but I've never been pregnant with twins."

"That makes two of us."

She laughed and opened the door. "Tim? Liam's here to see you."

His dad paused in the middle of raking leaves and waved. Liam went across the deck and down the steps.

"So glad you're here. I wanted to congratulate you myself, Captain." His dad stuck out his hand and pulled him in for an awkward shoulder hug.

"You knew?" Liam asked when they pulled apart.

"I may have heard something." Mac said and grinned.

"I haven't been gone from the department for that long. I still know a few people."

"Thanks." Liam cleared his throat.

Mac frowned. "What's wrong? You don't look like a man who has just gotten what he's been working toward for years."

Liam swallowed. How was he supposed to explain how hollow he felt? Sure, he was proud of making captain but after running out on Ellie the way he had, all he could think about was how much he'd hurt her. *Selfish much, McBride?* Why was he thinking about his own pain? He should be there comforting Ellie, helping her deal with her pain. Had he thought that, if he wasn't there, he'd be able to better handle the fear?

"What's on your mind, son?" His dad leaned against the rake.

Liam explained what had happened. He hated admitting his cowardice but he couldn't hide from it any longer. "Ellie found a lump and I shut down. I'm not sure I have the kind of courage you had to open myself again to love someone I might lose."

"It's not courage." Mac shook his head.

"Then what is it?"

"It's finding something that's more important to you than your fear." Mac met Liam's gaze. "Is Ellie that important thing for you, son?"

Ellie retrieved her jacket and closed her locker with a sigh. Liam had barely been gone twenty-four hours and the pain of missing him still throbbed, an ache that wouldn't go away. He'd texted earlier in the day but had been vague when she'd asked if he was coming back today, saying he would try but had some business to take care of first.

Had she pushed him too hard? Demanded too much? She pulled the jacket on and grabbed her purse. Maybe she wanted more than Liam could give. That wasn't his fault, nor was it hers. It was just…sad.

She stretched her neck, trying to muster up some energy as she dug around in her purse for her keys. Trudging out to her car, she glanced up and stopped in her tracks. Liam was leaning against her car, arms crossed, head bowed.

"Liam?" She continued walking toward him.

His head snapped up and he blinked, searching her face. "Hey."

She stopped when she was right in front of him. "Is everything okay?"

He reached out and rested his hands on her shoulders, gently massaging them. "It is now. Have you had any news yet?"

She shook her head, not trusting her voice. The look shining in his eyes was making something inside her spring to life, something that resembled hope. Hope was dangerous. Hope made you do things, say things. Hope could be devastating, even if you were careful.

He squeezed her shoulders. "We need to talk."

Talk. Yeah, they needed to talk, but for the moment she was relieved to see him. She did her best to tamp down the hope clamoring for freedom. He might want to talk about logistics or shared custody once the babies were born.

He was peering at her expectantly. Right. She hadn't answered him. "Okay. Come back to my place?"

"I have something I want to show you first, if that's okay."

She nodded, still trying to figure out his mood.

He took her hand in his. "Let's take my truck. We can come back for your car."

"W-what did you want to show me?"

"Our future," he said as he opened the passenger door.

Her mouth dropped open and she stared at him. He put his thumb under her chin and closed her mouth before giving her a chaste kiss.

"Liam, what in the world is this all about?" She still couldn't figure out his mood. He seemed a combination of excited and apprehensive. Or maybe she was crazy. Pregnancy hormones—times two!—were making her giddy.

"I need your opinion on something." He slipped behind the wheel but turned toward her instead of starting the engine. "I need to apologize for taking off on you. I shouldn't have done that."

"And I shouldn't have accused you of abandoning me." She sucked in a breath. "I may have overreacted."

He took her hand and brought it to his lips. "I should have explained myself better. I regret how I handled things with my mom, and yet I was doing the same thing with you."

"I know of a good support group for grieving families, if you're interested." She squeezed his hand. "Maybe we could both benefit from it, but first, I have to see what you want to show me."

He dropped her hand and started the truck. Although he didn't say anything else, he glanced at her several times as he drove across town. Clearing his throat, he made the turn into the Coopers' long driveway.

"Why are you taking me to your sister's house?"

"Meg's isn't the only house here." Liam pulled his truck up to the cottage-style home across the yard from his sister's house. Putting his truck in Park, he shut off the engine. Jumping out of the pickup, he hustled around to her side.

"Careful," he said as he helped her out. "This would have been better in the daylight but I couldn't wait until tomorrow."

She stared up at him, puzzled. "I don't understand what we're doing here."

He ran his finger under the collar of his jacket. "Like I said… I was picturing our future."

Her heart stuttered, then pounded so hard she was surprised it didn't jump out of her chest. She glanced down, expecting to see it flopping like a fish on the ground.

He made a sweeping motion with his hand to encompass the large, open yard between this house and his sister's. "I see kids—our kids and their cousins—running around this yard. Maybe even a dog of our own chasing after them. Baseball games, touch football, along with some hot dogs and burgers on the grill in the summer."

He turned so he was standing in front of her and took both her hands in his and cleared his throat. "I love you, Ellie Harding. No matter what. Now and forever. In sickness and in health. Will you marry me and live here with me?"

Her mouth opened and closed like that fish she'd been imagining a few moments ago. "But…but what about your job? Your house in Boston?"

"When Chief Harris called me in to tell me I'd made captain, we—"

"Wait…what?" She took her hand out of his and jabbed him in the shoulder. "You made captain and are just now telling me?"

He shrugged. "It wasn't important."

"How can you say that? Of course that's important."

"Not as important to me as you and our babies. This right here, with you, is what I want. Chief Harris is always asking me when I was going to sell him my three-decker and yesterday I told him to make me an offer. I tracked down the owner of this one and he's willing to sell. So whaddaya say, should we make an offer on this place?"

Overcome with emotion that her dreams were coming true, all she could do was shake her head and choke back a sob. All the color drained from Liam's face and she realized he'd misunderstood. She threw herself at him and began blubbering incoherently.

He held her and rubbed her back. Finally she raised her head. "I love you, too," she choked out.

He grinned, his eyes suspiciously shiny. "So, that's a yes?"

She nodded vigorously.

"Wait…" He set her away from him. "I was supposed to do this first."

He reached into his pocket and pulled out a ring. "It was my mother's. My dad gave it to me today. Will you marry me?"

"Yes."

He slipped the ring on her finger and kissed her. She pulled away first.

"I haven't gotten the all clear yet on the biopsy," she warned.

"And I don't have another job yet," He brushed the hair back from her face and dried her damp cheeks. "We'll work out all the details."

"McBride, are you telling me I just accepted a proposal of marriage from someone who is unemployed?"

"You're not going to let a little thing like that stop you, are you?" He frowned, then laughed. "I'm still employed and will have to divide my time for now. While I was waiting for you to get off work, my dad called to let me know the state fire investigator's office here in Vermont was looking for someone."

"Would that kind of work make you happy?"

He pressed his hand against her stomach. "I have all I need right here with you and these guys to make me happy."

"What if I don't get good news from the biopsy?"

"Then we'd deal with it together. I'm not going anywhere. Ellie. You've got the entire McBride clan with you, for whatever comes along."

Epilogue

Six months later

"Hey, bud, you didn't have to make this a competition to see if you could get here before your sister or your cousin," Liam whispered to his newborn son, Sean, who was staring up at him. He turned to the similar bundle cradled close on his other side. "And you, Miss Bridget, you'll be keeping all the boys in line, won't you?"

His newborn daughter twitched in her sleep and Liam leaned down to press a kiss to the top of her head. He glanced up at Ellie, his precious wife, who, despite the mad dash to the hospital several weeks early, lay smiling at him.

"You done good, Harding," he said, blinking back a sudden burning in the back of his eyes. "Or should I say 'McBride'? You're one of us now, Ellie."

"You didn't do so bad yourself, McBride," she whispered and sniffled, her lips quivering.

He swallowed and his smile faltered as he adjusted his precious bundles in his arms. "I hope both of you heard that, because it might be the last time she says something like that."

Ellie wiggled her feet under the covers. "Meg is going to be so jealous I can finally see my feet."

Liam shook his head and glanced down at his son. "Looks like the women in this family are just as competitive."

"At least now I can put on my own shoes." Ellie yawned and lay back against the covers. "Good thing you and Riley finished the nursery."

Liam nodded in agreement. The last few months had been hectic, what with a wedding, selling one house and buying another, and starting his new job as a state fire investigator. But he wouldn't have traded one minute of it for anything. Even having to wait for Ellie's biopsy results had been worth the nerves. And the celebration when the all clear came back had been—he grinned at the babies in his arms—best kept private.

"What are you grinning about over there?"

He shifted the babies and stood up. "I was thinking how lucky I am and how I can't wait to start this phase of our lives."

She lifted an eyebrow. "This phase?"

Coming to stand next to the bed, he gently lowered their son into Ellie's waiting arms. "Changing diapers, chasing rug rats around the yard, drying tears and retrieving Barbies from toilets."

Ellie yawned again as she cuddled her son. "I guess I better rest up. Sounds like I'm going to be busy."

Liam leaned over and kissed his wife. "I was talking about us. Ellie, we're in this together. For today and always. No matter what the future brings it's you and me together, sharing everything. Partners."

"Intimate partners," she said and laughed.

As always, her laughter drew him close and filled his heart and world with love.

* * * * *

IF YOU ENJOYED THIS BOOK
WE THINK YOU WILL ALSO LOVE

HARLEQUIN
SPECIAL
EDITION

Believe in love. Overcome obstacles. Find happiness.

Relate to finding comfort and strength in the
support of loved ones and enjoy the journey
no matter what life throws your way.

6 NEW BOOKS AVAILABLE EVERY MONTH!